She laughed, ... up to her mouth, now ... ceive his kiss. Those lips . . . and just a hint of moist, pink tongue . . . the instruments of his irritation for so many years, now offered up in invitation. Just waiting to be silenced, mastered, tamed. There was one certain way, a dark voice inside him argued, to make Lucy finally see sense.

Kiss her senseless.

His mouth crushed down on hers, and he felt her lips contract from that wide smile to a passionate pout. And when she opened her mouth to him readily, eagerly, Jeremy thanked God for lurid novels.

He slid his tongue into her hot, whiskey-bold mouth, exploring, demanding. She gasped against his lips, and he thrust deeper, took more, determined to drink in her sweetness until he tasted the bitter edge of fear. If she wanted lessons, he meant to give her one. He would teach her that desire was not a game; passion was dangerous sport indeed. He meant to push her until he sent her away—sent her scurrying back to her room to tremble beneath crisp white sheets and curl back into that high-necked virginal nightgown. And button that damned button.

Then her tongue stroked his. Cautiously, once. Again, with abandon. She was pulling him in, coaxing him on, stoking the fire in his loins with every darting caress. He answered instinctively, deepening the kiss. And a realization pierced him with all the sweet sting of requited desire.

This kiss was a dare.

And in the eight years he'd known her, Lucy Waltham had never once backed down from a dare.

GODDESS OF THE HUNT

A
Novel

Tessa Dare

BALLANTINE BOOKS • NEW YORK

A Ballantine Books Mass Market Original

Copyright © 2009 by Eve Ortega
Excerpt from *Surrender of a Siren* by Tessa Dare copyright © 2009 by Eve Ortega

Published in the United States by Ballantine Books, an imprint of The Random House Publishing Group, a division of Random House, Inc., New York.

BALLANTINE and colophon are registered trademarks of Random House, Inc.

This book contains an excerpt from the forthcoming book *Surrender of a Siren* by Tessa Dare. This excerpt has been set for this edition only and may not reflect the final content of the forthcoming edition.

ISBN 978-0-345-50686-3

Cover illustration: Doreen Minuto

Printed in the United States of America

www.ballantinebooks.com

OPM 9 8 7 6 5 4 3 2 1

For my husband.

CHAPTER
ONE

AUTUMN, 1817

A knock on the door in the dead of night could only mean disaster.

Jeremy pulled a pair of worn breeches on under his nightshirt and stumbled toward the bedchamber door. A fire? He didn't smell smoke. Perhaps a Waltham family emergency? An urgent message from his steward, maybe—unrest at Corbinsdale would not come as a surprise.

A memory assailed him, unbidden. Unnerving. His heart thudded wildly in his chest. He paused, clutching the door handle, cursing his body for recalling so quickly what he'd worked long years to forget.

Logic caught up to his racing pulse, reining it in. The dim glow of banked coals cast ominous shadows, but Jeremy forced the room into focus. This was not that night. He was in his usual bedchamber at Waltham Manor, not wandering Corbinsdale Woods. More than twenty years had passed, and he was no longer a boy. Whatever surprise awaited him on the other side of the door, he was fully equipped to face it.

When he slid back the rusted bolt and wrenched open the door, Jeremy was prepared for the worst.

"Hold still," came the whispered command.

He had an instant to register a feminine silhouette, a tangle of dark curls, and two hands grasping his shoulders. Then Lucy Waltham, the younger sister of his oldest friend, popped up on her toes and pressed her lips to his with such force, he stumbled against the doorjamb.

Good Lord. The girl was kissing him.

Well, he thought ironically, he'd been prepared for the worst. And of the many kisses Jeremy Trescott had experienced in his nine-and-twenty years, this was, undoubtedly, the worst.

Lucy kissed with her lips perfectly puckered and her eyes open wide. And if she lacked in finesse, she compensated with bold enthusiasm. Her hands were everywhere at once—tangling in his hair, skimming his shoulders, exploring the broad expanse of his chest.

This wasn't a kiss. It was a siege.

Furthermore, it was incomprehensible, wholly illogical, and a dozen different shades of *wrong*.

Somehow Jeremy's hands found their way to her elbows, and he wrested himself from her eager embrace. "Lucy! What the devil do you think you're doing?"

"Shhhh." Her eyes darted to either side, scanning the darkened corridor. Then her gaze tilted back up to his, narrowing with a disturbing intensity, and Jeremy fancied briefly—absurdly—that someone had painted a target on his face.

"I'm practicing," she whispered, her fingers tightening over his arms. "Let me try one more time."

She swooped up for another kiss, and he instinctively ducked, pulling her into the room and shutting the door behind them. In a more rational moment, it might have occurred to him that the impropriety of kissing his host's sister in the corridor would only be compounded by yanking her into his bedchamber. But Jeremy's faculties of reason had temporarily vacated Waltham Manor.

Lucy had, quite literally, kissed him witless.

"Did it work, then?"

He stared at her, mute with confusion. Did what

work? At the moment, it seemed that nothing worked, least of all his brain. Shock had frozen his limbs. He certainly couldn't force an answer from his lips.

Stepping back, she crossed her arms over her crimson velvet dressing gown and surveyed his form boldly. As her gaze traveled downward, Jeremy grew uncomfortably aware of his own dishabille, from nightshirt to worn breeches to bare feet.

A satisfied smile spread across her face. "It must have worked. You did pull me into your bedchamber." She reached for the door handle. "Very well, Jemmy. I suppose that's enough practice. I'll see you at breakfast."

She cracked open the door. Jeremy put out a hand and slammed it shut.

Shooting him a glare, she grasped the handle with both hands and tugged. "I beg your pardon. I'll be on my way, then."

"No, you won't." He leaned his weight on the door, effectively bolting it closed. Lucy might be used to flouting her brother's half-hearted attempts at guardianship, but Jeremy had four inches and two stone on Henry Waltham, not to mention an iron will. Lucy did not walk all over him.

He mustered his most autocratic, Earl-of-Kendall tone. "You are not going anywhere. You're going to sit down and explain yourself." She opened her mouth to object. He grabbed her by the elbow and steered her toward a chair. "But first," he said, "I am going to have a drink."

She stopped struggling under his grip and dropped gracelessly into the chair. "A drink," she repeated. "Why didn't I think of that? A drink would be just the thing, thank you."

Shaking his head, Jeremy strode to the bar and poured a single glass of whiskey. He downed half the liquor in one greedy swallow, closing his eyes to savor the burn spreading down his throat. When he opened them again, he looked around to assure himself this was, indeed, the same Waltham Manor he'd been visiting each autumn since Cambridge. Roughhewn beams scored the sloping ceiling. Muted tapestries covered the walls, and an unfussy, timeworn carpet obliged his bare feet. The room had not altered in the past eight years, any more than it likely had in the past one hundred.

In decor, in landscape, in the quartet of old friends enjoying their annual sporting holiday—Waltham Manor had remained a welcome constant in Jeremy's life. Until this year, when everything had changed.

"Why couldn't everything just go on as it was?" Lucy stirred the fire with a poker, sending swirls of agitated sparks into the air. "Why did Felix have to go and get married? He's ruined everything."

Jeremy drowned his reply with a sip of his drink. He would not have admitted it, but he rather agreed.

"It was all right when Henry got married," she continued. "Marianne's so busy with the children, at least she stays out of the way. But that shrew Felix married is going to expect to be entertained. And to make it all worse, she's brought along her sister, that Sophia."

"*Mrs.* Crowley-Cumberbatch and *Miss* Hathaway are, by all accounts, charming young ladies. One would think you'd be glad of their company."

She threw him an incredulous look.

"Or not." Truth be told, Jeremy wasn't glad of their presence, either. There was nothing precisely offensive about Felix's wife, Kitty, or her sister, Sophia. To the contrary, Sophia Hathaway was the epitome of an inoffensive, well-bred society beauty. A bit of meringue—insubstantial, but pleasing enough, if one's tastes ran to sweet. As Toby's apparently did.

Jeremy tossed back another swallow of whiskey and tasted the irony. Henry and Felix married, Toby on the verge . . . their bachelors' retreat had become a family house party. Well, if all his friends were determined to shackle themselves in marriage, at least he would be in no imminent danger of joining them. All three ladies at Waltham Manor were safely accounted for.

The sound of fingers drumming wood interrupted his thoughts. "Do you intend to drink the whole bottle yourself?"

Unless, of course, one counted Lucy.

And he did not count Lucy. She was neither eligible nor a lady. She was Henry's much younger sister and ward, and she was Jeremy's personal version of a biblical plague. She'd spent years devising ways to get under his skin. Now she was charging into his bedchamber and . . . and *practicing*.

Much as he wished to erase that kiss from his memory, he couldn't ignore it. Neither could he ignore the obvious implications of that word, "practicing."

He could, however, ignore her request for a drink. Jeremy refilled his own glass and carried it toward the hearth, dropping into the chair opposite hers. Raking a hand through his hair, he exhaled slowly. "I don't like to ask this. I dread your response. But for what, exactly, are you practicing?"

"Not 'what,' " she answered. "Who."

Oh, it only got worse. "For *whom* are you practicing, then? Some local youth? The vicar's boy?"

"For Toby, of course."

He gave a wry laugh. "For Toby? Why would you be kissing Toby? He's all but engaged to Miss Hathaway."

She hugged her knees to her chest, curling into a ball of red velvet and chestnut curls. The chair's masculine proportions dwarfed her, and her green eyes brimmed with raw, undisguised hurt. "Then it's true."

Bloody hell. Suddenly this bizarre nighttime visit

made sense. Jeremy punched the arm of his chair. Of all the irretrievably stupid things to say.

"My maid said she heard it from Toby's valet. I didn't want to believe her. I *couldn't* believe her. But it's true."

Jeremy had to look away. It was a matter of self-preservation. Lucy's countenance was a collection of pixie features set within a heart-shaped face—a face designed to display, unfiltered, every emotion of the heart within. One couldn't look at her without knowing exactly how she was feeling, and Jeremy didn't wish to know how Lucy was feeling. He preferred to keep a respectful distance from even his own emotions.

"How could he?" she squeaked.

Jeremy winced. Lucy sniffed loudly, and he took another slow sip of whiskey. She could not cry, he wanted to remind her. That was the rule—Henry's single exercise in authority. He'd allowed the chit to run roughshod over them every autumn, tagging along on their hunting and fishing excursions, parroting their curses, even taking nips off their flasks—under one condition. Lucy was not to cry. In eight years, he had never seen her shed a single tear. He prayed she wasn't about to start now. If there was one thing he couldn't abide, it was a crying woman.

He stole a glance at her. Damn it, her chin was quivering. "You're not going to start weeping, are you?"

"No." Her voice quivered, too.

Jeremy busied himself adding wood to the fire, stalling for time.

Curse Toby. This was all his fault. He'd always made such a pet of the girl. Every autumn, Lucy clung to Toby like a tick on a hound. He baited her hooks and taught her bawdy Latin conjugations. He brought her flowers and wove her crowns of ivy that went straight to her head. His Diana, Toby called her. Goddess of the hunt. Goddess he may have dubbed her, but the worship was all on Lucy's side. A young girl's harmless infatuation—that was all it had seemed. Obviously, to Lucy it had seemed much more. And now the task of disabusing her of all those romantic notions had somehow fallen to Jeremy. Just his luck. But also fitting, he supposed. If he'd ever harbored a romantic notion, which was doubtful, he'd been disabused of it long ago.

He clapped the dust from his hands and reclined in his chair. In his most magnanimous tone, he began, "Now, Lucy, you must understand . . ."

"Don't, Jemmy. Don't you dare speak to me as if I were a child. I ought to have come out two seasons ago. If only Marianne weren't perpetually confined. Perhaps I am not a genteel lady like Sophia Hathaway. But I'm not a girl any longer, either."

She stretched a bare foot toward the fire and absently flexed her ankle. The sinuous grace of the motion caught Jeremy's gaze. Caught it, and trapped it. He couldn't look away. She circled her foot idly, her skin glowing golden in the firelight. His eyes swept upward, tracing the sweet curve of her calf to where it disappeared under her dressing gown.

Then Lucy shifted, crossing her legs. Red velvet fell like a theater curtain, abruptly ending the show. A swift blow of disappointment caught Jeremy in the chest. The sensation drifted downward, mellowing to the familiar ache of thwarted desire. God, this night was simply rife with surprises.

"I suppose you're not," he muttered, tearing his gaze away and giving himself a mental shake. "Very well, let us speak as adults. You can begin by dropping that childish nickname and addressing me in a proper fashion."

"You mean by your *title*? I don't even remember your old one, let alone the new." She looked up at the ceiling.

"You can't possibly expect me to call you 'my lord,' Jemmy."

Jeremy sighed, abandoning any effort to soothe. "Then let us be perfectly plain. Toby is going to marry Miss Hathaway."

"But he can't! It isn't fair!"

He snorted. "Spoken like a girl, Lucy."

She ignored him. "I've always known I would marry Sir Toby Aldridge, ever since the day we first met."

"That's absurd. The day you first met, you were twelve years old."

"Eleven."

"Eleven, then. And Toby shot at you."

"He didn't shoot at me. He shot at a partridge I startled. He didn't know I was there, because—"

"Because you were following us after Henry forbade you," Jeremy finished impatiently. "Yes, yes. I remember it clearly."

Too clearly, he added in silence. He remembered everything about that day in painful detail. The glaring afternoon sun, the acrid odor of gunpowder. But he especially remembered the sounds. How could he forget? A frantic staccato of wingbeats, the crack of Toby's gun, a piercing shriek. The dreadful silence as all four of them charged through knee-deep brambles, only to find Lucy sitting in a clearing, unharmed and unrepentant.

Ensuing years had proven that near miss to be the beginning of a pattern. Lucy Waltham was always flirting with disaster, and therefore Jeremy had always avoided Lucy. He didn't want to be in the vicinity when disaster inevitably struck.

With a sniff, she reached out and took the glass of whiskey from his hand. Her fingertips grazed his wrist. So much for safe distances.

She rested her chin on one knee and stared morosely

into the amber-brown liquid. "What does Sophia Hath-away have that I haven't?"

"Besides impeccable breeding, accomplishment, and a dowry of twenty thousand pounds?" He extended his hand to retrieve his drink.

She downed a generous swallow of whiskey before relinquishing the glass. "She doesn't love him."

"More girlish fancies. This is marriage. Love is hardly required. They get on well enough, and their families will approve. She has wealth but no title; he is a baronet. It's a fortuitous match for them both."

"Fortuitous?" She narrowed her eyes. "Only you would speak of marriage as a prudent business arrangement."

"It isn't only me. It's society. Love matches like your brother's—they are the exception, not the rule. Ladies who insist on romance end up disappointed. You'd realize the truth of this, if only you—"

"If only I what? If only I were cold and jaded, like you?"

Jeremy clenched his jaw. "If only you had paid the slightest attention to any of those governesses Henry hired for you. If only you'd had some model of female behavior, aside from an overburdened sister-in-law and a senile aunt. If only you had a modicum of sense."

"If only I were like Sophia Hathaway."

"You said it. Not me."

She crossed her arms. "Well, I don't care what you—or society—say. I'm going to marry for love, and that means I won't marry anyone but Toby. I refuse to believe he could marry anyone other than me. He loves me. I know it, even if he doesn't yet."

"Lucy, the matter is all but settled. I expect he will propose any day."

"Then I shall have to act tonight." She rose from the chair and began pacing the floor. Her brow was furrowed, and she toyed absently with a lock of her hair, catching it between her teeth. It was a warning sign he'd learned to heed. Lucy always fidgeted with her hair when she was scheming.

She usually wore her hair up—for convenience, not fashion. But they hadn't yet invented the hairpin or bonnet that could contain Lucy's curls. They were forever working loose at the edges and winding between her fingers, finding their way to her lips. Now her hair fell in heavy waves down to her waist, rippling like a thick, luxurious pelt as she prowled the carpet's knotted fringe. She turned and swept back across the room, fluid fabric wrapping around her curves.

Curves. Great God. When had Lucy grown curves? Lucy was always a collection of bony, awkward angles, held together by sheer force of will. Now that hard frame of determination was cloaked in soft, supple, womanly curves. And she *and* her curves were parading about his bedchamber in a state of undress. At the ungodly hour of—he stole a glance at the clock on the mantel—two o'clock. The impropriety of the entire situation struck him with sudden force.

"You shouldn't be here. It's late, and you're . . . upset. Go back to your room and get some sleep. We can speak more on this tomorrow."

"Tomorrow may be too late," she said. "I can't take that risk. I'll have to do it tonight."

"You'll have to do what tonight?"

"Seduce him, of course."

Jeremy stared at her, dumbstruck. A log settled in the fire with a loud crack, and a flurry of red sparks shot out from the hearth.

Lucy stopped before the mirror. She untied her dressing gown and opened it, surveying the simple linen nightgown beneath with a dissatisfied expression. "Silk and lace would be better, I suppose, but I haven't anything finer." She made a quarter turn and looked askance at her reflected profile. Thrusting her shoulders back, she smoothed her nightgown tight against her torso until every swell and peak of her flesh strained against the sheer fabric.

Jeremy leapt to his feet, upending what remained of his whiskey onto the carpet. In a matter of two paces, he crossed the room and stepped between Lucy and her scandalous reflection, grabbing the edges of her dressing gown and wrapping them firmly about her waist. The third button of her nightgown was undone, and the thin fabric gaped to reveal a crescent of golden skin. He forced his gaze up to her face. "Don't tell me that . . . that *this* is what you're practicing."

She nodded. The cool intensity in her gaze told Jeremy that, ridiculous as the idea might seem to him, Lucy thought seduction an entirely sensible plan. He put his hands on her shoulders and willed authority into his voice. "Lucy, Toby does not love you."

"Yes, Jemmy, he does."

"What makes you so sure? Has he given you any reason to hope?"

"I wasn't aware that hope required a reason, any more than love. In case you have forgotten—I have no talent for hoping. I don't hope. I *know.* I *believe.* I *expect.* I know that Toby loves me. I believe we belong together." She jabbed a finger into the center of his chest. "And I expect you to understand."

Jeremy groaned. How was he supposed to reason with a girl—a *woman,* he corrected—who put no stock in reasons? "Lucy, Toby is quite fond of you." He realized he was still holding her by the shoulders. Retreating a step, he let his hands drop to his sides. "But fondness isn't love. Besides, what would you know of seduction?"

"Oh, I have a book."

"A *book?*" He pulled a hand through his hair. "Good

Lord, Lucy, I am not going to ask you where you obtained such a book or what pearls of wisdom it might contain." She opened her mouth to interject, and he silenced her with an outstretched hand. "In fact, I beg you *not* to tell me. Suffice it to say, I hope you will not heed the lessons of whatever lurid novel you've managed to get your hands on."

"I'll admit book learning has its limitations." She regarded him cagily, her gaze searching his.

"That's one way of putting it."

She inched closer. "Reading is certainly no substitute for practical experience." She drew nearer still.

"But . . . wait . . . Lucy, you can't possibly—" And then he blurted out a question directed more at God in heaven than at Lucy herself. "Why me?"

"You mean besides the fact that there's no one else? You're so proper, Jemmy, so cold. There are icebergs in the North Sea with less frost on them. If I can thaw you out, I'll have no problem seducing Toby."

"I assure you, you could not 'thaw' me, even if I wished to be . . . thawed. Which I don't." He retreated a step. Then two.

"Try to resist, by all means. I like a good challenge." She closed the distance again, her eyes lit with mischief. "I've learned to snare grouse and angle for trout. Is catching a husband really so different?"

Yes, Jeremy meant to insist, but somehow his jaw would only move up and down noiselessly, in a rather good imitation of—well, of a trout.

And then she caught him by his shirt and reeled him in, catching him up in that net of chestnut curls and kissing him within an inch of his life. Her lips attacked his with the same steely determination. But when she threw her arms around his neck and fell against him, the rest of her was soft, pliant, yielding. Silky strands of her hair slid over his forearm. Lush curves molded against his chest.

Before he could gather his wits to protest, she pulled away suddenly and studied his face.

"Well? Is it working?"

It was a simple question. And as Jeremy's mind recited the reasons why his answer ought to be an emphatic *no*, other regions of his body were decidedly saying *yes*. Good Lord, he was only a man. A man who, it seemed, had wasted the past several months not kissing anyone, and whose body was veritably leaping at the chance to end the reign of self-imposed monasticism. He shook his head firmly in the negative, hoping she would overlook the ragged breathing that argued otherwise.

Lucy was undeterred. She shot up for yet another attempt, but Jeremy caught her face in his hands. Her cheeks flushed soft and warm beneath his palms.

"Have you gone mad? This is not going to happen. It cannot happen."

"Well, of course *it* cannot happen." Her mouth spread into a grin, and her cheeks dimpled under his thumbs. Jeremy was seized by an unpardonable urge to trace those little laughing hollows with his fingers, explore them with his lips.

"Have no fear, Jemmy, I have no plans for *it*. Then *you* would have to marry me, and that would not do at all."

"It most certainly would not." He studied the face cupped in his hands. Her skin drank in the firelight and glowed like burnished gold. Her eyes danced with reflected flame, daring him to look closer, draw nearer. Who was this woman, and what had she done with Lucy? She felt like a stranger to him, and that was a dangerous thing. A stranger was fair game, for kissing . . . and more.

Jeremy began a short list of the reasons why Lucy was not—most definitely *not*—fair game.

Point one, she was the sister of his oldest friend.

Point two, his oldest friend was a crack shot.

"Listen to me," he said, giving her head a little shake. "If you have questions about . . . about the marriage bed, you ought to take them up with Marianne. Or you should wait for your wedding night, when your husband—who will *not* be Toby—can enlighten you. There will be no lessons on fishing for husbands or ensnaring men."

She smiled. A smug, maddening smile that Jeremy longed to shake right off her face.

"Do you understand me?" he demanded.

"Yes." She pressed her lips together briefly before they parted again in laughter.

"Then damn it, why are you laughing?"

"Because I think it *was* working."

That damned impish grin again. But this time he saw not the impudent smile, but rather what composed it.

Lips.

Full, sweetly bowed lips, flushed deep red with kissing and laughter. Lips that begged to be covered with his own.

He closed his eyes to the temptation, sliding his hands back to fist in her tumbled hair, as if by taming those curls he could control her. Control himself. But—sweet heaven. It was like plunging his hands into liquid silk, and behind his eyelids he saw those strands of exquisite softness stroking every inch of his skin.

His eyes snapped open. In desperation, he glanced downward, just to see if the third button of her nightgown was still undone.

And it was. Damn it, it was.

She laughed softly, drawing his gaze back up to her mouth, now tilted at the perfect angle to receive his kiss.

Those lips . . . and just a hint of a moist, pink tongue . . . the instruments of his irritation for so many years, now offered up in invitation. Just waiting to be silenced, mastered, tamed. There was one certain way, a dark voice inside him argued, to make Lucy finally see sense.

Kiss her senseless.

His mouth crushed down on hers, and he felt her lips contract from that wide smile to a passionate pout. And when she opened her mouth to him readily, eagerly, Jeremy thanked God for lurid novels.

He slid his tongue into her hot, whiskey-bold mouth, exploring, demanding. She gasped against his lips, and he thrust deeper, took more, determined to drink in her sweetness until he tasted the bitter edge of fear. If she wanted lessons, he meant to give her one. He would teach her that desire was not a game; passion was dangerous sport indeed. He meant to push her until he pushed her away—sent her scurrying back to her room to tremble beneath crisp white sheets and curl back into that high-necked virginal nightgown. And button that damned button.

Then her tongue stroked his. Cautiously, once. Again, with abandon. She was pulling him in, coaxing him on, stoking the fire in his loins with every darting caress. He answered instinctively, deepening the kiss. And a realization pierced him with all the sweet sting of requited desire.

This kiss was a dare.

And in the eight years he'd known her, Lucy Waltham had never once backed down from a dare.

She wriggled closer, grasping his shoulders and running one hand to the back of his neck. He growled as her fingernails raked lightly across his nape.

Some force pulled his hand downward. Regret, perhaps. The desperate need to regain control. A charitable impulse, truly—he had to convince her she was playing with fire. Fingers splayed, he laid claim to the small of her back and pressed her to him, drawing her body tight against his swelling groin. The pleasure was immediate. Intense. Not nearly enough.

Surely now she would squirm away, perhaps even scream.

But no. She was moving, yes. God, was she moving. Arching against him, moaning into the kiss. Cool velvet teased his fingertips; warm velvet caressed his tongue. Traitorous images flooded his mind. A crimson robe pooling on the floor. Buttons flying everywhere. He was in this kiss far too deep, and oh God, how he longed to sink in deeper still. It had gone all wrong.

This was . . . all . . . *wrong.*

Jeremy fought through the haze of lust, clenching his fist in her hair and tearing her away. An inch. He looked down at her face. This time, her eyes were closed.

"Lucy," he whispered hoarsely.

Her eyes fluttered open. They were green flecked with gold; dark, wild passion, glinting with laughter. He untangled his hand from her hair, released her waist, and stepped back, trying to think. His breath was ragged, his pulse thundering, and blood was rushing everywhere in his body except his brain. "Lucy," he tried again, "that was—"

"That was practice," she interrupted. A smile curved her lips. "Very good practice." She shifted her weight back on one foot, pushing the curve of her hip into relief and lifting her breasts for attention—an unconscious motion of raw sensuality.

It was wildly seductive.

Jeremy swore inwardly. What had he done? He'd opened the door to an awkward virgin, and not a half-hour later, he was sending away a temptress. It was as though he'd been handed an unloaded gun, only to pack it with powder and buckshot and—dear God—damn near pull the trigger. Scant minutes ago, she'd been harmless. Now . . .

Now Lucy was a danger to herself.

And if she stood there a moment longer, taunting him with those glittering eyes and those swollen lips and that flushed, kissable curve of her throat, Jeremy would be a danger to her.

What had he been thinking? He had mauled her like a brute. Never mind the fact that she had mauled him right back, or that the whole thing had been her idea. He was a gentleman, and she was—by birth if not behavior— a lady. She was his best friend's *sister*. He ought to be facing a pistol at dawn, or worse. A vicar across an altar.

She must have read the guilt in his eyes. "For heaven's sake, Jemmy. Henry's never going to know, unless you tell him." Smiling, she tied the sash of her dressing gown. "And I strongly suggest you don't. You'd never live it down."

"You," he said, grasping her by the elbow and steer- ing her firmly to the door, "are very late for bed." He cautiously scanned the corridor before guiding her through the doorway. She started to turn left, toward Toby's bedchamber. He caught her by the shoulders and swiveled her to face the opposite direction.

"Go to your room, Lucy," he whispered sternly. "I shall keep my door open all night—if you try to get to Toby, you'll have to get through me."

She flashed him a coy look which, in any ballroom, he would have taken for shameless flirtation. She was a quick study, indeed. "Are you suggesting that would be difficult?"

He gritted his teeth. "So help me, I will march you down to Henry's room this instant if . . ."

"Shhhh." She silenced him with a finger to his lips, glancing over her shoulder. "Very well, Jemmy," she whispered. "I suppose Toby will let Sophia unpack her valises before he drops to one knee. I can wait one more night."

Jeremy listened to her pad softly down the corridor and strained his ears until he heard the sound of a bolt sliding into place. He sagged against the wall.

It was some comfort to know Lucy slept behind a bolted door. But he would have felt entirely more at peace, were the bolt on the other side.

CHAPTER
TWO

Lucy Waltham's appetite was insatiable.

Henry liked to jest that when she married, he would provide her a dowry of two cows, six pigs, and two dozen chickens—just so her husband could keep her fed. It was only a joke, of course. In all likelihood, her dowry would be worth far less.

But no one would be jesting to say Lucy downed meals that would put a farm laborer to shame. Lucy lived hungry. She devoured every day. This appetite for life required a steady supply of actual food. She nicked hot rolls from the kitchen, rang for cold chicken at midnight, and spent long afternoons grazing in the orchards. And she never missed breakfast.

Marianne and Aunt Matilda were already at table when Lucy entered the breakfast room. Lucy leaned over to kiss Aunt Matilda's papery cheek. The old lady responded by taking a loud slurp of chocolate.

No one knew exactly how old Aunt Matilda was—Aunt Matilda least of all—but Lucy thought she was eighty if she was a day. She also thought Aunt Matilda the most beautiful woman she knew. Lucy's grandfather had built his fortune farming indigo in the West Indies, where Aunt Matilda had spent her youth. She still dressed head-to-toe in yards of the deepest indigo blue. Her spine had not curved one whit with age, and she kept her chin held high to balance a formidable turban. She smelled of ocean breezes and exotic spices and snuff.

Henry turned from the buffet bearing two plates. He froze momentarily, eyes wide in disbelief, before setting one plate before his wife. "Lucy, what on earth have you done to yourself?"

"Henry, hush," Marianne said. "I think Lucy looks lovely."

"Yes, lovely," Aunt Matilda warbled.

Lucy smoothed her palms over cool silk as she made her way to the sideboard. The dress had been made up by a London modiste nearly three years ago, for what was to have been her first season in Town. That was before Marianne learned she was with child for the second time. The gown had languished in Lucy's closet through that confinement, and then another—a bit of shimmering silk promise amid yards of everyday muslin. The pale blue fabric matched the shade of a starling's egg, and creamy lace edged the cap sleeves.

Her figure had rounded considerably in the three years since the dress had been fitted. Her breasts strained against the bodice, pulling the fabric taut. The neckline dipped scandalously low for morning.

It would do perfectly.

She really ought to wear silk more often. The gown flowed around her body, gliding over her skin like water. She touched a hand to her neatly coiled hair. Her maid had nearly dropped the hairbrush when she'd requested a more elegant style than her usual simple knot. The jewels were perhaps a bit much for breakfast. Her mother's opal earrings pinched on either side of her head. They were far heavier than she'd anticipated. Surely her earlobes would sag to her shoulders by noon.

But no matter. If jewels were required to outshine Sophia Hathaway, Lucy would drape herself in diamonds.

She had seated herself at the table when Felix entered

the breakfast room with Kitty on his arm. Sophia followed a few paces behind. Both ladies were attired in simple frocks of sprigged muslin. To Lucy's mind, they might as well have been wearing frogged blue uniforms with tasseled epaulettes. They were hostile invaders.

The enemy.

"My, my." Kitty eyed Lucy with amused disdain. "I had no idea breakfast at Waltham Manor was such a formal affair." She turned to Marianne. "Forgive me, Mrs. Waltham, I see we are underdressed."

"Not at all," Marianne replied. "Won't you be seated? Do you take tea or coffee? Or chocolate, perhaps?"

"What a charming breakfast room." Sophia settled into a chair opposite Lucy. "Such a delightful view of the park."

Kitty slid into the next seat down and unfolded her napkin with a ruthless snap. "The windows face full west," she said. "It must be unbearably warm in the afternoon."

Lucy smiled. "How fortunate then, that we take breakfast in the morning."

Kitty's eyes narrowed. She tapped her knife against her plate and spoke over Lucy's shoulder, addressing her husband. "Felix! Toast!"

Poor Felix, to be saddled with such a shrew for a wife. Lucy could not imagine enduring a lifetime of breakfasts across the table from Kitty's pinched face. The very thought curdled her cream.

She glanced over her shoulder at Felix. He traveled down the buffet, heaping food on his breakfast plate, humming a little tune as he went. Humming! His parents had certainly been prescient when they selected his Christian name. His sanguine temperament never faltered. If any man could smile through life with Kitty by his side, it was Felix.

Lucy cast a sidelong glance at Sophia, who was daintily stirring sugar into her tea. Sophia was a softer version of her sister. They shared the same golden hair and fair complexion. But where Kitty's nose tapered to a point, Sophia's sloped elegantly. Kitty's blue eyes had an icy glint, but Sophia's sparkled with warmth. She was, Lucy grudgingly allowed, beautiful.

No one would call Lucy beautiful. At least, no one ever had. Her cheekbones were too wide, her chin too pointed. Her skin was tanned and olive, not fashionably fair. She did have a few pleasant features, she thought. Her eyes were large, and fringed with long, dark lashes. Her teeth were straight. Nothing that would inspire poetry. In fact, she rather sounded like a prize mare.

Sophia accepted a plate of toast from Felix and picked up her butter knife. She held the solid silver in a dainty grasp, as though it might snap in two. With her perfectly buttered points of toast and her neat little nibbling bites, she looked the picture of feminine delicacy.

Lucy looked down at her own plate, piled high with eggs and ham, rolls and preserves. She lifted a forkful of eggs to her mouth and chewed unrepentantly. Battling Sophia Hathaway would require strength and wit, silk and jewels—and a hearty breakfast.

"Good morning, Jem," Henry said.

She looked up from her plate to see Jeremy entering the room. She nearly choked on her eggs.

His black hair was windswept, and he was dressed for riding, in a dark brown coat layered over an open-necked shirt and buckskin breeches. There had been a time when the men never bothered with neckcloths at Waltham Manor. In fact, they made a great show of tossing their cravats into the fire upon their arrival each October. But that was before Henry married Marianne. Since the addition of a lady to the party, the gentlemen dressed for meals punctiliously.

"Mrs. Crowley-Cumberbatch. Miss Hathaway." He made a terse bow in their direction. Apparently scandalized by his dishabille, the sisters repaid his greeting with averted eyes, busying themselves with their tea and toast.

"Lucy."

Jeremy fixed her with a dark look, full of reproach. A hot blush singed the tips of her opal-adorned ears. For a moment, Lucy felt as though she were sitting in the breakfast room wearing only her nightgown—or less. But if he meant to shame her, he would be sorely disappointed. Her lips tingled, and she slowly wet them with her tongue before flashing him a bold grin. He quickly looked away.

Oh, what fun it was to vex him. He made it so easy to do. Hunting and fishing were all well and good, but truly, Jemmy-baiting had always been her favorite autumn sport. Lucy viewed his staid countenance as an unending challenge. A smooth, thick-shelled egg that begged to be cracked. Any rearrangement of his features constituted a victory, be it a wince, a scowl, or that rarest of expressions—a smile. A smile that showed teeth counted double.

Last night had shown her an entirely new way to bedevil Jeremy Trescott. Not with girlish pranks, but with womanly wiles. Oh, yes. She'd cracked the egg last night, but good. His expression of befuddled desire was far more amusing than a wince or a scowl, or even a smile that showed teeth. That last kiss had to count at least ten.

She lifted her cup of chocolate to her lips. Closing her eyes, she pressed her tongue against the cool china rim, remembering the power of a proper kiss. Drinking in the hot, sweet richness, feeling delicious warmth spread down her throat and pool in her belly. And lower. She sighed into the cup. If Jeremy's kiss could rival chocolate, Lucy shivered to imagine how it would be to kiss—

"Toby!"

Lucy sputtered against the rim of her cup. She returned it to the saucer and picked up her napkin, dabbing her lips hastily.

"Good morning, ladies." Toby made a gallant bow in the direction of Sophia Hathaway. He wore a dove-gray morning coat and striped waistcoat. His snow-white cravat was perfectly tied. Lucy melted in her chair like butter on toast.

"Good morning, Aunt Matilda." He caught her wrinkled hand and kissed it. "You're looking lovely this morning."

"Yes," the old lady replied. "Lovely."

Lucy sat up in her chair. "Good morning, Sir Toby." She held out her hand.

"Good morning, Luce." Their eyes met, and his pleasant smile widened into a grin. Then he took her hand— and *shook* it.

Lucy sighed. This might prove more difficult than she'd anticipated. She tilted her head to one side, dangling one opal earring like a fishing lure. She'd confirmed last night that men were not so different from trout as they might like to think.

"How wonderful it is to welcome you back to Waltham Manor, Sir Toby." She patted the seat of the chair next to her. "Please, do take a—"

"Thank you, I will," Jeremy said, sliding into the chair and plunking his plate down next to hers. Lucy clenched her teeth and took hold of her butter knife. Yes, men were like trout. And Jeremy was one she dearly wished to fillet.

"*What,*" he asked, in a voice so deep it was nearly inaudible, "are you wearing?"

"I might ask you the same," she murmured behind her cup. "*Lord* Kendall."

"I thought you had forgotten my title."

"Forgotten it? Me? Perhaps *you* mislaid it. I'm certain I saw it lying about somewhere. Right next to your cravat."

His jaw tensed. "I was out riding. When I learned you were already at table, I thought it unwise to delay my own repast." His derisive glance wandered from her earrings to her neckline. "It appears my concern was warranted."

"When did you appoint yourself Toby's protector? He's a grown man, is he not?"

Toby returned to the table with coffee and toast. He sat down next to Sophia Hathaway and murmured something Lucy could not hear. Sophia smiled demurely and fluttered her eyelashes. The eggs scrambled in Lucy's stomach.

Jeremy reached for a dish of marmalade, obstructing her view. "Have you considered," he asked, "that it may not be Toby I'm attempting to protect?"

Before Lucy could summon a sufficiently indignant response, Felix interrupted. "What's our sport today, Henry?"

"It's a fine, warm day," Henry replied. "I thought a spot of fishing?"

"Just the thing!" said Felix. "Will you join us, Lucy?"

Lucy felt Kitty and Sophia staring at her. Well-bred ladies, evidently, did not fish.

"Oh, no! I assure you, Mr. Crowley-Cumberbatch, I have given up those hoyden pursuits of my youth." She turned to Toby. "I haven't been fishing in ages. I can't remember the last time."

"Really, Luce?" Toby sounded incredulous. "Henry—is it true?"

Henry sawed away at a slice of ham. "If you count six days as 'ages,' then I suppose it's true. But if you can't remember six days back, Lucy, and you've forgotten Felix's Christian name, I'm concerned for you. Perhaps you've been spending too much time with Aunt Matilda."

"Henry!" said Marianne. "Don't say such things in front of the poor dear."

"Oh, she has no idea." He leaned over and shouted in Aunt Matilda's ear. "Lucy's given up fishing, Aunt Matilda! She's going about dripping in silk and baubles. Next she's going to paint her face and run off to become an actress! Won't that be lovely?"

Aunt Matilda slurped her chocolate. "Lovely."

Lucy smiled and tightened her grip on her knife.

"Since the day is so fine, perhaps the ladies would enjoy a picnic by the stream," said Marianne.

"Oh, how delightful!" Sophia fairly jumped in her seat. "I'll bring my watercolors."

"Miss Hathaway is a very accomplished painter," said Toby. "Just the other week, she showed me a cunning little tea tray she'd adorned with . . . roses, was it?"

"Orchids." Sophia blushed.

"Do you sketch, Miss Waltham?" Kitty asked in a smug tone.

"Oh, yes. I adore sketching. And painting. I shall bring my watercolors, too." She knew one of those governesses had left behind some paints somewhere. Perhaps in the old schoolroom. Her thoughts were interrupted by a loud, rasping slurp.

"Lucy, pour Aunt Matilda more chocolate," said Henry. "She's sipping air again."

She rose from her chair, lifting the chocolate pot with as much grace as she could muster.

"I never knew you were an artist, Lucy," Toby said.

Lucy leaned forward as she filled Aunt Matilda's cup, giving Toby a view of her brimming décolletage. She made her voice low and breathy.

"Oh, but Sir Toby," she said, fluttering her eyelashes like mad, "there are ever so many things you don't know about me."

Her mother's opal earring slipped from her ear, landing in Aunt Matilda's cup with a splash.

"Don't laugh, Jemmy. Don't you dare laugh."

Drat. Given the endless parade of governesses that had marched through Waltham Manor, Lucy was forced to admit that she ought to have paid the tiniest bit of attention to one or two of them.

Jeremy stood over her shoulder, looking down at her easel. Her work of the past hour had resulted in a tolerably good likeness of a mud puddle.

She had meant to capture the autumn glory of a distant oak tree, its orange-red foliage branching across a clear blue sky. She had begun by coating the entire paper with a lovely wash of brilliant blue. It was an excellent sky. Bold, cloudless, and indicative of untapped creative genius. No mundane tea tray, no matter how cunning, could possibly hope to touch her sky.

But then she'd started in with the orange. Only, when she laid the brush to the still-wet sky, she did not get orange, but brown. Worse yet, the brown would not stay put in nice little leaf-like shapes. Watery brown rivulets streaked the paper like muddy tears. The more she attempted to fix it, the more hideous it became, until the entire painting was nothing but a soggy mess.

"Don't. You. Dare," she ground out.

He bent low over her shoulder, as if examining her work. There was something vaguely unsettling in the way he loomed over her, his broad shoulders blotting out the sun. She felt the sudden impulse to shrink away—or shrink closer.

"I would not dream of daring." The solemn bass of his voice resonated deep in her body, thrilling her in an intimate, unexpected fashion. An unwelcome fashion. "And neither should you. Daring only invites disaster. By all means, stick to watercolors."

She looked up sharply. Their faces were but a hand's breadth apart. Too close to gauge his expression. She saw only a collection of features. Black hair sweeping over a heavy brow. Full lips. A strong, square jaw. Blue eyes.

Bold, brilliant blue.

Lucy shut her paint box with a defiant snap. Proper, staid, insufferable man. Stick to watercolors, indeed.

"You're going about this all wrong," he said coolly. "A silk gown, watercolors . . . do you honestly believe they'll catch Toby's attention?"

"They worked for *her*." Sophia sat a few yards in front of them, near the edge of the stream. She bent over her own easel, where a study of cattails arching over the riverbank appeared delicate, detailed, and remarkably dry.

"You're not her."

"I can't believe you would presume to advise me on courtship. I haven't noticed you bringing a wife around."

"That's because I don't wish to marry."

She gave a sardonic laugh. "Oh, I see. Bachelorhood is your choice. It has nothing to do with your dearth of charm."

"This from the girl whose concept of a romantic overture is a bullet whistling overhead."

She leveled a paintbrush at him. "Don't bring up marksmanship. You're the worst of the four in that pursuit, too. But I suppose it's by design," she said. "You simply don't wish to shoot the pheasants?"

A strange expression crossed his face. One Lucy had never seen before. A flash of blue surprise, quickly crushed by his heavy brow. When he spoke, icicles hung from his words. "Believe what you will." He straightened to his full height. "Do what you will. It's none of my concern." He stalked off to rejoin the gentlemen.

Lucy was tempted to throw her paint box at his head. She would have hit her target, too. Unlike him, she knew how to aim.

Sophia interrupted her vengeful thoughts. "Are you finished painting, Miss Waltham? May I see?"

"Of course," Lucy replied, still quietly seething. She jerked the paper out from under the easel clips and held it aloft between her thumb and forefinger. And then she let go. "Oh dear." An obliging breeze dropped the painting into the stream. "What a shame. No matter. I can paint another just as lovely in a trice."

She had no desire to attempt another painting, now or ever. She folded her easel with harsh snaps, until the edge of her frustration dulled.

Sophia had returned to her work, dabbing at her painting with light, feathery brushstrokes. Kitty, having declared the sun too strong, sat cloistered in the shade of a beech tree upstream. Little Beth's latest bout of colic had kept Marianne in the nursery. Marianne was always in the nursery.

Blast refinement. Lucy yearned to lie back against the bank and gaze up at the sky. To flatten her spine against the ground until the grass towered above her, the cool earth warmed under her back, and her heartbeat pounded in her ears like a drum. She had to settle for leaning back on an outstretched hand. Her gaze, however, slipped straight to its natural resting place.

Toby.

He was wearing his hair a touch longer this year. The

thick, golden-brown waves just kissed the collar of his coat. Each autumn, the features of his face appeared more chiseled, more permanent in their perfection. He still moved with the sure, lithe grace that Lucy had always envied. Bronzed by the sun and aglow from within, Toby radiated masculine beauty.

She watched with envy as the gentlemen cast their lines, waded in the icy stream, joked and laughed with one another. Would it always be this way, from this year forward? The men enjoying the same easy camaraderie, with Lucy exiled to the margins of their attention? She plucked a stone from the grass and flung it into the stream. They'd passed so many pleasant autumns here, just the five of them. Why did the men have to ruin it all by getting married? First Henry, then Felix. And now Toby.

Her heart seized. She couldn't lose Toby. Eight years she'd loved him, ever since that first afternoon. Jeremy had it all wrong. Toby shooting at her had nothing to do with it. It was everything that followed, once the cloud of gunpowder cleared. Henry had yelled at her; Jeremy had glowered at her; Felix had probably made a joke. But Toby had *bowed* to her. Her ears still ringing from the shot, she'd barely registered the words of his gallant apology. But for the first time in months, someone had spoken *to* her, rather than *at* her or *about* her.

Toby had coaxed Henry into letting Lucy stay instead of sending her home. He'd fashioned a wreath of ivy and crowned her his Diana. Her, Lucy Waltham, a reed-thin girl with tangled hair and an ill-fitting mourning dress. A goddess.

And that afternoon, for the first time since long before her mother died, Lucy had felt happy. Not just happy. Weightless with bliss. Since that day, she'd never imagined loving anyone else. It wasn't an emotion she could slip into and out of, like a silk gown. Adoration wove through the fabric of her being like a golden-brown thread. Without it, she would surely unravel.

The thread pulled tight around her heart. Toby strode up the bank toward her, his expression intent. He reached her side, went down on one knee, and addressed her earnestly. "I have a question for you, Lucy."

She swallowed hard and nodded.

Toby reached into his pocket and withdrew something small and shining. He held it in his outstretched palm for her examination.

"Will this fly do for October, do you think?" He pulled a tackle box from behind his back and opened it. "Or would you suggest another?"

She buried her face in her hands. *Flies.* She was ready to promise him her heart, her life, her soul's devotion— and he wanted her opinion on fishing lures.

"Lucy?"

"Oh, Toby," she sighed, uncovering her face. "That's a may-fly. It won't do at all." She took the tackle box from him and began sifting through the assortment of artificial flies.

Sophia climbed the bank to join them. "How perfectly lovely!" she exclaimed, looking into the tackle box. "What are they made from?"

"This and that," Lucy answered. "Bits of wool and down. Hair from a dog or a calf. Feathers." She plucked a dazzling blue fly from the box and laid it on her palm. "This one I made with peacock feather, and a bit of iridescent shell."

"You made these?" Sophia took the peacock-feather lure and held it up to the light for examination.

"That's our Lucy," Toby said, smoothing a lock of hair from his brow. "So very clever. So very . . ."

"Cunning?" Lucy suggested.

"Cunning. Exactly so."

His nimble smile tugged at Lucy's heart. That was Toby. Never reproachful, never cross. Was it any wonder she adored him? With a single, effortless word or glance he could put her whole world to rights. To bask in that warm, brown gaze was to feel singled out, special. As though the sun shone for her benefit alone.

Blushing, she returned her attention to the tackle box. She plucked out a small fly and held it out to Toby between pinched fingers. A plump bit of black wool formed the body, and the tiny wings were fashioned from a single mallard feather.

"This is what you need," she said. "A thorn-tree fly. It may be less fancy, but the trout find it irresistible." She placed it in his outstretched hand, allowing her fingers to glide across his palm. Toby's gaze met hers. His eyes flashed with surprise, and perhaps—curiosity?

"Toby," she whispered, leaning closer. Daring him to do the same. His gaze dropped to her lips, and Lucy waited in breathless agony until—sweet heaven—his fingers curled tight around hers. So close, so close.

And then—disaster.

"Might I have a go?" Sophia turned from her examination of the peacock fly.

Toby dropped Lucy's hand. He turned those brown eyes on Sophia, and pink bloomed across her porcelain cheeks. Lucy went cold. She'd always known Toby had the power to make *her* feel special. But evidently he made Sophia feel special, too.

"You wish to try angling, Miss Hathaway?" he asked.

"Yes, if you will teach me."

"I'd be delighted."

He helped Sophia to her feet and offered his arm as they walked down the bank. Lucy watched through narrowed eyes as Toby attached the peacock fly to the hook and demonstrated the proper casting technique. He then handed the pole to Sophia, guiding her hands into position. They stood side-by-side, her shoulder pressing against his arm.

Sophia's line went taut, and she gave a startled cry as her pole dipped. Toby moved quickly to stand behind her and encircled her in his arms, placing his hands over hers to steady the fishing pole.

Lucy jumped to her feet. She could not bear to watch this—this *display* any longer. She turned away, walked a few paces, and then turned back in the next moment. Sophia recast her line under Toby's guidance. She hung on his every word and copied his movements, gazing up at him with rapt attention. Lucy rolled her eyes, but Toby appeared—gratified. Pleased. Taller.

What was it about helplessness men found so attractive? She supposed they must enjoy the illusion of superiority. Well, Lucy did not feel the least bit helpless *or* inferior, and her pride rebelled against the notion of feigning either state.

Oh, but she was going to do it anyway.

She took up a spare fishing rod and baited the hook with a thorn-tree fly. Jeremy observed her with a smug expression, which she pointedly ignored. She stepped gingerly onto a slender peninsula of rocky riverbed and cast the line into her favorite spot—a slight bend in the stream, where the waters gathered in a deep pool before braving the course of small rapids downstream. The pool's calm surface gave no hint of the fallen tree that she knew lurked beneath the water.

Lucy reeled in the line until she felt resistance. She leaned back and pulled, snagging the line on the underwater obstacle. Her boots scrabbled for purchase on the rocks, and she braced her heels.

"Help!" she called over her shoulder, in Toby's direction.

Felix came to her side. "Caught a big one, have you?"

She nodded, making a show of struggling with the imaginary catch. "Toby! Kindly help me reel it in?"

Jeremy came up behind her. "I don't suppose you want my assistance?"

"Certainly not." She sidestepped onto a large boulder. What was keeping Toby? He was certainly taking his time in disentangling himself from Sophia Hathaway. Lucy leaned back again, battling the phantom fish with all her might.

Henry joined the group and assessed the situation. "Your line's caught, Lucy. That's all." He took a knife from his pocket and pulled it open.

"Henry, no!" She frantically attempted to right herself.

Too late.

With a flick of the knife, Henry cut the line. Caught off-balance without a counterweight, Lucy pitched, reeled, and ultimately splashed headlong into the stream.

Cold. Freezing cold water. Ice-cold mortification.

Icy shock seized her ribcage like a vise, squeezing the air from her lungs. Lucy could not bring herself to care. She would gladly drown. Here, in the spot where she and Toby had passed so many pleasant afternoons. It would be a fitting end to her young life and vain hopes. For who in his right mind would marry such a perfect ninny?

Then several strong, meddlesome hands hauled her out of the water. Lucy went limp. There could be only one thing worse than dying of shame.

Surviving it.

She kept her eyes tightly closed as the men dragged her onto the bank. She heard voices. Henry, Sophia, Toby, Kitty, Felix, Jeremy. They all spoke at once.

"Fetch the blanket."

"Is she alive?"

"Henry, you ass."

"She's breathing."

"I wouldn't have imagined she weighed so much."

"Lucy, wake up."

She allowed her eyelids to flutter briefly—just long enough to glimpse Henry's face hovering above her. His eyes were troubled; his mouth a thin line. She shut her eyes again. More voices.

"What shall we do?" Toby asked, as strong fingers brushed her hair from her face and throat. Lucy quickly disguised her sigh with a cough. *Toby was touching her throat.*

"Leave her be," Henry ordered. "She's my sister. I'll see to her."

The touching ceased. Drat Henry. His brotherly affection always surfaced at the worst possible moment.

"Poor thing," Sophia said.

"Should we remove her boots?" Felix asked.

Silence.

"They say that, you know." Felix again. "If you're drowning, you ought to remove your shoes."

"I think that only helps while one is actually *in* the water," Kitty said.

"Lucy, wake up now." Henry gave her a rough shake. "Stop playing around. I swear you'll be the death of me, if I don't kill you first."

"You very well may have killed her this time." Jeremy's voice was gruff, and nearer than she would have supposed.

"Henry, just step aside. Let's get her back to the house, warm her up." Oh, now that sounded promising. Toby's voice warmed her from the inside out, like whiskey.

Lucy felt a pair of strong arms lifting her, tucking her body against a broad, muscled chest. Powerful strides carried her up the bank and across the uneven ground.

She sighed and nuzzled into his coat, breathing in the

deliciously masculine scents of leather and pine. Eyes closed tight, she mentally cataloged the position of each of his ten fingers on her body. A five-pointed star cupped her right shoulder; the other five formed a crescent curving around her upper thigh. The flexed muscles of his arms were thick ropes running across her back and under her knees, binding her to him.

She couldn't remember the last time she'd been carried. She must have been a girl, and a small girl at that. It had always been a matter of pride, for Lucy, to choose her own path. Whether walking or riding or driving the gig—she decided just how far she went and in what direction, and she found her own way back. Eventually.

But there was something strangely pleasant about surrendering to this strength, her eyes closed, her body limp in his arms. He could have been carrying her anywhere, or nowhere. But wherever he was going, Lucy was willing to be taken. She pressed her ear to his chest and listened for the distant rhythm of his heartbeat, beating faster to match his determined pace. Beating for her.

He trudged down an incline, and her body sank lower in his grasp with each step. Her cheek slipped from the rough wool of his lapel to the smooth linen of his shirt. His fingers bit into the flesh of her thigh. He broke stride briefly, tossing her body into a new, stronger grip.

"Oh!" she cried, falling against his chest with a soggy thud.

He stopped.

"Lucy?" His voice rumbled through his chest like distant thunder. It sounded different this way. Deeper. Darker. Slightly dangerous.

"Mmmm?" She kept her eyes shut tight and her cheek plastered to his chest.

"Are you finished playing Ophelia, then?"

No. It couldn't be. Her eyes flew open, and cool blue eyes met her startled gaze.

Jeremy.

"I thought Henry was jesting this morning, when he said you planned to pursue the stage. You have the madness bit mastered, but the drowning? That's a bit rich. There are fish in that stream that could take swimming lessons from you."

"I didn't *mean* to fall in." She wriggled in his arms. "Put me down."

"No." He pulled her back against his chest and resumed walking at a brisk pace.

"I said, put me *down*!" She beat against his shoulder with her fist.

"I said, no. You wanted to be rescued."

"Not by you!" Lucy jabbed her elbow into his ribs, levering her arm to increase the space between them. "Jemmy, I do not need to be carried." She growled with frustration. "*Put. Me. Down.*"

At last he complied without ceremony, fairly dropping her into the mud. To her added irritation, Lucy missed his warmth immediately. She hugged herself against the chill and looked around to get her bearings. The house's familiar Tudor façade winked at her through the Manor's iron gates. In the distance, the rest of the group crested a distant rise.

Jeremy shrugged out of his navy wool coat and draped it over her shoulders testily. The front of his shirt was wet. The thin linen clung to his chest, revealing every muscled ridge and hardened plane she had so recently—so mistakenly—molded her body against.

"You're making a fool of yourself, Lucy."

If her teeth hadn't been chattering so fiercely, she would have flung his coat back at him, along with a few choice curses. Leave it to His Lordship to dispense chivalry with a generous dose of condescension.

His disapproving glances at her drenched gown and sodden tangle of hair were wholly unnecessary. She didn't need him to tell her she looked a fool. Standing in the autumn breeze, dripping river water into her nankeen half-boots was a small clue. She was soaked to the bone with humiliation.

And why should he care?

She firmed her chin and glared at him. "You're jealous."

CHAPTER
THREE

Jealous? Jeremy wanted to laugh. It seemed he *must* laugh. To provoke Lucy, to distract himself—it didn't matter which. He only knew that if he didn't muster an ironic little laugh soon, or at least another insult, he might do something truly embarrassing. Like shake her, or kiss her, or just plain crumple to the ground with relief. He couldn't stop reliving that moment, when Lucy had tumbled into the stream and his stomach had plummeted with her.

Worse, he couldn't help noticing how she looked wet.

She looked furious and fiercely beautiful. Like a water nymph ripped from the river and set dripping on firm ground. Her hair had worked free of its pins once again, and the wet locks hung down her shoulders like thick, curling vines. Her face was pale, but her eyes glowed green like an ocean in a tempest, and her quivering bottom lip matched the shade of a frosted plum.

And that was the end of her. Lucy did not exist below the neck. Jeremy refused to glance further downward, because he knew what he would see. Wet, all-but-transparent silk clinging to full, high breasts, a sleek belly, rounded hips . . . he didn't have to look. He could picture her body well enough. *Had* pictured it through a sleepless night. He'd saddled his horse at dawn that morning, ridden breakneck across fields in hopes of leaving that image behind—only to find the same temptations served up to him over breakfast. It was useless.

Even if his mind could forget the sight of those sweet, maddening curves, his body recalled every inch of her as she felt pressed up against him.

He would not look. Would. *Not.*

Even though she was breathing hard, and he knew her chest would be likewise heaving. And even though she was cold and wet, and her nipples *must* be—

His eyes slipped.

Oh, God. They were.

Jeremy clenched his jaw and looked toward the horizon for some distraction. Ah, yes—Henry, her brother, making his way across the green. Henry would serve nicely.

What the devil had come over him? This was what came of spending the entire Season in Town without bedding a woman, for no earthly reason. Had he been expecting to receive a plaque from the Ladies' Society for the Promotion of Abstinence? The silver cup awarded for Reformed Rake of the Year? Whatever his perceived reward, Jeremy had spent the last few months polishing his self-control to a sterling luster. Unfortunately, he seemed to have left it in London.

And now, this water-witch—this *Lucy*—stood before him, accusing him of being jealous.

Lusting? Yes. Addled? Clearly. But jealous? Most certainly not.

Never before had Jeremy been happier to *not* be the recipient of a lady's affections. God forbid this hoyden-turned-siren unleashed herself in his direction. He doubted he would survive the experience.

Jealous. What a ridiculous notion. To prove the point, he conjured a vivid mental image of Lucy standing in her nightgown, craning up on tiptoe to kiss Toby, twining her fingers in his hair. He watched detached, a mere observer of a ribald opera revue, as in his mind's eye Lucy fell against Toby's chest. She parted her lips, Toby deepened the kiss, and Jeremy felt nothing. A bit of annoyance, perhaps—because Toby was kissing her all wrong. She arched into him and dug her fingers into his shoulders and made little writhing circles with her hips. Jeremy felt . . . almost nothing. Only the faintest suggestion of something. A flea bite. A tiny sting. Then in his mind, he heard Lucy give a breathy moan of passion, and somewhere deep and low in his body, something snapped. He was no longer an observer of the scene, but taking control of it. Taking control of her. *His* lips were covering hers. *His* tongue was teasing hers. *His* fingers were snaking between the buttons of her nightgown to curve around—

Good Lord, Henry walked unforgivably slowly. What did it take to light a fire under the man? His sister had nearly drowned.

Lucy was still glaring at him, letting that word—*jealous*—hang in the air, unchallenged. He ought to muster a defense. He ought to set her straight. He ought to take her inside and lay her down by the fire and strip her out of those wet clothes.

"You're jealous," she repeated, in an icy tone that cut straight through the heat of his desire. Her eyes flashed with fury. "You're a cold, unfeeling, heartless man. And you have no idea what it is to care for something—some*one*—so deeply. To be willing to admit it, to yourself and to the world. To make a complete and utter fool of yourself, if necessary. Real love takes real courage. I have it, and you don't. And you're jealous."

She brushed past him and stalked off toward the house. Jeremy stared after her, numb with shock.

"I take it Lucy's made a full recovery." Henry covered the last few paces to stand at Jeremy's shoulder. "What was that all about, then?"

Jeremy wished he could say. He shifted his weight

from one foot to the other; then shifted it back. "Henry, I think we need to talk."

"I think so," said Henry, eyeing him with amusement. "Explain to me, kindly, why my little sister is lecturing you on love."

The gentlemen convened their council over a bottle of fine brandy. Jeremy had drained one glass and was already pouring himself a second while his friends still savored their first sips. "Something has to be done about Lucy," he announced in a firm voice intended to convince no one more than himself.

"I've been trying to do something about Lucy for years now," Henry said, leaning back in his chair and propping his feet up on his desk. "I've quite given up."

"Did I miss something?" Felix asked. "What's the matter with Lucy?"

"Besides the fact that she's forgotten how to swim, fish, and dress appropriate to the weather?" Jeremy topped off his glass and sank into the chair closest to the fire. His shirt was still damp, and Lucy had absconded with his coat. "She fancies herself in love."

"Aha," said Henry. He turned to Felix and whispered loudly, "Apparently she and Jem had some sort of lovers' quarrel." Both men erupted in laughter.

Toby chuckled into his glass. "Lucy and Jem? Now *that's* amusing. But better Jem than that spotty son of your vicar, Henry. He wrote her some perfectly dreadful verses last year."

"The vicar's boy was writing Lucy verses?" Henry sat up in his chair, suddenly sobered. "Why does no one tell me these things?"

"I thought you knew." Toby shrugged. "And as I said, they were dreadful. Even if they weren't, Byron himself couldn't touch Lucy's heart, unless he came bearing pie along with his poems."

"Let's ring for tea and sandwiches, shall we?" Felix asked. "I'm famished."

"It was *not* a lovers' quarrel," Jeremy interrupted. "Lucy is *not* in love with me." He turned to Toby. "And neither is she in love with the vicar's son, you idiot. She's in love with you."

"Still?" Toby sipped his brandy. "Blast. I was hoping she'd taken a liking to someone new."

"You hoped no such thing." Jeremy set his glass down with a forceful clatter. "You know you encourage her. Just like you encourage everything in a skirt between the ages of thirteen and thirty."

"Jem," said Henry, "in case you haven't noticed, Lucy's been mooning over Toby for years now. Calf-love, that's all it is."

Jeremy groaned. "Henry, in case you haven't noticed, Lucy's not a girl anymore. She's grown out of calf-love. She's—" He stopped himself, edging away from that sentence as if it were a dangerous cliff.

Henry laughed. "Surely you're not calling my sister a full-grown cow?"

Jeremy took a breath and began again, slowly. As though speaking to a cow. "Lucy knows Toby is planning to marry Miss Hathaway."

Felix let out a low whistle. "That is a problem."

"Which one of you told her?" Toby asked, sounding faintly peeved.

"It wasn't me," Felix said.

"*I* certainly didn't." Henry frowned. "Are you sure she knows, Jem?"

Jeremy paused. He couldn't very well tell them how he knew that Lucy knew. There was no good way to tell Henry that his sister had visited his bedchamber in her dressing gown. There was no way at all to explain what had happened next. "There are four ladies in the house," he said with a shrug. "You know how ladies talk. She must know. And now that she knows—"

"She's jealous," Felix finished.

"Exactly. She's jealous." Jeremy took a triumphant swallow of brandy, pleased to finally hang that label where it rightly belonged.

"So she's jealous," said Henry. "I don't see why there's any call to *do* something about it."

Jeremy shook his head. Could there be another man so thick-skulled in all England? How Henry had managed to get through Eton and Cambridge, Jeremy couldn't guess. Actually, the answer was obvious. By sticking close to Jeremy. Not that Jeremy had begrudged him the assistance. Since their first year at Eton, Henry had been a friend.

Jeremy's choice of friends had given his father fits, if one could call the slight twitch of the jaw that preceded a monotone lecture a "fit." He could still hear the cool disdain in his voice. *Warrington,* he had intoned after Jeremy's first year at Eton, *it escapes me utterly why you should choose to surround yourself with that collection of miserable, low-born scamps. Who are their fathers? Tradesmen? Farmers? Not a title among them, save a mere baronet. You are in every way their superior, and if you tolerate their company at all, you should at least insist they address you by your title.*

But that was just it. Jeremy had not wanted to consort with other boys of his rank, nor be addressed as "Warrington"—the title that, in Jeremy's ten-year-old mind, still belonged to his older brother. Why should he suffer constant reminders of Thomas's death, when he could play with boys who knew nothing of it? Boys like Henry, Felix, and Toby.

Good friends, the three of them, but Henry most of all. Henry didn't allow him to sit brooding in his club when there was a prizefight to see, any more than he allowed him to stew at home over a failed wheat harvest when there were trout to be netted. Without stooping to methods so grating as cheerfulness, Henry simply refused to indulge his darker moods. But the same qualities that made him a valued friend made Henry a miserable excuse for a guardian. Now that Jeremy began to see what that blithe irreverence was costing Lucy, his humor was growing black indeed.

"You know how persistent Lucy can be when she sets her mind to something," he said testily. "She's going to throw herself at Toby at every opportunity. This afternoon she missed and hit the river instead. She's like to do herself in, and take a few of us with her."

"And what, precisely, do you recommend I do?" Henry asked.

"Not you," Jeremy said. "Toby."

"Oh, no." Alarm flared in Toby's eyes. "I'm not having *that* conversation with Lucy. I take no pleasure in breaking young ladies' hearts."

The other three stared at him.

"Well, I don't," he said defensively. "Of late."

"You don't have to break her heart." Jeremy was becoming exasperated. "At least, not to her face. You just have to propose to Miss Hathaway. Once you're engaged, Lucy will be forced to give up this absurd notion of seduc—*distracting* you."

"I shall be perfectly happy to propose marriage to Miss Hathaway," said Toby. "At the *end* of our holiday."

"Why the end?" asked Felix. "Kitty's been after me daily, asking when you're finally going to propose to Sophia. She thinks you've got the gout, you're so reluctant to bend a knee."

"I may as well be infirm, for all the fun I'll have once I'm engaged," Toby said. "I can't very well bag a bride in the morning and a pheasant that same afternoon.

Once I've asked for her hand, I'll have a hundred things to do. Go apply to her father in Kent. See my solicitor in Town. Make appointments with my tailor. Retrieve my grandmother's ring from Surrey. I'll be running all over England like a Norman invader, and that will spell the end of all amusement."

"What rot," Henry said. "Felix and I are both married, as you see, and we manage a bit of sport despite it."

"Yes, but you're *married*," Toby replied. "A married woman likes nothing better than to be left alone. A betrothed woman won't leave a man be. I'll be obliged to take ambling strolls in the garden and read poetry over tea, when I ought to be tramping through the woods, taking nips off a flask of whiskey."

"Courting can be a sport in its own right," Felix said with a sly smile.

Toby countered, "Yes, but blushing virgins are always in season." He rose from his seat and went to stand by the window, gazing out over the park. "Miss Hathaway is an enchanting creature. I admire her beauty and esteem her character. I may even love her. But this autumn is my last gasp of bachelorhood, and I mean to enjoy it. While there are still coveys in Henry's woods, I have no intention of proposing marriage to Sophia Hathaway."

"And what about Lucy?" Jeremy asked.

"Oh, don't worry. I shan't propose to her, either."

Jeremy regarded his friend through narrowed eyes. Toby's brand of reckless charm wore well on a youth of one-and-twenty, but it ill became a gentleman nearing thirty. Not that the young ladies had ceased swooning in his direction. Falling in love with Sir Toby Aldridge was still a rite of initiation for debutantes. But this wasn't another simpering heiress they were discussing. This was *Lucy*.

He turned to Henry. "Aren't you the least bit concerned for your sister's welfare?"

"Of course I'm concerned for her welfare. I'm her guardian."

Jeremy snorted.

"You're making too much of this," Henry said. "So Lucy is infatuated with Toby. It's an all-too-common affliction. One many a girl has survived, with no lasting ill effects."

"Unless you count near-drowning."

"She's mistaken Toby's kindness for some deeper emotion," Henry continued, ignoring Jeremy's remark. "It's entirely understandable. She ought to have had her season by now, and fallen in and out of love a dozen times. As it is, she's a complete innocent."

Jeremy snorted again. Obviously Henry did not know about *the book*.

"She feels left out," Henry went on. "She's surrounded by ladies who are either happily married or engaged." He waved off Toby's interjection. "*Nearly* engaged. She wants a bit of romance all her own." Apparently satisfied with this deduction, Henry saluted his own ingenuity by pouring another round of brandy. "It will pass."

Jeremy felt creeping tendrils of madness winding around his brain. *It will pass?* Henry couldn't possibly know how wrong he was. And Jeremy couldn't possibly tell him. "And in the meantime?" he asked. "You just allow her to keep up these . . . these antics?"

"Jem has a point there," said Toby. "I can't very well have Lucy hanging all over me if I'm meant to be courting Miss Hathaway. A bit awkward, that."

Henry shrugged. "I don't see what else there is to do."

"Perhaps you should invite the vicar's son to tea," Felix suggested.

"Impossible," said Henry. "He's off to Oxford."

Jeremy shook his head. This conversation was becoming nonsensical. He glowered at Toby. *Selfish ass.* So cocksure of captivating any and every woman's affections. Of course he saw no reason to rush a proposal. The idea of Miss Hathaway refusing him would never cross his mind. It would serve him right if she did.

Toby noted Jeremy's sullen expression. "Don't look at me like that! It's not my fault, you know. If you find Lucy's 'antics' so annoying, why don't *you* distract her?"

"Please." Jeremy tipped his glass to drain the last of his brandy, then lowered it slowly. Henry was giving him the most distressing look.

"That's not a bad idea," Henry said.

"What's not a bad idea?" asked Felix.

"Jem distracting Lucy." A mischievous grin spread across Toby's face.

"Oh, no." Jeremy rose from his chair and stepped behind it, as though the wing-backed barrier of civility might shield him from their lunacy. "If by 'distract,' you mean—*distract*—and if by 'Lucy,' you mean Henry's *sister* . . . the answer is no. No."

"Relax, Jem," Henry said. "We're not suggesting you court her in earnest. Just pay her a bit of attention. Take her on an amble through the garden. Read her one of Byron's poems."

"And don't forget the pie." Felix was enjoying this far too much.

"You can't be serious, Henry." Henry had never been a model guardian, but this strained the definition of the term. "Are you honestly suggesting—*inviting* me to play loose with your sister's affections?"

"Her affections?" Henry laughed. "As if *you* could engage Lucy's affections. It's nothing so dreadful. Her pride's been bruised, and she wants a bit of admiring. Just do your best to stand in for the vicar's spotty son."

Good Lord, had Henry *met* his sister? Lucy was many things, but easily dissuaded was not one of them. She'd invested eight years in this misplaced adulation, and if Henry thought a few pretty words would snap her out of it now, he was a bit late on the draw.

"You'll not touch her, of course," Henry added, his voice deep with mock warning.

A bit late on that one, too.

"Come on," Toby pleaded. "Do a man a favor. I'd do it for you, were our situations reversed."

"I don't doubt you would," Jeremy said. "But oddly enough, Toby, I've never aspired to your example of conduct."

They were closing in on him, all three of them wearing expressions of great amusement. Jeremy began to feel a bit desperate. "It won't work," he protested.

"Are you so out of practice then?" Toby taunted. "You typically cut quite a swath through the *ton*, but not this season. Perhaps you're just not up to the task?"

Jeremy's hands were fists at his sides. His right itched to connect with Toby's jaw. The left had distinctly lower ambitions. "My *ability* is not in question."

Henry clapped him on the shoulder and smiled. "Good. Then it's settled."

CHAPTER
FOUR

"Come to call me a fool again?" Lucy asked from behind her book. "Or perhaps you've devised a fresh insult?"

Jeremy pulled a chair up to the hearth. Aunt Matilda dozed on a nearby divan, her turbaned head slumped to her chest. The turban's indigo plume dangled in front of her nose, and each rattling snore set it dancing in the breeze.

After this afternoon's dousing, Lucy had traded her ruined silk gown for a simple dark-green dress with—thankfully—a modest neckline. Her hair was braided into a thick rope of chestnut that tapered to a gentle curve at her waist. A leather-bound volume hid her face from view. She had maintained this studious attitude ever since the group retired to the drawing room following dinner, but Jeremy hadn't seen her turn a single page.

He maneuvered a chess table into the space between them and began arranging the pawns in neat rows. "I did not come to insult you. Quite the opposite." He leaned forward across the game board, as though preparing to spill a great secret. "I've come to seduce you."

She peeked at him over the top of her book. Her eyes flared momentarily before narrowing to slits. "I prefer insult to ridicule."

He shrugged and continued arranging the chess pieces. "Perhaps I simply want a game of chess."

She snorted in disbelief and glanced over toward the card table, where the Hathaway sisters were on the verge of bankrupting all three gentlemen. "Henry put you up to this, didn't he?"

Jeremy's fingers tightened around a black rook.

"I don't want your pity, Jemmy." Lucy snapped her book closed. "And what's more, I don't need it."

She met his eyes directly, and the force in her gaze nearly knocked him off his chair. Her green eyes were clear and alive with intelligence, not red or brimming with tears. He shook his head, chiding himself for underestimating her resilience. Lucy had not sequestered herself to nurse her wounded pride or lament her disappointed hopes. She was plotting her next move.

"I'm not here to pity you. Nor am I acting at Henry's behest." Jeremy placed the last pieces on the board. "I have my own reasons to speak with you."

She rotated the chessboard to situate the white pieces before her. Winding her braid around her right hand, she advanced a pawn with her left. She glanced up at him through thick, curving eyelashes. "To apologize?"

To apologize, indeed. Lucy ought to be thanking him. He intended to bring a swift end to this absurd scheme of her brother's. At dinner, he had suffered winks from Henry, grins from Toby, Felix's jab to the ribs—even Marianne's sly expression when she seated Lucy at his elbow. Well, Henry could make accomplices of every last footman, for all Jeremy cared. He'd be damned if he'd spend his holiday reciting Byron in the garden, simply to coddle their consciences. Neither did he intend to stand watch in the corridor each night, or keep fishing Lucy out of danger. If neither Henry nor Toby were man enough to simply tell her the truth, Jeremy would.

He brought out a pawn to meet hers. "I've come to tell you the good news. Toby will propose marriage to Miss Hathaway at the end of the holiday."

"*That* is the good news?" She moved a bishop across the board, claiming a black pawn. "I can scarcely contain my joy. Please excuse my display of wild jubilation."

"At the *end* of the holiday, Lucy. Weeks from now. Any attempt to prevent the engagement would be futile"—he continued speaking over her objection—"but if you insist on trying, you have ample time. There is no need to commit a brazen act of seduction. Or subversion."

"On the contrary." The corners of her lips curled in an impish grin. "With so much time at my disposal, I can commit more brazen acts than ever."

"And do you suppose brazenness is a quality Toby seeks in a wife?"

His barb hit home, and Lucy's mouth thinned to a line. She glanced over at the card players. "What *does* he see in her?"

"As I told you, she is beautiful, accomplished, and—most importantly—wealthy."

"And these are the qualities that inspire a man to the heights of passion? A large dowry and cunning tea trays?"

"No, they are not the qualities that inspire a man to passion. They are the qualities that inspire a man to propose."

Lucy studied the chessboard, twining the curled end of her braid around her fingers and touching it against the corner of her mouth. Her tongue flicked out from between her parted lips, drawing on a strand of hair. Jeremy shifted in his seat.

"We seem to be back where we began," she said.

"How so?"

"I have no dowry or tea tray to inspire a man to propose. Therefore, I shall have to summon the qualities that inspire a man to passion." She looked up at him, green eyes dancing with reflected firelight. "And those would be?"

If he were being honest, Jeremy would be forced to tell her that the saucy gleam in her eye was a powerful start. And that the way she kept teasing that stray chestnut curl with her tongue—nibbling it, sucking it, drawing it into her mouth—had him feeling *inspired* indeed.

But Jeremy had no particular desire to be honest. In fact, he heartily wished to change the subject. And if he managed to change Lucy's mind in the process, so much the better. "It isn't only Miss Hathaway's dowry," he said. "I believe Toby does feel a genuine attachment to her."

Lucy looked disbelieving. She moved her bishop across the board. "You can't expect me to believe it was love at first sight."

"Not at all. More like the second." This captured her attention. She leaned forward slightly in her chair. Jeremy bent over the chessboard and lowered his voice. "Toby was first introduced to Miss Hathaway at a dinner party at Felix's house. She was every bit as lovely and charming as you see her now. She made trifling conversation at dinner and played the pianoforte afterward, quite capably. Toby took no notice." He moved a knight into play.

"And the second time?"

"The second time we were all in company, we met at a ball. On that occasion, Miss Sophia had a bevy of admirers surrounding her before the first set. Toby was instantly enthralled. For weeks afterward, he spoke of nothing but Miss Sophia Hathaway. He was quite insufferable."

Lucy looked nonplussed. "So you're telling me Henry should host a ball?"

He sighed. "I'm telling you to stop flinging yourself at Toby's feet. A man doesn't want to stoop to love. He wants to reach higher, stand taller. He desires something more than a woman. He wants an angel. A dream."

"A goddess?"

"If you will."

Her voice grew wistful. "Toby always called me a goddess. His Diana. Goddess of the hunt."

"She was the goddess of chastity, too," he scoffed. "But no matter. You're beginning to comprehend the principle. The allure of the unattainable. You'd be foolish to keep flashing your . . . your *charms* at Toby so brazenly. Men want what it seems they can't have."

And God help him, he was a man. He wanted what he could not have. That must be the reason Jeremy felt himself growing stiff at the mere mention of Lucy's *charms*. Lucy was unattainable, he reminded himself for what must have been the nineteenth time that day. And whatever strange allure she held, it logically proceeded from that fact. Not from her enticing, womanly curves, or her golden, petal-soft skin. Not from the obvious challenge of her flinty spirit or the veiled invitation in her smoky voice. And most definitely not from her lips—those lush, bowed, dusky red lips that Jeremy now knew to be formed for something wholly apart from stinging retorts. Sweet, sensual kisses that stirred a man's blood and tasted of wild, ripe fruit. Forbidden fruit.

It was all too true. *Men want what it seems they can't have.*

Lucy leveled her green gaze at him. "Jealous."

He groaned inwardly. Not that word again. He was not—*not*—jealous. He began piecing together an objection, but she spoke first.

"I comprehend you perfectly. I need to make Toby jealous."

He stared at her. Not comprehending.

"You said yourself that he never looked twice at

Sophia until she showed up with a throng of suitors. That's what I need. A suitor. A throng of them would be preferable, but I suppose one will have to do." She wound the braid around her finger and began toying with it again. "Too bad the vicar's son is off to Oxford. He's positively mad for me."

She stared at the carpet, brow furrowed. Then she raised her head and locked gazes with him. "It will have to be you."

"Me?"

"I know, I know. It sounds ridiculous, but there's no one else. It's nothing so terrible. Just pretend to court me for a while. Until Toby realizes he loves me."

"I could court you forever, and that plan would never work."

Lucy sank back in her chair and folded her arms. She exhaled forcefully. "I suppose you're right." She regarded him with an expression that struck Jeremy as uncomfortably close to disdain. "No one would ever believe it."

Jeremy couldn't decide which facet of this disturbingly familiar conversation should perturb him more. To begin with, there was the repeated insistence that, heedless of his own feelings or principles, he must perforce strike up a counterfeit courtship with Lucy. Then there was the fact that he once again came in second to the vicar's spotty son in his desirability for this appointment. Most galling of all, however, seemed the general skepticism of his ability to convincingly woo even a country-bred innocent.

His pride spoke ahead of his judgment. "You could not be aware of it, Lucy, but I do have a certain reputation. The others here, they are used to watching me seduce ladies in Town. They expect it. It will strike no one as surprising, should we take up a flirtation." This was mostly true. Of course a flirtation would not strike

Henry, Toby, or Felix as surprising, since they had all insisted he begin one.

Lucy sat up in her seat. "Jemmy—are you trying to tell me you're a rake?"

She burst into laughter. Had she not been laughing at *him,* Jeremy would have thought it an altogether pleasant sound. "I don't believe it," she said, shaking her head.

She reached toward the chessboard, and he caught her hand in his. "Believe me," he whispered. "When I wish to be, I can be very convincing." He followed the seam of her fingers with this thumb, tracing slowly upward until he reached the soft cleft below her knuckles. He watched as her eyes widened and her lips parted. Then he stroked the spot lightly—a quick, circular caress— and she made a little sound, half gasp and half sigh.

That little sound—that tiny, panting breath—was very nearly his undoing. Jeremy knew that sound. It was the tumbler of a lock falling in place, the charged crackle between lightning and thunderbolt, the hiss of a candlewick the instant before it comes alive with flame. An incomplete sound. A sound that promised—and begged for—more. Lust blazed through him, and he dropped her hand as if burnt.

Lucy crossed her arms and sank into her chair, her eyes studying his face. Then she smiled—a sly, kittenish curling of the lips that looked to be the devil's own grin.

Jeremy swore inwardly. He ought to rise from his chair that instant and walk away. It was true that Henry and Toby had urged him to do exactly as Lucy suggested, but he had no duty to oblige them. Lucy was not his sister. She was not his admirer. But through some absurd twist of fate and fishing line, she had become his problem.

Because he knew Lucy. She would go after Toby, with or without his help. The alternative to this ruse, in her eyes, involved a certain high-necked shift and bold flashes of bare, golden skin. And Jeremy found he didn't like that alternative. At all.

"So you'll do it," she said slowly. "You'll pretend to court me."

"*Pretend,*" he stressed, sighing heavily. "Yes."

Lucy smiled.

She liked this plan. She liked it very much. It made perfect sense. Seeing Toby with Sophia Hathaway had propelled her to new heights of jealous desperation. It had propelled her into a river. If any ploy could make Toby see her in a new light, this one could. And better still, the plan offered a source of amusement in the bargain. A chance to needle Jeremy to distraction.

She viewed Jeremy's expression—his usual stern, sober veneer. An irresistible challenge. Yes, she liked the plan very much.

She allowed a few moments to pass in silence. Time to crack the egg. "So, Jemmy—just how in love with me are you?"

She was rewarded with an expression of sheer panic. Oh, this was going to be fun.

"I beg your pardon?"

"And I accept your apology," she teased. She captured his knight with her rook. "Check."

He stared at her with an expression of utter bewilderment. One would think he'd never played chess before.

She took pity on him. "It's just that, if you're to be my suitor, I'd like to know exactly what level of devotion I can expect. Are you merely admiring? Thoroughly besotted? Completely and utterly lovestruck?"

He exhaled with obvious relief. "Let's not get carried away," he growled, moving his king out of danger. "Besotted should do."

"Besotted it is, then." She repositioned her rook.

"Check." She leaned closer and whispered, "I do believe a besotted suitor would let me win."

"Never." He captured her rook with his queen.

The smug set of his jaw charmed his lips into the curve of a smile. Lucy was strongly tempted to stick out her tongue at him. She doubted, however, that sticking out one's tongue was how a lady treated a besotted suitor. At least, not when prompted by a fit of petulance. In a moment of passion, however . . . sticking out one's tongue appeared to be *de rigueur*. Her face flushed with warmth.

There was a burst of applause from the card table. Lucy turned to watch as Sophia laid the winning card and raked in the pile of tokens from the middle of the table. Toby took her hand and kissed it before leaning closer to murmur something in Sophia's ear. Something that made her smile and blush bright pink. Roses on porcelain, with a halo of gold. An angel. A dream.

"It's your move," Jeremy prompted.

"I don't feel like playing anymore. I'll finish beating you tomorrow."

He followed her gaze to the table, where Toby and Sophia's heads were bent close together as she examined the cards in his hand. "Lucy, you have to accept—"

She cut him off with a look. She picked up her book and held it out to him. "Here. Read to me."

"Read to you? You must be joking."

She tossed the book at him, and he caught it instinctively. "A *besotted* man would read."

He glanced at the cover. Smirking, he read the title aloud. "*Methods and Practice of Leporine Husbandry?* Lucy, tell me this is not *the* book."

"No, it is not *the* book." She wrapped her shawl about her shoulders. "It is merely the *first* book I picked up."

He shook his head. "I suppose I should be grateful it isn't Byron."

He opened the volume at random and began to read in a slow, steady voice. Lucy leaned against the side of her chair, pressing her cheek against the upholstery. Her eyelids fluttered shut. The room melted away. Exhaustion claimed her, and she slipped into that drowsy place between wakefulness and sleep. There, in that half-dream world, she could almost recapture those few blissful minutes from earlier that day, when the same deep voice had rumbled through rough fabric. When she had imagined herself to be safe and protected, wrapped in the arms of the man she loved.

It was a very pretty dream.

CHAPTER
FIVE

"There's something I've been meaning to ask you, Jem." Henry fell in step alongside Jeremy, his worn Hessians treading briskly through fallen leaves and shriveled ferns. "It's a question I've been pondering for quite some time, and—well, you know I value your opinion."

He pulled up, gripped the brim of his beaver, and turned to Jeremy with a serious expression. "Does this hat make my face look round?"

Behind him, Felix and Toby doubled with laughter.

"Jem, d'you suppose," Felix wheezed, "that pink ribbons would suit me better, or lavender?"

"Oh, definitely lavender," Toby answered, schooling his expression to one of mock sincerity. "I'm sure Jem would agree that ginger hair and pink ribbons are a horrid combination."

Jeremy steeled his jaw and inhaled slowly through his nose. "I am carrying a loaded rifle, you know."

"No good, Jem. We all know you piss with better aim than you shoot." Toby brushed by him, digging an elbow into Jeremy's side as he passed. "You're no marksman. But clearly you missed your calling in millinery."

"Need I remind you," Jeremy said, his grip tightening around his gun, "that this was *not* my idea? I recall someone pleading with me to do a man a favor."

"And I hereby nominate you for sainthood," said Henry, clapping him on the back. "You're a better man than I. No humanitarian cause could possibly entice me to escort three ladies bonnet shopping."

Good Lord, thought Jeremy. He would never live this down. And his friends didn't know the half of it. They'd only seen him driving the barouche back from the village, buried under tittering ladies and pink hatboxes. Thank God they hadn't seen him hunched over a tiny tea table laden with dainty cream-filled cakes, or holding up three lengths of satin ribbon—one in either hand, the third caught in his teeth—just so Lucy could stand back three paces and compare them from afar.

And it didn't end there. The events of the past three days formed a chain of small degradations. New links were added hourly, as Lucy spun ridiculous fantasies of how a besotted man ought to behave.

A besotted man, according to Lucy, would gather hundreds of hawthorn berries from a thorny hedgerow, happily sacrificing several hours and a nearly-new coat for the distant promise of tart, seedy jam.

A besotted man, evidently, would sit by his lady's side at the pianoforte and turn pages for her—even if the only tune his lady knew was a vulgar drinking song, which she played from memory at a dirge-like tempo for nearly an hour straight.

A besotted man would share his brandy.

A besotted man would pet the cat.

A besotted man would *smile*.

And a besotted man would give up a perfectly fine afternoon of sport to take the ladies shopping.

How had he let the ruse get so out of hand? He was the Earl of Kendall, for God's sake. He employed six-and-twenty footmen—in London alone—to heed his every command. Now he catered to the whims of a despot in dotted muslin. Being in league with Lucy was a fate far worse than truly being besotted. Bedraggled, bedeviled, beleaguered—he felt each in turn, and often all three at once.

A dozen times a day, Jeremy resolved to break off this farce of a flirtation. He could never quite bring himself to do it. His friends' ribbing and his own bruised pride notwithstanding, the plan was working admirably. Aside from purchasing an obscenely ugly bonnet, Lucy had not, to his knowledge, committed any further reckless acts. She had not invaded Toby's bedchamber.

But Jeremy couldn't keep her out of his.

As if Lucy's capricious demands weren't punishment enough by day, the true torment began at night. At night, she drove him utterly mad—in dreams. Indecent, immoral, exceedingly vivid dreams. Dreams of creamy flesh and berry-stained lips. Dreams of satin ribbons and silky skin, sliding under both hands and caught in his teeth. Dreams of brandy-scented breath coming hot on his neck and bawdy lyrics urging him on. Dreams that aroused him so powerfully, they roused him from sleep, slick with sweat and aching for release.

Damn it all, a man of nine-and-twenty should have long outgrown this sort of adolescent panting. Jeremy thought he *had* outgrown it. As a youth, he'd enjoyed his share of frantic fumbles with chambermaids and village girls. Then it was off to Cambridge, where they'd all studied gambling and wenching with greater diligence than philosophy or physics. Add in a year spent sampling the delights of the Mediterranean. Then it was back to Town, back to the *ton*.

Time, his father had charged him, to settle down and select a bride. He needed to produce an heir, secure the line—and the promise of an earldom and one of England's most sizeable fortunes meant Jeremy might look as high as he pleased. A suitable bride, in his father's opinion, would have been a lady of fair face and delicate breeding, from established lines and old money. A hand-some catch.

A trophy.

As usual, his father had been disappointed.

Jeremy attended the requisite balls, the musicales, the dinner and card parties. And he pursued ladies, yes. Eminently unsuitable ones. Willing widows, mostly, with no wish to remarry. The occasional talented actress, an elite courtesan or two. Every conquest held a double thrill—satisfying his own desires while thwarting his father's.

Then, two years ago, he'd returned to London as the Earl of Kendall. It took only a few more meaningless trysts to realize the thrill was gone. His father was dead. The ladies themselves had no complaints, and the matchmaking mamas had all but given him up. The only person he was disappointing was himself.

Besides, he had an estate he needed to learn to run, before neglect ran it into the ground. Jeremy took the desire and penned it safely away. He had considerable experience caging unwanted emotions. He reasoned he could keep lust locked up, as well.

Ha. It had taken one kiss. Well, three kisses. The first was rather bad; the second, a vast improvement. And God in heaven, the third . . . Lust had sprung free of its cage and now roamed his body at will. A year's worth of pent-up desire, unleashed in a heartbeat. And in those dozen times a day that Jeremy longed to call off this ill-conceived plan, it was always the lust that roared *no*. He tried to believe he had better, nobler reasons for keeping Lucy out of Toby's bedchamber. Perhaps he did, some-where, in some forgotten recess of his mind, filed under Gentleman. But a wild, savage, lust-crazed Beast was currently prowling the earth in his skin, and the idea of Lucy in any man's bedchamber—other than his own—incited the Beast to violence.

Jeremy raised his gun to his shoulder, took aim at a distant tree stump, and fired. Chips of rotten wood exploded into the air. Henry, Toby, and Felix stopped in their tracks and stared at him as though he had burst into song.

"There was a pheasant," he said.

Three heads swiveled in unison to regard the cratered tree stump, then turned back to face him. Henry opened his mouth to speak, but Jeremy silenced him with a look.

The Look.

There were few aspects of his father's demeanor Jeremy found worth imitating, but The Look was one of those few. Like it or not, he had inherited his father's ice-blue eyes and heavy brow. With a bit of practice, giving someone The Look came as easily as flexing a muscle.

The Look meant different things at different times, depending on the recipient and the occasion. It could mean, "Hold your tongue." It could mean, "Lift your skirts." On one particularly memorable occasion, it had meant, "Put down the damned candlestick before you embarrass us both."

But whatever The Look meant, it conveyed authority. The Look said, without equivocation, *I lead, and you follow.*

There was only one person in Jeremy's acquaintance who remained utterly impervious to The Look. And damn, if she wasn't leading him around by a satin ribbon.

"He's giving you that look again," Sophia whispered.

Lucy raised her head from her book. "Who is?"

"Lord Kendall, of course," Sophia replied, dipping her quill in a pot of ink. "He's quite taken with you."

"You mean Jemmy?" Lucy looked up to catch Jeremy glaring at her from across the drawing room. She grinned and winked, and he looked away. No doubt he was still smarting about the ribbons. Or the cat hair on his coat. Perhaps the brandy. It couldn't be that she'd stolen his sherry trifle at dinner. He had never cared for dessert. Whatever was irking him, it must be something truly dreadful. Marianne sat down to the pianoforte, but he scarcely took note.

"Oh, he is quite taken with me," she answered Sophia in a matter-of-fact tone. "He's thoroughly besotted."

At last, *someone* had noticed, even if it was the wrong person entirely. Lucy had put Jeremy through the paces of a besotted suitor for three days now, but Toby remained oblivious. For that matter, so did Henry, Marianne, Felix, and Kitty. It was unspeakably maddening. She might have eloped with a gardener ages ago, and no one would have noticed.

"You call him by his Christian name?" Sophia raised an eyebrow. "So very brave. Perhaps even a bit wicked." Her mouth twitched in a strange smile.

Wicked? Lucy had forgotten. She was speaking with an angel. Why, in heaven's name, had she chosen to sit near the escritoire? She ought to have known Sophia Hathaway would be seized with the urge to write letters. Lucy yearned to be truly wicked and escape with her book to the window seat, shutting out Sophia and society with one yank on the plum-colored drapes.

"I've known him for ages," Lucy said. "Since I was a girl. He wasn't even the Earl of Kendall then. He was Viscount Something-or-other."

"Warrington," Sophia said, putting quill to paper with a delicate touch. Lucy watched as sweeping strokes and precise loops flowed from Sophia's quill. Even her penmanship was perfect. Lucy hated her with a wicked, inky-black passion.

"Hmm?"

"Viscount Warrington."

"Oh."

Sophia laid her quill down on the table and stretched her hand. "Correspondence can be so tedious," she said. "Nothing drains the joy from a happy memory like the act of committing it to paper ten times over. Don't you agree?"

"I wouldn't know," Lucy answered, returning her attention to her book. "I don't write letters."

"None at all? Whyever not?"

Lucy shrugged. "I've no correspondents."

"Surely you must have," Sophia said. "What about your friends from school?"

"I never went to school. I always had governesses."

"Do you not still write to them?"

The suggestion brought a smirk to Lucy's face. "No," she replied. "We weren't especially close."

"Well, you shall have at least one correspondent soon."

"Oh, really? Who?"

"Me," Sophia said, glancing up from the letter. "I shall be inconsolable if you do not write *me* after we leave."

"Yes, of course," Lucy muttered. She turned a page of her book and inched her chair in the opposite direction, as if insincerity might be catching. The very idea of writing letters to Sophia Hathaway was absurd. As if they were friends!

"And you may not forget me," Sophia warned with a sly smile, "no matter how many new friends you will make, once you're a countess."

The word gave Lucy a jolt. "A *countess*?"

"Come next season, you'll be the darling of the *ton*. Everyone will be desperate to meet the woman who captured the elusive Earl of Kendall."

"No, they won't," Lucy clipped. "Because he will *not* be marrying me."

"Why not?" Sophia looked disbelieving. "You said

yourself he's thoroughly besotted. He's an earl. He's wealthy. He's your brother's friend."

"He's cold. He's stern. He's forbidding."

Sophia lowered her voice. "Yes, but isn't that what makes him so attractive? In that strong, silent way, of course. Just to look at him, I'd imagine he has all sorts of dark, thrilling secrets."

Lucy didn't like Sophia speculating on Jeremy's "dark, thrilling" secrets. Mostly because she knew there were none. Lucy had known him for eight years now. She knew everything there was to know about Jeremy Trescott, and none of it was the tiniest bit thrilling.

Except his kiss. Lucy grudgingly admitted that his kiss was, indeed, just the tiniest bit thrilling. Days later, she still felt that kiss in her toes. And that Look of his—the same glare that had always bounced right off her glib indifference—now penetrated her poise, setting off a queer humming deep inside her.

"Rich, handsome, titled . . ." Sophia ticked off the attributes on her fingers. "He's a magnificent catch, by any standard."

"Who, Jemmy? If he's such a magnificent catch, why don't you want to marry him?" Now *that* would solve matters nicely.

"If he looked at me the way he keeps looking at you," Sophia whispered, "I might."

Lucy clapped her book shut in one hand. She turned her gaze back to Jeremy, only to find that he was indeed giving her that Look again. And this time he did not look away. Their gazes held, locked, deepened. She tried to imagine seeing him for the very first time—viewing him as Sophia did, just a fortune and a title and dark, imaginary secrets. She nearly laughed aloud with the absurdity of it.

But then Jeremy's gaze shifted, scanning down her body in an unhurried fashion, almost as though his mind didn't know his eyes had gone wandering. And Lucy realized he was not looking at her as though seeing her for the first time. He was, she fancied, looking at her as though he'd seen her many times before—in various states of undress. A potent awareness coursed through her veins, and with it spread a most curious sensation.

Lucy felt as though she were seeing *herself* for the very first time.

"Cousins," Sophia blurted out, tugging Lucy from her reverie. "Surely you have cousins to write."

"None on my mother's side. On my father's side, there's Aunt Matilda—" She nodded toward the corner, where her aunt was opening a silver box encrusted with lapis lazuli to gather a generous pinch of snuff. "But she never married. My grandfather farmed indigo in Tortola. I suppose I do have cousins there, but we've never met. At any rate, they would be far older than I."

"Tortola!" Sophia's eyes widened. She propped her chin on one hand and stared unfocused toward the bank of mullioned windows. "How romantic. If I had cousins in Tortola, I would write them a letter every week, if only for the pleasure of imagining its voyage across the sea. My little missive—my tedious scribbles of everyday life—tossed about on the ocean, washing up on a distant, sandy shore." She sat up abruptly, her hand dropping to the table with a dull thud. "Or pirates!" she exclaimed, giving a tiny shiver. "Imagine—my letter falling into the hands of pirates."

Lucy eyed Sophia with amusement. "What a vivid imagination you possess."

"Yes." Sophia's face grew wistful, and she tapped her quill against the inkpot. "I rather wish I hadn't. It's a curse, to imagine so many wonderful things and never see them come true."

An uncomfortable silence followed, during which Miss Hathaway's demeanor made a swift progression from pensive to morose. And a strange sensation filled Lucy's breast. Something uncomfortably close to *sympathy*.

Impossible. Sophia was the enemy. One didn't sympathize with the enemy.

But then the enemy sniffed and bit her lip, and the horrifying truth became inescapable. It *was* sympathy. How vexing.

"I don't expect the pirates would know how to read it," Lucy said, obeying the strange compulsion to cheer her companion. "But if you're so enamored of the notion, you're welcome to write my cousins for me."

"May I?" Sophia perked immediately. She drew out a fresh sheet of paper and dipped her quill. "What are their names?"

Lucy paused. "I don't remember."

"What was your father's brother's name?"

Lucy thought for a moment. "George, I believe. After my grandfather."

"Then his son must be George as well." Sophia put her quill to paper. "Dearest Cousin George," she read aloud, pausing briefly before beginning to scribble again. "We are enjoying fine weather." She paused again. "My brother's annual hunting party is underway. This year Waltham Manor is enlivened by the company of Mrs. Crowley-Cumberbatch and her sister, Miss Hathaway." Sophia gave Lucy a sidelong glance as she dipped her quill.

"Miss Hathaway is a delightful and charming lady," she went on. Her lips slowly shaped each word as her quill danced frantically across the page. "We are already the best of friends. In fact, she has recently implored me to address her by her Christian name, Sophia."

She cast Lucy a wide smile, which Lucy repaid in a rather bewildered fashion. Sophia's eyes sparked with sudden inspiration, and she dipped her quill yet again.

"I write you to invite you, dearest cousin, to my upcoming wedding. While the engagement is not yet formalized, it cannot be long. By the time this letter reaches you, I will very likely be Lady Lucy Trescott, the Countess of Kendall."

"No!" Lucy glanced about the room to see if anyone had heard. Fortunately, Marianne had reached a rather lively section of her sonata.

"No?"

Lucy swallowed her objection in a great, bitter lump. When had pretending to flirt with Jeremy become pretending to marry him? "My full name is Lucinda," she said. "Lady Lucinda Trescott sounds much nicer, don't you think?" She could barely pronounce the name without cringing.

"Lady *Lucinda* Trescott, the Countess of Kendall," Sophia corrected. "I hereby invite you to my wedding. But since this letter will not reach you for an age, I also hereby accept your regrets and express my fondest wish that you might have been in attendance. I am certain it will have been a lovely occasion."

Lucy laughed despite herself. Still, she was eager to change the subject. "But what about the pirates?"

Sophia dipped her quill again and furrowed her brow. "A warning to pirates," she said sternly. "Although my new husband is one of the richest men in all England, he is also among the most fearsome. If you have any ideas of kidnapping the author of this letter to hold her for ransom, I advise you to abandon them. Blackbeard himself quakes in his boots—"

She stopped writing and looked to Lucy. "Is it boots, or boot? Did Blackbeard have one leg, or two?"

"I believe he had two."

"Blackbeard himself quakes in his *boots*," she continued, "at the merest mention of Evil-Eye Jem, the Plundering Earl."

Lucy clapped both hands over her mouth to keep from laughing aloud. "The Plundering Earl? People don't really call him that?"

"No, I made it up just now. But he does have the most scandalous reputation. My mother forbade me to waltz with him. Not that he ever asked." Sophia glanced toward Jeremy and lowered her voice to a whisper. "Has he tried to plunder *you*?"

Actually, Lucy longed to confide, *it was rather the other way around.*

Marianne beckoned Sophia to the pianoforte. Toby approached with an outstretched hand, and Sophia reached to accept it. As she stood, she leaned over and whispered in Lucy's ear—

"If I were you, I'd let him."

CHAPTER SIX

"All Englishmen salute the hound," Henry belted out in a mocking baritone, nudging his bay into a trot. Felix matched his pace, adding his tenor to the song.

"Who, when his lady runs to ground, gives dogged chase o'er dell and knolllll . . ." They pulled their horses to a stop and drew out the note in a two-part harmony that strained the meaning of the word. "To burrow in his vixen's hole!" they bellowed at last.

An airborne pinecone knocked the triumphant grin off Henry's face.

"Watch yourself, Waltham!" Toby called. "We've ladies among us."

Henry looked over his shoulder with an expression of feigned innocence. "Ladies?" His glance fell on Sophia. "So we have." He tipped his hat, arching an eyebrow in Lucy's direction. "My apologies, *ladies*," he said sardonically, weighing heavily on the dubious plural. Then he touched his crop to the gelding's flank, heading into the woods. The pups raced ahead of him, ears flopping in the wind.

Jeremy saw Lucy wince, and he beat down the surge of sympathy that rose in his chest. Really, what could she expect? For eight years, she'd wheedled her way into the company of gentlemen and demanded equal treatment. On any previous autumn day, she would have paced Henry across the fields, riding astride in borrowed breeches and gilding the profane verses with her clear soprano.

Now Lucy wished to be a lady. She'd donned a russet velvet riding habit and brown leather gloves, piled her curls on top of her head, and somewhere, somehow conjured up a sidesaddle. It was, he owned, a vast improvement over her jewels-and-silk folly a few days previous. But she couldn't expect the men to change their behavior as quickly as she changed her clothes. She certainly had no business feeling affronted if they didn't.

She sniffed. "I knew I ought to have worn breeches. Do I look so ridiculous, then?" She glanced at Jeremy. "You've been staring at me all afternoon."

Staring? He hadn't been staring. Had he? *Damn.*

"Not ridiculous," he said, accepting the invitation to appraise her form openly. "You look . . ." *Soft. Lovely. Strangely delicate and quite frankly, bewildering.* "Different."

She gave him a rueful look. "And those are the words of a besotted man. No wonder Henry's mocking me."

Jeremy sighed. He wished he could ride ahead with Henry and Felix and leave that pained expression behind. But a besotted suitor, as Lucy decreed, would ride alongside his lady. For once, her notions of courtship proved correct. Toby had not strayed from Sophia's side since the party departed the stables. The four of them skirted the edge of the woods, the gentlemen flanking the ladies as they rode through the fringe of a mowed barley field.

With reluctance, Jeremy nudged his mount closer to hers. "Henry is an ass." Not the most conciliatory phrase he might have uttered, but it was sincere.

Shrugging, she tucked a wisp of hair behind her ear. "Henry is Henry. And he may be an ass, but he's also my brother."

"Precisely." He lowered his voice. "He should treat your feelings with more care."

"He does care," she muttered. "He just . . . isn't good at it." Her chin lifted. "And who are *you* to talk about tender feelings?"

Jeremy meant to reward her cold remark with an equally cold silence, but Miss Hathaway spoke, ruining the effect. "That song the men were singing," Sophia said. "I don't believe I've heard it before."

"Miss Hathaway, allow me to apologize for Mr. Waltham's crass behavior," Toby said in a buttery tone. "We are unused to the company of ladies on these excursions."

Lucy's nose twitched, and she tossed her head.

Jeremy trained his gaze on the horizon. He'd learned his lesson. It was useless to offer her soothing words. Lucy always took as she pleased, even when it came to offense.

"There is no need for apology," Sophia replied. "I should like to learn the words, that's all." She arranged the folds of her emerald-green skirt over her mount's dappled flank. Her face brightened as she turned her horse into the woods. "Oh, look! Have they found one?"

None of Tuppence's whelps had succeeded as yet in sniffing out a fox, but it appeared one brindled pup had managed to surprise a squirrel. Both hound and quarry scuttled underfoot, causing Lucy's mare to rear and buck.

Jeremy lunged to grab the reins, but Lucy didn't need his assistance. With a quick jerk on the bit and a soothing word, she had the horse calmed within seconds. She repositioned herself in the saddle. Her velvet riding habit slipped easily across the leather, making a little shushing noise that Jeremy found anything but calming.

Lucy turned and caught him staring. She arched an eyebrow.

He cleared his throat. "Since when do you ride sidesaddle?"

"Since this morning."

"This morning? No wonder your horse is skittish."

"Thistle is *not* skittish. I've ridden her astride, bareback, and standing up. I expect I can ride her sidesaddle." Lucy patted the mare's neck and ruffled her gray mane.

"Standing up?"

Jeremy supposed he must appear sufficiently shocked, because she smiled for the first time all day. "Only once," she said, her green eyes teasing. "On a dare. And it was years ago. The steward's son—"

Her voice trailed off as her eyes fixed on something behind him. Jeremy turned to follow her gaze. He saw instantly what had captured Lucy's attention. Toby and Sophia had dismounted in a small clearing some paces away. A shaft of sunlight pierced the trees, bathing the couple in luminous gold. Toby was working something between his hands, and Sophia sat on a fallen tree, looking up at him with a radiant expression. They exchanged smiling words that Jeremy could not hear, and then Toby held his creation aloft for a moment before placing it gently atop Sophia's head.

A crown, woven of ivy.

Toby took Sophia's hand and kissed it. Jeremy swore under his breath.

"Lucy—" he began, turning back to her.

Or to where she had *been*. He caught only the cracks of snapped twigs and a glimpse of russet velvet and gray mare disappearing through the trees. Jeremy turned his horse in pursuit, leaning over the stallion's neck to duck a low-hanging branch.

Lucy urged her mare on, riding hell-for-leather across

the barley field. Bent low over the mare's neck, her chestnut curls blown loose and streaming behind her, she burned a path across the field toward a gap in the hedgerow. Jeremy was tempted to let her go. Let her ride out all the hurt and come back calmer.

But then he remembered that little shush of velvet slipping over leather. The sound echoed in his ears and crawled down his neck, setting every hair on end. It wasn't called a breakneck pace for nothing. One misstep—one stone in a barley field—could send her flying.

Jeremy nudged his horse into a gallop. In a flat-out race over open country, her mare was no match for his mount, and the gap between them narrowed.

Then he saw the stile.

A low wooden fence bridged the gap in the hedgerow. Beyond it, a steep slope led down to the orchards. It would be a difficult jump for any rider, under the best conditions. For a rider in a holy fury, on a skittish horse, riding sidesaddle for the first time in her life, it was certain disaster.

Jeremy hauled on the reins, pulling his horse to a halt in the middle of the field. "Lucy! Stop, damn it!"

He groped for a more impressive threat to hurtle in her direction, but it was too late. She pushed the mare into a jump. Jeremy heard the hollow clatter of hooves clipping wood. Then horse and rider disappeared from view completely.

His stomach gave a sick lurch. Panic twisted in his chest, squeezing the air from his lungs. For one black, unending moment, his heart refused to beat. Then it roared back to life at a thundering gallop, and he dug his knees into the horse's sides until his stallion matched the pace.

The top rail of the stile had been knocked from place. Jeremy's mount easily cleared what remained of the fence, landing with a dull thud on the other side and careening instantly into a headlong skid down the rocky slope. The moment his horse found solid footing, he dismounted. Lucy was nowhere to be seen.

The orchard was laid out in neat rows of trees that formed a crosshatch of leaf-paved avenues. He plunged into the grove, searching through empty branch-framed corridors until he glimpsed Thistle, grazing riderless beneath a distant pear tree. He strode toward the mare, expecting at any moment to trip over a lifeless heap of russet velvet. It seemed an age since he'd drawn a breath. His brain felt woolly. The edges of his vision grayed.

Then he saw her.

She stood with her back to him, resting one shoulder against the trunk of a tree. Just relaxing in the orchard, perfectly serene, as if she hadn't just watched Toby crown Sophia his goddess. As if she hadn't just nearly broken her neck. As if Jeremy weren't about to vomit his breakfast on his boots.

"Oh, Jemmy," she said, "how do you do it?"

He hadn't the faintest notion what she meant. How did he do *what*? At the moment, he was not entirely certain how he managed to stay upright. The leaden weight of anxiety that had been crushing his chest had sunk through his gut, churning the contents of his stomach. Now it seemed to hang somewhere in the vicinity of his knees, making his legs weak, unsteady. He picked a tree near hers and sagged against it.

"How do you do it?" Lucy turned and pressed her back against the tree, staring up into the canopy of orange leaves. "How do you go through life and just—not *care*?"

That did it. He was going to throttle her. Fist his hands in that russet velvet, crush her close, wrap his hands around the delicate, golden skin of her throat—

and throttle her. Right after he leaned against this pear tree for a while.

He stared blankly down a row of trees, his breath heaving in his chest. How did he do it? How, indeed. However it was that he managed to go through life and just, as Lucy so kindly put it, not *care*—Jeremy couldn't seem to remember. He'd utterly forgotten. Damn.

"I never thought I'd envy you," she said. "Never in a million years. You're so composed, so serious. So cold."

His hands balled into fists. How dare she? How dare she burst into his room and kiss him and dive into a river and invade his dreams and make him go shopping and throw herself headlong into danger and lean back against a pear tree in a dress the exact color of her hair kissed by fading sunlight? How dare she make him forget? Damn it all. Damn her for making him care.

"I want to go cold," she said. "All these feelings— they're like flames inside me. I'm tired of getting burnt. I don't want them anymore. I want to put out the fire and just go cold. I never imagined I'd envy you, but today . . ." Her voice wavered. "Today, I do."

He barely heard what she was saying, but he couldn't turn away. Her green eyes were clouded with hurt, threatening to burst into a storm of tears. *Don't cry*, he willed her silently. "Don't cry," he said aloud.

She bit her lip and blinked hard. "I don't cry."

But even as she spoke, her chin began to quiver. And somewhere deep and low inside him, panic began to build. He'd been here too many times before—watching a woman shed tears for a man he could never replace. *Look away*, he told himself. *Better yet, just leave.* He wasn't a boy any longer; he didn't have to suffer this scene again. But he couldn't look away, and he couldn't leave. He was down and defenseless, and she was so damned beautiful, reclined against that tree. If she cried . . . He couldn't let her cry.

"Stop being so dramatic, Lucy." She winced. Jeremy squared his shoulders. He tried again. "You're making a fool of yourself."

It worked. In an instant the sorrow in her eyes gave over to fury. She straightened her spine and took two paces toward him. Jeremy breathed a small sigh of relief. He knew how to deal with an angry Lucy.

"Did I call you cold?" she asked. "You're worse than cold; you're cruel. And what's more, you're afraid. I'll be a fool, again and again, but I would never be like you. Not for a thousand Tobys."

"Afraid? Me? You're the one who's hiding from the truth."

"Hiding from the—" Fury made her grow an inch. "I don't hide. From anything."

He snorted. "You don't hide. You didn't hide when you let the cows into the oatfield, then? You didn't hide when you lost Henry's signet in the coal grate?"

"This is completely different. I was a girl then. I'm not a girl any longer."

"You're still hiding, Lucy. Hiding behind silks and jewels and sidesaddles and outrageous behavior. All because you're afraid. You're afraid to drop these ridiculous games and simply tell Toby how you feel."

"I was on my way to do that on the night you arrived," she said. "*Somebody* stopped me."

"You weren't on your way to tell him the truth. You were on your way to trick him into marrying you."

Lucy's mouth fell open, but she said nothing. Jeremy took another step toward her. He knew he ought to turn away, but his feet wouldn't move in any other direction. He'd stopped the tears. The danger had passed. But it wasn't enough. There were things she needed to know. If she wanted to call him cold and cruel, then he would acquaint her with the cold, cruel truth.

"I'll tell you why you haven't told him," he said, inching closer to her, backing her up against the trunk of the tree. "Because you know—deep down, Lucy, you *know*—he doesn't feel the same. He doesn't love you. And if you had an honest conversation with him, you would have to face that fact. So long as you keep up your games and your schemes, you can imagine he cares for you. That's why you won't tell him the truth. *You're* afraid."

"You're wrong," she seethed. "Wrong in every possible way. I'm not afraid. I'm in love. You wouldn't know love if it struck you in the face. And I'm mightily tempted to strike you, just to prove the point."

Jeremy leaned closer, bracing his arm against the tree behind her, caging her between the tree and his body. "Go ahead," he taunted, offering her his cheek. "Strike me. It won't work."

He lowered his voice to a secret. "You know why it won't work? Because you're not in love with him, either. You're afraid of that truth, too. You don't love Toby." She opened her mouth to reply, but he cut her short. "Oh, you *want* him—like a girl wants a sweet or a shiny new toy. But you said it yourself, Lucy. You're not a girl any longer."

Her eyes widened. The daylight was fading, mellowing to an amber glow. The air was heavy with the scent of pears. Her face was scant inches beneath his; her lips, scant inches beneath his. Lucy's cheeks flushed red beneath the gold. She tilted her face to his, and her eyelids fluttered closed. An invitation he knew well.

He tucked a curl behind her ear—so she could hear him and believe every word. "If you really loved Toby," he said, "you wouldn't be standing here under a tree, waiting for another man to kiss you."

Her eyes flew open, but she didn't pull away.

"I'm right, Lucy," he whispered hoarsely. "You know I'm right."

She placed her gloved hand flat against his chest. Jeremy waited for her to push him away. She would have to push him away, because there was no part of him that wanted to be anywhere else. Every inch of his body was acutely aware of hers—so near, so warm, so ripe. Her hair, tumbling over her shoulders in glossy chestnut waves. Her breasts, rising and falling against his chest with every breath. Her lips, deep red and slightly parted, inviting his kiss. Her hand splayed over his heart, the touch electric even through layers of linen and leather and wool.

She would have to push him away.

Instead, she curled her fingers around his lapel. And pulled him in.

CHAPTER
SEVEN

Lucy wanted him to plunder her.

Even though he was wrong, in every possible way. The wrong man, in the wrong place, and just wrong, all wrong. Even though it was wicked, and she knew she was acting the farthest thing from an angel or a dream.

She wanted to be a goddess—*someone's* goddess. And here he was, worshipping her with his gaze if not his words. And when she touched him, she had the power in her fingertips to make him tremble. She wanted to be kissed. She wanted to be *wanted*. She wanted those strong, full lips to stop spouting wrongheaded nonsense and start kissing her instead.

She pulled him against her and watched his sky-blue eyes darken to the deepest indigo, then close in a sweep of ebony lashes. His warm male scent embraced her, the clean aromas of leather and pine blending with musk. He bent his head by slow degrees, until his brow rested against hers. They traded the same breath back and forth. And when his lips finally bridged the last bit of distance between them, it felt like the end of a kiss rather than the beginning.

Lucy closed her eyes. She let the world contract to the unbearable softness brushing against her lips and the feel of rough wool clutched in her hand. She wouldn't remember anything before that moment, and she wouldn't think about the future. She wouldn't think about what he'd said. She wouldn't think—she would only feel. She would shut everything out and let only him in. The taste of him and the warmth of his mouth.

His mouth, claiming hers in a tender kiss. His lips, ranging over hers in a series of slow, teasing tastes. His tongue, sweeping into her mouth again and again in a gentle, rhythmic dance. She pressed her body against his solid chest, burrowing closer, nestling into his strength and warmth. He groaned against her mouth and tore his lips from hers.

Lucy kept her eyes shut tight. She didn't need to see him. She could *feel* him looking down at her, the heat of his gaze wandering over her closed eyes, her flushed ears, the hollow of her throat where her quickened pulse beat. She kept her eyes shut tight and her lips slightly parted, and she waited. Because she knew he would come back.

He did. And this time, there was no gentle dance, no teasing or tenderness. He pressed himself against her, pushing her against the trunk of the tree until the ridges of bark bit into the flesh of her back. His lips claimed hers in a scorching embrace. He thrust his tongue into her mouth again and again and again, stealing her breath, stealing her very presence of mind. He cupped her face in one hand and angled it back, taking more of her, and she clung to his lapel as if the scrap of fabric were her only tether to the earth.

This wasn't Jeremy Trescott. This wasn't any man she knew. He was some wild, dangerous, plundering stranger, and she was a wanton, pagan goddess being ravaged under a pear tree. He broke away from her mouth, kissing a trail of fire along her jaw. He groaned her name against her ear, and it sounded foreign, forgotten—two random syllables sliding over her skin like a pair of hot, seeking lips. She didn't know who she was. Who he was. Didn't care. The world had contracted to the warmth of a kiss and a clutch of rough wool, and there was no one else.

But there was.

There was someone else.

Someone—or *someones*—treading over dry leaves, drawing nearer, talking to one another. Lucy exhaled in a sharp hiss. Jeremy froze, his face buried in her neck, his lips pressed against the soft place under her ear.

"They must have come this way," a voice was saying. "That's Jem's horse."

Toby.

"Perhaps we shouldn't follow them," Sophia replied. "Perhaps they wish to be alone." Her voice took on a coy inflection. "Lovers sometimes do."

Toby chuckled. "Not these lovers."

They must be only a few rows away. In a matter of paces, they would turn their heads and discover Lucy and Jeremy, clinging to one another, molded to the bark of the tree like lichens. Lucy released her grip on Jeremy's coat and pushed against his chest.

He didn't budge.

"Get off," she whispered.

He didn't move, just covered her body with his own and pinned her to the tree. "No."

"They're coming." Desperation tweaked her voice. "They'll see."

"Let them see," he whispered roughly. "You wanted this game. You wanted besotted. You wanted him jealous. Let them see."

Lucy squirmed against him, to no avail. His bulk trapped her. She heard footsteps approaching. She shut her eyes, held her breath, and buried her face in Jeremy's coat.

The footsteps stopped. Lucy did not move. She did not breathe. The silence stretched to an eternity. Then, finally, the footsteps resumed. They hastened, grew fainter.

She heard Sophia's laugh fading into the tree-lined avenues. "Not *those* lovers, hmm?"

Lucy shoved against Jeremy's chest again, and this time he fell back. His face was blank. The expression in his eyes was, as usual, unreadable.

"You were right." She jerked the fabric of her riding habit back into place. He eyed her warily as she wound her hair into a simple knot. "You were right about one thing." She backed away from him. "We're through playing games. I'm going to tell Toby the truth."

"So—do I tell him the truth?"

Toby leaned over the billiard table and lined up his shot. A swoop of golden-brown hair fell over his brow, and he flicked it out of his way with a quick jerk of his head.

"Tell whom the truth?" Jeremy asked. "About what?"

"Henry." Toby pistoned his arm. The cue ball hit its mark with a sharp crack, and the red ball caromed off the far bank and into a side pocket. "Do I tell him what I saw this afternoon in the orchard?" He stood up and leaned on his cue, regarding Jeremy with a cool gaze. "For all he teases Lucy, he'd not want her trifled with. She is his sister, you know. Or had you forgotten?"

"I hadn't forgotten." Jeremy reached into the pocket and withdrew the red object ball. He placed it on the spot and stalked the perimeter of the table, deliberating his best shot. "Nothing happened."

Toby laughed. "Come on, Jem. I know the difference between nothing and something, and that was definitely not nothing."

Jeremy kept silent and leaned over the table to size up his shot.

"You didn't speak to her once during dinner," Toby

continued, "and she never so much as glanced at you. We're in the drawing room all of ten minutes before she retires early, and you develop a sudden passion for billiards. Two people never work so hard at saying nothing unless they are avoiding *something*. Come on, Jem. What were you thinking?"

Toby's tone was glib, but each smooth word pricked Jeremy's conscience. He primed the cue between his knuckles, sliding it back and forth. Hesitating.

Damn. What *had* he been thinking? The answer to that question was plain. He hadn't been thinking at all. He'd kissed Lucy. Not once, but twice—and he'd goaded her into kissing him back. He had known she'd be too stubborn to back down, and he'd taken advantage of it. Taken advantage of *her*. He'd pressed her up against that tree and savaged her like a brute. Then, in a moment of either utter madness or just plain idiocy, he'd *allowed people to see*. Not merely allowed it. Insisted on it. Made a public exhibit of his reprehensible behavior. Loomed over her like a buck guarding his doe in rutting season, staking a claim to his female.

An animal. He'd been reduced to an animal. For the better part of a week, Lucy had picked at the threads of his self-control with every saucy look and reckless act, and his gentlemanly restraint had frayed perilously thin. Now the fabric of politesse was ripping apart, exposing the lust-crazed beast that lurked beneath. The naked, sweating beast that hungered, thirsted, craved, demanded, would not be denied.

Good Lord. Even engaged in self-recrimination, he was tearing off his clothes.

He pulled back the cue, the muscles of his shoulder straining against the seams of his shirt. Ivory cracked against carmine. The balls spun out into futile trajectories, missing the pockets completely.

Lust. It had to be lust. That was the only possible explanation for this behavior—this complete lapse of conscience and control. It could be the only name for this need that quaked through him whenever she was near. The need to possess her. Claim her in some primitive, irreversible way and send every other man on earth straight to the devil, with Toby leading the procession.

But there was something else. There had to be, much as he hated to admit it. If simple lust transformed him into a panting, feral creature whenever he came within ten paces of the chit, then logic argued for a simple cure. Increase the distance between them. Leave. It couldn't be more straightforward. Saddle his horse and ride off for London with the dawn. Find some comely little courtesan with chestnut hair and gold-green eyes to paw and pummel until his lust was slaked.

It wouldn't work, Jeremy knew. He couldn't even muster the desire to try. He'd been saddling his horse at dawn every morning, and he couldn't reach the border of Henry's lands without feeling a visceral tug pulling him back to the Manor. And then there had been that terrifying moment in the orchard. Not the yawning black minute when he'd been convinced she was dead. The true panic had started when he found her alive, and this need had roared to life as well. The need to snare her, trap her, pin her to a tree, anchor her with his body, and above all keep her *still*. Keep her from bolting off breakneck and dragging him along by that blasted satin ribbon now cinched around his gut.

This wasn't a blind, mindless craving for anything woman and willing. This was needing with a name. It was a force beyond lust. It was Lucy.

He wanted Lucy.

Lucy wanted Toby.

And Jeremy didn't want to talk about it.

"Don't mistake me," Toby continued with grating nonchalance. "You've done an admirable job keeping

Lucy distracted, and I do appreciate your sacrifice. But there's no call to get carried away. A little kiss—it's nothing to one of our usual set of ladies in Town. Harmless. But Lucy's different. She's not been out in society. You don't want to risk her feelings."

Jeremy couldn't believe his ears. Surely Toby—the *ton*'s most ruthless flirt—did not mean to lecture him on the delicate sensibilities of young ladies. Surely Toby was not attempting to enlighten *him* on the distinctions between Lucy and every other lady in England. *Lucy is different.* If there was one truth in Creation on which Jeremy needed no further convincing, it was that one. "Since when," he asked in measured tones, "do you care about Lucy's feelings?"

"Of course I care about Lucy's feelings. No one wants to see Lucy hurt. That's what this was about, remember?"

Jeremy swore and let his cue clatter to the table. "This was about *you*," he seethed, "and your vain, infantile, self-absorbed determination to finish your holiday before getting engaged." He tugged on the front of his waistcoat and attempted to compose his expression.

Toby crossed to a side table and uncorked a decanter of brandy. "Calm down, Jem," he said, pouring two generous glasses. "I expect I'm just jealous."

"Jealous." Jeremy choked on the word. "You can't possibly mean you—"

"Ridiculous, isn't it? I haven't even kissed her yet. *Me.* I've kissed a hundred girls if I've kissed one, and I've yet to share a tender moment with the lady I mean to marry."

Sophia. The blood rushed back to Jeremy's knees. *He meant Sophia.* "I thought you said a little kiss was nothing to a lady of the *ton*. Harmless."

"A kiss *is* harmless. But if I start with one kiss, I'm not certain I'll stop—and I can't vouch for her safety then."

Jeremy cocked an eyebrow at his friend and accepted the drink offered him. "Running a bit low on self-control, are you?" Thank God he wasn't the only one. He eyed his glass suspiciously. Perhaps there was something in Henry's brandy. He *had* gotten his wife with child three times in five years.

"I'm in torment," Toby said, pulling a grimace. "Seeing her every day, living under the same roof . . . You couldn't possibly understand."

You'd be surprised.

"She was uniformly enchanting in Town, of course. But there, she was one of a dozen beautiful ladies in any given salon or ballroom. Here . . . here, she sparkles like a jewel among coals."

Jeremy rolled his eyes. If only Lucy could hear herself compared to a lump of coal.

"Thank heavens for geometry," said Toby.

"Geometry? What has geometry to do with anything?"

"That's what I think of when I feel myself losing control. When she's right there, and so tempting . . . I turn my mind to geometry. You know—theorems, proofs, all that."

"Yes, I understand geometry," Jeremy said. "What I don't comprehend is why *you* should claim to understand it. You're worthless at mathematics. Always were, even at Eton."

"Precisely. Old Fensworth held my ballocks over a flame all fifth form. Always hated me, the miserable, arthritic cur. To this day, I can't think about geometry without breaking into a cold sweat. That's why it's the perfect cure for ardor."

Jeremy considered whether this geometry cure might work for his own situation. The trouble was, he'd always been rather good at geometry. Latin, on the other hand . . .

"And we're always together, and too frequently alone," Toby continued, ruffling his hair with one hand. "If Miss Hathaway knew the thoughts running through my head, she'd be . . . terrified, I imagine. Sophia is a delicate flower. Innocent. Refined. I can't very well drag her off into the bushes for a tumble." He shot Jeremy an accusatory glance over his glass.

It was the orchard, not the bushes, Jeremy longed to retort, but he didn't think it wise. Neither would it be wise to point out that he had not *tumbled* Lucy, when without Toby's well-timed interruption he might have done just that.

"A lady of her breeding doesn't allow such liberties," Toby continued. "Nor should she. Sophia Hathaway is an angel. Pure as the driven snow, and I wouldn't have it any other way. I don't dare even kiss her before we are engaged." His lips curved in a sly smile. "And therefore we may become engaged quite soon."

"That tempting, is she?" Miss Hathaway met every accepted standard of beauty, but Jeremy failed to see the attraction beyond aesthetic admiration. But then, he and Toby had never shared the same taste in women. And suddenly, Jeremy found himself exceedingly grateful for that fact. "What about the sport?" he asked. "I thought you were determined to exhaust every covey in Henry's woods before you would even contemplate bending a knee."

Toby frowned. "It was never about that, Jem. It's just that becoming betrothed is quite a step, you realize. A rather momentous decision, as decisions go. And for once, it's actually my decision to make." He swirled the brandy in his glass thoughtfully. "Consider our lives. We didn't choose to be born. Our titles were destined for us before we could utter our Christian names. We certainly didn't select the time or manner in which we inherited them, or we wouldn't have done so yet."

Jeremy tipped his brandy. Toby didn't know the half of it. His title had been destined for someone else entirely. Jeremy ought to have been an earl's second son. Instead of reading up on crop rotation, he should have been deflecting bayonets at Waterloo. Or chasing an opera singer around the Continent, squandering the family fortune along the way.

Toby continued, "We'll have precious little to say about when our children are born, or even how many we'll have. We won't choose the hour or day that we die." He drained his glass and set it down.

"We have this choice to us, though—whom we marry, and when. I've a mother and three older sisters, each more unnaturally competent than the last. They've never needed me to carry any burden besides the title. This may very well be the first choice in my life of any import, and considering the nature of marriage, it's like to be my last for a goodly length of time. My engagement is my decision to make. And it may be damned selfish of me, Jem, but I'm not going to make that decision for anyone else's convenience. Not Lucy's, or yours, or even Miss Hathaway's. There will come a moment— and perhaps rather soon—when I simply know it's time. When I can't live another hour without securing Sophia's hand. That's when I'll propose, and not a blasted minute before."

Jeremy stared at his friend. There must be something in the brandy, he thought. For a moment there—almost a solid minute—Toby had sounded *thoughtful*. "You're right," he said finally, taking a slow sip from his own glass. "That is damned selfish of you."

Toby's face cracked into a wide grin. He picked up his billiard cue and reset the balls. "You know, being in love isn't half bad, Jem. I can't imagine why I avoided it so assiduously all those years." He took a wild shot that missed both balls completely.

"Can't you?"

"Must be the brandy," Toby replied with a sheepish smile. The smile faded, and his gaze sharpened. "You never answered my question. About this afternoon. What do I tell Henry?"

Blast. Jeremy had hoped he'd forgotten that question.

"You tell Henry nothing." He picked up his cue and chalked it, trying to keep his tone light. "There's nothing to tell. Lucy's not infatuated with me, she's furious with me. That's why we're not speaking. The little game is over."

"Gave you a swift kick in the shins, did she?" Toby chuckled. "Or perhaps a few feet higher? Good for Lucy. Good for you, too, I suppose. Lucy's had her taste of romance. I'll propose to Sophia soon. You're off the hook."

Off the hook. Toby was right. He ought to feel relieved. No more ribbing from his friends. No more "besotted suitor" nonsense. Lucy said it herself. *We're through playing games.*

"And I must admit, I'm relieved as well," said Toby. "I wasn't at all looking forward to discussing that scene with Henry."

"Discussing what scene with Henry?" Henry strolled into the room and crossed immediately to the brandy. Toby looked to Jeremy, eyebrows raised.

Jeremy gave Toby a slight shake of the head. The game was over. There was nothing to be gained from upsetting Henry over a few kisses. Jeremy leaned over the table and focused his gaze on the ivory cue ball. "He's talking about your Aunt Matilda," he said. "You've got to put a stop to her wandering, Henry. Toby woke up last night to find her standing over his bed in her shift."

Toby turned away from the table and coughed violently into his sleeve. Jeremy held his shot.

"Really?" Henry asked.

His outburst subdued, Toby turned back with a solemn face. He shuddered dramatically. "Gave me nightmares."

Henry laughed. "I suppose you'd better bolt your door tonight, man."

"Better yet," said Jeremy, "you should station a footman in the corridor. Be certain she stays put." He plunged his arm forward, his thoughts focused on an entirely different *she*. His cue ball banked off the far side of the table, then banked again to the left; glanced off the red object ball, sinking it into a corner; then connected with Toby's cue ball and chased it spiraling into a side pocket.

Henry gave a low whistle of appreciation. "Well played," he said, sipping his drink. "And a footman it is."

CHAPTER
EIGHT

"Oh, well done!" Sophia gasped, breaking into applause.

"There's nothing to it," Lucy said, fitting another arrow to her bow. It was highly satisfying to finally have the better of Miss Hathaway in some acceptable, ladylike occupation. Sophia might hold the advantage in painting, embroidery, cards, and writing letters, but Lucy had her bested when it came to archery. There weren't many people Lucy couldn't best at archery. Come to think of it, there weren't any that she knew.

Lucy raised the bow to her shoulder and drew back the string. "If you want to hit the target, it's as simple as that—wanting it. Some people will go on and on about proper technique. They will analyze the line of your arm, the way you hold the bow, the length of time you take to release. Absolute rot, all of it. I simply look at the center of the target, and I *want* it. I focus and I wait and I want it. I wait until the rest of the world falls away, and all that's left are my arrow and the target and the wanting." Her gaze narrowed, and her speech slowed. "And when I want them to collide so desperately that I can feel the arrow want it, too . . . *then*, I release." She let go the string and watched the arrow zing home.

Sophia applauded again. "Magnificent! Shall we have another go?"

"If you like. I'll just retrieve the arrows."

"I'll walk with you." Sophia linked her arm in Lucy's, and Lucy regarded her warily. The two set out across the green toward the target—a fat punchinello, its clownish colors playing against a curtain of dark forest.

"I'm terribly envious of you, you know," Sophia said as they walked. The morning was gray and cloudy, and traces of the previous night's frost still lingered on the ground. Damp sucked at Lucy's toes through her boots.

"It's only archery," she replied.

"Oh, no," Sophia giggled. "You're brilliant with a bow, to be sure. But it isn't that skill I envy."

"Then what?"

Sophia lowered her voice to a whisper, although there was no one to hear. "Yesterday. In the orchard. We saw you."

"Oh. That."

"Was it terribly thrilling? How did it feel? How did he *taste*? Did he touch you . . . *all over*?"

Lucy gaped at her companion. She thought surely Miss Hathaway must be teasing—but no. Sophia's expression was all honest, eager inquiry. She wasn't even blushing.

She briefly considered answering the questions frankly. It was powerfully tempting. She had been furious with Jeremy the day before, when he insisted they be seen. Now she reviled him thoroughly—because he'd been right. Toby would finally look at her not as a girl, but as a woman. And Lucy could finally discuss the churning tempest of sensation a kiss could unleash with some one . . . even if that someone was the enemy.

Was it terribly thrilling? Yes, devil take it. Devil take *him.* Yes.

How did it feel? Wicked and wonderful. Like a swarm of bees humming under her skin, tickling the nape of her neck and the backs of her knees. A few straggling stings pricked her memory even now.

How did he taste? Like hot rolls straight from the oven, washed down with whiskey.

Did he touch you all over? No. But Lord, had she wanted him to.

Lucy considered it a great tragedy that she had let nearly twenty years of her life go by without kissing anyone. She was greatly impatient to try it with the man she actually loved. It had been tempting the previous night to set her original plan in motion, but she wouldn't give Jeremy the satisfaction. She could win Toby's heart without trickery or temptation. She needed only the opportunity, a few minutes alone with him. And, evidently, she needed to find that opportunity before Sophia found hers.

"If only I were so fortunate," Sophia was saying. "I've been waiting and waiting for a passionate moment, but Sir Toby is a model of propriety." She said this with such obvious distaste, Lucy thought she might as well have said, *Sir Toby has the pox.*

"You haven't let him kiss you?" she asked, almost afraid of the answer.

"I would have," Sophia replied with annoyance, "but he hasn't even tried."

Lucy felt a little thrill burn down her neck, and she squeezed it between her shoulder blades, standing taller as a result. Toby couldn't possibly be in love with Sophia. He hadn't even tried to kiss her. Why, she and Jeremy felt nearly nothing for each other save animosity, and they had shared five kisses now. Each one better than the last.

"Sometimes he looks as though he might," Sophia continued. "His eyes go all glassy, and he stares at my lips." She screwed her features into a cross-eyed mask, and Lucy laughed despite herself. "But then—nothing. He clears his throat, gives his neck a little quirk, and then changes the topic of conversation entirely. To geometry, of all things!"

"Geometry?" Lucy was baffled. What Toby knew about mathematics could fit on the head of his stickpin. She tried to imagine him holding an actual conversation on the topic. She failed utterly.

"Absurd, isn't it? He'll have to kiss me someday. I suppose he is waiting for our betrothal."

The hot little thrill between her shoulder blades turned to ice. "Do you expect him to propose soon?"

"Any day now, Kitty says."

"You don't sound overly excited about the idea."

They reached the painted bull's-eye, and Lucy began plucking arrows from the straw-filled target. She closed her hand around a shaft that had landed dead center. She froze. But of course. How had she not thought of it before? All this time she had been trying to prevent Toby and Sophia's engagement, she had been aiming at the wrong target. Even if Toby was determined to propose marriage to Miss Hathaway, it did not necessarily follow that Sophia was wedded to the notion of accepting him. She turned to Sophia. "You don't want to marry him, do you?"

Sophia shrugged. "Oh, I expect I do. At least, everyone else expects me to. Kitty goes on and on about what a splendid couple we make. Sir Toby *is* very handsome, and most affable. We converse on all manner of subjects and never disagree. And there is the title. When we marry, I shall be Lady Aldridge—that will satisfy."

"Will it?"

Sophia bit her lip and stared off toward the horizon. "Oh, Lucy, I fear it won't. Sir Toby admires me, I know. But I don't wish to be merely admired." She looked back at Lucy, eyes lit with mischief. "I want to be desired. I want true passion. I want what you have with Lord Kendall."

Lucy choked back a laugh. Whatever Sophia's fantasy of "true passion" looked like, it could not possibly resemble the truth of matters between her and Jeremy. But the truth of matters was beside the point. If her apparent happiness with Jeremy would lead Sophia to seek happiness with a man other than Toby—Lucy would effuse romantic bliss. "Should you like to hear about true passion, then?" she asked, turning to walk back across the green.

Sophia clutched her arm tightly. "Oh, yes! Tell me everything. What do you feel when he draws near? Does your heart start to flutter madly? Do you feel as though you might swoon?"

"The farthest thing from it," Lucy replied truthfully. "Swooning would be the wrong thing entirely. When a man kisses you, you want to be awake. That's how you feel when a passionate man draws near. *Awake,* every inch of you. Awake, and . . ." She searched her mind for an appropriately lurid word. "Tingling," she finished in a whisper.

"Tingling?" Sophia's ivory cheeks blushed bright pink.

"Tingling. *All over.* Every forgotten little corner of your body tingles like mad. Even the spaces between your toes."

"Just from being close to him?"

Lucy nodded.

"And then?" Sophia said. "When he touches you, what then?"

Lucy considered. "Lightning," she said. "All the tingles rush together in one bracing shock. And the shock travels straight to the center of your chest and squeezes out all your breath. And just for the tiniest moment, you fear that you won't remember how to breathe, ever again."

Sophia shivered against her arm, and Lucy smiled.

My, but what great sport it was to corrupt the angelic Miss Hathaway.

"And then?" Sophia asked, breathless.

"Then—if you're lucky—he kisses you, and you forget breathing altogether."

They reached the end of the green, and Sophia fitted an arrow to her bow. "Go on," she urged, pulling on the string.

"And then," Lucy said slowly, "it's quite like drawing back a bow. You feel everything in you pulling tight, and there's a, a . . . *wanting* building somewhere deep inside. The whole world starts to fall away." She curled her hand into a fist, closing her fingers tight over the memory of a rough wool lapel. "Until there's just you and him and . . ."

"And the wanting," Sophia finished, releasing an arrow that landed just left of center. "Yes," she sighed, "that's exactly how it felt for me."

Lucy jerked her mind back into the present. "But I thought you said Toby hadn't kissed you!"

"He hasn't." Sophia fitted another arrow to her bow, her eyebrow arching to match her bowstring. "That doesn't mean I've never been kissed."

"But—" Lucy sputtered. "By whom?"

"Prepare yourself for something truly shocking." She narrowed her gaze at the target. "Last year, my . . ."

"Don't!" Lucy clapped her hand on Sophia's arm. The bow went slack.

"Well, it isn't *that* shocking," Sophia said, disappointed. "I daresay you'll be able to sleep at night after the telling."

"No, not that." Lucy scanned the woods behind the target, her gaze roving through the backdrop of brown and green. There it was again. A flash of deep blue where none belonged. "It's Aunt Matilda. She's gone wandering again."

She charged off across the green, vaguely conscious of Sophia trailing behind her. "Aunt Matilda!" she called, crunching into the undergrowth. The sound of snapping twigs drew her to the left, and she pushed deeper into the wood, her eyes searching the path ahead for any glimpse of indigo.

"Does she do this often?" Sophia dodged a low branch.

"Yes," Lucy replied testily. "Whatever Henry is paying her nurse, it's three times too much. Really, how difficult can it be to keep one doddering old lady in place? It's not as though she's especially quick on her feet."

Lucy spied a blue turban bobbing through the trees ahead. "There she is." She cupped her hands around her mouth. "Aunt Matilda!" The turban kept bobbing.

"I don't think she heard you."

"No, she never does. She's completely deaf."

"Oh. Then why do you shout at her?"

Lucy bristled with irritation, but she held her tongue. She redoubled her pace on a leaf-strewn game trail, leaving Sophia to struggle through the brush on her own. Really, she would humor Sophia up to a point, but she would not be made to look stupid.

"Oof!"

An unseen something caught her ankle, sending her sprawling onto the forest floor. Her fingernails dug into spongy moss. She didn't need Sophia to make her look stupid, she thought ruefully. She made a right idiot of herself on a regular basis.

She rolled over gingerly. Her ankle was caught on—or rather, caught *in* something. She tugged against the resistance, and a sharp twinge of pain was her reward. Lucy sat up and pulled up the hem of her skirt to investigate. A slender cord looped around her ankle above the boot; a little noose drawing tighter with every motion she made.

"Blast," she muttered as Sophia rushed to her side.

"Lucy, what is it?"

"It's a snare." She yanked at the noose, working her fingers under the cord. "Do you see Aunt Matilda?"

"No . . . Oh, yes."

"Would you kindly go after her, please?"

"I don't think it's necessary."

"Whatever do you mean?" Lucy unlaced her boot and slipped it off, then began easing the noose over her stockinged heel. "Of course it's necessary. We don't want to lose her. I'll be right along."

"We won't lose her. She's already found."

Lucy looked up from her foot in exasperation. A cutting retort twitched on the tip of her tongue. Couldn't Sophia dispense with the coy remarks? It wasn't as though Toby were around, after all.

Oh. But he was.

Toby and the other three men were walking toward them. Henry led the way, Aunt Matilda's arm tucked firmly in his. Felix and Toby chatted companionably as they followed. Jeremy brought up the rear.

"Hullo, Lucy." Henry came to a halt and loomed over her. "Did you need rescuing, too?"

"No," she huffed, finally sliding the loop of cord off her toes and jamming her foot back into her boot. "It's a snare, is all. I had my eye on Aunt Matilda, and I didn't watch where I was stepping."

"Who's setting snares in this part of the woods?" Felix directed his question at Henry.

Henry shrugged. "Tenants, I suppose."

"Poachers, you mean," Jeremy said. His voice was low and terse.

"If you call a man a poacher who traps a hare to feed his family from time to time," said Henry, "then I suppose they're poachers. I'm of a mind to turn a blind eye, myself."

"It isn't me who calls them that. The law does." The gravity in Jeremy's voice pulled it down to a growl. "This is your land. If you turn a blind eye to the law, you encourage lawlessness. People—" he pointed at Lucy without turning his gaze, "get hurt."

Henry made a dismissive snort. "The law would send a man to Australia for the sake of a few miserable animals. Should I have all my farmers transported because I begrudge them a few hares? This isn't Cambridge, and I'll thank you to end the lecture. As you said, it's *my* land. And Lucy's fine."

Jeremy's hand curled into a fist at his side. "How do you know Lucy's fine?" he demanded. "You haven't asked. And you should—"

Lucy cut him off. "Actually, no one's asked." She took the hand Felix offered and scrambled to her feet, brushing dirt from the sleeves of her spencer. "But Lucy is fine. The only person Henry should be sending to Australia is Aunt Matilda's nurse. Really, Henry. This makes the third time this month."

Everyone turned to stare at Aunt Matilda, who had taken advantage of the pause to forage in the folds of her skirt for her snuffbox. Sophia went to her side and placed an arm around the old lady's shoulders.

"She doesn't even have a cloak, the poor dear."

Aunt Matilda snorted and sighed her way through a pinch of snuff. "Lovely."

Jeremy shrugged off his coat and thrust it at Sophia. With a parting glare at Henry, he turned and stalked off in the direction of the stables. Lucy was glad to see the back of him. And not because his broad, muscled shoulders looked so irritatingly splendid rippling under the crisp linen of his shirt. She knew he was furious with her over the incident in the orchard. He'd scarcely glanced in her direction since the previous afternoon. If he had any sense, he ought to be furious with himself. Being seen together was his grand idea. But angry with her or angry with himself, he had no reason to pick nonsensical rows with Henry. Poachers, her foot.

Ouch. She winced as she shifted her weight. Her foot.

Sophia draped Jeremy's coat over Aunt Matilda's shoulders, and the frail spinster disappeared into its large proportions. She looked like a column of brown wool topped by an indigo turban.

"We'd best get her back to the house," Felix said. "The wind's picking up. It looks like rain." He led the way back toward the Manor. Henry and Sophia followed, shepherding Aunt Matilda between them.

"Are you all right, Lucy?" Toby asked. "You're not hurt at all?"

"Of course not." She took a firm step forward, and her twisted ankle exploded with pain. She faltered, but suddenly Toby was there, shoring her up with his arm.

His arm, stretched across her back. His hand, curled around her waist. His everything, right there up against hers.

If her ankle weren't throbbing, Lucy would have jumped for joy. She was brilliant. Had she truly chided herself for tripping in that snare? Had she honestly felt shamed to have triggered a device designed to trap small-brained rodents? Well. She had never been more wrong. Stepping in that little noose was the cleverest thing she'd done in an age.

"My ankle . . . It seems I've twisted it." Lucy tried another step. The pain felt less intense this time, but she winced dramatically for effect.

"Just lean on me."

In a perfect dream, she would have been swept off her feet and carried back to the Manor. But this wasn't a dream, she reminded herself with every pain-hobbled step. This was live, waking, in-the-flesh reality, and what was more—it was her *chance*.

She had so much to tell him. Where to begin? She dreamt up and discarded a series of bold declarations.

Toby, I've loved you since I was a girl. Too much in the past, she told herself. Talk about the present.

Toby, you can't marry Sophia Hathaway. Probably best not to mention the enemy. Focus on the future.

Toby, make me your wife and you'll never be sorry. I'll warm your bed, and I'll give you beautiful babies, and we will never—well, hardly ever—disagree. Lucy chewed her lip. Perhaps a bit too forward?

Figuring out *what* to say was only half the problem. The other half being, carving out a moment to say it. Toby was nattering on incessantly as they made their slow progress toward the house.

"It's a bit of luck we decided to cut our hunting short this morning," he was saying. "We were over toward the eastern edge of the woods, and the sky kept growing darker. A proper storm brewing, Henry thinks. This wind has a boar's teeth, I'll say. Odd time of year for it. Not unheard of, mind you. Was it three years ago we had that snow just before fox season began? Maybe just two."

Lucy opened her mouth to tell him it had been four, but she never had the chance.

"Yes, it's fortunate we headed back when we did. Exceedingly so. Imagine," he said, "you might have been here in the woods with a wayward aunt and a twisted ankle and rain about to fall . . ."

Now the topic of weather was getting somewhere. *Yes,* she thought, nodding enthusiastically. *Imagine the peril.* She would have been perfectly fine, of course, but a few protective masculine instincts could never go astray.

"Imagine," he said, "poor Miss Hathaway wouldn't have known what to do."

Poor Miss Hathaway! Lucy groaned.

Toby's steps and speech drew to a halt. "I'm so sorry. Am I walking too fast?"

"No . . . Well, yes. It's just—" She looked up at him. He gazed down at her. His eyes were clear, patient brown with just a hint of gold—and nothing at all of glass. She licked and pursed her lips, but his gaze never slipped from hers.

"Do you find me pretty?"

The words were out before she could stop them. Out and echoing through the woods, ricocheting off the trees, ringing through the silent space between them. She couldn't take them back. Wouldn't wish to, if she could. Toby's brow wrinkled in surprise. Tension knotted in Lucy's stomach.

"Why . . . yes, of course." He cleared his throat. "You're a very pretty girl, Lucy."

There. He'd said it. She was pretty. Sir Toby Aldridge found her pretty. Lucy was perfectly satisfied. She'd never need to hear it again.

"Really?" Once more wouldn't hurt.

"Really and truly." The words flipped off his tongue so lightly, she despaired that he didn't really mean them. But then he cupped her chin in his hand, and his gaze wandered slowly over her face. Lucy held her breath.

"You've the most lovely eyes," he said quietly. "And that hair—" He smiled and tucked a curl behind her ear. "A man could get lost in that tangle and never find his way out."

Their lips were just inches apart. So close. If she only craned her neck a bit . . . and then he would bend his head a fraction . . .

Oh, but would he? She couldn't tell. He'd been chattering on like a bedlamite, but he hadn't spoken one syllable of geometry.

"Next Season," he said, "you'll go to London, and you'll have a pack of suitors nipping at your heels. Henry will have to fend them off with a stick."

"And you?"

"Me?"

"Where will you be next Season?"

"Right there with you." He brushed a finger down her cheek and smiled. "I'll bring my own stick."

Then he turned his gaze to the path and began walking again. Though her ankle felt nearly well, Lucy clung to him more tightly than ever.

They walked along in silence. The sky was growing dark. A bitter wind bit through the fabric of Lucy's spencer, but a smile warmed her face. Next Season, Sir Toby Aldridge would beat her admirers away with a stick. The very thought was ridiculous and barbaric and the most romantic thing she'd ever heard. Of course, the question remained . . . would he be bludgeoning half the *ton* for the sake of brotherly affection or out of jealous love?

Right now, it didn't matter. Next Season could go hang. Toby had called her pretty, and his arm was tight about her waist. Right now, this felt like all she had ever wanted.

Oh, Toby, the truest words came to her now, *you're the only person in the world who makes me feel perfect just as I am. Who never scolds or reproaches or wants me to change. And if you marry Sophia Hathaway, I fear I'll go my whole life without ever feeling this way again.* She gripped his coat tightly. *Toby, if I lose you, I'm afraid I'll lose me, too.*

But these words, her pride would never let her speak.

As they finally neared the house, Toby asked, "How does your ankle feel? Much improved?"

She nodded. The throbbing in her ankle had subsided. All that remained was a faint tingling.

Lucy frowned. She *must* be in pain. She must have broken a bone, and the shock had rendered the rest of her body numb. Because she'd just walked a quarter-mile tucked under Toby's arm, and as surely as her ankle tingled like mad . . . she didn't tingle anywhere else.

CHAPTER NINE

The storm broke that afternoon.

Jeremy tried to outride it, but the rain caught up with him in the south fields. It was a long, wet, muddy ride back to the Manor. Cold rain drenched his shirt and waistcoat, plastering the linen and silk to his skin. Just as well he no longer had his coat. There was nothing more vile than the smell of damp wool.

And the cold felt good. The rain felt good.

He'd ridden off in a blind rage, furious with Henry beyond all reason. And he knew, from years of experience, that the only thing for anger like this was to ride. Ride hard and fast, until he shook off the demon breathing down his neck. Or a cold rain washed it away.

He was getting damned tired of watching Lucy get hurt. In the space of a week alone, she'd almost drowned in the stream and nearly been thrown by a horse. It was completely irrational, that seeing her tripped up by a bit of cord should send him into a chest-seizing panic.

But it had. Of course it had.

Jeremy could walk the seven continents of the Earth and the nine circles of Hell and never hear a more sickening sound than the dull twang plucked from a trip-wire. Because in his mind, that sound would always echo with the deafening crack of a gunshot. Followed by the most terrible, haunting sound of all—not a warning, not a scream. Just silence. Years of silence.

He told himself it could have been anyone. Had it been Sophia, or Aunt Matilda, or even Toby who tripped the snare, he would have reacted the same.

But that would be a lie. Lucy was different. As he returned to the stables, drenched with rain and drained of anger, Jeremy saw it clearly—exactly why he'd kept her at arm's length ever since the day Toby nearly shot her head off. Lucy had "impending disaster" written all over her, and Jeremy had seen his share of disaster for a lifetime.

But Lucy refused to stay at arm's length. She'd kept nagging him, provoking him, pestering him about fishing lures and chess. And now she'd burst into his room and thrown herself straight into his arms. That safe distance narrowed to the thickness of two layers of linen. And beneath the linen were soft, maddening curves and smooth, golden skin. Lust had roared to life inside him, but something else, too. Something he didn't care to examine too closely, didn't wish to name.

When he finally entered the Manor, dripping rainwater and tracking mud across the parquet floor, Jeremy couldn't even bring himself to go straight to his chamber and attend to his appearance. No, he had to see *her* first. Assure himself that she wasn't lying abed with a broken ankle or sitting there yet in the woods, chilled through with rain.

He found her in the drawing room. He found everyone in the drawing room. And judging from their shocked stares when he entered, they all found him quite a sight.

Felix broke the stunned silence. "Enjoy your ride, Jem?"

"Quite." The room fell silent again—except for the faint sound of dripping.

Jeremy's eyes went to Lucy where she sat in the window seat. She looked dry and well enough—and inconveniently fetching, wrapped in a lacy, pearl-gray shawl that slipped off one shoulder. She avoided his gaze.

Everyone else, on the other hand, wouldn't stop staring at him.

"My coat?" Jeremy asked.

"Gave it to your valet," Henry said.

"Right." A rivulet of rainwater trickled down his brow. Jeremy dabbed it with his fist, resisting the urge to shake like a wet dog. "Well then, I'll just go change."

"Don't take overlong," Marianne said, having collected her composure. "We're about to play parlor games. The perfect way to spend a rainy afternoon. Don't you agree?"

Jeremy didn't agree at all, but he gave a politic nod. He'd rather be drawn and quartered than spend the afternoon playing parlor games. They wouldn't miss him. He'd simply slip up to his chambers and conveniently forget to return. Nothing so simple.

He shifted his weight, and his foot squished softly in his boot.

"Just because the weather's turned," said Sophia, "it doesn't mean the men must give up their sport completely. We can still arrange for a bit of hunting." She arched her eyebrow in Toby's direction. Toby's attention, however, was focused on the window seat. He was looking—staring, really—at Lucy. Jeremy decided there was no reason to beat such a hasty retreat. He'd already ruined the carpet.

"What are you on about?" Kitty asked her sister.

"This is a grand old house, and I've been desperate to explore it," Sophia continued. "Why confine our games to the parlor?" Her eyes twinkled, and her mouth crooked in a mischievous smile. "Let's play hide-and-seek."

At this, Lucy looked up. Her gaze met Toby's, and then they both looked away in an instant. Damn. Just what had passed between them while he was out racing demons?

He remembered Lucy's last words to him in the orchard. The words that had erased his kiss from her lips and turned her soft, supple mouth to stone. *I'm going to tell Toby the truth.* Surely she hadn't.

Lucy's gaze flickered back up to Toby. Then she turned back to the window, staring out unfocused at the rain. Slowly winding a lock of hair around her finger and raising it to her lips. Thinking. Scheming.

Surely she hadn't—yet.

"A nursery game?" Kitty toyed with one of her bracelets. "Why don't we just play cards instead?"

"Oh, no," said Henry, looking from Kitty to Sophia. "I can't afford it. One more afternoon of cards with you ladies, and one of you will own Waltham Manor."

"I think it's a capital idea, Sophia," said Felix. "But I warn you all—I know just the place to hide. You shan't find me for days."

"The larder?" Lucy asked, still staring out the window.

"Wh—?" Felix colored. "No. I wasn't thinking of the larder at all. How absurd." He picked up the poker and stirred the fire, muttering an oath into the flames. "The larder, indeed."

"Then it's settled." Sophia drew straws from the tinderbox and began cutting them with her penknife. "We have only to choose a seeker." She bunched them together in her fist and offered them around. She started in Jeremy's direction, but he warned her off with a slight shake of his head.

His refusal did not appear to offend Miss Hathaway. When she offered the straws to Toby, however, she shifted her hand slightly. A different sort of look passed between the two. Jeremy was not the least bit surprised when, once the last of the straws had been handed round, Toby held up the shortest one.

"Ah, Toby," said Henry. "I always suspected your straw was the shortest."

Marianne kicked him under the table. "Henry! We're in polite society!" She cast an apologetic glance at Kitty and Sophia. The sisters schooled their expressions to innocence.

"We're about to play a nursery game," Henry grumbled, rubbing his shin. "Just trying to get in the spirit of things."

Sophia clapped her hands together. "Let's begin, shall we? Sir Toby, you must count to one hundred—very slowly, mind. We must have ample time to find our hiding places."

"Don't concern yourself, Miss Hathaway," said Henry, lurching out of his chair and pulling down his waistcoat. "*Very slowly* is the only way Toby can count. In fact, I doubt he'll make it to one hundred without losing his place and beginning again at least twice." Marianne dug an elbow in his ribs. "Ow!"

Toby smirked. "I'd come over there and thrash you, Waltham, but I shan't waste the effort. Your wife's doing the job admirably."

"I shall be hidden before Toby counts ten," Lucy said, rising from the window seat. She sidled up to Toby with a pointed look and a little smile. "With a sore ankle, I can't stray far. I expect I shall be terribly easy to find."

Jeremy winced. Flirtation did not become Lucy in the slightest. She employed feminine wiles with all the subtlety of an elephant stamping a waltz. If Aunt Matilda herself failed to comprehend that invitation, he would have been surprised.

He told himself he shouldn't care. The rest of the party might be preparing to commence this childish diversion, but he was through playing games. Lucy wasn't his sister or his admirer. She wasn't his problem. She wasn't his *anything,* he told himself sternly. She wasn't his at all.

Toby stood flanked by Lucy and Sophia. Both ladies regarded him expectantly, pulling his attention in two opposing directions. He cleared his throat. "I suppose we all understand the object, then." His glance flitted from one lady to the other. He looked like a man being stretched on a rack.

Devil take it. Jeremy turned on his soggy heel and quit the drawing room, heading swiftly for the stairs.

"That's cheating, Jem," Henry called after him. "But don't think your head start will do you a bit of good. You're leaving a trail of rainwater."

Lucy waited in her wardrobe.

She had always thought of it as her wardrobe, even though it had actually belonged to her father. Even though it wasn't in her chambers, and it held none of her clothing. The wardrobe sat in an alcove of the first-story corridor, facing the door to Henry's study, and it was usually empty—except when she occupied it.

She leaned against the wood paneling at the back of the cabinet. Lacy ribbons of light filtered through the latticework at the top of the doors, dappling the pear-green muslin of her frock with spots of gold. She shut her eyes and inhaled deeply, drinking in the secret scents that never faded—teasing hints of spice and tobacco and sea salt and rum. The smells of Tortola, as she dreamed it must be.

Her father had brought back the cabinet from the West Indies, when he came home to Waltham Manor.

Lucy could never imagine how a ship had managed to stay afloat carrying the monolithic wardrobe. As a girl, she'd had to grasp the carved handle with both hands and lean back on her heels just to wrench open one massive door.

The wardrobe's exterior was carved with vines and leaves and flowers that blossomed across the surface in sinuous, pagan patterns. Lucy would swear that they grew and shifted ever so slightly with time. Inside, however, the ebony panels were solid and smooth. Like polished stone, but warm to the touch. A deep, black cave shot with arrows of light.

Countless hours she'd spent closeted there. Hiding from nursemaids and governesses. Evading blame for mischief she'd wrought. Listening to Henry and his friends drink and talk well past the hour of her bedtime. Waiting for her mother to die.

Even as she grew older and taller, the space inside the wardrobe never seemed to shrink. There was always room for two. Two of her. There was Lucy—troublesome, orphaned, hoydenish Lucy—and there was the other girl. The better girl. The girl who would push open the ebony door and walk out onto a white, sandy shore in Tortola, swinging hand-in-hand with her mother on one side and her father on the other. The girl who was beautiful and elegant, with fair skin and yellow hair and perfect, unskinned knees. The girl who was really a princess, asleep—waiting for her golden-haired prince to come and wake her with a kiss.

Lucy sighed. She was almost twenty and no longer a girl. Her parents were dead, and she would never see Tortola. Her skin was olive, and her hair was brown, and she'd skinned her knees yet again that morning. And if her golden-haired prince didn't come for her today . . . he never would.

Lucy knew precisely why Sophia had suggested this

amusement. She wanted to find a dark, hidden corner of the house and then corner Toby. Sophia wanted her moment of passion.

But what did Toby want? More to the point, *whom* did Toby want? Lucy had felt his gaze on her in the drawing room. She had caught him staring more than once, and the look on his face was wholly unfamiliar. Wholly unfamiliar, and therefore wholly unreadable. She fought the temptation to leave her hiding place and go seek him out. If he knew her at all, he would know she'd be here. If he wanted to find her, he would. And if he didn't . . . he didn't.

She heard heavy footsteps approaching. Slowing. Stopping in front of the wardrobe.

Both doors of the wardrobe swung open, scattering the darkness.

"Lucy, come out of there." Jeremy loomed over her, his dark silhouette filling the ebony frame.

"Go away," she squeaked, raising her hand to her eyes and blinking against the flood of harsh light. "Find your own hiding place. There's a lovely cupboard under the stairs where they keep the mops. Go drip there."

"I know what you're up to, Lucy," he said, his voice a dark warning. "I thought the time for games was over."

He came into focus as her eyes adjusted to the light. Black hair hung over his brow in thick, damp locks, making a stark contrast with the pale blue of his eyes. He'd changed into a dry shirt—hastily, it would seem, and without the assistance of his valet. The starched linen hung open at the collar, exposing wisps of dark hair curling around the notch at the base of his throat, and the hard ridge of his collarbone running toward either shoulder. His cuffs were unfastened, upturned, and her gaze followed the corded muscles of his forearm nearly up to the elbow.

Her eyes shot back up to his face. "I didn't suggest the game, now did I? That would be Marianne and Sophia's idea. Go harass one of them." She pushed at his chest with both hands. She might as well have pushed against a boulder.

But boulders weren't warm. And boulders didn't smell like rain and leather and pine. And boulders didn't send jolts of electricity humming through her body, tingling all the way down to the tips of her toes and even the spaces between.

Lucy felt something swift and sudden growing inside her, curling in the pit of her belly. Then the sound of voices down the corridor gave it a name. *Panic.* Panic it must have been, and no other earthly emotion—because only blind, unthinking desperation could have possessed her to do what she did next.

Her hands, still flat against Jeremy's immutable chest, gathered into fists. She pulled on his shirt, hauling him into the wardrobe with her, then let go with one hand to pull the ebony doors shut. The temperature inside the space instantly increased.

She backed him into a corner of the wardrobe, still clutching his shirt in one hand. With the other, she jabbed a finger in the center of his chest, just an inch below that indecent, gaping collar and the nest of dark curls it framed.

"*You* said I should stop playing games. *You* said I should tell Toby the truth about how I feel. So here I am, waiting for my chance to do exactly that, and now *you* are ruining everything." Her hand balled into a fist, and she beat on his chest. "You. Are. Ruining. Everything."

She looked up at his face. A shard of light pierced the latticework to illuminate his eyes. A sunbeam glancing off ice. "Everything," she repeated, beating on his chest with both fists this time. He didn't flinch. He didn't even blink, damn him.

Exasperating man. Lucy was tired of his stony composure. She was tired in general, and muddled with heat and this wicked tingling, and her head felt thick and heavy. She couldn't think. Couldn't have *been* thinking clearly at all, for she let her head fall against his chest, the crown of her head resting against that warm patch of skin and hair.

Still he had no answer, spoken or otherwise. They stood there in the wardrobe, cloaked in dark and quiet, for moments that dragged into minutes. The silence chafed on Lucy's sanity. For one thing, in the absence of speech, there was too much else to hear. His breathing—a slow, husky resonance that teased her ears as his chest rose and fell against her. Her heart—thumping against her ribs so loudly she was sure he heard it, too. The ceaseless hum of electric excitement coursing through her body.

On another count, the silence became increasingly unbearable because of what Lucy didn't hear. Footsteps in the corridor. Ebony doors creaking open. Toby's voice. She shuddered to think of being found in this position, but she began to question whether she'd even be found at all.

"How did you know I'd be hiding here?" Her voice was a whisper, but it echoed through the darkness they shared.

She felt him shrug. "You've always hidden here. Whenever Henry was on a tear to thrash you. When that mangy hound died. Was it Farthing?"

"Sixpence."

"Oh."

Lucy felt something square and hard settle against the top of her head. His chin, she realized.

"He didn't remember," she whispered into his chest. "Why didn't he remember? You did."

He brought his hands to her shoulders, sending twin bolts of sensation straight to her center, squeezing out all the breath from her lungs. "Perhaps he just didn't come looking for you."

"You did."

She felt his body tense. He hooked his thumbs under the edges of her cap sleeves and pulled her back to face him. Her hands slid off his chest and fell to her sides, still clenched in fists. "I came looking for you, yes. To stop you from doing something foolish." His cool glare ignited Lucy's pride.

"Foolish? We're playing a nursery game. It's foolish by nature."

"Something . . . compromising."

"Such as being found in a wardrobe with a half-dressed man? Or discovered in an amorous clinch under a tree? Well, thank you for appointing yourself guardian of my reputation."

"Damn it, Lucy. You pulled me in here. You—"

She cut him off. "Why did you carry me?"

"What?"

"The other day, when I fell in the river. Why did you pick me up and carry me back? Why not Toby? Why not Henry or Felix?"

"I wish I knew," he said, his voice rough. "I should have made you walk, you little minx. Obviously I wasn't thinking."

"Were you thinking yesterday? When you followed me into the orchard?"

"Apparently not. I haven't been thinking clearly all week." His thumbs pressed into the flesh of her arms. "I've run myself ragged trying to look after a scheming chit with an eye toward complete ruination."

"Don't pretend to be vexed with me. You're only vexed with yourself."

"Explain to me," he said through gritted teeth, "why I should be vexed with myself."

A saucy lilt crept into her voice. "Because you like yourself better when you're not thinking. And it's driving you absolutely mad."

He moved toward her, his face crossing into shadow. "If anyone's driving me mad, it's—"

She shushed him by putting her fingers to his lips. "I'll tell you a secret," she whispered, slowly tracing the shape of his mouth with her fingertips. "I like you better when you're not thinking, too." His lips parted, and she let her thumb slide into the corner of his mouth.

Lucy didn't know what was coming over her. She told herself it was the rush of power, this palpable power she had over him. It felt infinitely preferable to confusion or heartache. Or perhaps she kept chipping away at his glacial composure because she craved what seeped through the cracks. Hints of a different man altogether—someone dark, fierce, thrilling. That sense of danger that rose from deep inside him, and the excitement of teasing it to the surface. The taste of it in his kiss.

No, thought Lucy. It was only habit. She'd spent eight years mastering the art of provoking Jeremy Trescott. It was a game, a sport. It had nothing to do with emotion or sentiment or, God forbid, love. Nothing at all.

There was a pause. A brief moment of silence and heat. Lucy inhaled, drawing a slow, thick breath of leather-scented steam. Sweat beaded on the back of her neck.

Jeremy swore under his breath. He slid his hands from her shoulders down to her back and crushed her against him. Her breasts flattened and ached against his hard chest. His thigh wedged between her legs. Soft muslin shifted over muscled strength, kindling a burning ache between her thighs.

"What are you doing?" She squirmed against him, and the tiny movement sparked an inferno of sensation. "Oh," she said weakly. She already knew the answer. The answer that fell from his lips the moment before his lips fell on hers.

"Not thinking."

CHAPTER
TEN

Jeremy was through thinking. Ever since he'd been pulled into this cursed wardrobe, his mind had been racing in a dozen directions at once.

He'd tried to remember who he was. He was Jeremy Allen Dumont Trescott, the sixth Earl of Kendall. He was a gentleman and a peer of the realm. He was a man of nine-and-twenty, not a randy youth. He was a man who would never want for anything—not wealth, property, influence. But he was kissing this woman as though his life depended on it, devouring her mouth with a desperate hunger.

He'd tried to remember who *she* was. She was Lucy Waltham, Henry's sister. She was a gangly hoyden, an impertinent chit, a perpetual thorn in his side. She was nineteen years old, and she was not even out. And she was kissing him back with an innocent passion that made his knees buckle and his head spin.

He'd tried to remember where they were. They were in Henry's home, where he was a guest. They were in a wardrobe in the middle of the corridor, where anyone might—in fact someone *should*—come by at any moment and fling open the wardrobe doors and expose his perfidy to the world. And they were drifting into the corner of the wardrobe, tongues tangling and bodies melding as one.

And when all other efforts at rational thought failed, Jeremy tried to remember Latin. *Basio, basias, basiat,*

basiat, basiamus . . . I kiss. You kiss. He kisses. She kisses. We kiss.

That's when Jeremy gave up on thinking. He couldn't remember the conjugation for "they kiss," and he didn't bloody well care. The wardrobe was only big enough for two, and for this moment, the wardrobe was the world. *I, you, he, she . . . we.* No one else.

She tasted wild and sweet, like pears and honey and the fresh air after rain. He stumbled backward, pulling her with him into the dark corner of the wardrobe. His hands roved over her back as he ravished her mouth. Tiny ridges teased his fingertips. *Laces.*

The very thought was wicked and depraved.

Good thing he was not thinking.

He tore his lips from hers, slowly kissing his way down her throat as his hands wandered down the length of her back. His fingers lingered over each taunting eyelet of her dress, and his lips savored every delicious inch of her neck. She threw her head back and wove her hands into his hair. His fingers found the knot of lacing at the base of her spine and teased it apart while he teased the hollow of her throat with his tongue. He wrapped the end of the lace around his finger and slowly pulled as he ran his tongue up the length of her neck.

She sighed with pleasure, and the dress sighed loose from her body, and Jeremy thought he would be completely undone.

He brought his hands to her shoulders and pulled her away slightly. Her hands fell back to her sides. Shadow cloaked her face and body, but thin shafts of light filtered through the latticework to gild her silhouette. A single curl of hair glowed russet against her brow. A petal of light floated over her cheek. A thin ribbon of gold undulated over her shoulder as her chest rose and fell with each breath.

Beautiful.

The word echoed through his mind, filled his breath, danced on his lips. But he didn't dare speak it aloud. So long as the silence held, this moment would as well. His hand went to that golden ribbon of light rippling over her shoulder. He traced it with his fingertips, watching the light move over his bronzed skin and the green fabric of her sleeve. Then he slowly ran one finger up the ridge of her shoulder, toward her neck, and hooked it under the edge of gaping muslin.

He waited. Waited for her to stiffen or startle. Waited for her to step away or protest. She didn't. He eased the fabric down an inch. Two. A bit more—just enough to let that golden ribbon of light slide over smooth, bare skin. He traced it with his fingers once again, and she shivered at his touch.

Jeremy had charmed the frock off many a woman, but this was uncharted territory. Some provided eager assistance; others put on a show of resistance. Lucy did neither. She merely waited in the darkness. He stroked her shoulder again with his thumb, and again she shivered. A shiver of fear? Of delight? He couldn't tell. Perhaps she didn't know, either.

Then her hand went to his chest, slowly exploring up to his neck, wending inside his open shirt. Her fingertips grazed the ridge of his collarbone. The touch whispered warm and soft over his skin, like breath. Her hand stilled on his shoulder. Then her thumb swept over his flesh in a bold caress, and Jeremy shuddered. Sank against the solid ebony panel and trembled like a leaf. Trembled with the softness of her touch, exquisitely tender but not at all timid. Trembled with the knowledge that she was unlike other women, that she didn't know how to play coy or loose. She wanted him to touch her. She wanted to touch him. That was the simple truth of it—and the truth left him trembling with unbearable need.

He fanned his fingers over her shoulder and dragged his hand slowly down, dragging the bodice of her dress down with it. Beneath the latticed light, down into shadow, where touch was his only guide. The fabric resisted briefly; then a rougher tug convinced it to give way. He dipped his fingers under the edge of her stays, and the firm swell of her breast sprang into his palm. She drew in her breath.

He cupped her breast gently, letting the warm weight of it fill his hand. He ran his thumb over her flesh. She was soft. So soft. Unimaginably sweet to touch, like sugar melting under his fingertips. He brushed his thumb over the taut peak of her nipple, and she gasped. He brushed it again, and she sighed. Then he pressed his thumb against it, rolling and teasing the straining flesh until she moaned.

He wanted to kiss her. Cover her mouth with his, make her moan again and again, and drink in that honeyeyed sound. But then her finger flickered over the tight bud of his nipple, and he was powerless to move. She repaid all his sweet torture, and he let her. Let her tease him within an inch of his sanity, pinching and pressing until he ached with longing.

When he could take no more, he lifted her breast in one palm and pushed her hand from his chest with the other. He bent over her breast, nuzzling against that sweet softness in the dark, and then he drew her nipple into his mouth.

Dear God. Merciful heaven.

It wasn't just that she tasted warm and sweet and beautiful and pink. It was more than the way she bent her head over his, so that her curling hair tumbled around him, brushing against his neck and cheek. It wasn't how she gasped and panted against his ear and his loins throbbed with every hot little cry.

It was the way she melted into his body and clutched

his shoulders with both hands, clinging to him as though he were her anchor to the earth. As though without him she might float away or fall apart or die. And as he worshipped her breast, suckling and tonguing her lush, sweet flesh, a question—sly and sinister—whispered through his mind.

Who was he to her, here in the dark? Was he himself, or a stranger, or—most terrible to contemplate and altogether probable—someone else known to them both?

If he called her by name . . . would she know his?

"Lucy," he breathed.

Even her name was a kiss. An erotic, depraved collection of sounds. He murmured her name again and again, slowly kissing it over her breast. Licking the L over her nipple, pursing his lips around the sensual, rounded vowel, and releasing the name in a hiss of hot breath.

She was soft, sighing heaven in his arms, but he was wicked and damned and it wasn't enough. He wanted more, *needed* more. More of her.

He kissed his way back up her neck and brought his hands to the neckline of her dress, gathering the fabric of both sleeves. He hesitated, his grip tightening over the muslin until it threatened to tear. Then her tongue flicked a silent plea against his ear, so lightly he might have imagined it, once.

Twice, he could not mistake.

With a strangled groan, he wrenched her bodice and chemise down over her shoulders. She pulled her arms free, letting the sleeves dangle at her hips. Then her hands flew to the edge of his shirt, and with one swift tug she yanked it free of his breeches and thrust her hands underneath to splay across his chest.

Pleasure pierced him in ten sharp darts as her fingers pressed against his flesh. Ten little fires ignited on his skin, burning straight through to his core. And then—oh, God, and then. Those ten tormenting fingers began to move. Roaming over his skin, spreading trails of flame over every inch of his torso. Pressing against his nipples, curling through the hair that covered his chest and tracing its trail down the center of his abdomen.

Then her hands slid around to his back, and she leaned against his chest. She brushed her lips over the base of his throat. Again. Again. Her kisses fell like raindrops in a desert, sizzling on his scorched flesh. He bent his head, and his mouth found hers. And then the storm broke.

She was draped over his thigh and writhing in his arms, her fingernails biting into the flesh of his back as he plundered her mouth. Her breasts rubbed against his chest through the single layer of linen. His hands wandered over the smooth skin of her back, pulling her closer, crushing her deliciously soft body against his hard chest and aching groin. He reached down to cup the firm swell of her backside with both hands and pulled her hips against his.

She gasped, startled. Then she arched against him again, and the gasp became a moan. Jeremy was on fire, and her breathy moan threw brandy on the blaze. He held her to him, kissing her neck and the delectable curve of her bare shoulder. She rocked her hips against him over and over, until her breath came in little pants.

She sought his lips and covered them with her own, and he tasted the desperate question in her kiss. She was racing toward an unknown destination, and she needed him to show her the way. And God, did he want to show her. He would show her just what it was she craved. He would bring her to that peak of pleasure, where no other man had taken her. She would be his and no other's, and she would know which man had taken her there.

She would say his name.

"Lucy," he groaned against her mouth. He let one hand slide down her leg.

Mine, he thought, gripping her thigh as she arched against him again. He fisted his hand in the fabric of her skirt, rucking it up to her knee. His hand snaked under the folds of skirt and chemise, curving around her stockinged leg. *Mine,* he vowed, sliding his fingers up her thigh, to where the rough stocking ended and smooth, supple paradise began. Her flesh quivered under his fingers. She broke away from their kiss and let her head fall against his chest.

"Lucy." His voice was low and hoarse. "Lucy, look at me."

She lifted her head, but shadow obscured her face. He couldn't see her. She couldn't see him. They were two strangers huddled together in the dark.

He wrapped his hand under her bare thigh and lifted her against him, rolling out from the wardrobe's dark corner. In one swift move, he reversed their positions, pinning her against the back panel of ebony. Shards of light decorated her face and danced over the tops of her breasts. She stared into his face, her pupils wide, the green of her eyes nearly eclipsed by black. Her lips were swollen and dusky red. *Mine,* he thought, taking her mouth in a greedy kiss. She welcomed his tongue with her own, but he pulled away. He wanted to see her face, to watch those beautiful lips as they shaped the syllables of his name.

He slowly lowered her, letting her sink back onto his thigh. She arched against him with a little moan. Then she melted back against the ebony panel, and her eyes fluttered shut. Jeremy moved his hand under her skirt, skimming his fingers over the smooth crest of her thigh. She bit her lip as his fingers traveled slowly up, into moist heat and tight curls. Then his fingers brushed over her mound, and her eyes flew open.

"Yes," he said, rubbing lightly again. She shuddered, and her breath caught in her throat, but she held his gaze. *Yes*.

Dear God, it would be so easy. A few buttons, one quick thrust, and she would be his. All his. But as badly as he wanted her—as much as his loins ached and his heart pounded and his whole body shook with desire— he didn't want her that way. She had to come to him.

She had to come for him.

He worked his fingers against her slowly. "Oh," she sighed. "Oh, God."

Mine, he willed silently, sliding a finger into her molten core. Her mouth fell open. Her gaze was pleading. *Call my name. Not God's, or the devil's, or any man's in between. Mine.*

Through the thick, musky fog of desire, Jeremy was vaguely aware of noises. Muffled noises from without the wardrobe. Footfalls. Voices. But he slid his finger further into her hot, slick sheath, and her little strangled cry was the only noise in the world. She clutched his shoulders tight.

Call my name, he thought.

"Toby," she squeaked.

He froze. Her fingers dug into his flesh. His finger slid out of hers.

"He's coming," she whispered, wriggling out of his embrace. She flattened herself against the back of the wardrobe and hugged her arms over her naked breasts.

The footsteps came to a halt directly outside the wardrobe.

"And Lucy must be here." Toby's voice was muffled by thick panels of ebony, but unmistakable. As was Sophia's voice asking,

"How do you know?"

"She always hides here," came the reply. "Come out, Lucy," Toby called.

Lucy looked to Jeremy, her expression panicked. "Do something!"

Do something. How Jeremy longed to do something. Many things. The first thing was to send his fist crashing through the ebony door, grab Toby by the throat, and strangle him. The second thing was to gather Lucy into his arms and find the hot, slick place where he'd left off. And then the third thing . . . oh dear Lord, the third thing.

The ebony doors began to swing apart, and a thin crease of light shone through. Jeremy grabbed the bolts that held the door handles in place and yanked the doors shut. He held the bolts in white-knuckled grasps while unseen hands tried again, rattling the doors in their frame.

"That's odd," Toby said. "It must be locked."

The doors stilled, and Jeremy's grip on the bolts relaxed. Then the crease of light rent the darkness again, and he clutched at the bolts once more. This time, he didn't dare let go. Not until the footfalls resumed and the voices faded. Not for several moments after that.

When he finally looked back toward Lucy, she had her back to him. She was shrugging back into her chemise and dress, drawing the sleeves up over her shoulders. Jeremy longed to rip them back down. But instead he pulled her laces tight and tied them in silence. He placed his hands on her waist and kissed the back of her neck. "Lucy," he whispered.

She pulled away.

"He remembered," she said softly. "He remembered after all."

CHAPTER
ELEVEN

Lucy lay flat on her back, staring up at the ceiling. She lay atop the brocade counterpane, her hair spreading across the pillows like a fan. If she turned her neck slightly, she could see the untouched dinner tray sitting on her writing table. Surely the food had long gone cold.

She was still wearing the same green dress she'd put on that morning. Her bath had been drawn, her hair unbound—but when Mary had reached to untie her laces, Lucy had practically slapped her hand away. Ridiculous, she now chided herself. Utterly absurd—the idea that without those thin layers of muslin and lawn, her maid would somehow *know*.

Oh, but how could she not? How could anyone not *know* just by looking at her? That was why she had fled—hurried straight from the wardrobe up to her bedchamber and never returned to the drawing room. She hadn't gone down to dinner, sending Mary instead to relay some excuse about her injured ankle. She might never show her face in public again—because everyone would *know*. Surely it was stamped across her forehead in big, red letters that spelled out . . .

What, exactly? She'd sat at her dressing table for a long hour, studying her reflection by candlelight, trying to discern that word.

Wanton? Kissing a man was one thing. A very pleasant thing. Tempting a man to kiss you was another thing, and equally grand. But this . . . this went beyond anything. She'd hauled a man into an enclosed space, made short work of her clothing, and thrown herself at him so hard she would stick. Lucy had never claimed to be an authority on the definition of ladylike behavior, but she knew the difference between good breeding and . . . well, just plain *breeding.*

Fool? Perhaps that was the word. Because the letters to spell out "great bloody imbecile" probably wouldn't fit. If Toby married Sophia Hathaway, Lucy would have no one to blame but herself. She could have spoken with him as they walked back from the woods, but she hadn't. She should have sent Jeremy away when he burst into her wardrobe, but she didn't. She hadn't and she didn't, and she couldn't understand for the life of her why.

Ruined? Lucy knew most people would think so. But she wasn't concerned about what most people thought. At the moment, she cared only for the opinion of two particular people. Well, perhaps three. She herself was foremost among them. And Lucy didn't feel "ruined" in the slightest. She felt distinctly, deliciously *improved.*

The other word picked at the frayed edge of her mind. She tried to push it away. But it always came back, that word. The simplest label of all, and the most unthinkable yet.

His.

Just thinking the word set her to thrumming like a plucked bowstring. Her whole body vibrated with the awful, unbearable truth of it.

She'd been branded. She was his. Wasn't that what she truly feared the world would read on her face? Hadn't his lips written it over her body and his touch burned it into her skin? Even now, she felt his mark, raw and itching under the fabric of her dress. Scored over and over across her flesh.

His.

His wanton. *His* fool. *His* alone, and ruined for anyone else.

Lucy blinked at the ceiling. Then she pressed the heels of her hands against her eyes and blotted out the world.

Damn.

Damn him. Damn her. Damn, damn, damn.

It wasn't supposed to be this way. She wasn't a thing to be claimed. A quarry to be bagged. She'd never wanted the indignity of a Season in London. The miserable ordeal of being preened and plumed and paraded about the *ton*. The humiliation of waiting for some strutting peacock to cross the ballroom, shove a ring on her finger, paste his name over her own, and stamp "His" on her forehead for the world to read. The abject shame of it if no man even tried.

She was Diana. She was the goddess of the hunt. She wanted to choose. She *had* chosen, Lucy reminded herself. She had chosen Toby. Familiar features floated up into the darkness behind her eyelids. Golden-brown hair. Chiseled cheekbones and a dimpled chin. Laughing eyes and a generous, smiling mouth. *Hers,* she willed. All of it, *hers*. She wanted him with every ounce of her will and every inch of her body.

Every inch . . . except the little tingling patch of flesh beneath her left earlobe. That bit of her wanted someone else. Someone else's lips. Not that generous, smiling mouth, but stern, stony-set lips that melted to fire against her skin. Against that tiny, traitorous inch of her flesh that declared itself *his*. She put her fingers to the soft hollow of her neck, and her pulse quickened under her touch.

Another piece of her rebelled. A random ridge of collarbone seceded from her will. She ran her fingers along that razor-thin republic that now lived for the weight of a heavy brow and the bracing chill of damp hair, cool and dark as ebony. Not hers any longer, but *his*.

And then her breasts were rising up against the oppression of her bodice. Yearning to be liberated into his hands. She flattened her own palms over them, and her nipples peaked in protest. *His, his,* they insisted in tandem. Lucy was outnumbered. Her resolve was falling apart, and her body dissolving with it. Her mind was swirling with shadows and shards of latticed light, and she felt the dark secret of his caress burning on her skin. Rekindling that hot ache between her legs. The place where his tender assault had laid waste to her will. The place that so easily, so readily might have been *his,* yearned to be *his* even now.

If Toby hadn't come . . . Her whole body flushed with the question, burned to know the answer. Her hands strayed lower, smoothing over her belly.

A light knock at the door yanked her out of the memory and out of the wardrobe . . . again. She sat up in bed.

"Lucy, it's me."

Lucy slid back the bolt and cracked open the door. Sophia stood in the corridor, wrapped in a blue silk peignoir. Her golden hair was loose, flowing over her shoulders in soft waves.

"May I come in?"

Lucy opened the door in a silent invitation, and Sophia entered.

"I came to see if you were feeling better," she said, flouncing onto the edge of the bed. She eyed Lucy's stockinged ankle dubiously. Then her gaze wandered up to Lucy's flushed cheeks. "But I daresay you are," she said, arching an eyebrow. She smiled. "In fact, you look very well indeed."

Lucy sat down at her writing table and plucked a roll from the dinner tray. She bit off the end and chewed furiously. Lord, but she was hungry.

"You disappeared this afternoon," Sophia accused.

"And so did Lord Kendall. You cannot expect me to credit coincidence."

Lucy took another bite of bread and shrugged.

Sophia bounced on the edge of the bed. "Lucy! You know you must tell me what happened."

"Nothing happened."

Sophia pouted. "I know the difference between something and nothing," she said, reclining back on her elbows. "And the look on your face does not come of doing nothing."

"Doesn't it?" It was just as Lucy had suspected. One look at her face, and Sophia *knew*. She would never be able to leave her chamber again. Then she recalled Sophia's aborted "shocking" tale that morning. "So tell me about *something*," she said, "and I will tell you whether this afternoon fits the definition."

Sophia toyed with the lace neckline of her peignoir. "Shall I tell you about Gervais?"

"Gervais?" So *something* had a name.

"He was my painting master. And my tutor in the art of passion." She sighed and laid flat on the bed. "Divinely handsome. Lean and strong, with jet-black hair and silver eyes and long, sculpted fingers. I was madly in love with him. Perhaps I still am."

Lucy choked on her bite of roll. She poured herself a glass of claret and threw back a healthy swallow. Then another. When she had drained the glass, she drew her knees up to her chest and coiled into her chair. Sophia was still lying flat on the bed, staring up at the ceiling. Her bare feet dangled over the edge, and she flexed her ankles idly.

"Well?" Lucy prompted. "Surely you don't mean to stop there."

"It all started with sketching," Sophia said to the ceiling. "I was doing a study of Michelangelo's David. Just a little charcoal sketch from a plate in a book. I couldn't quite capture the muscles of the forearm, and I became so vexed. Gervais tried to explain it to me, but he couldn't put the words into English, and I failed to comprehend his French. Then suddenly he stood up, stripped off his coat, and rolled up the sleeve of his shirt. He took my hand and placed it over his wrist. He dragged my fingers over every inch of his forearm, tracing every tight cord of muscle and sinew. He was so solid, so strong . . ."

Sophia rolled over onto her side, propping herself on one elbow. "You will think me wicked, and I don't care. You will be right. I am wicked. I wanted to rip off his shirt and touch him all over."

Lucy did not think Sophia wicked at all. Given her own similar reaction in the wardrobe, she thought Sophia wholly sympathetic. In fact, the pattern of behavior was vastly reassuring. Sophia wasn't to blame, and neither was she. Clearly the sight of a well-muscled forearm incited a woman to utter depravity. How else to explain the invention of cuffs?

"And did you?"

Sophia's mouth crooked in a half smile. "Not then. Only much later." She traced the counterpane's brocade pattern with her fingertips. "I sketched him, you know. *All* of him."

"All of him? Even—"

"Yes, even. And I let him sketch all of me."

Lucy clapped a hand over her mouth and laughed into her palm. And Toby thought Sophia's *tea tray* was cunning? This took the term "accomplishment" to a whole new level of meaning. "You didn't."

"Oh, but I did." Sophia placed her hand over her heart. "And after he sketched me, he painted me."

"You mean a portrait? Or a miniature?"

"No, no. He did not paint my likeness. He painted *me*. I took off all my clothes and stretched out on a bed, and he stroked every last inch of me with paint. He said I was white and smooth, like a blank canvas. *His* canvas. He painted little vines curling over my belly . . ." Sophia's fingers drew a twining circle over her stomach. Then her hand traced over the curve of her breast. "And flowers here—lavender orchids." She shut her eyes and sighed. "I feigned the grippe and refused to bathe for a week."

Lucy gaped at her in awed silence. Questions stuck in her throat. When Gervais had been stroking Sophia with paint, had he stroked her *there*? And had she felt the same unbearable, wondrous ache that Lucy had felt . . . still felt even now? And had Mr. and Mrs. Hathaway never heard of chaperones?

Sophia rolled flat on her back again and clasped both hands over her heart in the throes of romantic agony. "Oh, Gervais," she sighed. "He loved me. He did. *Je t'aime,* he would say. *Je t'adore, ma petite.* He said it over and over again while he . . ."

Sophia's voice trailed off, and Lucy wanted to scream. "While he what?"

Sophia threw her a superior look. "Don't you know?"

"Er . . . yes, well." Lucy blushed. "I mean, were you discovered?" Good heavens, and here Lucy had thought *she* was ruined. A bit of fumbling in a wardrobe was nothing to a torrid affair with a tutor. And with a Frenchman! Society would never forgive Sophia that, were it ever known. Her twenty thousand pounds could go hang. Were such a scandal ever made public, no gentleman of the *ton* would have her.

The hairs on Lucy's neck stood on end. *Toby wouldn't have her.*

"Oh, no," said Sophia. "We were never discovered. We quarreled, and I sent him away."

"Quarreled? Over what?"

"Sir Toby had asked permission to court me, and my

parents were overjoyed. I was desperate. I told Gervais I wished to elope. We might have a little cottage by the sea. Spend our days painting and our nights making passionate love. Our own piece of paradise." She shivered. "But Gervais refused."

"But why, if he loved you?"

"He doubted my devotion. He said that I would live to regret marrying him, that the pain of scandal and poverty would overshadow our joy. I told him he was wrong. I pleaded and begged and shouted and kissed . . . but I could not move him. So I sent him away." She put her hands over her face. "Oh, Gervais!" she whimpered. "*Mon cher, mon amour*. Forgive me."

Lucy poured herself another glass of claret.

Sophia uncovered her eyes and flung her arms out to either side. "I have tasted passion, Lucy," she said, her voice matter-of-fact. "And now that I have—I do not know how I shall endure a bland society marriage. Take a lover, I suppose. But the very idea seems so . . . gauche."

"You feel no passion for Toby," Lucy said, taking a careful sip.

"How could I? He professes to care for me, but then he scarcely looks at me. A kiss on the hand, a pretty phrase here or there . . . all so measured, so proper. Nothing of true desire." Sophia sat up. "I have no grand expectations. I do not expect the sort of raw, animal passion I knew in the arms of Gervais. That can only come once in a lifetime."

"Truly?" Lucy wrinkled her nose. "Just once?"

"But if only Sir Toby would show me a glimmer of hope." Sophia drew her legs onto the bed and crossed them under her. "Just one gesture of pure, unfettered romance. That's all I wish. Tear off his coat. Fold me into his arms. Sweep me off of my feet. But no, never, not once. I was so hoping the moment would come this afternoon. I didn't hide at all, you know. I counted ten and went straight back to the drawing room."

"Really? And what did you do?"

"The most shameless things imaginable. I offered to help him count. He only smiled. I said, 'We mustn't have you peeking,' and then I leaned over the divan until my bosom nearly fell out of my dress. And he put his hand over his eyes! I went to him and took his hand away and kept it in my own. I was ever so brazen, and what did he say? What topic sprang first to his mind?"

"Geometry?"

"Worse! *You*!"

"Me?" Lucy's head spun. Or perhaps the room was spinning around her. Whichever the case, she wanted it to keep whirling forever. She tipped her wineglass to her lips and drained the remaining liquid.

"Yes, you. He just gave my hand a little squeeze and said, 'Let's go find Lucy.' In that moment, I truly hated you." Sophia glared at her, then turned her gaze on the half-full decanter at Lucy's elbow. "Do you intend to drink that all by yourself? I wouldn't hate you nearly so much if you'd share."

Lucy smiled. Sophia Hathaway was welcome to hate her all she wished. So long as Toby didn't. She refilled the wineglass anyway and handed it to Sophia, who swallowed the contents in one long draught and then held out the glass for more. "You're still ahead," Sophia replied to Lucy's look of amusement.

Lucy poured again, her thoughts swirling like wine in a glass. Toby felt no passion for Sophia. Sophia cared nothing for Toby. And Gervais . . . Gervais was the answer to a prayer. A sign from above. It would be wrong to ignore a sign, Lucy told herself. Wicked indeed.

"Oh, Gervais," Sophia lamented into her second glass of claret. "If only I could . . . oh, but it is impossible. We live in different worlds."

"Nothing is impossible, if you want it badly enough. You must write to him." Lucy pushed aside the dinner tray. She opened the drawer of the writing table and drew out a sheet of paper and a quill.

"Write to him?" Sophia looked up sharply. "A letter? What an idea. I couldn't possibly."

"Why not?" Lucy uncorked a bottle of ink.

"It's only . . . he's not . . . I really *couldn't*." Sophia chewed her thumbnail. "Oh, but I must."

"You must." Rising from her chair, Lucy held out the quill.

Sophia shook her head. "No, you write. My hands will tremble."

"All right." Lucy sat back down and dipped the quill in ink. "How do you begin?"

"*Mon cher petit lapin*," Sophia dictated.

"If I'm going to do the writing, it will have to be in English. My French is abysmal."

"Very well," Sophia sighed. "My dear little rabbit."

Lucy did not move her quill. "Surely you're joking."

"Not at all."

"Your *rabbit*? And a 'dear, little' one at that? Are you certain you wouldn't prefer to begin with something a bit less . . . furry? 'Dear Gervais' seems a likely choice."

"But it's what I always called him," Sophia insisted. "And if the letter is in your hand, and in the wrong language, he has to know it's truly me somehow."

Lucy shrugged. "My . . . dear . . . little . . . rabbit," she said, scrawling the words as she spoke. "And then?"

"Forgive me, my darling," Sophia continued, reclining again on one elbow and gesturing grandly with her wineglass. "I regret our quarrel more than you could know. Sir Toby is nothing to me. You alone are—"

"Just a moment," Lucy interrupted. "You're speaking too fast." She wrote furiously. "You . . . alone . . . are . . . All right, go on."

"You alone are my love. I cannot forget you. I think of you constantly by day, and your face fills my dreams each night. I long for you. I long for your touch. When I close my eyes, my body remembers the warmth of your hands." She paused to take a large sip of wine. "When I taste wine, my lips remember your kiss."

"Ooh, that's very good," Lucy said, dipping her quill.

"Thank you. It just came to me." Sophia studied her glass of claret. "This is very good wine."

"Go on, then."

Sophia paused a moment before speaking. "Doubt not the depth of my feeling, nor the constancy of my love. Come to me, I beg you. Make me yours in every way."

Lucy smothered a small laugh.

"What?" asked Sophia.

"It's only . . . I thought he had already done that. Made you his in every way."

Sophia tossed her head. "Oh, Lucy," she said knowingly. "There are ever so many ways we hadn't tried yet."

Lucy's eyes widened. She turned her attention back to the paper.

"I shall await you this night," Sophia continued, "and every night thereafter." She waited for Lucy's quill to cease scratching. "All my love—no, wait. All my *undying* and *everlasting* love . . . Yours and yours alone . . . Signed, your little cabbage."

"Dear Lord." Lucy looked over her shoulder at Sophia. "First rabbits, now cabbage?"

"It sounds lovely in French."

"I suppose I'll take your word for it."

"It does. *Ton petit chou.*"

Lucy shook her head. "Cabbage it is. Or rather, cabbage you are." She blew lightly over the paper until the ink was dry, then folded it. "The direction?"

Sophia gave an address which Lucy dutifully transcribed. She turned to Sophia, lifting the decanter and one eyebrow, and Sophia eagerly held out her glass. Lucy poured out half the remaining wine into the glass. The rest she drank directly from the decanter.

"*À notre santé,*" said Sophia, raising the glass to her lips. "*Et à l'amour.*" She drained the glass and let it slip from her hand as she reclined fully. "I do believe I'm drunk."

Lucy laughed. "I do believe you are."

Then Sophia rolled over onto her stomach and buried her face in her forearm. Her shoulders shook. It took Lucy more than a few moments to realize she wasn't laughing, but sobbing.

"Sophia?" Lucy sat down gently on the bed. She reached out and patted her shoulder awkwardly, searching her mind for some comforting words. *Blast.* Yet another area in which her comportment was lacking. She wasn't particularly accomplished in comfort—neither giving nor receiving.

"Oh, Lucy, what shall become of me?"

"Why, you'll elope with Gervais. You'll have your little cottage by the sea. Painting, making love. Rabbits, cabbage. You'll be brilliantly happy."

"If only I could believe you." Sophia raised her head. Her eyes and nose were red. She sniffed loudly.

"Believe me," Lucy said. She stretched out next to Sophia on the bed, lying flat on her stomach and stacking her arms under her chin. "You don't want to marry Toby anyway. If he catches the slightest cold, he takes to his bed and moans as if he'd succumbed to the putrid fever. He'd take your dowry and spend it all on new boots. Or lose it at cards. He's hopeless at cards."

"Oh, don't go making me like him!" Sophia smiled and wiped her cheeks. "It all seemed so different once, didn't it? When we were girls? As if only we imagined something and wanted it deeply and believed it with all our hearts, it would come true."

She pulled back the counterpane and nestled under the sheets. "When I was a girl," she said, flipping her golden hair over the pillow, "I had a porcelain doll called Bianca. And I always knew that Bianca could become real. If only I minded my nursemaid and ate all my porridge and believed it with all my soul, she would one day spring to life. She would walk and talk and play with me like a real girl."

Her brow wrinkled. "She never did, of course. But it's funny—I'm still not sure why. There's the obvious answer—because Bianca was never more than a piece of china and a few scraps of cloth. But somehow I remain unconvinced. Perhaps it was just because I never ate all my porridge."

Lucy pulled back the other edge of the counterpane and crawled beneath the covers. "When I was a girl, I used to think that if I closed my eyes tight and wished hard enough, I would open them and find myself in Tortola."

Sophia shut her eyes and nuzzled into the pillow. Her voice grew thick with wine and sleep. "You were braver than I. I thought Venice."

CHAPTER
TWELVE

Lucy cracked open the door and peeked out into the corridor. The footman stationed opposite Aunt Matilda's chamber sagged against the wall, powdered wig listing at a sleepy angle. She coughed quietly, but the footman did not move. If she strained her ears, she could discern the faint rhythm of his snoring.

She stepped into the corridor and gently shut the door behind her, leaving Sophia to her wine-soaked dreams. Moving as swiftly as possible without extinguishing her candle, she padded down the hall. She kept her gaze trained on the threadbare carpet until she reached the head of the stairs.

Her slippers brushed lightly over timeworn wood as she descended the stairs in surefooted silence. With a nimble hop, she bypassed the third step from the bottom. It creaked, she knew—and even louder than usual in damp weather.

She paused at the bottom of the staircase. The rain had slowed as the night wore on, but the wind howled fierce as ever. An icy draft swirled over her neck. She clenched the letter between her teeth for a moment, pulling her shawl tight around her shoulders. Sometimes Waltham Manor seemed constructed of lace, rather than stone and mortar.

She ducked into Henry's study. The fire had banked to ashy coals that blanketed the room in a faint red glow.

Lucy placed the candlestick on the burled walnut desk-top. She stood still for a few moments, blinking and waiting for her eyes to adjust to the dim light. An oval, gilt-edged tray came into focus before her, as well as the handful of sealed envelopes that awaited tomorrow's post.

Lucy pulled open the top right drawer of the desk and began to rummage through it. The drawer brimmed with quills and ledgers and rumpled correspondence. Finally her fingers closed around the bit of sealing wax she sought. She held it over the candle until the red wax softened and oozed, and then she dripped a large red seal over the paper's flap.

She held the letter flat in the palm of her hand and blew lightly over the cooling wax. This was it. Her future. Lying right there in the palm of her hand, disguised as an innocent scrap of paper and a few scrawls of ink. She leaned over to place it on the salver with the rest of the post, but something made her pause.

What if Gervais didn't come?

Lucy straightened and clasped the letter to her chest.

Perhaps his noble instincts would win out. Perhaps he didn't love Sophia any longer. Perhaps he had moved to another address. Once the letter was posted, the letter was gone. Her future would be in the hands of a French painter with a penchant for cabbage. To hear Sophia tell it, those hands were rather capable—but still.

She needn't post it, Lucy realized. Simple misdirection would serve her purpose far better. She had only to show the letter to Toby, and his plan to marry Sophia would be banished instantly. Her twenty thousand pounds would have all the allure of twenty thousand sharp sticks in the eye. No painted tea tray could alter that fact.

But Sophia would be heartbroken. And ruined.

The room was cold and drafty, but Lucy began to flush. Her brain felt warm and muddled. Something was wrong with her. She pressed the back of her hand to her forehead. Perhaps she was ill. She must be taken with brain fever, because she couldn't think at all. She couldn't think what to do, and this was a situation that definitely required her to do *something*. Didn't it?

Lucy felt herself falling into halves, her will divided. The sensation was wholly unfamiliar and greatly alarming. This was worse than brain fever. This was indecision. Indecision was not in her makeup. She had always known what she wanted, and she had always known how to get it. She didn't stand waffling in drafty rooms in the middle of the night when she could be warm and snug in her bed, dreaming sweet dreams that would soon become realities.

But then again, she'd never held her future in the palm of her hand. If she felt indecision for the first time now, it could be because this was the first real decision she had ever faced. And wasn't this what she had always desired? To choose?

Lucy considered her options. She thought about posting the letter. She thought about shoving it under Toby's door. She thought about throwing it into the fire and watching it curl into ash. She mentally walked through each alternative, hoping one would simply feel right.

But none of them felt right, or even simple.

A week ago, she would have known what to do. A week ago, doubt was as foreign to Lucy as friendship, or a kiss. Before, every piece of her—heart, mind, body, soul—lived for one purpose. For one person. But then she'd stolen into another man's bedchamber, and then Sophia had flounced into hers—and in between, a hundred terrible, wonderful things had happened. Suddenly, every piece of her—heart, mind, body, soul—had grown bigger, stronger, with needs and wants and demands of its own.

And that one purpose—that one person—was no longer enough to hold all the pieces together.

She let herself think the unthinkable words. Let them bubble up from deep inside her and seep quietly through the cracks in her resolve. Only here, in the dark, where she could change her mind and take them all back with no one the wiser.

I'm not in love with Toby.

Her heart kept beating. The candle kept burning. The earth did not open and swallow her whole. She tried the words again, aloud this time, but softly. Just a whisper, swirling through the air like candle smoke.

"I'm not in love with Toby."

It was so easy. Too easy. She nearly laughed aloud with the absurdity of it. The relief of it. Lucy felt as though she'd spent years clinging to a rope for dear life, dangling and twisting in the air with each fickle breeze—only to finally let go and fall all of two inches to land on solid ground.

Or solid ebony.

Her gaze shifted to the doorway. Through the doorway and across the corridor, to the shadowed alcove that hid her wardrobe. Only it wasn't her wardrobe any longer, she knew. It was *their* wardrobe.

She had nowhere left to hide.

And even though she half expected it—even though it made perfect, unquestionable sense—when Jeremy rounded the doorway, saw her, and halted mid step, Lucy was caught completely unprepared. If she had known how the sight of him would send a shock wave rolling through her body, she would have grabbed the desk. If she had anticipated how splendid he would look—wearing a black coat thrown carelessly over an open shirt, his dark hair so touchably tousled—she would have lit more candles. And if Lucy had had the faintest inkling that this man would turn her plans to chaos and her will to water and her knees to absolute porridge, she would never have crept into his room and kissed him that night, less than a week past.

She would have done it years ago.

Her shawl slipped to the floor.

Jeremy's heart lurched in his chest.

She wore the same dress. Even in the dim glow of a single candle, he recognized it. He would know it in the dark. The same light-green muslin he had hungrily peeled from her body and then re-laced with sharp tugs of regret. At the realization, his body reacted quickly, violently. His mouth went dry. His chest grew tight. His breeches, as well.

She wore the same dress. She had not bathed. All the places he had touched, all the places he had kissed—something of him lingered still. On her. Inside her.

She hadn't washed him away.

And God, she had never looked more beautiful. Flickering light kissed over her cheeks, her brow, her lips. Her hair tumbled over one shoulder in a chestnut cascade. Her skin drank in the candlelight and glowed. Or perhaps the candle drank in her beauty and burned.

"Oh," she said finally. "It's you."

"Were you expecting someone else?"

"No." Her gaze flitted away for an instant, but then came home to his. "Not really."

Jeremy wanted to step closer, but his feet wouldn't move. He'd come here intending to leave, but he knew he couldn't do that either. He would stand on this bit of ground until the candle guttered or the sun rose or the manor walls crumbled to dust at their feet.

He wasn't going anywhere.

"What are you doing here?" she asked, her voice smoky with warmth.

She wanted to know what he was doing here. Jeremy paused, considering his response. It didn't seem wise to tell her exactly what he was doing there, at that precise moment. *Picturing you naked*, should he say? Or perhaps, *recalling the exquisite softness of your lips against my skin*? She probably wouldn't care to hear, *cupping my hands around the memory of your breasts.*

He cleared his throat and flexed his hands at his sides. No, it was probably wise to confine his answer to what he had *meant* to do here. Before the sight of her, and the dress she hadn't changed, had changed everything. "I was going to leave a note for Henry."

"You were going to leave Henry a note."

He nodded.

"But now you're not."

He shook his head. "I'm not."

"What changed your mind?"

"You're here." It was part of the truth. The whole of it being, *you're here, and I can't bear to be anywhere else.*

She stiffened. Her eyes narrowed. "Well, I'll clear out then. Leave you to your note." She pushed back from the desk. Catching the paper between her teeth, she crouched down to gather her shawl.

He was at her side before he realized he'd taken a step. "Don't."

She stood up, swinging the shawl around her shoulders. With the paper still grasped in her teeth, she flipped her hair out from under the pearl-gray wool of her wrap. Finally she took the paper back with her hand. "Don't what?"

"Go."

A strand of hair was caught in her mouth, and she blew it out with a gust of breath. Jeremy smelled wine. "I *am* going. You've no need to growl at me." She started to turn from him, but he caught her wrist.

"Don't. Go." He forced the words from his throat.

Her face softened. "Oh."

She looked at his hand where it gripped her wrist. He released her abruptly. He wanted to grasp far more than her wrist, yearned to pull her into his arms. But he wouldn't. He couldn't watch her flee from him again.

"I only mean," he said, straightening his coat, "you came here for some reason, I presume."

"I was going to post a letter." She held up the folded paper.

"You were going to post a letter."

She nodded.

"But now you're not."

She tapped the letter thoughtfully against her bottom lip. "Actually, I hadn't quite decided."

Without thinking, he reached out and took the letter from her hand. If she kept tapping it against her lip like that, he would have to kiss her. No decision involved. He just would. Of course, now that he held the paper in his own hand, Jeremy realized he scarcely needed the tapping letter as provocation. She was too close. So close his mouth ached to taste her. She would taste like wine. He thought about taking a step back. He didn't.

"You don't write letters," he said, sliding his thumb across the uneven wax seal. The sensation instantly recalled the puckered satin of her nipple. His breath hitched. He ought to step back. He couldn't.

"I don't write letters. It's Sophia's. She's in love. She wants to elope."

"With Toby?"

Lucy bit her lip. "No."

He broke the seal and unfolded the paper. She made

no effort to stop him. He perused the contents quickly and refolded the letter before shoving it inside the breast pocket of his coat. "You can't do this, Lucy. I won't let you."

"Why not? If Sophia's in love with another man, doesn't she deserve to be happy? If she's in love with another man, doesn't Toby deserve to know?"

Her eyes were guileless green, but Jeremy saw red. "Don't pretend this is about them. You don't give a damn about what Toby or Sophia deserve. This is all about you. You think that if Sophia's out of the picture, Toby will turn to you. He won't."

Her eyes glimmered, and she lifted her chin. "Why wouldn't he? Because I'm not elegant and accomplished? Because I have no dowry?"

"Because," he said roughly, grabbing her by the shoulders. The soft wool of her shawl slid under his fingers. "Because I won't let him."

He inched toward her, closing the distance between them until the lapels of his coat grazed the bodice of her dress. He waited. She didn't pull away. Slowly, tenderly, he slid one hand from her shoulder to her neck, tangling his fingers into her hair and cradling the back of her head. He made a small circle with his thumb, stroking the silken flesh behind her ear. She sighed somewhere deep in the back of her throat, and the sound made him weak. Her wine-stained lips parted, and her tongue darted out to moisten them.

He bent his head to hers, and her eyes widened. "Oh, don't."

Jeremy recoiled as if stung. He released his grip on her shoulder. His hand went slack in her hair. He pulled his head away.

Then her hands were around his neck, tugging him back down.

"Don't let him."

* * *

Lucy dragged his lips onto hers. Had it truly been only hours since she'd tasted them last? It felt like months. Years.

And it felt right. So right. Damn the letter and everyone else. This, this alone was right.

His lips were firm and warm on hers, but motionless. And closed. One of his hands hovered over her shoulder, the other somewhere behind her head. Lucy could feel their warmth, but not their weight. Not his touch. He was hesitating, she knew. Fighting the kiss, fighting his desire. She could feel the struggle in his chest as it rose and fell against hers.

She pulled his bottom lip into her mouth, sucking gently. He groaned somewhere deep in his chest, and the sound made her bold. She caught his lip between her teeth and nipped. Harder.

His lips parted. At last. She slid her tongue into his mouth, tasting whiskey and relief. She burrowed into his open coat and pressed her breasts against his chest. And when his hands still hesitated, she grabbed hold of his shoulders and jumped. Hopped straight up off the floor—and never came back down, because he caught her in his arms. Just as she'd known he would.

Oh, yes. Finally. One strong arm wrapped around her waist. One hand cupping her head. His lips, moving over her mouth again and again. His tongue, caressing hers. Every inch of his hard, heated body pressed against her, supporting her weight. Heaven. It was night and dark, and his kiss was pure heaven, but Lucy didn't see stars. She saw clouds. White, feathery clouds and blue, blue sky. Blue like his eyes. Her feet would never touch the ground again. She would float on this cloud for the rest of her life. Longer than that.

She hooked her legs around his waist. His hand slid

down to cup her backside, and he pulled her tight against his groin. She still didn't see stars. She *became* a star, free-falling through dark desire, exploding into white-hot light and flame. He lowered her down onto the desk, his hips still locked with hers. He was kissing her neck now, running his tongue up to her ear.

Then he pulled away. He leaned over her, bracing himself on his hands. Candlelight illuminated one side of his face. He looked half man, half dangerous shadow—and Lucy wanted him all.

"Touch me," she whispered. *God in heaven, touch me before I burn straight through this desk.*

He winced. "Do you hear something?"

Lucy heard many things. She heard her heart hammering in her chest and her pulse thundering in her ears. She heard his ragged, panting breaths. She ground her hips against his. There. She heard a groan.

He shut his eyes and clenched his jaw. And then Lucy heard it, too. Footsteps above them. Not just a few, but many. Footsteps thundering down the stairs. The creak of the third step.

"Not again," she said, covering her face with her hands. "This is becoming ridiculous." She unwrapped her legs from his waist, and he stepped back. "Well?" she asked, sitting up. "What do we do?"

He shrugged, running a hand through his hair. "You could hide under the desk."

"Are you daft? This is my house. I'm not hiding under the desk. If anyone's hiding under the desk, it's going to be y—"

He clapped a hand over her mouth. His voice was low and gruff, and she felt it rumble through her, down through her chest and between her thighs. "Hide, don't hide. Do as you wish. But whatever you do, you'd better do it quickly."

He removed his hand. They looked at each other.

Lucy gave herself a shake. She opened her mouth to swear at him, but he cut her off again. This time with a kiss, raw and possessive.

"Don't," he said, his voice husky as he tore his lips from hers. "Don't hide."

CHAPTER
THIRTEEN

When Henry entered his study, Jeremy was seated at the desk, sharpening a quill by the light of a single candle. Lucy sat perched on a corner of the desktop, studying a paper by the glow of a few red coals. If Henry had been an observant guardian, he might have taken exception to the fact that his friend and his sister were alone in a room at an ungodly hour of night, studiously avoiding one another's gaze. He might have noticed that their clothing was rumpled and their hair mussed and their breathing labored. He might have seen that the paper in Lucy's hand was blank.

But Henry was not observant. He wasn't even much of a guardian.

"Oh, good," he said. "You're both awake."

Lucy stared at her brother. He had breeches pulled on under his nightshirt and a loose-fitting greatcoat slung over all. His dark brown hair stood up at wild angles.

"Jem, come with us," Henry said. "Lucy, go find Marianne. She's checking the house."

Lucy looked at Jeremy. He merely blinked at her, his expression blank.

"Come on then," Henry said impatiently. "She can't have gotten far. The rain's stopped at least, but this wind is the devil's own bitch."

"Aunt Matilda." Lucy and Jeremy spoke as one.

Jeremy followed Henry's lead, pausing at the door to cast Lucy a parting glance, intense and unreadable. She wrapped her shawl about her shoulders and took up the candle before venturing out into the corridor.

Marianne greeted her at the bottom of the staircase. Sophia was descending the steps, the hem of her blue silk peignoir skimming above her bare feet.

"How long has she been missing?" Lucy asked.

"We don't know for certain," said Marianne. She knotted the sash of her dressing gown with brisk tugs. "Her nurse left her at ten, and it's well past midnight now. Henry's taken all the men out in search of her."

"Two hours." Sophia shivered. "She could be halfway to the village by now."

Lucy glared at Sophia and placed an arm about Marianne's shoulders. "I'm sure she's no such thing. She's probably just ambled into an unused room and gone to sleep. We'll find her."

"I'll keep searching down here," Marianne said. She turned to Sophia. "Miss Hathaway, would you be so kind as to search the upstairs rooms with Lucy?"

"Of course," Sophia answered. "I'll wake Kitty as well."

"Thank you."

Lucy mounted the stairs two at a time, with Sophia scampering up behind her. She headed down the East corridor, where the guestrooms were located. Most of them were in use at the moment, but a few surplus chambers remained untouched. Perhaps they would find Aunt Matilda curled up between a divan and its dust-cover.

"Lucy!" Sophia grabbed her elbow as they entered an unused chamber. Lucy shook her off and began lifting the sheets from the furniture and checking in the cupboards.

Sophia cornered her by a bookcase. "Lucy, where did you go? What did you do with the letter?"

Lucy paused. It took her a moment to remember

which letter Sophia meant. It took her another few moments to recollect its current home—the breast pocket of Jeremy's coat, snugly tucked between the layers of fabric, nestled against his hard chest. It then took her a long minute to recover from that image.

"You didn't put it with the post, did you?" Sophia grabbed her by the shoulders. "Tell me you didn't post it."

"Why? Didn't you want me to?"

"Of course not!"

"But what about Gervais? How is he going to know to come for you if he never receives the letter?"

Sophia let out a strangled sigh. "Gervais is never going to come for me. Gervais doesn't exist."

"What?"

"He doesn't exist. I made him up. My real painting master is a balding prig called Mr. Turklethwaite. I'd lighten my tea with paint before I touched his forearm, let alone any other part of his body." Sophia shuddered.

Lucy was stunned. "But, the letter . . ."

"Was *your* idea!" Sophia exclaimed in a loud whisper. "I thought you were suggesting a bit of fun, just like you proposed writing that letter to the pirates. I thought you understood." Her face softened. "All that talk about wishing for something so hard it would come true . . . Lucy, I thought you *understood*."

"I do," she said, thinking of her own infatuation with Toby. Lucy took her friend's hand and squeezed it. "I do understand. Oh, but how did you ever invent such a sordid tale in the first place? The sketching, the . . . the *painting*! The rabbits and cabbage!"

"The *wine*." Sophia rolled her eyes. "And, so long as I'm being momentarily honest, the envy."

"Envy?"

"Yes, of course, envy! You're getting kissed under

trees and worked over in cupboards, and I'm getting lessons in geometry!"

Lucy smiled despite herself. This probably wasn't the moment to tell Sophia she'd just been kissed to distraction in Henry's study. "But if Gervais isn't real," she asked, "then whose address did you give?"

"My *modiste*'s." Sophia cringed and let go of Lucy's shoulders. "Oh, I'll be ruined," she moaned, putting one hand over her eyes.

"Don't be ridiculous. Your name wasn't on the letter. It isn't even in your hand."

Sophia uncovered her eyes. "You're right. But how brilliant! Madame Pamplemousse sells more gossip than gowns. That letter will end up in the scandal sheets, and all of England will be mad to find out who wrote it. We'll be the talk of the drawing room all winter long. We'll be infamous!" She grabbed Lucy's hand in hers. "Oh, tell me you posted it!"

"I didn't post it."

"Well give it to me, then. I'll post it myself."

"I can't." Lucy brushed past her and exited the room. She went down the corridor to the next room. The latch rattled in her hand. It was locked. She turned around and jumped at the sight of Sophia's nose three inches from hers.

"What do you mean, you can't? Where is it?"

"Er . . ."

Lucy was saved by a series of male shouts emanating from the courtyard. She crossed the corridor and entered the first open room. She hurried to the window and wrenched it open. Footmen scurried about in the courtyard, brandishing torches and shouting directions to one another.

Sophia put a hand on Lucy's shoulder and leaned over her, craning her neck. "They must have found her."

Lucy turned from the window and started back

toward the door. She froze in her tracks. This was Jeremy's room. She looked around. The fire was banked and growing dim. The bed had not been slept in; the counterpane remained unwrinkled. There were no personal objects to speak of. No book lay on the bedside table. No flask awaited filling at the bar. No discarded cravat hung from the corner of the mirror. Only two objects in the room evidenced his occupancy.

Two valises, standing at attention by the door.

He was leaving.

"Well, come on then." Sophia tugged at her elbow, and Lucy followed numbly.

Of course, Lucy thought as they hurried down the corridor. Of course he was leaving. Why else would he be leaving a note for Henry in the middle of the night?

"What's all this, then?" Kitty stepped into the corridor, rubbing the sleep from her eyes with one hand and clutching the neck of her dressing gown with the other.

"Aunt Matilda," Sophia called over her shoulder as they breezed past. "She's wandered off again. All the men are out searching for her."

Lucy and Sophia started down the stairs, and Kitty hurried after them. "Wait!" she called.

Sophia stopped, and Lucy halted likewise. They stared at Kitty.

Kitty huffed. "Well, I'm not going to be left here all alone." She planted one hand on her hip and leaned against the banister.

"Come along then," Lucy said with a shrug, resuming her progress down the stairs. *Really,* she thought. Kitty was insufferable. One would think she'd missed her invitation to a garden party.

Lucy led the sisters out through the manor's massive front door. Cold seized her instantly. The wind whipped straight through her thin shawl and dress. Moonlight filtered through a lace of clouds overhead, and she blinked as her eyes adjusted to the dim silver glow. She hugged her arms across her chest and hastened to follow the line of torch-bearing footmen into the garden. She turned slightly and noticed Marianne had joined the other ladies.

Dread shivered through her as they wove through the garden behind the bobbing beacons of flame. Dread and shame. Because although she ought to have been consumed with fear for Aunt Matilda, the true source of Lucy's dread was the sight of those valises in Jeremy's bedchamber. He was leaving.

Her slippers were wet through, and her feet felt like blocks of ice shuffling under her. They prickled with pain. The rest of her was numb. He was leaving, and the wintry wind felt like an ocean breeze in Tortola compared to the chill wrapped round her heart.

The footmen wound their way through the garden hedges, finally gathering around a circular flagstone terrace with a fountain at its center. Oblivious to the cold, the fountain's nymph and satyr cavorted in their perpetual summer, their bronze bodies weathered to a muted green. Seated at the fountain's edge, Aunt Matilda shivered inside a vast black coat. Jeremy's coat.

Lucy and Marianne rushed to Aunt Matilda's side.

"Poor dear," said Marianne, wrapping an arm about the old lady's shoulders.

Lucy grabbed her aunt into a fierce embrace and held on longer than she'd planned. Her usual Aunt Matilda smell, tinged with spice and chocolate and snuff, mingled with *his* scent. Lucy buried her face in the lapel of the coat, breathing in leather and pine and sweet reprieve. He might be leaving, but he hadn't left yet. He couldn't leave without his coat.

"How long do you suppose she's been here?" Sophia asked, looming over Lucy's shoulder. "She must be freezing."

Lucy reached into a great black sleeve and found one of the old lady's papery hands. "Her hands are ice." She rubbed the chilled, bony fingers between her own.

She looked around. The men stood at the edge of the terrace, conferring with the servants. Kitty went to Felix's side and assailed him with questions. Lucy was dimly aware of Henry gesturing with a torch and saying something about a pallet and blankets. Her attention was largely drawn to a tall figure in the shadows behind her brother. A broad-shouldered silhouette framed by white linen that gleamed in the moonlight. She couldn't see his face, but she could feel his gaze on her, burning through the midnight chill.

Then Toby emerged from the shadows and strode into the circle of light.

Oh, thank God, Lucy thought. Thank God she already knew she didn't love him. Because in the eight years she had spent admiring his physical beauty, Toby had never looked more splendid. He wore a greatcoat that gaped in front to reveal a bare chest. The torchlight bronzed every muscled plane and contour of his torso. His golden-brown hair was windblown and wild. He looked magnificent and pagan, like a piece of garden statuary brought to life. Lucy felt pagan just looking at him.

Beside her, Sophia gasped. "Oh," she said. "Oh, my."

Toby brushed past Felix and crossed directly to Sophia. He eyed her from head to toe, his gaze lingering over a few areas in between. "God in heaven, look at you." He shook his head slightly and jerked his eyes back to her face. "You must be freezing."

Sophia nodded slightly. Her gaze did its own share of wandering and lingering over his bare chest.

Toby stripped off his coat and flung it around Sophia's shoulders. He stood bare to the waist in the bitter night wind, but Lucy could have sworn she saw steam rising from his body.

"Better?" he asked Sophia hoarsely.

She nodded.

"Do you feel warm?"

"Everywhere," Sophia breathed. She stared up at him, entranced. "Everywhere . . . except my feet."

Toby looked down to where Sophia's bare feet met the cold flagstones. Without a word, he hefted her into his arms and settled her against his chest. The blue silk of her peignoir flowed over his arms like a waterfall, and her golden hair fanned over his bare shoulder.

"Better?"

Sophia nodded again and made a small squeaking sound, presumably of agreement. Toby looked into her face and swallowed hard.

"Oh, bloody hell," he said, as though it were poetry. And then he kissed her.

Lucy knew the polite response would have been to look away. Study the cobbled path beneath her feet. Admire the swan-shaped topiary. Stare up at the night sky. But a polite response was beyond her at the moment. She gaped openly. And since no one around her remarked on the flagstones or the hedges or the stars overhead, she assumed she was not alone.

At last, Aunt Matilda broke the stunned silence. "Lovely."

"Felix!" Kitty prodded her husband in the ribs. "Don't you think you should do something?"

Felix snapped his jaw shut and looked to his wife. "Oh, very well." He took off his own coat and held it out to her. Kitty shook her head and looked at him as though he were mad. "You don't mean for me to pick you up?" he asked, his face uncertain. "I'm not sure I—"

"Not me." She jerked her head toward Toby and Sophia. *"Them."*

Comprehension made its slow journey across Felix's face. "Right," he said softly. Then, a bit louder, "Ahem."

Toby and Sophia remained joined at the lips and oblivious to all else.

Felix raised his voice. "I say, Toby." No response. "Toby!" he fairly shouted.

Toby reluctantly broke the kiss. He kept his eyes closed and his forehead pressed against Sophia's. "What is it, Felix?"

Felix shuffled his feet. "Sorry to interrupt, man, but I believe this is where I'm supposed to remind you that's my sister-in-law you're . . . holding." He absorbed the pointed look Kitty gave him. "Was there something you meant to ask her?"

"Right." Toby opened his eyes and straightened away from Sophia's flushed face. He cleared his throat. "Miss Hathaway," he began, shifting her weight in his arms, "It has been many months now that I have admired your elegance and the beauty of your . . ." His gaze wandered down her form. "Your character. The attachment I feel toward you transcends . . ." He looked back up at her lips and paused. "Transcends . . ."

Sophia smiled and bit back a small laugh.

"Oh, bloody hell," he said again, bending his head to hers and stealing the laughter from her lips. "Marry me?"

Even if she'd wished to, Sophia could not have uttered a reply. Toby was keeping her lips occupied. Her lips, and—from the looks of things—her tongue, as well. But somehow she managed a muffled squeak of acceptance. Really, Lucy thought, Sophia's whole body bespoke acceptance.

"Well, then," said Felix. "That's settled. Carry on." As if either Toby or Sophia cared one whit for his permission. If they kept up like this any longer, Henry had better send the footmen off for a vicar and special license, instead of a pallet and blankets. Lucy told herself once again that she ought to look away. But from the general silence, it seemed no one else was looking away either.

But someone was. Someone was looking at *her*. And the hot intensity of his gaze set Lucy ablaze with conflicting sensations. She felt stripped naked and exposed to the cold. She felt blanketed in warmth. She felt bolted to the stone beneath her, and she felt like running into his arms. In one second, she went numb with shock; in the next, every inch of her body burst into exquisite awareness. His gaze was holding her together and tearing her apart, and Lucy's heart raced so fast, she feared it would break.

Her heart was breaking.

Jeremy watched Lucy watch her life's dream slip away. No matter how hard he stared, no matter how hard he willed her to look away, she wouldn't. Her eyes were riveted to Toby's imbecilic display of ardor and bare chest. She turned deathly pale. Then she flushed. She shivered with cold, but he saw the sheen of perspiration on her brow.

Her heart was breaking, and there wasn't anything he could do. She wasn't his sister. She wasn't his betrothed. She wasn't *his*, and that was the whole damned problem.

Any of the others—they could have done something, but they didn't. No one cared. Toby, self-absorbed ass that he was, had shuffled his feet for weeks over this proposal, waiting for his perfect moment, only to choose *now*, of all times. Felix, who ought to have tossed Toby's self-absorbed ass into the fountain for mauling his sister-in-law, had the nerve to laugh. And Henry—oldest friend or no, Jeremy hated him. He was no excuse for a guardian and only a poor imitation of a brother. His sister's heart and hopes were being ripped to pieces in front of him, and he was either too stupid to notice or too insensitive to care.

Two footmen hastened toward the fountain, bearing a pallet between them.

"Come on, then," Henry said. "Let's get back to the house. I'm freezing my stones off out here."

Lucy and Marianne took Aunt Matilda by either arm and helped her onto the pallet. As the footmen carried her away, a scrap of white fluttered to the ground.

"What's this?" Kitty bent over and picked it up. She turned it over and lifted the broken seal. "There's no name." She unfolded the letter, and Jeremy felt his gut twist into a knot. Her eyes began to scan the page, and she clapped a hand over her mouth. "Oh goodness." Her eyes widened.

"What is it?" Felix asked. He tried to look over her shoulder, but Kitty turned away. She read further.

"Oh my," she said, her lips curling into a feline smile.

Felix grabbed the paper from her hand. He held it at arm's length and knitted his brows. "My . . . dear . . . little . . . *radish*?"

"No, no." Kitty grabbed the paper away from her husband. "It says 'rabbit,' not 'radish,' you simpleton."

Felix shrugged. "Looks like 'radish' to me."

"Oh, Felix, that is clearly a 'b.' My. Dear. Little. Rabbit," Kitty read aloud, jabbing her finger at each word.

Jeremy looked at Lucy. Lucy was looking at Sophia. And Sophia was clinging to Toby's neck in wide-eyed terror. She bit her lip and gave Lucy a barely perceptible shake of the head.

"Give me that," Henry said testily, leaving Aunt Matilda to his wife and reaching toward Kitty. Kitty reluctantly put the letter into his outstretched hand. Henry took it and shook the creases from the paper with a flick of his wrist. He lowered his torch to provide better reading light. "No wonder you can't decipher it. This is Lucy's handwriting. But it's rabbit. Definitely rabbit." He shook the paper again.

Jeremy looked back to Lucy. Now hers was the expression of wide-eyed terror.

"My dear little rabbit," Henry read in a booming voice. "Forgive me, my darling. *Darling?*" He shot an amused glance over the paper and continued. "I regret our quarrel more than you could know. Sir Toby is nothing to me. You alone are—" He stopped reading and looked up at Lucy, eyebrows raised.

"Henry, stop," she pleaded.

"You alone are my love," he continued with a smirk, affecting a girlish tone.

"Henry," Marianne warned.

Lucy looked to Jeremy, panic written across her face. Jeremy ran both hands through his hair. Damnation, this was like watching a rider thrown from a horse and being powerless to stop it. Helplessness roiled in his stomach like bile. What could he do? He couldn't very well tell Henry it was Sophia's letter. He would have to explain *how* he knew it was Sophia's letter, and he'd ruin two ladies in the space of one minute. Even he wasn't that great a rake.

"I cannot forget you," Henry continued in his high, mocking voice. "I think of you constantly by day, and your face fills my dreams each night."

Jeremy frantically tried to recall the exact contents of the letter. Perhaps it wasn't as damning as he remembered. Perhaps Henry would simply laugh and chalk it all up to girlish fancies.

"I long for you," Henry crooned. "I long for your . . ." His grin faded. His mouth thinned to a line. "I long for your *touch?*"

Jeremy groaned. Damned they were.

Henry skimmed the remainder of the letter, muttering more damning phrases as he read. "I remember the warmth of your hands . . . When I taste wine, I remember . . . I shall await you tonight . . . Make me yours in every way . . . *Cabbage*!" Henry held up the paper and shook it at Lucy. "What's the meaning of this?"

"Henry, please," she begged, shooting a glance toward Sophia. "Can we discuss this inside?"

"No, I think we had better discuss this now."

Lucy shook her head. "Henry, you don't understand. It isn't real." Her voice grew shrill with desperation. "It isn't even mine!"

Sophia burrowed her head into Toby's shoulder. Kitty clutched Felix's arm with glee.

Lucy buried her face in her hands. Her shawl slipped off one hunched shoulder, and Jeremy watched the ridge of her neck shiver into gooseflesh. Damn Henry. She was cold and heartbroken, and Jeremy was incensed. It was all mixed up inside him—this need to protect her; the desire to possess her. Anger and lust wrestled in his chest, spurring his heart into a furious rhythm. He wanted nothing more than to go to her. Cover her. Warm her. He had no coat, but he had his body. He had his hands and his lips and his tongue.

"Well if this letter isn't yours," Henry demanded, "then whose is it?"

Jeremy strode forward, calmly took the letter from Henry's hand, and said the only word that mattered. The word that had been echoing through his mind and his heart and an ebony wardrobe for the better part of a week.

"Mine."

CHAPTER
FOURTEEN

Lucy uncovered her face. *No.* He hadn't just—

Oh, but he had.

Jeremy stood next to Henry, letter in hand, wearing an expression more grave and determined than she had ever seen him wear. And that was saying something.

Felix grabbed the letter out of his hand, laughing. "Good one, Jem. As if you'd ever be Lucy's dear little radish."

"Rabbit." The low threat in Jeremy's voice would have sent a hare bounding for its hole. He took the letter back, but in the next instant Henry had snatched it again.

"Oh come now, stop joking." Henry smoothed the paper against the front of his coat and then held it before his face. "You honestly expect us to believe that Lucy is . . . your little *cabbage*?"

Jeremy clenched his jaw. He briefly closed his eyes and opened them again. "I'm rather fond of cabbage."

"Really?" Felix asked. "Terribly bland stuff, I've always thought. Of course, it's not so bad when stewed with a bit of salted pork. Or pickled in brine, that's all right, too. But—ow!"

Kitty removed her elbow from her husband's side.

Lucy finally caught Jeremy's gaze. "*What. Are. You. Doing?*" she mouthed.

He gave her a serious, inscrutable look. Then he turned away.

Lucy shook her head. She couldn't understand it. Jeremy had just sentenced himself to a lifetime of merciless teasing. Henry, Toby, Felix—they would never let him live that letter down. Endless rabbit jokes would be made at his expense. Countless dishes of cabbage would be served up for his benefit. But Jeremy had taken it anyway. He had purchased that letter at the cost of his dignity, and Lucy knew he would rather have walked through fire. It was either the most utterly idiotic act she'd ever witnessed, or the most breathlessly romantic.

Perhaps both.

Henry perused the letter in his hand. "Your touch, your kiss, make me yours in every way," he read. He looked up from the paper and regarded Jeremy with a skeptical expression. "You say this is your letter, Jem. I don't suppose that means you intend to answer for it?"

Jeremy nodded. Lucy's heart thumped wildly in her chest. Answer for it? Whatever did Henry mean? Surely they wouldn't be so idiotic as to fight? Or *duel*? The idea froze the marrow in her bones. She clutched her shawl with both hands. Jeremy couldn't shoot a pheasant from six paces. Not even one that was already dead.

But Henry's look to Jeremy was incredulous, not murderous. And, Lucy assured herself, even if he did believe Jeremy had compromised her, Henry would never challenge him to a duel. It just wouldn't be sporting.

Henry folded the letter with an odd air of leisure, all trace of joking gone from his voice. "You're really accepting responsibility for this? And all the implications?"

"I'm accepting responsibility for *her*." Jeremy crossed to stand beside Lucy, so close she could feel his radiant, masculine heat. Then, in a lower voice, he added, "It's about time someone did."

Henry's eyes sparked. "What the hell is that supposed to mean?"

Lucy desperately wanted an answer to the exact same question. And the answers to a few questions of her own. She grabbed Jeremy's cuff and tugged until she pulled his gaze down as well. His eyes pierced her with their clear blue intensity, robbing her of the breath to manage anything above a whisper. *"What are you doing?"*

He took her by the elbow and turned her slightly away from the group. "I'm sorry, Lucy. I know this isn't what you wanted. But it's the only way."

"*What's* the only way?"

Jeremy's only answer was to wheel her back to face Henry. The two men stared at one another in silence. Lucy finally excavated a shred of courage from the pit of her belly, then summoned the tone to match. "Will one of you please tell me what the devil is going on?"

Jeremy's hand slid down to grasp hers. "We're getting married," he said, never taking his gaze from Henry's.

"*What?*" Lucy tried to untangle her fingers, but he only tightened his grip. Yanking her close, he tucked her hand into the crook of his elbow. Lucy watched, stunned, as her fingers curled over his forearm of their own accord. As if they belonged there.

Jeremy finally looked down at her. "We're getting married," he repeated. His voice rumbled through her body, sending little shivers along her skin that had nothing to do with cold.

"*Married?*" Lucy felt all the blood rush from her head. The more he insisted on repeating this ridiculous notion, the easier it became to imagine. But that didn't make it right. If only they could speak alone, she could explain that the letter was all lies and claret. Sophia's reputation, Toby's engagement—nothing stood to be damaged, save Lucy's dignity. And surely Jeremy wouldn't think that a cause worth proposing marriage.

Not that he had exactly *proposed* anything.

She dug her fingers into his arm, clutching the idea desperately. "But . . . But don't I have something to say about it? Shouldn't we have a moment alone? I don't re-call accepting any proposal!"

"It's a bit late for romance, Lucy." Henry held up the folded letter and fixed her with a reproachful look. "It would seem you've already granted your consent."

Say something, Lucy prodded herself. This was the moment to tell the truth. She had only to tell Henry, and everyone else, that the letter implied nothing more than two fanciful girls drinking too much wine. Sophia cer-tainly wasn't going to come out and say it—she probably thought this turn of events would make Lucy ecstatically happy.

But it didn't. Did it? Surely "ecstatically happy" would feel more like summer sunshine, or a shower of rose petals. Not like a hedgehog digging burrows in her stomach. Happiness wasn't the reason Lucy felt herself melting against Jeremy's arm. It was just that the night was cold, and he was warm.

Warm. And strong. Oh, and distractingly handsome. Her gaze climbed the edge of his jaw, shadowed with night and stubble. His full, strong lips, dusky in the moonlight. She watched his breath curl into vapor where it met the cool air. Like a kiss dissolving into the night.

Lucy shook herself. She had to object. The very idea was nonsensical. Whatever misplaced notions of duty or propriety had spurred Jeremy to claim that letter—what had they to do with her? She wasn't a lady. Certainly not the sort of lady an earl would marry. She wasn't elegant or accomplished or wealthy. Her only tenuous claims to beauty were wide eyes and straight teeth. If she hadn't come downstairs with that letter, none of this would have happened. He would have left Henry his note and then . . .

And then he would have left entirely.

His belongings were already packed. She shivered anew, the memory of those two valises chilling her to the bone. If she protested now, there would be no second chance. He would leave. And by the light of day, he would surely realize the absurdity of this very scene. He would shudder to think he'd nearly married a dowerless hoyden.

Say something, her mind screamed. But her voice just wouldn't obey. Lucy's grip tightened over his arm. She wasn't ready to let him go.

Looking askance at the others, Henry approached Jeremy and lowered his voice. "You're certain this letter belongs to you, Jem? It wouldn't do to let a simple misunderstanding decide the rest of your life, you know. For God's sake, you're an *earl*."

"Yes," Jeremy replied, his own voice firm. Firm, and deliciously dark and determined, and strong enough to drive all objections straight from Lucy's mind. "I'm an earl. And Lucy will be a countess."

Silence.

Lucy felt everyone staring at her. No one said a word. Really, she thought. It was more than a bit rude. From the way they all gaped at her, one would think he'd announced something truly shocking. Something like, "Lucy is a spy for Napoleon," or "Lucy only has six months to live," or "Lucy has decided to take up the harp."

She forced her chin out. Well, now she couldn't possibly protest. Now it was a matter of pride.

Marianne recovered first. "Two engagements in one night. How exciting!" She rose from the edge of the fountain and crossed to Lucy's side. "How wonderful," she said, kissing Lucy on the cheek.

The others mumbled words that sounded vaguely congratulatory.

"And when will the blessed event take place?" Henry asked.

"Friday," said Jeremy.

"*Friday*! *This* Friday? Two days from now?" This outburst would have mortified Lucy much less had it not come from her own lips.

"Friday," he repeated, eyes still fixed on Henry. "I'll ride to Town in the morning for the license."

Henry wore an expression Lucy had never seen cross his face. Not mocking, not doubting, not cynical or wry. Simply blank. "Very well."

"I'll need an early start, then," Jeremy said, looking around the group. "If you'll excuse me." The men nodded.

Jeremy unlatched Lucy's hand from his arm and turned to her. Determination carved a deep furrow in his brow; his eyes shone so sincere, they were heaven's own blue. And Lucy suddenly realized that without saying yes—without even being asked—she'd somehow become engaged. To be married. To him.

The whole of her life up until this evening, the enormity of her future—all of it clamored for admittance to this brief swatch of time, resonated in the tingling heat of his skin against hers. Lucy's breath caught in her chest. Her pulse pounded a dull roar in her ears, and every beat echoed a lifetime. This one thrilling, terrifying moment stretching into forever.

"Take care, Lucy." Jeremy bent his head and brushed a warm kiss against her fingers. "I won't be long." Then he let go of her hand and walked back toward the house, leaving her alone.

Lucy realized, too late, that she ought to have said something in the way of farewell, or at least met his eyes before he turned away. She ought to have watched him go and cemented the memory in her mind. But she hadn't thought of any of those things. She'd been too preoccupied staring stupidly down at her hand. The hand he had kissed.

And when at last she was back in her bed, staring up at the ceiling and wishing she'd pulled from him some kind of reassuring glance, or said a single word to him a bit kinder than *"Friday,"* she blew out the candle, rolled onto her side, and laid her cheek against that hand. And then she did the most silly, girlish, ridiculous thing imaginable.

She kissed it back.

CHAPTER
FIFTEEN

Two days passed.

Very slowly.

There were a few hours that rushed by in a rustle of silk and sewing pins. The task of packing her belongings filled a half-dozen trunks and most of an afternoon. But even when her hands were occupied, the frantic workings of Lucy's mind stretched each second into an eternity. Past, present, future—her brain tried desperately to grasp all three at once and bind them together into something that resembled certainty.

She relived every minute she'd spent in Jeremy's company—every argument, every glance, every meal.

Every kiss.

She tried to imagine what he might be doing that very moment—riding to London, procuring the license, meeting with his solicitors.

Soaking in his bath.

Then her mind ventured forth into the uncharted void of the future and wandered there for hours. Springtime in London, summer by the sea, winters at Jeremy's estate—the location of which Lucy dearly wished she could recall.

A year's worth of nights in bed.

Every minute—waking or asleep—Lucy guessed and second-guessed everything that had occurred in the past week and everything that lay ahead. In her memory Jeremy looked so improbably handsome, she feared disappointment when he actually appeared. He'd been so determined that night in the garden, but would his resolve survive two days' separation? She expected his return any moment and imagined that event in a thousand ways, wonderful and not.

When she went out for her Thursday morning ride, she knew he couldn't possibly be coming back yet. But searched the horizon for his figure anyway. She imagined him galloping toward her on his stallion, man and beast moving as one. Power, grace, and purpose—intent on one destination. Intent on her.

Then at breakfast, she imagined him rounding the doorway and fixing her with that same cold blue stare of disapproval he'd worn the morning after they'd kissed. He looked over her olive skin and her ill-fitting gown and her mother's earrings and saw her for the impostor she was. Then he turned on his heel and left.

Later, Lucy stood on a stool in her bedchamber while her maid pinned the hem of a borrowed gown. In her mind, Jeremy burst through the door, ripped the dress from her body, and tumbled her onto the bed without speaking a word. Lucy's involuntary gasp at this vision drew concern from the maid, but a straight pin conveniently shouldered the blame.

And that afternoon, as the sunlight began to fade, Lucy strolled through the orchard. She leaned back against a pear tree and shut her eyes. Long minutes she stood there, waiting for him to come find her. Waiting for his kiss.

Then afternoon became evening, and Lucy began to worry that he wouldn't come at all. She suffered silently through dinner. Afterward, she declined to play cards and repaired to a corner of the drawing room instead, to hide behind a book. She tried to imagine what might have kept him away. Perhaps he hadn't been able to procure the license. Perhaps he'd changed his mind entirely—come to his senses and realized he couldn't make an awkward, penniless hoyden his countess. Perhaps his horse had stumbled in the dark and he lay in a ditch by the side of the road, staring up at the stars and whispering her name with his dying breath.

Lucy snapped her book shut and shook herself. That third "perhaps" was a horrible, horrible thought to have. And it was horribly, horribly wrong of her to prefer it to the second.

Then she looked up, and he was there. Standing in the doorway wearing a rumpled greatcoat and polished Hessians and his usual inscrutable expression. For the first time in two days, the whirring gears in Lucy's mind ground to a halt. And the churning fire in her belly roared to life.

If he had looked improbably handsome in her memory, he looked impossibly so now. Oh, but handsome wasn't the word for it. A handsome face, one could gaze upon for idle enjoyment, simply admiring the ideal features and pleasing symmetry. And although his features were as strong and well-balanced as ever, this—this was something altogether different than handsome. There was nothing pleasing or idle about it. One glance at him, and her stomach began pitching and rolling like a cork tossed about in a stream. She could scarcely stand to look at him, but she could hardly turn away.

And surely he hadn't grown four inches taller in two days. Surely it was only the fact that she was sitting and he was standing that made it seem so. But he looked so tall and broad-shouldered he nearly filled the doorframe; so solid and strong he might just be the cornerstone of the whole blasted house. Lucy blinked and bit the inside of her cheek, just to be sure she wasn't dreaming.

After nodding his greetings to the card players, Jeremy approached her where she sat by the hearth. He was fresh from the stables, she could tell. When he bent over her hand, she could smell the cool wind that lingered in his hair and his clothing. His hand felt chilled as it lifted hers; his lips a curious mixture of frost and heat as he kissed her fingers. His eyes held hers for only a brief moment. Just long enough for Lucy to read the same strange combination of coolness and warmth mingled there.

"Lucy," he said simply. As if only to confirm that he had not wandered into the wrong drawing room on the wrong manor and kissed the wrong lady's hand.

Then he released her hand, straightened, and turned away. The instant he turned, she wedged her hand between her thigh and the cushion of her chair. But her elbow still trembled, rattling against her ribs in the most mortifying manner.

Henry rose from the table and tugged on his waistcoat. "I've spoken with the vicar. He'll be here tomorrow at ten."

"Good," Jeremy replied. "I had my solicitor draw up the papers. But I'd rather discuss them in the morning, if it's all the same to you. It's been a long day, and I'm wanting a bath."

"And a stiff drink, I'd expect." Henry sat back down and picked up his hand of cards. "We'll see you in the morning, then."

Jeremy took his leave of them quietly, then turned back to her. "Lucy," he said again, nodding curtly. Then he was gone.

Lucy crossed her arms over her chest and sank back into her chair. What had just happened? She'd spent a full two days alternately dreaming of and dreading this moment, and now it had come. And passed. And aside from a little kiss that had turned her arm to jelly, it seemed she would receive no further insight into Jeremy's state of mind until he showed up in the morning to marry her. In her best and worst imaginings—

whether he rejected her or fell at her feet or pinned her to the bed—at least she had known where she stood with him.

And what did she know now? It was confirmed, twice, that he remembered her name. He still intended to marry her, she gathered. That was all.

Another night of rumination and conjecture stretched endlessly before her. If there were any answers to be found in the cracks of her ceiling, Lucy knew she would have divined them by now. She would surely go mad by morning.

His bath drawn, Jeremy divested himself of his coat and cravat before setting to work on his cuffs. He heard the door swing open and turned his head to glimpse a familiar swirl of crimson velvet and chestnut curls. Lucy shut the door, turned, and flattened herself against it, clutching her dressing gown closed at the neck.

"I need to tell you something."

Jeremy's hand froze. He had been in the process of rolling up his shirtsleeve, but he began to roll it back down. "Do you want to call it off, then?" *Damn.* He hadn't meant to blurt that out.

Her brow wrinkled. "Do you?"

"I asked first."

"Yes, but you brought it up. Have you changed your mind?"

"Lucy, I'm here. I have the special license and the marriage settlements. I rode three hours in the dark. I haven't changed my mind."

"Oh." She softened against the door. "I didn't come to call it off."

Relief flooded through him. Muscles knotted from hours of riding and days of uncertainty began to work loose.

Jeremy rubbed the back of his neck, slowly shaking

his head. She wanted to know if he'd changed his mind. How could he change his mind, when his mind had nothing to do with this? He was not thinking. He was acting. He was claiming. And most distressing of all, he was *feeling*.

He could have returned that afternoon. He'd finished business with his solicitor that morning, procured the license the day before. The letters he'd spent all afternoon writing could just as well have been written from Waltham Manor, or a week later for that matter. But he'd dawdled over them, waiting to leave until the sky was dark and the day nearly gone.

And when he'd arrived, he'd needed to see her immediately. Once he had, he'd felt equally compelled to leave. She hadn't said a word to him, and that suited him fine. Because if he didn't give her the chance to speak, she couldn't have a chance to say no.

But now she was here, and she didn't want to call it off, and how Jeremy was going to keep from kissing her senseless that instant, he didn't know. Good Lord, it had been hard enough to keep from doing so in the drawing room, with six people looking on. Now here she was again in that damned red velvet robe, and they were all alone. In his bedchamber. A ragged sigh escaped his lips.

She heard it. "Perhaps I should go. You must be tired."

"I am tired," he answered honestly. "And you should go. But before you do, I have something for you."

"Really?" A surprised smile spread across her face, and she stepped away from the door.

Jeremy reached into the pocket of his coat where it hung over the back of a chair. He pulled out a small velvet box and held it out to her. She stared at it, but made no motion to take it from his hand.

"What is it?"

"Well, opening it would be a certain method of finding out." He picked up her hand where it dangled at her side and turned it palm-side up. He placed the box flat in her palm. She simply stared at it, then looked up at him with eyebrows raised.

"For pity's sake, Lucy. It won't bite you." He took the box out of her hand and opened it himself. "It's a betrothal ring. I thought you should have one." He glanced at the mantel clock. "Although, considering there are only eleven hours remaining in our betrothal, it now seems a bit silly."

She stared at the ring nestled in its box. A single, round-cut ruby glowed like an ember against the black velvet, flanked by flashing diamonds. Still she made no move to take it. Finally Jeremy plucked the thick circle of gold from its bed and cast the box onto the table. He picked up her hand again and pushed the ring over her finger. "I suppose I should have chosen an emerald to match your eyes. But for some reason, the color red stuck in my mind."

He released her hand. Lucy took a step toward the fire and lifted the ring before her face. She slowly twisted her hand back and forth, inspecting the stone in the firelight. The crimson sleeve of her dressing gown pooled down around her bare elbow. Jeremy's blood pooled down to his groin. "If you don't like it, I'll buy you another," he said.

"Another?" She looked up at him, eyes wide. "And you would, wouldn't you?"

He shrugged. "One for every finger, if you wish."

"I don't need any others. I don't even need this." She smiled and arched an eyebrow. "But you're never getting it away from me now." Looking down at her hand, she waggled her fingers again. "I've never seen anything so beautiful."

Nor I, Jeremy thought. The firelight gilded the lines of her profile and filtered through her hair, dusting a ruby-red halo over her curls. Her neck curved gracefully over the ring as her eyes sparked with pure delight. She looked one part magpie, one part Madonna.

She glanced up at him suddenly. "Sophia doesn't have a lover."

Jeremy blinked. "What?"

"That's what I came to tell you." Her words came out in a high-pitched rush. "That letter—it was all lies. Just a product of her wild imagination and too much claret. She hasn't been compromised by anyone. I can explain it all to Henry. We don't have to marry."

He paused. "Let me be certain I understand you. You think I offered to marry you to save *Sophia's* reputation?"

"Well, and Toby's engagement. He is your friend, isn't he?"

Jeremy winced. Even now, when she was betrothed to him and wearing his ring, he hated the sound of that name on her lips. But perhaps he'd mind hearing Toby's name less, if once—just once—Lucy would speak *his*. "Our friendship doesn't extend that far."

"Oh." She stared down at the ring again. "Then why are you doing this?"

He deliberately skirted her question, moving toward the bar. "It's as I said. Ours may not be the most conventional of betrothals, but it seemed only fitting that you should have a ring."

"Not the ring. *This*," she said, looking up and gesturing into the space between them. "Why are you marrying me?"

He sighed. "Lucy, it's not Sophia's reputation that's endangered. It's yours. After what almost happened in the wardrobe . . . and what nearly happened in Henry's study . . . I have a duty to you, as a gentleman."

"A duty," she repeated numbly.

"An obligation. Of honor."

"Honor." She straightened. "So you're just being noble, then."

"Yes. Or, no." Jeremy set a glass on the table and filled it with whiskey. He corked the decanter and reached for the glass. Suddenly Lucy was there at his shoulder. "I've been acting rather ignoble, is the heart of the matter. And I'm sorry that you have to pay for it. But it's the only way."

She frowned, taking the glass from his hand and sipping thoughtfully. "But surely it isn't. What almost happened in the wardrobe . . . what nearly happened in Henry's study . . . No one knows, but the two of us."

"There's what happened in the orchard. Toby and Sophia saw that. They could tell Henry."

"And you think Henry will care?"

"Whether he cares or not doesn't matter. He *should* care. We *should* marry. It's the proper thing to do."

She looked unconvinced. "I've never been one to do the proper thing."

Jeremy set out another glass and uncorked the decanter again, willing his hand to remain steady as the amber-brown liquid swirled slowly into the glass. "If you must know, there is another reason I'm marrying you. One that has nothing to do with duty or honor."

"And what would that be?"

He fixed her with a steady look. "What almost happened in the wardrobe . . . What nearly happened in Henry's study . . ." He paused. "I want it to happen."

A fierce blush spread from her neck to the tips of her ears. She took a rather large swallow of whiskey. "You . . ." She sipped again. "You *want* me."

"Yes."

Her gaze slanted away, then came back to his. "You want *me*."

"Yes," Jeremy repeated impatiently. "How many times do you want to hear it?" Not too many more, he hoped. Just speaking the word, watching her blush . . . Raw lust powered through his body, stiffened in his groin. As though his verbal admission were a call to arms.

Something changed in Lucy's eyes. Her gaze sharpened, focusing on his with an unnerving intensity. She set her whiskey down, and glass met polished wood with the resounding crack of a decision. Her hand went to his where he still gripped the decanter.

"I don't want to *hear* it," she said, her voice as warm and insidious as smoke. Her fingers skimmed over his wrist, the touch warm and soft, almost too light to be real. Like the sweetest of dreams. She curled her fingers over his forearm and pulled gently until he released the decanter. "I want to feel it."

She took his hand in both of hers. "Have you noticed," she asked coyly, turning his hand over, "that we are forever being interrupted at the most inopportune moments?" She began tracing lazy circles on his palm. Jeremy's groin throbbed with each swirl of her thumb.

"Lucy, no." The words came out strangled, hoarse. He cleared his throat and willed authority into his voice. "We can't. We shouldn't."

"Why shouldn't we? As you said, we're to be wed in eleven hours." An impish grin spread across her face, bracketed by saucy dimples. "And then I'll never have my chance to be a brazen seductress. What a shame that would be. I read a book and everything."

She raised his hand to her lips and kissed the tip of each finger, one by one. When she reached his thumb, her tongue darted out from between her lips and flickered across the tip.

Jeremy groaned. What the hell kind of book had she been reading? "Lucy," he said darkly. He meant it to sound as a warning, but instead it came out more like a plea. He wrenched his hand from her grasp and laid it on her shoulder. "I am trying to behave in an honorable fashion. We are not married yet. We are in your brother's house. I won't do this to him. I won't do this to you."

"Even if I'm asking you to?" Her green eyes glimmered up at him. Emotion swelled uncomfortably in his chest. "We're about to be married. Maybe duty is reason enough for you. But it isn't enough for me."

Fear clawed at his heart. Jeremy tightened his grip on her shoulder. She wasn't getting away from him now. "It isn't only duty. I told you as much."

"You did. And I heard it. But right now . . ." She put her hands on his chest, and he winced with pleasure. "I want to feel it."

"You want to feel it," he repeated slowly.

"Yes."

He slid his hands to her waist and crushed her to him. Her lips parted in a gasp, and he covered them with his own. He devoured her mouth, thrusting deep with his tongue. Deep, to taste through the sharp bite of whiskey. Deeper, to drink in the sweetness beneath. He was so damned hungry for her. Ravenous. Starving. He felt like a man who hadn't eaten in days.

"There," he said gruffly, holding her tight against the hard ridge of his erection. "Can you feel that?'

She nodded.

"Good." He released her waist. His hands fell to his sides. "Now go."

She shook her head. Her face was flushed; her eyes, smoky. She picked up one of his hands. "Now feel me," she said, dragging his hand over the swell of her breast.

Jeremy knew he shouldn't. But devil take him, he couldn't help it. His fingers moved of their own accord, kneading her breast gently through the thick plush of her dressing gown. The feel of soft velvet sliding over the softer flesh beneath had him teetering on the brink of madness.

He had to stop this, he told himself. They would marry tomorrow. He could wait one more night. He was going to do this the right way, in the proper order. Wed, then bed. Some base, primitive Beast in him might have started this business, but he was resolved that the Gentleman in him would finish it. Lucy deserved no less.

But still his fingers roved over the velvet-cloaked swell of flesh. Her sharp gasp told him he'd found her nipple. He stroked it again, teasing the flat circle of flesh into a straining peak. Teasing the frayed remnants of his sanity.

Jeremy shut his eyes, searching for the shreds of his restraint. Damn it, nothing did this to him. Especially not a woman. Self-discipline, strength of will, resolve—they weren't just empty words to him. They were a way of life. They were how he'd survived while his father lived and how he'd succeeded after his death. They marked him apart from his wastrel peers who gambled away fortunes in the hells and brothels of London. They made him a sought-after lover amongst women who didn't want love. They made him who he was.

But she made him forget. She made him forget himself completely. And the longer he stood there—massaging her sumptuous flesh with his palm, rolling her nipple under his thumb, listening to her breathy sighs—the harder it became to remember. If there was one single reason why he shouldn't haul her to the bed that instant, Jeremy couldn't recall it.

Then suddenly she stepped away. Just in time. He regained a tenuous hold on the remnants of his willpower. He felt the urge to reach out and pull her back, but he checked it. Barely.

She was staring up at him with heavy-lidded eyes. Her lips were swollen and dusky red. She rotated her neck in sensuous motion, tossing her hair back over her shoulders. Her hands went to the belt of her dressing gown. She loosened the knot.

Oh, God. He knew all too well what was under that robe. That high-necked virginal nightgown with its dozens of buttons. He'd wanted to rip that shift off her even that night. He'd dreamt of doing so more than once.

He ought to object. Words stuck in his throat. He stared, mesmerized, as she untied her belt. Then crimson velvet rained down like hellfire, and Jeremy knew he was damned, damned, damned. No high-necked virginal nightgown. No nightgown at all.

Just Lucy.

Every part of him longed to go to her, but his feet were bolted to the floor. His jaw worked, but he couldn't speak. If there was any sound in the room besides the wild pounding of his pulse, he couldn't hear it. She had him utterly bewitched. She'd rendered him immobile, deaf, and dumb.

But he was mercifully not struck blind.

He'd devoted an inordinate amount of time in the past two days to picturing Lucy naked. He had amassed a fair amount of evidence to inform this mental image. He knew how she felt pressed up against him. He'd touched almost every part of her, albeit in the dark. But nothing had prepared him for the glorious sight of *all* of her.

Her body was like no other woman's he'd seen. And he'd seen his share of unclothed women. But be they ladies or courtesans or women of the stage, compared to Lucy, they all shared an almost indolent softness. A fragility that somehow rang false. Lucy was rounded in places and sleek in others. Firelight delineated the sculpted tone of her shoulders and arms. Her breasts were round and firm; her belly tight and flat. Supple, sweetly curving hips flared into firm, muscular thighs. She was softness and strength. Power and mercy.

A goddess.

And then she held out her arms and called to him. And he heard her. Even through the thick haze of desire, he heard her—because she spoke straight to his heart. His feet were in motion before he'd drawn breath. In a moment, he had her swept up in his arms. A second after that, they were tumbling onto the bed. And as he lowered her onto the soft nest of pillows, she whispered it again. The word he'd been longing to hear from her lips for so long it felt like forever. The one simple call he was powerless to deny.

"Jeremy."

CHAPTER
SIXTEEN

Lucy fell backward onto the bed, the heavy weight of a man on her chest and a ponderous burden thrown off her shoulders.

Thank God that had worked, she thought. There were no cards left in her hand after *that*. Was there some way to feel more naked than naked? If so, she had felt it. For a long, terrible moment, she'd begun to doubt he'd respond at all.

But respond he finally did, and in quite thrilling fashion. Now his lips and his tongue were responding all over her. And something hot and hard was making demands of its own against her thigh.

He was everywhere at once. One hand kneading her breast, the other cupping her bottom; his mouth doing indescribable things to the soft hollow beneath her ear. He wedged his thigh between her legs, and she gasped at the sensation of smooth buckskin and hard muscle pressed against her delicate flesh. He ground against her. Sweet, aching pleasure spread up through her belly and down to her curling toes.

"Jeremy." His name fell from her lips again and again as he rained hot kisses over her neck. It was important for her to say it aloud, for the same reason she'd come to his room, placed his hand on her breast, brazenly dropped her robe. So he would know—so *she* would know—that she wasn't a passive player in this turn of events. No one could force her to slip a thimble on her finger, much less a betrothal ring. Lucy may not have had a proposal, but she did have a choice.

And she chose *him*.

"Oh, Jeremy," she sighed against his ear. He was rolling her nipple under his thumb and dragging his teeth over her earlobe, and her whole body began to hum with wanting.

She ran her hands down his back, savoring the feel of solid muscle beneath soft linen. Then she fisted her hands in the fabric and tugged it up, wild to get closer to him. Desperate to feel the smooth heat of his skin against hers. She had worked his shirt almost up to his shoulders when he suddenly pulled away. He sat back on his heels, straddling her leg.

Lucy's hands fell to her chest, covering her breasts. She watched as he gathered his shirt, yanked it over his head, and cast it aside.

She let her gaze wander over him. Slowly. Greedily. Possessively. He was hers. All hers, tonight and thereafter. Every muscled ridge of his shoulders and chest. The dark, curling hair that tapered down to his navel, then trailed lower still. And the fascinating, pulsing prominence in the front of his breeches. Lucy was greatly tempted to stare. With some effort, she pulled her gaze back up to his face, framed with black, ruffled hair and anchored by clear blue eyes, now dark with desire.

Dark, and focused intently on her hands. Or thereabouts. It took Lucy a moment to realize it was probably not the sight of her hands that captivated him, but rather what heaved beneath. She let her palms slide slowly to her sides, revealing her breasts.

He sucked in his breath.

Her nipples hardened under his gaze, contracting to taut, aching peaks, straining toward him, begging for his hands, his mouth, his tongue. If he didn't stop staring and start touching her soon, Lucy felt certain she would go mad.

She reached up for him, gliding her palms up the thick trunks of his arms and letting her fingers feather over his chest. He groaned and leaned over her, caging her between his elbows. Lucy gasped at his sudden, enveloping heat. Sliding her hands around his neck, she pulled his lips toward hers.

He suddenly resisted. "I haven't bathed."

His expression was so adorably earnest, she had to laugh. "I don't mind." She pulled his face down to hers and rubbed her cheek against his jaw. The rough beginnings of a beard rasped against her skin. She brushed open-mouthed kisses up to his ear. "In fact," she whispered, licking his earlobe, "I like it."

She inhaled deeply, drinking in his scent. The scent she'd been craving for two endless days. That heady aroma of saddle leather and whiskey and night wind raked through boughs of pine. She buried her face in his neck, ran her tongue down the rigid tendon there, tasting salt and musk. Then she kissed her way back up his throat, blessing the world for the mercy of an unwashed man. *This* man, who had ridden hard in the dark to her, bringing jewels and the wind and the sweat of his body.

She felt him swallow and tense as she nuzzled his throat. She let her head fall back on the bed. His eyes fixed her with a wild, almost feral look.

"Lucy." Her name tore from his chest like a threat, or a prayer. Then he fell on her, pinning her under his weight, and she realized too late what it had really been.

A warning.

He took her breath away. Literally. His chest crushed hers, flattening her aching breasts and forcing the air from her lungs. His tongue filled her mouth, thrusting and demanding and stealing even her startled gasp. Then his hips ground against hers, working in between her legs, nestling into the cradle of her thighs, and she lost all thought of breathing. She lost all thought.

He rocked his hips against her, growling deep in his throat. Suede-soft buckskin teased over her inner thighs. Solid heat throbbed against the cleft of her legs. He rocked again, and pleasure lanced through her. Sharp, slicing joy.

Suddenly, he abandoned her mouth and raised up on one elbow. "Lucy . . ."—he swallowed hard between panting breaths—"You do understand what's going to happen? Someone has explained it to you?"

Lucy laughed. "Of course. The book explained everything."

His voice deepened. "Everything?"

Between the note of delicious danger in his voice and the way her intimate places pulsed around each syllable, she began to wonder if *The Memoirs of a Wanton Dairymaid* hadn't been a bit vague. But regardless of the details, she knew she had a firm grasp of the basic concept. "Jeremy, this is a farm. I've helped Henry breed hounds for years. I understand how mating is accomplished."

Now it was his turn to chuckle. "Yes, well—it's a bit different between a man and a woman."

"Because it's done face-to-face?"

He smiled slightly. Rather wickedly, she thought. "Usually."

Before Lucy had any chance to wrap her mind around *that* casual statement, he continued, "It's not the act itself that's so different. It's more what happens beforehand."

"Beforehand?"

He kissed his way down her neck, his tongue dallying in the notch at the base of her throat. "I need to make you ready for me," he murmured.

"I think . . ." Her voice trailed off as he lightly nipped

her shoulder. "I think I *am* ready." She was completely naked, in his bed, *under* him. How much more ready could she be? She hooked her legs around his. "I'm ready."

A muffled laugh against her neck was his only reply. Then he dropped lower, dragging his mouth down to her breast, and Lucy was not inclined to interrupt.

Please, she heard herself sigh. Her fingers slid into his hair, tangling and twining through the thick, black locks.

He drew her nipple into his mouth, and pleasure shot through her. His tongue circled the tight crest of flesh, flickering over the tip. Lucy arched against him, her grip tightening in his hair. He pursed his lips around her and pulled, wrenching a cry from deep in her chest. He suckled her greedily, teasing and tonguing without mercy, until she writhed under him, against him. And just when she began to believe he would never stop—and she began to believe she wouldn't mind—he released her nipple.

Kissed his way slowly across the tender valley of her chest.

Let his tongue ascend the slope of her other breast to its taut, aching peak.

And did it all over again.

Lucy gave up. She stopped wrestling the pleasure. It lost its sharp edges and melted to liquid, and she simply let it flow. Let it swim through her in sinuous, curving currents. Felt it swirl out to her fingers and down to her toes and up to the tips of her ears. Quivered as it tumbled faster, gathered momentum, and rushed back to pool between her thighs. She dimly heard herself murmuring words. Maybe his name. Maybe hers. She had no idea.

But when he left her breast and began kissing a serpentine path down her belly, she fell silent. She drifted down with him, her awareness floating below the rippling pleasure of his kiss. He sank between her thighs, the breadth of his shoulders pushing them wide. His breath tickled against her soft curls and the tender flesh they guarded. She felt his fingers, parting her gently. And then the hot, hooking joy of his tongue.

Oh, my.

Oh my oh my oh my. The book had definitely not mentioned *this*. This, she would have remembered. This, she would have underlined. His tongue flickered against her, and she cried out. Rather loudly.

He rose up on his elbow. "Lucy, hush. Someone might hear."

She nodded, and he bent to taste her again. His tongue danced over her tender flesh, and pleasure rocked through her in a great, glittering wave. She cried out again. Louder.

She clapped a hand over her mouth. "I can't help it," she whispered when he rose up again. "It's your fault, you know." He had his fingers on her now, caressing her. He swept his thumb over that unbearable, sparkling place in tight, nefarious circles. Her head rolled back onto the pillow. "Oh, God."

"Should I stop?" he asked, sliding a finger into her.

"God, no." His finger dipped deeper, working slowly in and out. Lucy moaned against the back of her hand.

Then he was next to her, kissing his way back up her body, stretching out alongside her. Hard heat throbbed against her hip. His tongue flashed into her ear. The heel of his palm rocked against her as his finger worked in and out and in and out, and Lucy . . . Lucy was *ready*. Ready, willing, eager, prepared. Hot, liquid anticipation coursed through her veins. She was sinking through dark and wild and wet and hot, and she was ready, ready, ready. Ready for something to happen. Ready for it to never end. Never never ever ever end.

Waves of pleasure rocked through her. Flooding her, filling her. Forcing out everything else. Her hand fell away from her mouth, and a helpless cry surged from deep in her belly, wrenching into her throat. He clamped his lips over hers and took her cry into him. Joy, confusion, frustration, fear—she poured them all into one long, rapturous cry against his mouth. And he took it all. Took everything she gave, drinking it in, probing deep with his tongue to leave nothing behind.

He caressed her softly as she floated back down. Back into herself.

Oh, my.

Her body felt wonderfully languid, but soon restless questions churned in her mind. How could he know her body so well—so easily stir sensations it had taken her sixteen years to discover on her own? Ones she'd never discovered at all? How did she go about learning *his* secrets, making *him* ready? And was this truly just preparation? What pleasure came next?

So many questions, and she lacked the words to even phrase them. When at last she thought she could trust it again, she tried her voice. "Jeremy?"

"Yes?"

"What is it called, that . . . that thing that just happened to me?"

He paused. "Well, there are several words for it."

"Only several?" Lucy marveled. "I would think there'd be hundreds. Thousands might not be enough."

He nipped her ear playfully. "What? Weren't a few of them in your book?"

Lucy batted his shoulder with her palm. "I thought we discussed the limitations of book learning." He kept nibbling her earlobe. She sighed and ran her fingertips down the strong muscles of his arm. "And it can happen to you?"

She felt his arousal throb in his breeches, prodding

against the curve of her hip. "Yes," he murmured against her neck.

"But it didn't . . . not yet."

"No."

"Then why are you just lying there?" She pushed him away slightly and turned to meet his eyes. "How can you stand it?"

A strangled laugh tore from his chest as he rose to his knees. "With great effort."

She rolled onto her side and reached for the fastenings of his breeches. Her hand brushed over the stiff, straining bulge in front. It jumped. Lucy was fascinated. She rose up on her elbow, working the buttons loose with her other hand. He finally took the task from her, freeing the last few buttons, pushing the fabric down over his hips. Leaving her hand free to explore.

And what she discovered, she would have never imagined. The hardness and strength, yes. He was hard and strong, in general. But the delicate softness, she could have never dreamed. Velvet soft, and lightly ridged. Like a kitten's ear. She let her palm glide over his length. He jerked away from her hand, and she curled her fingers around him tight. So he couldn't get away.

He exhaled forcefully. A rough, faintly dangerous sound. "Lucy, we don't have to do this. We can wait." He closed his eyes briefly, then opened them again. "*I* can wait."

"Whatever for?" She stroked him again, and he made a low growl in the back of his throat. "You want me, don't you?"

Brushing her hand away, he kicked out of his breeches and lay down on his side, facing her. Staring into her eyes with a look so deep, so intense, Lucy's whole body came alive with tingling. The narrow space between their bodies crackled with electricity, and when his hand shot out to cup her face, the shock sparked to the soles of her feet. "God, Lucy," he said roughly. "You can't know how I've wanted you."

"Can't I?" She slid closer to him, until her nipples just grazed his chest. "Tell me," she whispered, gliding her hand down his muscled back and over the taut swell of his buttocks.

He shuddered as she gently squeezed. "Not enough words." His hand slid around to fist in her hair, and he angled her head back to trail hot kisses along her neck. "I would need more than several," he murmured, his tongue weaving a wicked path downward. "Thousands might not be enough."

"Then show me." Lucy hooked her leg over his, tightened her grip on his backside, and rolled onto her back, pulling him with her. He settled between her legs, grinding his hard, pulsing heat against her mound. Pleasure echoed through her as she arched against him, and their moans mingled in an urgent kiss.

He rested his forehead against hers. "Lucy, I can't—" His breath rushed over her face, hot and thick, like steam. He swallowed hard. She could feel him *there*, pressing against her entrance. Poised to make her his.

"There is no going back from this," he said, his voice strained. "If it isn't . . . If you aren't . . ." He nudged closer still, sliding into her a bit. She ached around him. Ached *for* him. He gritted his teeth. "Just push me away."

She slid her hands to his hips and pulled. "Never."

And then he was in her, swift and sudden and strong. Filling her, stretching her.

He stayed there, motionless, atop her. In her. His chest struggling against hers as they each fought for breath.

"You aren't hurt?" he asked.

She shook her head. "Should I be?"

"I . . . I don't know."

This admission sent Lucy into a bit of a panic. "What

do you mean, you don't know?" she asked, pushing on his shoulders until he rose up to meet her eyes. "You said you were a rake! Don't tell me this is the first time you've—"

"Of course it's not." Jeremy clenched his jaw. "But I've never bedded a virgin before. And I had been given to understand it's painful." Lucy regarded him quizzically. "For the woman," he clarified.

"Oh." Lucy closed her eyes and fell quiet, assessing. Sifting through the myriad overwhelming sensations to judge if any qualified as pain. As if they sensed themselves the subject of enquiry, her intimate muscles tightened around him. He groaned.

"I'm not hurt," she said. "I feel . . ."

He sucked in a ragged breath. "You feel what?"

"That's all." She opened her eyes. "I *feel*." She uncurled her fingers from around his arms and skimmed them up to his neck. "I feel *you*."

He rocked against her gently. Exquisite pleasure washed through her body. Yes, she felt *him*. And he felt like heaven.

He withdrew slightly and thrust into her again, deeper this time. Into the very heart of her. She clutched his neck and cried out against his ear.

His whole body went rigid, and Lucy wondered for a moment if she'd done something wrong. Then Jeremy looked down at her, his gaze searching and anxious, and a sharp stab of emotion caught Lucy in the chest. It hurt *him*, she realized. It hurt him to think he'd hurt her. "No pain," she assured him between panting breaths. "Only you."

He held her tightly, tenderly, while her body learned to accommodate his, resting his forehead against her brow and dropping a light kiss on her cheek. And when he gently withdrew and thrust again, Lucy closed her lips over her cry, sealing it into a moan. Again and again he stroked into her. She buried her face against his shoulder and felt the sweet ache building once more.

He moved faster and harder, and she began to move with him, arching into each stroke with a gasp of delight. Her fingers sank into his shoulders. She heard a loud moan. It was probably hers, but he made no reproach. They were both past caring. She felt it starting again—that wondrous flood of pleasure that welled up from deep inside her, welled up from *him*. His breathing grew rough. His thrusts rougher, too. Until the dam broke and the flood took her and they drowned together in bliss.

He collapsed onto her, sinking her into the bed with his weight. They floated there together, simply breathing. And Lucy tried to collect the pieces of her body, scattered like branches after a storm. One leg she found twined around his. A few fingers she located tangled in his hair.

And just when she began to believe that she was all still there, if somewhat rearranged, another flood began. This one didn't start from her womb, or from him. It began in her heart. A strange and powerful deluge of emotion burst forth and filled every inch of her body, until she trembled with the terrible task of containing it. And it wouldn't stop. It only kept coming. There was no reprieve. It flowed in great rivers out to her limbs and pounded in waves through her still-quivering core. It swelled her lips and thundered in her ears and welled up in her eyes. And it was too much to hold, impossible to dam.

It spilled over into her soul.

CHAPTER
SEVENTEEN

"Oh, I hate you!"

Sophia bent over Lucy's betrothal ring, wearing an expression of fascinated envy. "You just have to stay one step ahead of me, don't you?" she asked, flinging away Lucy's hand.

Lucy remained seated at the dressing table, watching Sophia's reflection pace back and forth in the mirror. Above her, Sophia's lady's maid muttered violent threats around a mouthful of hairpins. Lucy's curls, like her thoughts, were particularly unruly this morning. The diminutive French maid was undaunted. She attacked with Gallic determination, yanking and twisting the chestnut locks into an elaborately coiled coiffure for the wedding.

The wedding. Lucy's scalp prickled at the thought. *Her* wedding.

"First," Sophia ticked off on her fingers, "you're miles ahead of me in kisses. Then I get engaged in the garden, in perfectly scandalous fashion. One would think I'd have the advantage of you there for at least a solid hour, but no. Ten minutes later, *you* get engaged in the garden. You're about to get married before my father's even granted his consent. And now you've even beaten me to the ring. I shan't have mine until Toby can retrieve it from Surrey. And even then, it won't be half so fine."

Lucy smiled at her friend's pouting tirade. "Must I remind you," she asked, "that I would not be engaged *or* getting married *or* wearing a betrothal ring at all, had you not invented that ridiculous letter?"

"It was *your* idea." Sophia paused at the window and leaned against the glass in a petulant pose. "And don't sound so put out. I did you a grand favor." She toyed with the tassel of the amber-colored drapes. "You're disgustingly happy; don't try to pretend otherwise."

"Very well," said Lucy. "I shan't." She picked up one of her mother's opal earrings from the dressing table and smiled at her reflection as she secured it in place, remembering the delicious sensation of Jeremy's teeth nipping her ear. Her nipples hardened instantly, straining against the ivory silk of her bodice.

Had it truly been only a few hours since she'd left his bed? Already it felt like weeks. God, she missed him. Even worse than she had the evening before, after two unending days. Just thinking of him, she felt a dull ache cinch in her breast. And a hollow warmth kindle between her thighs. Fleeting memories teased through her mind, like flickers of firelight in the dark. His hand on her breast. His tongue in her ear.

"Just look at you," Sophia said. "You're so happy, you're blushing bright pink with it. If I didn't know better, I'd think you taken with fever."

Lucy pulled a face and pressed a hand to her forehead in feigned agony.

"And," Sophia continued, sweeping back across the room to stand behind her, "Lord help us all, it must be catching." She locked gazes with Lucy in the mirrored reflection. A reluctant smile played across her face. "I'm even happy *for* you."

The maid jabbed the last hairpin into Lucy's upswept locks. Lucy stood up and twirled slowly for Sophia's appraisal.

"You do look lovely," Sophia said, standing back to

judge the effect. "The ivory suits your coloring hand-somely. And it fits like a dream. One would hardly know the gown is made over."

Lucy went to the full-length mirror and surveyed her reflection. Ivory silk clung to her body like a second skin, the bodice scooping to reveal more than a hint of cleavage. The skirt fell from an empire waist, skimming the curve of her hips before draping in a smooth column to the floor. Opals dangled from her ears, and jewels flashed from her fingers. Her hair was heaped and coiled in a classical Grecian style and wound with silk ribbon. The wisps that hung loose were not wayward stragglers, but carefully styled curls designed to lure the eye down the gentle slope of her neck.

"Just think," Sophia said. "In a few hours, you'll be a countess."

Lucy watched her reflection blanch. A countess. Her? The words "Lucy" and "countess" just didn't seem to belong in the same breath. They scarcely seemed to be-long in the same room. Lucy suddenly realized she'd never even met an actual countess. How in the world could she become one? Her heart began to pound against her stays, and she felt the urge to run for her wardrobe and hide.

But she couldn't hide from *him* there.

She steadied herself and took a deep breath, scrutiniz-ing her reflection anew. The same steady green eyes looked out from a heart-shaped face, framed by sweep-ing cheekbones below and dark brows above. Her olive skin flushed rosy pink, and when she smiled, her teeth gleamed in a straight row. She was still Lucy after all.

And even in her mother's earrings and a borrowed gown, she felt, for the first time in her life, as though the beauty belonged to her. She stopped worrying that she might teeter in the heeled slippers or trip on the heavy, satin-lined skirt. Her center of balance had shifted somehow. Her hoyden's frame was still sturdy beneath the silk, but stronger than yesterday. Shored up with kisses and bolstered by passion. Strong enough to carry the formidable burden of elegance.

It still terrified her, this notion of becoming a countess. But Lucy thought she just might be able to manage it, so long as she was *his* countess.

"It's as though that dress were designed for you," Sophia said.

"I'm fortunate that Marianne's proportions are so similar to my own."

"You're fortunate in general." Sophia's voice grew wistful.

Lucy regarded her friend, feeling a slight pang of guilt. All of Waltham Manor had spent the past two days readying itself for this impromptu ceremony. Any celebration of Sophia's engagement had been lost in the bustle of wedding preparations. And she'd been so absorbed in her own thoughts, Lucy had scarcely spoken with her friend. Their last true conversation had taken place over a bottle of very good claret.

"Aren't you happy, too?" Lucy asked.

Sophia's mouth quirked. "I expect I am."

"You certainly got your moment of passion, didn't you?" Lucy arched an eyebrow and grabbed Sophia's wrist playfully. "Bare-chested passion, no less. Even Gervais would be hard-pressed to top *that*."

Sophia bit her lip and smiled. "Oh, yes. A passionate moment, indeed." She pulled her wrist from Lucy's grip and hugged her arms across her chest. Her brow creased. "It's just . . ."

Lucy paused a long moment before prompting, "What?"

"Toby adores me. Worships me, even. He goes on and on about it."

"And that's bad?"

"I know, I know. It seems ridiculous to complain about being the object of such ardent devotion." She walked to the bed and sat down on the edge. "And I suppose I don't mind hearing I'm beautiful. But when he starts composing odes to my purity and perfection, I don't even recognize the woman he's describing. I'm not at all certain it's me. If he truly knew what I'm like, inside . . ." She gave Lucy an ironic smile. "Beauty goes no deeper than a reflection."

Lucy rose from the dressing table and perched carefully next to Sophia on the bed. Ivory silk settled around her like a cloud. "But that's the wonder of it, don't you think? That he sees qualities deep inside you—hidden, beautiful things you didn't know were there."

Like passion, she thought. And tenderness. The grace to carry off silk and jewels. And that perfectly wondrous pleasure he'd shown her last night. The one he'd given her three different times, and for which she'd teased from him three different names—one of them even in French. Now those were the sort of vocabulary lessons a girl could enjoy. Perhaps she might make an accomplished lady yet. She sighed languidly.

Sophia's eyes widened as she studied Lucy's face. "Curse you, Lucy Waltham," she said with a knowing look. "There you go again. Now you're hopelessly ahead of me."

Lucy slanted her gaze to the floor. A hot blush suffused her cheeks and chest. Of course Sophia would *know* just from looking at her. Wouldn't everyone? Their first joining she might have composed her face to conceal, but the second time? Oh sweet heaven, the second time. Really, it would be a miracle if the whole Manor hadn't *heard* the second time.

Lucy chewed her thumbnail, cringing. "Is it so obvious?"

"Of course it is! It's written all over your face."

Sophia jabbed a finger into Lucy's arm. "You," she accused, "are truly in love."

"Oh." Lucy's hand dropped to her lap. "Oh, that."

In love? With Jeremy?

"Don't try to deny it," Sophia said. "You're a terrible liar. You must let me give you lessons in deceit someday, Lucy. It's a more useful accomplishment than embroidery, by far."

Lucy had no wish to deny it. She'd had every intention of falling madly in love with him soon. She'd simply been waiting for a spare moment to make up her mind to do it. The same way she'd decided on Toby. She would set her mind and will to the task of loving her husband. Beyond reason, beyond argument.

But she hadn't set her mind to this. Her will had not even been consulted. Whatever this was she was feeling, it came from some fundamental layer of her being. *Beneath* reason, *beneath* argument. She loved him in the same way that her lungs drew breath, or her heart pounded in her chest. And indeed, now that Lucy was aware of it, every breath and heartbeat resonated with the elemental truth.

I love Jeremy.

Her whole body flushed with a giddy awareness. Lucy wondered which part of her had known it first. Her hand, when he'd kissed it that night in the garden? Her arms, when she'd pulled him into the wardrobe? Her lips, perhaps, when he'd kissed her under the pear tree? Or maybe even her feet, when they'd steered her to his door that night and not Toby's?

She bent her head and grinned, flexing her toes inside her slippers. Clever, clever feet.

Sophia sniffed. Lucy looked up to see her friend's eyes welling with tears.

"Oh, it's nothing," Sophia said, shaking her head. She looked up at the ceiling and pressed a knuckle to the corner of her eye. "I just always cry at weddings. Don't you?"

"No," Lucy answered honestly. "But then, I don't cry. Ever."

Sophia sniffed again and straightened her shoulders. "Well, then," she said, brightening. "I'm glad I did not buy you handkerchiefs for a wedding present." She stood up and reached for a paper-wrapped parcel. "You're going to love this." Her grin widened as she undid the knotted twine. She removed the paper and unfurled the contents in a dramatic cascade of scarlet silk.

"It was made up for Kitty before her wedding, but she thought it tawdry and vulgar. Fit for a trollop, she said." Sophia dangled a flame-red negligee. "I, of course, thought it perfect." She pressed the scrap of a nightgown up to her body and posed before the mirror. The neckline plunged in dramatic fashion, and on one side a wide slit climbed nearly to the hip. Black lace formed the thin shoulder straps and edged the hem of the whole scandalous affair. "There's a matching dressing gown, too."

Entranced, Lucy reached out to touch the shimmering fabric. It flowed over her fingers like water.

"Poor Felix, hmm?" Sophia raised an eyebrow and lowered her voice. "And fortunate Lord Kendall. He's going to rip it off you, I just know it. And when I see you next, I want to hear every thrilling detail."

Lucy laughed. She would miss Sophia's elegant brand of madness. "You know, I have a gift for you, too."

"Really?"

Lucy went to her chest of drawers. She pulled open a drawer, cast aside a great tangle of stockings, and pried up the false bottom to reveal the hidden cache beneath.

"You're going to love this," she said, flashing Sophia a sly smile as she carefully removed her prize. "It's a book."

*   *   *

"Are you taking her to Corbinsdale, then?" Henry propped a boot on his desk and leaned back in the chair. He riffled through the papers Jeremy's solicitor had prepared.

Jeremy nodded. "Until the Season starts."

"Lucy will prefer the country anyhow. She's not coming to you with any dowry of note, but at least she won't cost you much. You'll not need to spend vast sums on jewels or gowns." He chuckled. "I can't picture Lucy swanning about a ballroom."

Jeremy yanked on his cuff. "Perhaps you could, if you'd ever allowed her to attend a ball."

Henry shot him a look over the sheaf of paper. He resumed reading in silence.

While Henry read, Jeremy set his mind to the task of dressing Lucy for her first ball. It seemed a safer occupation than what he'd been doing for the past half hour, which was picturing Lucy naked. He'd held her bare body for the better part of the night, and only a few papers and a vicar stood between him and the enjoyment of Lucy's nudity for the better part of a lifetime. One would think he'd be able to rein in his thoughts and his arousal for the intervening hour. One would be wrong. And the fact that he faced Henry over his desktop—the same burled walnut desktop he and Lucy had nearly *polished* three evenings previous—wasn't helping matters.

He closed his eyes briefly. There was no safe place to let his gaze linger. The rolls of smooth vellum recalled her skin. One glance at the post, with its round, red, bumpy seals, and his thumbs itched for the feel of her nipples. And the tableau of quill dipped into inkwell led his mind to places that were patently obscene.

No woman had ever done this to him. Jeremy had known lust. He'd known wanting. He'd known the sweet release of thwarted desire at long last fulfilled. And on its heels, he'd known the inevitable languor. Boredom. The sluggish satisfaction that lingered for days or weeks—until a fresh conquest stirred his blood.

Well, he had lusted for Lucy. He had wanted her with a feverish need beyond anything he'd ever experienced. And now, he'd known the sublime joy of her body. Twice. He'd reveled in the sweet music of her love cries while he made her come. Thrice. She'd held nothing back from him, showed him no fear. Only innocent passion and an unblinking trust that made his heart ache with the beautiful mercy of it. He'd meant to be gentle, and he had managed it—somewhat—the first time. But the second time . . . Sweet heaven above, the second time. Her passionate response and keening cries had stripped him of all gentleness, and he'd thrust into her tight, slick embrace again and again until he lost himself completely.

And he was anything but satisfied. As for languor or boredom, Jeremy suspected those two words had been permanently removed from his vocabulary. After she'd left his bed, he'd nestled against the linens where her warmth and her sweet scent lingered, and he'd dreamed of her in brilliant, luminous color. He'd awoken hard and aching for her, as if they'd never made love. He'd tasted every inch of her, but he only hungered for more. Jeremy doubted he could ever get enough of her.

But starting in—he glanced at his pocketwatch— about forty minutes, he'd make it his life's ambition to try.

"You really mean to do this, don't you?" Henry waved the sheaf of papers at him.

"Hmm?" Jeremy shook himself out of his reverie.

"All these past two days, I've been waiting for you to flinch. Cry off. But you really mean to do it." Henry sighed heavily and tossed the papers on the desk. "I can't let you, Jem."

"You can't let me what? If there's some problem with the settlements, it can be easily remedied."

"I'm not quibbling with the settlements, man. I can't let you marry Lucy."

Jeremy stared at his friend, dumbstruck.

"This is absurd," Henry continued. "I'm looking at these papers—properties, trusts, titles . . . You can't honestly mean to do this."

Jeremy didn't give a damn about papers. Or titles, or property, or trusts. The only thing he wanted was to slide back into that hot, silken heaven where none of it mattered. Where he forgot it all. Where he forgot his own name, until she gave it back to him in breathy moans.

Henry let his boot fall to the floor and hunched forward over the desk. "Jem, I know I asked you to show Lucy a bit of attention. I didn't mean for you to go marrying her. She's a good girl, but she's not the sort of wife you'd want."

Jeremy felt violence rush through him in a blur of red, pounding in his blood. He checked the powerful urge to run Henry through with his own letter opener.

"You're an earl," Henry continued. "You're supposed to marry a lady from an established family. Someone with money, connections. You've held off marriage longer than any of us. I don't suppose it's simply because you hadn't found the right penniless country chit."

The violence surging through Jeremy's blood took on the potent charge of panic. Sweat beaded under his cravat. He willed his voice to remain steady and took a slow, deep breath. "Henry, I'm betrothed to Lucy. I'm going to marry her."

A light knock preceded the gentle creak of the door. A

familiar voice asked, "Marianne said you wanted to see me?"

Jeremy stood and turned, just in time to watch Lucy float into the room in a cloud of ivory silk. And then he forgot how to breathe entirely.

He noticed her hair first—the profusion of dark coils crowning her head, and the dangling tendrils that teased his gaze lower. To her cheek, where a rosy blush drifted under translucent gold. Along the delicious slope of her bare neck. Down to where her gown's neckline ought to be. Down lower, to where her neckline actually was— where ivory silk clung to warm, sweet flesh like a dream.

Jeremy would have thought she could never look more beautiful than she had the night previous, in his bed. And indeed, she didn't, not quite. But damned close. And there was a completely different thrill to this beauty. It affected him in a strange new way. Lucy looked her most glorious when naked and well-loved, of course. But that was a private display for his eyes alone. This morning, she would stand at his side before man and God alike, radiant as an angel. No one could look at her and not be struck by her loveliness. This wasn't desire, swelling up in his chest, replacing the breath in his lungs.

It was pride.

"Good morning, Jeremy." She smiled at him, a coy twinkle in her eye.

Jeremy nodded in reply, not trusting his voice. But inwardly, he agreed that it was, indeed, a very good morning. For the first time since she'd left his bed, he began to imagine something other than passion-filled nights—a lifetime of pleasant mornings. And when he thought about starting each day like this, hearing those words drop sweetly from her lips, knowing that smile was for him alone—this particular morning got even better. "Good" did not begin to describe it.

Henry stood. "Lucy, I'm glad you're here. Come in, take a seat."

She shook her head, smoothing the skirt of her gown. "I'll get wrinkled."

"Suit yourself." Henry shrugged and dropped back into his chair. "But you needn't be concerned about the dress. I've just been explaining to Jem that I'm going to do you both a favor and put an end to this farce right now."

"What do you mean?" Lucy asked. "What farce?"

"This!" Henry gestured toward them both. "This engagement! This wedding!"

Lucy threw Jeremy a stunned glance. Jeremy cleared his throat. "Henry, I don't think—"

Henry waved off his objection. "I've thought it all through. No one even knows you're engaged, but the eight of us. Felix and Toby can keep their ladies quiet, I think. Lucy's reputation needn't suffer. I'll take her to Town in the spring, and she'll have her Season. You'll both be free to marry when and where you choose. Everyone's happy."

Happy? Was the man daft? Jeremy couldn't quite name the sick feeling rising in his chest, but he felt tolerably certain it wasn't happiness. "Henry, listen. I've no intention of crying off. I'm going to marry Lucy. I have an obligation to her, and to you."

Henry scowled. "Leave off with the nobility, will you? I know that ridiculous letter wasn't yours." He rose from his chair and rounded the desk, making the apex of their small triangle. His voice softened. "Jem, you're my best friend. Lucy, you're my only sister. I know each of you better than anyone else does, I'd wager. And I know you'd drive each other utterly mad."

Lucy's expression went from stunned to outraged. "Henry . . . I can't imagine what you mean."

"Of course you can! You've been sniping at each

other for eight autumns now. Do you expect me to believe that would suddenly change?" Henry took a step toward his sister and lowered his voice. "And if Jem will forgive me for saying it, Lucy—all these years, you've been sniping at his amiable side. You think he's overly sober here at Waltham Manor? That's your future husband on *holiday*. Here, he's a bit cold. The rest of the year, he's a veritable glacier." He cast a withering look in Jeremy's direction. "There's more to him than you know, Lucy."

It was a true enough statement. True enough that Jeremy wasn't at all certain how to reply. He just stood there, frozen, waiting for Lucy's response.

Her brow wrinkled as she shifted her gaze back and forth between them. "I'm certain there is," she said. "And I'm equally certain there's more to me than he knows. What confuses me, Henry, is how that concerns *you*."

Henry strode back to his desk. "Damn it, Lucy, of course it concerns me. Don't you realize that most men would jump at the chance to marry their sister off to an earl? I'm trying to do what's best for you."

And that was the crack that broke the ice.

Jeremy gave a harsh laugh. "Well, that would be a novelty. Come on, Henry. You've never done what's best for her. You ought to have sent her to school, taken her to Town, given her exposure to culture and society. She's years overdue for her debut. And now you claim to know what's best for her?" He walked to Lucy's side and laid his hand on the small of her back. It was vital, somehow, to touch her that instant. Claim her. He fancied she leaned against his hand slightly.

"Lucy has never had the opportunities or security she should have had," Jeremy continued. "I can provide for her. I can take care of her."

Lucy bristled away from his touch. "Who says I need anyone to take care of me?"

Henry ignored his sister, keeping his steely glare locked on Jeremy. "Oh, yes. You have money. Is that what you're saying? You don't need to remind me that you could buy and sell Waltham Manor with the spare change under your barouche seat cushions. And any other lady would be thrilled to attach herself to your bank account. But this is Lucy we're discussing. She doesn't care about jewels or silks or luxuries."

"How would you know?" Jeremy demanded. "You've never offered her any luxuries. Perhaps she'd like to go about dripping in jewels. Perhaps she'd enjoy the life of a countess."

"Oh, would she?" Henry turned to his sister, a wry smile spreading across his face. "Do you really want to be a countess, Lucy? Think about it carefully. A countess can't spend all afternoon climbing trees in the orchards. A countess can't take the hounds out for a romp and come back with muddied skirts. A countess doesn't go fishing."

Lucy frowned. "I should think a countess can do as she pleases." She looked to Jeremy. "Can't she?"

Jeremy sighed. This wasn't the best time or place to have this conversation, but he supposed it would have to happen eventually. "No, Lucy. Henry is right. Corbinsdale is . . . well, it's not Waltham Manor. You can't behave there the way you're accustomed to behaving here."

"What do you mean?" She crossed her arms over her chest. "Why not?"

Jeremy's hands flexed at his sides as he groped for the best way to explain. Marrying her meant taking her into his protection. Not just providing for her materially, or rescuing her from weeks of watching Toby fawn over Sophia—he meant to keep her physically safe. He still hadn't recovered from watching her trip a measly snare three days ago, let alone that breakneck ride through the orchard or her bath in the river. The thought of Lucy set loose on Corbinsdale land, with all those bluffs and boulders, not to mention the tenants . . . well, Jeremy couldn't think it. It was unthinkable.

"You'll be too busy," he said. "You'll have a house-hold to manage, servants to oversee. The Abbey's a very large estate." *One of the largest in England,* he refrained from adding.

"Yes, but it's been running quite smoothly without a countess for years now, hasn't it? And surely even a countess can take her horse out for a good gallop once in a while. Or take a stroll through the woods when the mood strikes."

Jeremy's hands balled into fists. If there was one thing Lucy was never going to do, it was wander Corbinsdale Woods at her leisure. He'd lost far too much to that god-forsaken forest already. His knees felt oddly weak, but he made his voice firm. "No, Lucy. A countess can't. Not *my* countess, anyway." And even though he knew it wouldn't faze her in the slightest, he threw in The Look for good measure.

Lucy recoiled as if she'd been slapped. "Well," she said quietly. "Perhaps Henry is right. Perhaps I'm not cut out to be *your* countess at all. Maybe we should for-get all about it."

Now it was Jeremy's turn to wince. Forget all about it? Impossible. He could outlive Methuselah himself and never forget last night. The tickling warmth of her breath against his ear; the satiny feel of her thighs wrapped over his hips. The miraculous joy of pouring his seed deep inside her, making her forever his.

And there it was. She was *his* now. It didn't matter a whit whether she cared for him or not; whether she wanted to be a countess or an actress or a spy for the Crown. She was his, and he wasn't letting her go.

"It's too late," Jeremy said quietly. "Isn't it, Lucy?"

He watched her eyes flare with comprehension. Then Henry stepped between them. "No, it's not too late," he said. "You see? Already it's starting. Jem, you live to order people around. Lucy, you can't abide being told what to do. Perversely enough, I happen to care deeply for you both. And I'll not see you shackled in a miserable marriage just to satisfy propriety."

"Miserable or no, we're getting married. And it's nothing to do with propriety," Jeremy said pointedly. "Nothing at all."

Henry yanked down the front of his waistcoat. His eyes narrowed. "I could withhold my consent, you know. She isn't of age."

Jeremy exhaled slowly and tried a less subtle approach. "Henry, you can't. You don't understand. Lucy is compromised."

"We just went through all that. Forget the damn letter. We can quell any idle chatter. Hardly anyone in the *ton* even knows her name, let alone cares enough to gossip about her."

Jeremy stepped closer, until they stood toe to toe. He spoke slowly and clearly, his voice a near-whisper. "Henry, listen to what I'm telling you. Lucy is compromised."

Lucy rushed to his side and clutched his sleeve. "Jeremy, please don't—"

Without turning his gaze from Henry, Jeremy shook off her grip. "Lucy is compromised by me. We must marry. She could be with child."

CHAPTER
EIGHTEEN

Lucy watched her brother change colors as he absorbed this information. His tanned, weathered face first blanched, then flushed bright red. Finally—slowly—he turned to her. She couldn't bear to meet his gaze.

"Oh, Lucy. Really? With . . . with *him*?"

Eyes averted, she hugged herself and gave a small nod.

Henry swore, pacing off toward the window. "Here? In my house? When the devil did this happen?"

Jeremy sighed. "I could answer that, but I don't think you really want to know."

Henry swore again, redoubling his pace. "*How* did this happen?"

"And with three children, you ought to know that much already," Jeremy said. When Henry stopped short and glared at him, he added, "I'm marrying her, Henry. I'll make things right."

"Make things *right*? I . . . You . . ." Henry moved to Lucy's side. "God, Lucy. I can't even find words. I'm so . . ." He clenched and unclenched his hands. "So . . ."

"Angry," she supplied, staring into the carpet. "Disappointed in me."

"Sorry." His hand gripped her shoulder, and she looked up into shining green eyes. If she hadn't known better, she would have thought him close to tears. "Lucy, I'm just so damnably sorry. This shouldn't have happened."

Shocked, she accepted his rough, one-armed hug.

"Henry, that's . . . that's sweet of you." Now *there* was a sentence she'd never expected to utter. "But I'm glad you're not angry, because I'm perfectly—"

"Oh, I'm angry. Just not with you." Releasing her, he turned to Jeremy. "She's my sister. And I thought you were my friend. For God's sake, what kind of man compromises his friend's sister?"

One who is shamelessly seduced. Lucy bit her lip. Perhaps she ought to defend Jeremy, but how could she begin to tell Henry the truth?

Henry's hands balled into fists. "So help me, Jem. I've a powerful urge to . . ."

Jeremy widened his stance. "Just do it."

And before Lucy had any chance to protest—or to consider whether she even wished to protest—Henry drove his fist squarely into Jeremy's gut. Lucy flinched with the sick thud. Bile rose in her throat.

Jeremy put his hand on the desk and leaned over it, taking shallow breaths. "Feel any better?" he rasped, addressing the carpet.

Henry stalked off toward the window. "No."

"Well." Jeremy sucked in another breath. "That makes two of us."

"Three." Lucy choked on the word. She didn't know which of the two men she hurt for more. Neither could she decide which one deserved the greater share of her anger. She only knew this argument was careening toward disaster, and if it didn't stop now, things could never be the same. "Please stop this," she said, "before you say things you can't take back."

Henry stared out the window, his gaze unfocused. "Something's just occurred to me, Jem. I could kill you."

Lucy closed her eyes. "Like that."

"It'd be within my rights to call you out," Henry continued in a cool tone. "Everyone knows you can't aim worth piss. I could shoot you where you stand."

Lucy's heart stalled. "Henry, no."

Jeremy spoke over her protest. "Yes, you could. But I'd ask you not to. Not for me, but for Lucy. In case there's a child."

Henry said nothing. He tapped a finger against the window's frosted pane.

Jeremy straightened. "I'll take care of her, Henry. The way she deserves."

The way she deserves? Lucy stifled a bitter laugh. Did she *deserve* this humiliation? Did she *deserve* to see the two men she loved, best friends since boyhood, turned against one another in violence? Worse—to know she was the force driving them apart?

Henry fixed Jeremy with a cold stare. "You bastard. You dare suggest she'll be better off with you, because you can buy her fine gowns and rings and carriages? You've *ruined* her. She'll have to marry you now. You've left her no choice. But don't dare look down your nose at me and act like you're doing the Waltham family a grand favor." He walked to the door and opened it.

"Henry, wait." Henry halted in the doorway. Jeremy took a deep breath. "You're right. This is my fault. I've behaved in an unforgivable manner toward you both." He cast Lucy a brief glance, then looked back at Henry. "I am sorry. I'd undo it all if I could."

His words hit Lucy like a punch to the gut.

Henry turned to look Jeremy in the eye. "And to think," he said, "for a moment there, I looked forward to calling you brother."

Wincing, Jeremy leaned on the desk again. Lucy stared at him, her slippers fixed to the carpet, her voice muted by shock and anger and hurt. And somehow, this bitter silence between the three of them felt worse than an argument, more punishing than blows.

Finally, in a weak voice, Jeremy ended it. "I'm sorry, Lucy."

Shaking her head slowly, Lucy backed away. "Like you said, Jeremy—it's too late."

She brushed past her brother's outstretched hand and fled the room. But Jeremy's words followed her down the corridor, echoing with every crack of heeled slipper on parquet. *I'd undo it all if I could.*

Lucy reeled to a halt, collapsing against the paneled wall.

They'd shared a night of unfettered passion. She'd discovered undreamt pleasure in his arms. And after the pleasure, a quiet, blissful peace. He'd made her feel desired and cherished and safe. Beautiful, for the first time in her life. He'd stroked every inch of her body, and he'd touched her heart.

And he'd undo it all if he could.

She rushed up the stairs to her room, slamming the door behind her. She pressed her hands flat against her belly, desperate to quell the sobs rising in her throat. She would *not* cry.

He'd never claimed to love her, she reminded herself. He'd only said that he wanted her. And now he'd got her. *Her,* Lucy—an incorrigible hoyden with no title or connections or dowry worth noting. Not even a painted tea tray. He'd wanted her, and he'd had her, and now he had to marry her. Not for himself, but in case there was a child.

It was too late.

Oh, what a fool she had been! Teasing him all this time with kisses and retorts, chipping away at that cool veneer, thinking she discerned something hidden inside him. Something intriguing, irresistible. A fierce, fiery passion only she could bring to the surface.

Even worse, she'd imagined he discerned a secret side to her. Not the impertinent girl, but a woman with whom he wished to share his life. A lady, fit to wear silk and jewels. And, against all evidence to the contrary, some hidden quality that made her worthy of the title countess.

But he didn't, because he didn't love her. She loved him, and he didn't love her. He'd undo it all if he could.

She wouldn't.

Lucy drew a deep, deliberate breath. Despite the hollow despair spreading through her body, she knew she would do it all again. She'd become a brazen seductress, just as she'd planned from the start. She'd trapped herself a husband. He was hers now, and she'd be damned if she'd let him go.

And so, a half-hour later, she stood before the vicar in a borrowed dress and her mother's earrings, uttering the phrases "I do," and "until death us do part," with weaker spirit than she typically ordered the curricle. Jeremy, his face drawn and pale, scarcely looked at her. Henry, standing behind him, refused to meet her eyes at all. The vicar, presumably grieved for his spotty son, maintained an attitude of pious melancholy as he mumbled his way through the rite.

When Jeremy took her hand and slid a thick gold band over her finger, Lucy felt all the blood rush from her head. *Breathe,* she ordered herself. She had never been the swooning sort, and this wasn't the time to begin.

She inhaled deeply, drawing inspiration. *I love him.*

She exhaled slowly, her heart deflating. *He doesn't love me.*

Back and forth, breath to breath, the tandem truths cycled through her for the remainder of the ceremony. Inhale; exhale. *I love him; he doesn't love me.*

Then the vicar blessed their clasped hands, invoked the power of everything holy, and declared them man and wife. Jeremy's hand tightened over hers by the slightest degree. Lucy glanced up and met his blue eyes for the briefest instant, and her litany was disrupted by the tiniest word.

I love him.

He doesn't love me—

Yet.

Jeremy could scarcely look at her. Even pale and trembling and presumably angry as hell, Lucy still took his breath away. And breathing was difficult enough at the moment, with his gut still knotted around the impression of Henry's fist.

How had this gone so horribly wrong? For the past two days, Jeremy had been telling himself he would make Lucy happy, protect her from Henry and Toby and other insensitive idiots. But now he realized that was a lie. The truth was, he'd been crazed with lust and spurred on by anger, and he hadn't been thinking of her happiness at all. He'd insisted on their betrothal, insisted on this lightning-fast ceremony, never pausing to consider Lucy's wishes. She'd come to him last night apprehensive and doubting, seeking comfort in physical pleasure. He'd known it. Hadn't he spent years doing the same? He should have conquered his lust and sent her away. But he hadn't, and now Lucy would pay the price.

A fresh twinge of pain twisted his gut. *Insensitive idiot.*

When the vicar had done his worst and the thing was finished, Jeremy leaned in to kiss his bride. But as he drew near, Lucy's lower lip quivered. And at the last moment, he brushed his lips against her cheek instead. He wished so desperately to take her into his arms, kiss the frown from her lips, and somehow make everything right.

But after the papers were signed and terse congratulations offered around, it was Henry she sought out.

Henry who consoled her. Brother and sister drew away from the rest and huddled in quiet conference for some minutes' time—at the end of which, Henry pulled her into a grim embrace.

Jeremy walked over to them.

"Lucy," Henry was saying, his green eyes dewy with emotion, "if you are ever unhappy, you have only to say the word. You're always welcome at Waltham Manor. Write to me, and I'll come for you at once." He shot a look at Jeremy. "Your home will always be here."

"Her home is Corbinsdale now. And we'd best be underway." Ignoring Henry's stony glare, Jeremy addressed his wife. *His wife.* "Can you be ready to depart in an hour?" She nodded. "Then I shall see to the carriages."

Two and a half hours later, Lucy finally emerged from the Manor. Jeremy noted with disappointment that she had changed from the ivory silk gown into a sage-colored frock and brown pelisse. More suitable for traveling, he supposed. But far more interesting than the type of fabric that covered her arms were the two parcels wriggling beneath them. She held a squirming puppy tucked firmly in each elbow.

Behind her followed a seemingly endless procession of footmen. Each came bearing a trunk or a tower of hatboxes; save one hapless fellow, who clutched a snarling cat. A groom suddenly appeared from the direction of the stables, leading Thistle by the reins. And just when Jeremy began to think his bride intended to bring every blessed creature from Waltham Manor along for the journey, out came the most curious bit of baggage yet.

"You're bringing your Aunt Matilda?" The old lady doddered out from the Manor. Lucy thrust a wriggling puppy into Jeremy's hands, freeing one arm to wrap about her aunt.

"Of course I'm bringing her. I can't very well leave her

here, can I? You know Henry's incapable of minding her properly."

"Yes, well . . ." He didn't know how to object. He could point out that they hadn't discussed this matter. But then, he hadn't given Lucy any opportunity to discuss anything. He cleared his throat. "Your aunt is quite welcome, of course. I was only surprised." He looked down at the pup gnawing a hole in his new glove. "And the dogs?"

Lucy tossed her head. "They're all the dowry I have, I'm afraid. I'm given to understand they'll make excellent foxhounds. They're from Henry's best lines."

He handed the dog to a liveried groom. "With the trunks," he directed.

"Oh, no!" she cried, clutching her own canine bundle to her chest. "They must ride with us, of course! Else they'll be terribly frightened."

"Lucy, the barouche is not six months old. The upholstery is still like new."

She lifted her chin. "And . . . ?"

He heaved a deep breath. "And . . . I suppose it's large enough to accommodate a few pups. And a cat. And your aunt." He paused. "But not your horse. On that point, you cannot move me. I'm afraid Thistle will have to walk."

At that, her lips curved a fraction. Jeremy's heart swelled in his chest. He would do anything to make Lucy smile again.

But he couldn't. As the carriage trundled down the lane, taking them away from Waltham Manor, he watched all the joy drain from her face. She craned her neck to catch a last glimpse of the rambling Tudor façade, then turned back to him.

"Is it a long journey, to your estate?"

"If the roads are dry, we should arrive in time for dinner tomorrow."

She blinked. "Tomorrow?"

Jeremy swore silently. She'd likely never been outside a twenty-mile radius of Waltham Manor, and here he was hauling her off to a place she'd never seen. He ought to have taken her to Town. She would have been only a half-day's journey from home. But he'd been absent from Corbinsdale so long already. If he took her to London, he'd only have to leave her there while he attended to the estate. And he didn't want to leave her.

He didn't want to be parted from her at all. He wished he'd purchased a smaller carriage, so she wouldn't be so damned far away, seated across from him on the black tufted upholstery. He despised frail, little Aunt Matilda for taking what ought to be his place, next to her. He hated the furry beast curled in her lap, enjoying her fingers' soft caress. And even were he seated beside her, he would resent the very fabric of their clothing for coming between her skin and his.

An inch of space between them would be one inch too many. The only thought preserving his sanity throughout the interminable journey was the thought of holding her in his arms that night, with nothing—not an inch of space or stitch of clothing—between them. He planned, in excruciatingly vivid detail, how he would kiss and stroke her until her cheeks bloomed pink again and the saucy sparkle returned to her eyes. Perhaps this wasn't the marriage she'd wanted. Perhaps he couldn't give her everything she deserved. But Jeremy vowed to lavish upon her that which he could offer—material comforts and physical pleasure. And it damn near killed him when they arrived at the coaching inn that evening and his wife declared her intent to spend the night—their wedding night—sleeping beside her aunt.

"I'm sorry," she whispered at the door to their suite. "I didn't realize we'd be stopping overnight. You know how she wanders. I need to stay with her."

"Are you certain? I can put two footmen in the corridor. Four, if you wish. One of the inn's serving girls can stay with her." Jeremy realized he sounded a bit desperate. He didn't really care.

Lucy bit her lip, avoiding his eyes. "We're in a strange place. She might wake up and become confused. I can't leave her alone."

You can't leave me alone, he wanted to argue. Never in his life did Jeremy expect to envy an ancient, turbaned invalid. But damn it all, he did. He was besotted *and* jealous. "Of course," he forced between his teeth, straining the childish petulance out of his voice.

Of course.

She didn't want to be near him. He couldn't get close enough to her, and she desired nothing but separation. It wasn't as though he could blame her. He'd rushed her into this marriage and whisked her away from her family and home. She needed time, Jeremy told himself. She needed space.

Lucy had more than enough space. Too much space, she thought to herself the next morning, as the carriage rattled down the road. The way was mottled with ruts and stones, and she bounced off the barouche sides like a billiard ball. Aunt Matilda lay flat on the seat across from her, sleeping through the entire ordeal as only the very young or impossibly old are able to do. If Jeremy had not insisted on riding with the liveried outriders, he might have been next to her, holding her tight against his solid frame. Not that she wished him to.

Lucy scarcely understood her own behavior of the last four-and-twenty hours. Ever since the argument with Henry, she'd been operating in a state of near-panic. She'd barely made it through the ceremony. Afterward, she'd clung desperately to her brother, embracing him with a girlish adoration she thought she'd long outgrown. His sudden tenderness surprised her, as had his offer to come for her whenever she wished. Lucy hadn't known whether to bless him for his kindness or curse him for his obvious belief that her future held little but misery.

When the time had come to depart from Waltham Manor, she'd panicked by trying to take as much of it with her as possible. Clothing she never wore, books she never read, and all of these creatures, both furred and turbaned.

Then she'd balked at her husband's company on their wedding night. She thought of his expression last evening as they parted—that intent gaze that made demands, even as his words released her. She'd seen the wanting in his eyes, heard the deep undertone of desire in his voice. The memory made her shiver even now.

Shiver, and frown. She apparently passed Jeremy's exacting standards whenever they approached a bed—or a desk, or a wardrobe, or a tree. Why did he want to alter her behavior in every other regard? He wanted the real Lucy in the bedchamber, it would seem, but everywhere else, he wanted her to change.

She ought to have listened to him from the first. *A man doesn't want to stoop to love,* he'd said. *He wants to reach higher, stand taller. He desires something more than a woman—an angel; a dream.*

Lucy sank into the barouche cushions with an ironic laugh. If he thought she would blithely assume the role of a demure countess, he would have to think again. It would never work. She'd learned that much from chasing Toby, at least. If Jeremy had wanted an elegant lady, he ought to have married one. It was too late now, indeed.

She stroked the plump tabby sprawled across her lap. If only she could stop loving him. Take back her heart, by sheer force of will. But her will had no say in the matter, it seemed. Love pulsed in her blood, filled her every breath. Inescapable, irreversible. Something had changed inside her, and she would never be the same.

Nothing would ever be the same. Not her life, not her home, not her relationship with Henry. And that circle of friendship that had formed each autumn, surrounding Lucy with security and affection—it was broken forever. What did she have left?

Nothing, save the smallest, most irrational glimmer of possibility. She shut her eyes, recalling that instant during the wedding ceremony when Jeremy's hand had closed warm and strong over hers, and she'd felt a strange flutter inside her chest. A winged bit of optimism, rising up through despair.

She thought it might be hope.

Lucy opened her eyes and sighed. She'd never had any talent for hoping. But this seemed the time to learn.

The roads were dry, and they made good time on the second day of their journey. Still, the days being short in late autumn, it was full dark by the time they reached Corbinsdale Abbey.

The assembled house servants greeted them with polite applause. The housekeeper, Mrs. Greene, stepped forward.

"My lord," she said, curtsying. "My lady. Welcome to Corbinsdale." Jeremy watched the matronly housekeeper eye Lucy with curiosity. He cleared his throat. Her gaze jumped back to him, a bit guiltily. "The chambers are all prepared, my lord."

"My lady's aunt has come to stay with us." Jeremy indicated Aunt Matilda. "You may put her in the Blue Suite. She will require two nursemaids."

Mrs. Greene's eyes widened, but she composed herself quickly. "Very well, my lord. Dinner is ready to be served whenever you wish."

"In one hour, then." He dismissed the housekeeper with a nod.

Jeremy ushered Lucy and her aunt up the stairs. As they gained the landing, a score of footmen leapt into action below, hurrying to carry their trunks and belongings up the service stairs. By the time they climbed the last of the steps and turned into the corridor, a maid awaited them at the entrance of the Blue Suite. Aunt Matilda's trunks were already lined up by the door. A footman snapped the last dustcover from a settee as they entered the room.

"My goodness," said Lucy. "How efficient."

With hands clasped and turban level, Aunt Matilda inspected her new surroundings. The windows were hung with dark blue velvet draperies, and the furniture was upholstered in blue-and-white toile de Jouy. Screens painted with pastoral scenes of nubile shepherdesses flanked the large hearth. "Lovely."

Jeremy offered Lucy his arm and steered her across the corridor. "These are our chambers," he said, ushering her into the sitting room. A fire crackled in the fireplace, throwing a muted amber glow over the French mahogany furniture and medieval tapestries. "This sitting room is shared. My apartment is to the right, and your chambers are through there." He indicated the door on his left. Lucy nodded, wide-eyed. "I've had a lady's maid hired for you. The best available in London."

"I see," she said quietly. Jeremy scarcely recognized the expression on his wife's face. If he didn't know it to be impossible, he would say Lucy looked overwhelmed.

He ushered her toward her chambers. "Why don't you take some time to refresh yourself and change for dinner? You must be hungry."

She smiled, looking a bit herself again. "Hungry isn't the word. I'm famished."

He laughed. "Well, then. Be quick about it."

Forty minutes later, Jeremy emerged into the sitting room, bathed and dressed in a black evening suit. He stood in the doorway, gazing at his wife. Lucy sat in an upholstered armchair, staring absently toward the fire, her chin propped in her hand. She wore a gown of pale yellow silk, and her hair had been brushed and twisted into a simple knot. In this attitude, unaware of her observer, she looked lovely and unguarded and utterly forlorn.

A wave of anguish surged in his chest. This was their first night in their new home as husband and wife, and the medallion-shaped carpet between them might as well have been an ocean. For the first time in his life, Jeremy wished he possessed some facility for charm. He couldn't help but imagine that a few well-phrased words, spoken in a smooth, conciliatory tone, would put everything to rights. But Jeremy hadn't a clue which words those might be.

He sighed. Toby would have known.

Lucy noticed him then and stood, a forced smile tightening her face. With a mute nod, Jeremy offered her his arm. He was glad he could offer her that much, at any rate. The security of marriage, a well-appointed home, a fine meal. Not everything a wife might wish, but things any woman needed.

He escorted the two ladies downstairs to the dining hall. As they entered, Lucy swallowed audibly. The long, rectangular table was laden with silver, china, and gilt-edged crystal. A half-dozen liveried footmen lined either side of the room. Jeremy steered Lucy toward the end of the table. A footman drew back her chair. As she began to sit down, the servant pushed the chair toward the table. Lucy collapsed into the seat with a startled yelp. She flushed bright pink. The footman faded back into the wainscoting.

Jeremy decided to help Aunt Matilda into her chair himself, situating her at Lucy's left elbow. He then traversed the length of the table to take his seat at the opposite end. He nodded to a servant, and the soup was served.

"What sort of soup is this?" She dipped a spoon into her bowl warily. "I didn't know soup came in this shade of red."

Jeremy tasted it. "Lobster bisque," he confirmed.

He watched as Lucy took a cautious sip from her spoon. She swallowed slowly, running her tongue over her bottom lip. Then she looked up at him, true delight shining in her eyes for the first time that day. "Oh," she sighed in a breathy voice. "Oh, Jeremy."

Jeremy very nearly dropped his spoon.

She took another bite. "Mmmm," she purred, closing her eyes in ecstasy. "This is divine."

The napkin in his lap stirred.

By the time Lucy moaned her way through her second bowl of soup, Jeremy was in a state of hard, aching arousal. He was certain his face must be lobster red. But it didn't end there. Lucy expressed her delight over each successive course with unrestrained enthusiasm. And there were seven courses. Jeremy wasn't certain whether he wished to throttle his French chef, or double his wages. He barely managed to choke down his own meal, his appetite for food eclipsed by an entirely different sort of hunger.

Then came dessert.

Jeremy never ate dessert. He therefore had nothing to do but watch his wife eat dessert—some confection of cherries and cake and chocolate from the Devil's own recipe book.

"Oh my God," she exclaimed, upon taking her first bite. "Oh, this is heaven." She licked a bit of cream from the corner of her mouth. "Jeremy, you must taste this." She leaned forward, giving him a full view of her bosom.

He motioned to the servant for wine.

Good Lord. If it weren't for the footmen lining the walls and her Aunt Matilda sitting beside her, Jeremy would have crawled down the table, yanked his wife from her chair, and had her right there, next to the saucer of clotted cream. He downed his drink quickly, hoping the liquid in his glass could douse the fire in his loins.

That was an imbecilic notion, he chided himself a moment later. One didn't throw spirits on a blaze. When Lucy squealed around another mouthful of chocolate, twelve servants and one senile aunt began to look like surmountable obstacles. The raw, animal lust in him was roaring to life, feeding on wine and breathy moans of delight, growing stronger by the minute.

He had to conquer the Beast. She was fatigued and heartsick and away from home for the first time in her life. She'd refused him last night, and he would not—he told himself sternly—he would *not* make demands on her. Henry would be only too happy to take her back to Waltham Manor the instant she asked. If Jeremy pushed her now, he just might push her away forever. No, Lucy was anything but missish or tentative, and she was no longer innocent, either. When she wanted him—*if* she wanted him—she would come to him. Just as she had before.

By what supreme force of will he pieced together enough gentlemanly reserve to calmly escort his wife back to her chambers, Jeremy could not say. And she could never know what effort it cost him, to school his voice to diffident calm and casually bid her good night. But it left him weak. Weak in his bones, in his mind, in his heart.

"You must be tired." He unwrapped her hand from

his arm. "Rest as long as you like in the morning. I'll see that you aren't disturbed."

"Thank you," she answered, a wry note in her voice. "I suppose I'll sleep easier that way. Knowing I shan't be disturbed."

And there it was, his dismissal. Quick and curt and razor-sharp. He brushed a quick kiss across her cheek. A tiny taste, sweeter than any French chef's concoction could ever aspire to be. "Sleep well, then," he said.

At least one of them would.

CHAPTER
NINETEEN

Nothing ruined a perfectly fine autumn morning like waking up as a countess.

Lucy sat up in the enormous, canopied bed and stretched her arms languidly. She had not made much investigation of her suite the night before. The room had been rather shadowy, and her mood likewise dark. Even this morning, light struggled through the window glass. Heavy pewter-toned drapes absorbed all the warmth and energy from the sunlight, permitting only feeble illumination of the chamber. The room seemed cloaked in an indoor fog.

Rising from bed, she strode to the window and pulled back the drapes. Brilliant sunlight dazzled her eyes, and—once she had ceased blinking—a breathtaking landscape beckoned. At Waltham Manor, the fields and hedgerows covered the low hills like a rumpled quilt—comfortable, domestic. This place was wild. Craggy bluffs blocked the horizon; a narrow gorge carved a path through the woods. Boulders dotted the countryside, pressing up through soil like giant teeth.

The landscape called out—nay, *demanded* to be explored. And who was she to refuse? After hastily donning her riding habit, Lucy spied a velvet purse and a folded paper on the desk. She picked up the purse and shook it gently, eliciting the rattle of coin. The note was from a Mr. Andrews, the steward, and it declared this to be Lucy's pin money for the coming month. Lucy unknotted the pursestring and emptied the contents onto the table.

Damnation.

It was three times the amount Henry gave her in a year. Lucy stared at the pile of notes and coin, resentment welling in her breast. Absurd, she knew. Most ladies would have been delighted to receive such a generous allowance. But to Lucy, the money felt like a test she had already failed. What the devil was she to do with it all? How many bonnets and ribbons could one lady purchase? She backed away from the table, suddenly desperate to get out of doors.

"Good morning, my lady." The housekeeper curtsied in the doorway. "I hope you were able to rest." A maid swept in, bearing a silver breakfast tray, which she deposited on a nearby table. The housekeeper continued, "You'll be wanting to go over the household accounts, His Lordship said. Shall I come back in an hour with the ledgers?"

Oh, and now Lucy really had to escape.

She nodded mutely, but once the lace-capped matron had disappeared, Lucy snatched a pair of buttered rolls from the breakfast tray and embarked on an epic adventure.

Finding her way out of the Abbey.

Pride, and the need for stealth, kept her from asking the servants for directions; surely Jeremy must have already left the house, or she would have stumbled across him by her third pass down the corridor. Eventually, however, she managed to exit the grand house via a back way—and from across the kitchen gardens and down a dirt lane, temptation winked.

The stables.

Thistle would still be somewhat fatigued from the journey, but a leisurely ride was exactly what Lucy desired. Surely Jeremy could not object—she would even ride sidesaddle. But when she reached the stables and began searching the stalls for her sweet, plain-featured mare, Lucy looked in vain. Thistle was nowhere to be seen. When she asked the groom to locate her mount, he directed her instead to a gleaming white gelding with haunches of carved marble and ribbons braided into his mane.

Ribbons!

"He's been groomed jes' for you, my lady. His Lordship said Paris here was to be set aside for your particular use."

"Did he now?" Lucy gritted her teeth. It was one thing for Jeremy to foist pin money and household ledgers upon her—but to replace her beloved Thistle with this equine dandy? Insupportable.

"Shall I saddle 'im for you, my lady?"

"No. That won't be necessary." Fuming, Lucy kicked a loose board at the bottom of the stall.

Something on the other side kicked back.

Intrigued, Lucy walked slowly over to the next stall. There stood a magnificent black colt, stamping and snorting and whinnying with restless energy. The animal's nostrils flared as Lucy held out her hand, and he nosed it roughly before giving her fingers an impatient nip.

Fiend, Lucy read from the small plaque above the colt's stall. Perfect. She smiled to herself and turned to the groom. "I'll take this one out instead."

Jeremy slowed his mount to a walk when he reached the pebbled bank. The river wound through a narrow valley here, tumbling over small rapids under a mantle of fallen leaves. On the other bank, steep bluffs rose from the river's edge. Rocky outcroppings and lopsided trees covered their face. It all looked much the same as he remembered.

But it felt different, somehow.

He'd experienced the same curious sensation, surveying the western fields with Andrews that morning. A field harvested of its barley looked much the same as one harvested of wheat in years previous. A new irrigation ditch here or there scored the soil, but there was nothing so remarkably altered it could account for this feeling he had, of looking on Corbinsdale with new eyes.

It wasn't a sense of optimism, precisely. The landscape looked no more smooth or accommodating, now that he'd brought home a countess. So far, marriage itself was a rather rocky affair. But although Jeremy's mind was still full of problems, they were *new* problems. And therefore the world, and these woods in particular, appeared—not better, exactly—but different. He couldn't dwell on past tragedy when he had a marital crisis to solve in the present, it would seem. Perhaps now he, and Corbinsdale, were ready to move into the future.

Then a sharp crack jerked Jeremy's attention to the craggy bluffs. And he found himself right back in a twenty-year-old nightmare.

"Lucy?" Jeremy did not want to believe that it was his wife, the figure scaling the precipitous outcropping on the other side of the stream. But he would know that russet velvet habit and tangle of chestnut curls anywhere. And really, he admitted with a tortured groan, who else could it possibly be?

"Lucy!" he shouted again, nudging his horse into the stream. If she heard him, she did not acknowledge the call, but continued picking her way up the rocky slope. Dear God. If she fell from there, with those boulders below . . .

She disappeared around the far side of a pointed outcropping. Jeremy's heart raced as he spurred his mount to give chase. He rounded the corresponding bend in the river . . .

And then his heart stopped beating.

She was climbing up to the hermitage.

A centuries-old cottage perched on a rocky ledge, the hermitage had been built by the Abbey's monks as a place for solitary prayer and reflection. Fashioned from stones and built to hug the sloping terrain, the tiny dwelling looked like a natural part of the bluff itself. A thin chimney leaned mostly heavenward. Two glazed windows were dark with grime. To anyone else, it must present a harmless, even a romantic picture. No doubt Lucy would think it an irresistible invitation to explore. There had been a time Jeremy had thought so, too.

But not anymore.

He slid down from his horse, landing in knee-deep icy water, and began scaling the bluff in pursuit. "Lucy!" he called up at her, cupping his hands around his mouth. "Lucy, what the hell do you think you're doing?"

She heard him this time and looked up sharply. Jeremy cursed his idiocy. He should never have drawn her attention away from her feet. She stepped on a loose rock and lost her footing, swaying perilously above him. Dread hollowed out his chest. Arms flailing, Lucy caught herself on a jutting lip of rock.

"Stay right there!" Jeremy ordered. *Good God, let her listen,* he half-cursed, half-prayed as he resumed his own climb. For once in what seemed fated to be an abbreviated life, give Lucy the sense to follow a simple command.

At last he reached her side, huffing for breath and weak with fear. And his wife had the audacity to look cool and calm and unjustly beautiful, flashing him the sweetest smile he'd seen in three days. "Hullo, Jeremy. Isn't it a lovely day?" She tilted her head up at the hermitage. "Let's explore it together, shall we?"

"*No.*"

Lucy blinked, obviously surprised by the vehemence

of his reply. Jeremy swore. He took a breath and tried again. "It's in disrepair," he offered lamely. "It may be unsafe."

"Oh, I'm certain it's fine. All fashioned of stone like that? It looks like it's been there for ages already. I doubt we could topple it if we tried."

Jeremy summoned his sternest voice and The Look to match. "I said, *no*." This time, she frowned. Good. At least the message was sinking in. "There's nothing of interest up there, I promise you. But if you must see it for yourself, you'll have to wait for another day. I'll have Andrews see to its condition first. No one's been up there in years."

Twenty-one years, to be exact. Not since he and Thomas had played there as children. Not since the small cottage had been the staging ground for fishing expeditions and military campaigns and the occasional Arthurian quest. Not since the night two boys stole out of the Abbey to retrieve a forgotten treasure from the hermitage, but only one returned.

A sharp whinny drew Jeremy's attention to the stream bank below. He watched that devil of a black colt go charging off through the woods, dragging the reins behind him. Never to be seen again, no doubt. He turned to his wife. "You rode . . . *that* horse . . . here?"

"Well, I would have ridden Thistle," she replied hotly. "But it appears she's been declared unsuitable for a countess."

"Fiend is eminently unsuitable, and you know it. It's a wonder you weren't thrown." He glared at his wife. Her riding habit gaped in the center, and he could glimpse the smooth globe of one breast overflowing her bodice with each angry breath. The exact sort of observation he ought to avoid. Averting his eyes, he took Lucy by the hand, guiding her back down the slope. "Where are your escorts?" he demanded.

"You mean those two grooms you employed to trail ten feet behind me and drive me absolutely mad? I bribed them to leave me alone." She gave him a smug look. "I used my pin money."

"Well, I hope you gave them enough to buy bread all winter," he replied, helping his wife ease her way around a boulder. "Because you've just cost them their posts. Lucy, you will *not* go riding—or walking, or driving, or anything else—unescorted. You will *not* saddle horses other than those I've approved. Or you will not go out at all."

She made an indignant gasp as he lowered her to the riverbank. "You can't just keep me locked up in that Abbey, like the villain in some melodrama!"

"Oh, can't I?" He whistled through his teeth, and his horse splashed through the river to his side. "I'll stop playing the villain, Lucy, when you stop playing the fool." She winced, the fire in her eyes doused with dismay. A small stab of guilt caught him between the ribs, but he wasn't about to stop now. Not when he was finally getting through to her. Lucy needed to understand that he was not jesting, and he was not going to chase her down from cliffs every day of their marriage. His heart just couldn't take it.

He grabbed his mount's reins and looped them over the pommel. "Can't you do something . . . something *feminine* for once? You've unlimited funds, a whole staff of servants. Plan the dinner menus. Redecorate the house. Embroider a cushion or two. Take the carriage into the village and buy something you don't need. Learn to be a lady, for God's sake!"

Silence.

Those green eyes trained on him like two flintlock rifles. Twin patches of crimson blazed on her cheeks. Her lips parted—no doubt to deliver a scathing retort—and in the instant before he lost himself completely and silenced those lips with his own, Jeremy wrapped his hands about his wife's waist and heaved her up on his horse. Then he swung himself into the saddle behind her, took the reins in one hand and his wife in the other, and dug his heels into his horse's flanks.

"I'm taking you home. *Now.*"

Lucy was numb with shock.

Well, not completely numb. She would have liked to have been completely numb—and then she might have conserved all her concentration for anger, instead of being so annoyingly distracted by the sensation of Jeremy's arm lashed about her waist, or his chest pressing warm and strong against her back.

She hadn't realized how much she'd been craving his touch.

Lucy couldn't even decide whether she was more angry with him, or with herself. He hadn't said anything new or surprising—he'd only said it all a bit louder than he had in Henry's study. He wanted her to change, to become a genteel lady. It angered her, even saddened her, but this much she already knew.

No, she was definitely more angry with herself. Because she couldn't help but lean against him. Closing her eyes, she melted into his strength, breathing in his masculine scent and cursing her body for the traitor it was. Each rolling equine stride stoked her desire, and when the horse's sudden change in gait caused her to slip, he gathered her to him roughly. Now wedged firmly between his thighs, Lucy could not mistake the hard ridge of his arousal pressing against her bottom.

Well. Evidently *that* part of him found her sufficiently feminine.

She wiggled against him and heard his breath catch in his chest. Heat swirled through her body. One word, one touch—even a suggestive glance thrown over her shoulder, and Lucy knew she could take the reins in this struggle, alter their destination entirely. And it was powerfully tempting to just give in, to satisfy the hot, liquid wanting that coursed through her veins.

But it would be a hollow victory. She'd learned that much, at least. Because beneath her wanting lay a deep, uncharted reservoir of emotion—and beneath his, only regret. Perhaps a deep, abiding wish for his wife to take up embroidery, or order new wallpaper. Lucy felt the futility of it keenly, and still the temptation grew. She yearned to feel his body stretched out over hers and imagine, if only for a few minutes, that the connection went deeper than skin against skin. This wanting began to feel perilously like a need.

She sat up, pulling away from him. She squeezed her eyes shut and searched within her until she found the blade-sharp edge of her anger, and she clenched her fists around it tight. He'd taken her from her home, her family, her circle of comfort. All she had left was her independence, and she'd be damned if she'd surrender that. She hadn't pledged to abandon all pride on their wedding day, and neither did she recall any vows regarding needlework. He might be able to restrict her movements, but he couldn't change her, just by keeping her indoors.

No, Lucy smiled to herself. She could wreak plenty of havoc from within four stone walls.

When they reunited for dinner that night, Lucy watched Jeremy's face. He scanned the platters of food covering the table. Roast venison, duck confit, sauced vegetables, braised lamb, sautéed trout. Exactly the same dishes served the night before, down to the small saucer of clotted cream.

"Lucy, didn't the housekeeper consult you about the dinner menu?"

"She did."

"And didn't you have any suggestions? Any different dishes to request?"

"No," Lucy said, sitting down. "I couldn't possibly imagine a finer meal than we had last night. So when the housekeeper asked me what dishes I'd prefer, I just asked for all the same things again." And she intended to order the same the next day, and the day after that, and every day in the foreseeable future. That would teach him to demand she plan menus. Tomorrow, she would see about embroidery.

"*All* the same dishes?" A strange look crossed his face. More apprehension, she thought, than displeasure. "Including dessert?"

"Oh, especially dessert." The footman snapped open a napkin and draped it over her lap. Lucy smiled. "Shall we begin?"

She meant to kill him. Jeremy felt certain of it.

His wife intended to eviscerate him daily by flirting with bodily injury right before his eyes. Then by evening, she meant to devour his self-control, one dainty bite at a time. And she would do it with a smile.

If he survived a month of this marriage, it would be a miracle.

She took a slow, seductive sip of soup, and Jeremy felt a hunger growing inside him that was anything but gustatory. With each subsequent course, it only grew. Each little sigh and moan of delight that fell from Lucy's lips slid straight down the table and landed in his lap. By the time they reached the dessert course—at the conclusion of which, Lucy extended her moist, pink tongue to lick the last bit of chocolate from her spoon—he thought he would spill in his breeches.

When she announced her desire to retire early, he was relieved. Every hour spent in her company was beginning to feel like torment. She was less accessible and more tempting now than before they married. Before they married, he hadn't known what he was missing. He'd had a fair idea, of course. But now that he truly knew—now that the contours of her body were etched on his memory and the scent of her skin infused in his blood—every minute he spent in her presence was a minute he longed to spend inside her.

He could wait for her, he told himself. Really, he had no choice. After their row this morning, he'd half-expected to find her writing a letter to Henry that afternoon. But no, she seemed resolved to stay. So far. He would do well to acquire a talent for patience, it seemed, along with a taste for lobster bisque. But the waiting was torment. Pure, sweet, agonizing torment.

And they'd only been married three days.

CHAPTER
TWENTY

The torment was only beginning.

After nearly a week of cold shoulders and lobster bisque and the inexplicable proliferation of needles jutting out from every chair and settee, Jeremy awoke one morning to a loud thunk.

Followed by a scream.

Scrambling from bed, he grabbed his dressing gown and shrugged into it as he crossed the bedroom and antechamber in quick strides. He threw open the door of the sitting room and was greeted by another piercing shriek.

He blinked. Bright sunlight flooded the room, blinding him. It was several moments before his eyes adjusted sufficiently to discern the tableau before him. The source of the shrieking was the chambermaid, who stood wringing her hands in the center of the room. By the window, Lucy lay on the floor, tangled in yards of pewter-gray velvet that had recently served as drapery.

"What the devil is going on here?"

The chambermaid put her hands to her mouth and wailed into them. Jeremy brushed past her and strode to his wife. "Lucy, are you injured? Are you daft? Are you mad?" She brushed her hair out of her face and glared up at him. Her eyes affected him the same way the sunlight had, a minute earlier.

She was blindingly beautiful.

Jeremy's curse died in his throat. He'd scarcely seen

his wife all week—she'd kept steadfastly to her chambers ever since that first morning, save her nightly performance at dinner. And it was the first time since their wedding that he'd seen her hair unbound, tumbling around her shoulders in those riotous chestnut waves. The first time he'd seen her ears flush pink, as only passion or anger could make them do. And that fiery challenge in her eyes—it was a spark to dry tinder. Desire singed the hairs on his chest as it blazed a path to his groin.

He recovered his breath and held out a hand to her. "What in God's name are you doing?"

"I'm changing the drapes," she said, ignoring his hand. She began to disentangle herself from the swaths of heavy fabric. "You did say I should redecorate."

"Yes, but now? Before breakfast?"

"How can one enjoy breakfast in this . . . this *tomb*?" She unwrapped a corded tassel from about her wrist. "It's still the Dark Ages in here."

"You needn't eat breakfast here at all," Jeremy said. "There is a breakfast room, if you'd ever care to venture out of your suite and locate it."

She ignored him and yanked on a length of unyielding gray swag. When it refused to give, he saw that the fabric was caught beneath an overturned chair. He righted the chair and held it up in his hands. "You were standing on a chair?" He tossed the chair aside, and it landed with a clatter. The chambermaid shrieked again. "You were standing on a chair and pulling the draperies down by *hand*?"

No answer. Lucy had untangled herself from the voluminous velvet, and now she set to straightening her dressing gown around her seated form. She wore that same crimson robe that plagued him in his dreams. She looked up at him briefly, and then away in an instant.

He stood over her, lowering his voice to a growl. "If

you wish the draperies to be taken down, you will ask the servants to do it. You will not stand on the damned chair and fall and break your neck."

"I haven't broken my neck. I haven't broken anything."

"Then why are you still on the floor?"

She closed her eyes briefly, and then looked up at the ceiling. "I *may* have twisted my ankle."

Swearing softly, Jeremy crouched down and hiked the layers of dressing gown and shift to her knees. Her left ankle looked red and slightly swollen. "Damn it, Lucy."

"It's nothing," she said. "If you'll just help me up, I need to go . . ."

With another muttered oath, he swept her up in his arms and began carrying her toward her bedchamber. "You are not going anywhere."

"Jeremy! What are you doing? Put me down this instant, you . . ." She squirmed in his grasp, wriggling against him. He tightened his grip around her thigh. "You addle-brained brute!"

The chambermaid resumed her wailing, and Jeremy shot her The Look. "Send for the doctor," he said evenly.

Lucy beat on his shoulder with her fist. "Jeremy, no! Put me down. I am perfectly fine, damn you."

He ignored her and spoke to the maid. *"Now."* She scurried from the room, taking her irritating whimpers with her. He carried Lucy through her anteroom and into her bedchamber, depositing her on the edge of her bed.

"That was wholly unnecessary." She jerked the coverlet over her legs. "I don't need a doctor." Her eyes flared with fury, and her chest lifted with each quick, shallow breath. Jeremy braced himself on his hands as he leaned over her semi-reclined body, boxing her between his arms. He could smell the sweet scent of her hair, like pears and honey. He could taste the venom on her pouting, dusky red lips.

And he could hear her scathing words echo in his ears. *I don't need a doctor.* She didn't need a doctor, she said. She didn't need pin money or a new wardrobe or soup in any color other than red. And she most assuredly—he suffered the reminder daily—didn't need his *help*. He was getting damned tired of hearing what Lucy didn't need from him.

"I will tell you what you need." He bit off the words, his own breath heaving in his chest. "You need to stay right here, in this bed. You need to see the doctor. You need to stop performing physical labors that servants should do. And you need to start keeping yourself healthy and whole for more than two days at a crack."

"But—"

"And—" He leaned closer, until they were nose to nose. Until he could feel the angry heat of her body. "You need to learn some propriety. When we are alone, you may call me whatever vile names you wish. But in company or in front of the servants, you *will* address me as 'my lord.' "

She gasped with outrage. Jeremy straightened, turned on his heel, and walked back to his own chambers, slamming the door behind him. Just in the nick of time. If she opened her mouth to object once more, this addlebrained brute would need to kiss her speechless.

Lucy winced as brusque hands prodded her ankle.

"So *you're* the doctor?"

"Of course not." The young woman perched on the edge of the bed looked up sharply. Wide-set brown eyes regarded her with silent ridicule. "My father is the doctor. I assist him by seeing to minor cases when he is occupied treating people who are *truly* injured. As is the case this morning. A man lost half his hand in the mill."

She sniffed, and the freckles scattered across her nose bunched together. "I suppose," she said, flexing Lucy's foot back and forth, "you think he should have come to attend you anyway, you being the Lady of the Manor."

"Not at all," Lucy answered, taken aback by her obvious hostility. "I told my husband that I did not need to see a doctor. He would not listen to reason."

With the back of her hand, the young woman swept back a wisp of amber hair. "Men seldom do."

"What's your name?"

"Hetta Osborne."

"I'm Lucy Waltham . . . Trescott."

Miss Osborne regarded Lucy with raised eyebrows. She then glanced around the bedchamber. Drapes yanked from their windows lay in heaps on the floor. The furniture was pushed into a jumble near the hearth.

"I'm redecorating," Lucy said lamely.

"So I see."

No, she didn't. She couldn't possibly see. No one could understand what had possessed Lucy to go careening about her suite like a madwoman, pulling drapes from the windows and tapestries from the walls. Lucy didn't understand it herself. She only knew that after a week of her self-imposed seclusion, she'd dreamt of a fog. A thick, dark, choking fog that filled her lungs and wormed into her ears and tightened around her neck—and when she'd awoken tangled in the bed linens, she'd been seized by a desperate craving for light. Bright light and fresh air.

Miss Osborne circled her ankle in one direction, then the other.

"Really, it feels perfectly fine," Lucy said.

The pain in her ankle had subsided shortly after her fall. Her encounter with Jeremy—from that, she would require a bit of time to recover. First, from the sight of him wrapped in his dressing gown, the wedge of naked chest framed by dark blue fabric; his bare, sculpted legs below the hem. It was obvious that he wore little beneath the robe. If anything. Did he sleep nude, Lucy wondered? Of course, he had done so the night she'd slept beside him, but . . . even alone? And in nights to come, how would she be able to sleep at all for wondering?

If the sight of *his* legs wasn't distracting enough, then he'd hitched up her own robe and touched her ankle in that exciting, possessive manner. Oh, and the marvelous displays of brute strength—tossing aside the chair, picking her up as though she weighed nothing, looming over her on the bed. Bright light and fresh air were instantly forgotten. *He* was what she'd been craving.

"Did that hurt?" Miss Osborne asked suddenly.

"No. Why do you ask?"

"You moaned."

Lucy felt a blush rising on her cheeks. "Did I?"

Curse the man, even as he'd berated her she couldn't focus on his words. She'd been too busy fantasizing. She'd wanted to slide her hands inside that gaping robe, reach around his broad shoulders, and pull him down on top of her. Until the end of his diatribe, when he'd brought up that "my lord" nonsense. So infuriating. And infuriatingly arousing. Lucy squeezed her eyes shut and exhaled her frustration.

"There's nothing wrong with you." Miss Osborne let her ankle drop to the bed. She threw Lucy a sideways glance as she picked up her gloves. "Not with your ankle, at least."

Lucy sat up and regarded the young woman at her bedside. Miss Osborne wore a patterned frock and curry-colored spencer. A few pins held her dark-blond hair in a simple knot, and she wore no jewelry or ribbons. She couldn't have been much older than Lucy, but she projected an enviable air of capability. She tugged on her gloves with precise, efficient movements.

"Why don't you stay for tea?" Lucy asked. "You've come all this way."

"Thank you, no." Miss Osborne stood, picking up a small black valise. "I'm already behind schedule, and it's a long walk back. I've a confined woman to visit and a seeping wound to dress. There are some people in the county with real injuries, you realize."

Lucy smiled. At last, someone in Corbinsdale who did not regard her with veiled disdain. Miss Osborne held her in open contempt. What was better, she hadn't even curtsied or called her "Lady Kendall" once. And she'd just offered Lucy the one remedy she needed most—an escape.

"If you can wait for me to dress," Lucy said, "I'll drive you."

If Miss Osborne held Lucy in contempt, she regarded the lacquered phaeton and team of perfectly matched black ponies with complete derision. Not to mention the pair of liveried outriders trailing a polite distance behind. Still, she did not seem to begrudge the offer of a ride. And when Lucy gave the team full rein to thunder down the road, she could tell Miss Osborne's respect for her increased tenfold. From "next-to-nothing" to "perhaps-a-mite."

It felt wonderful to be outdoors at last, inhaling the crisp autumn air. Lucy drew the phaeton to a halt before a small crofter's cottage. Four children came running out, followed by their rotund, waddling mother. Lucy rummaged behind the phaeton seat for one of the baskets she'd asked Cook to prepare. A smile warmed her wind-chilled face. Even Jeremy could not find fault with this outing. This was what Marianne had done, visiting the tenants with baskets of food and sweets for the children. Lucy felt more like a countess already.

She turned back to the children, anticipating the squeals of joy her treats would no doubt elicit. They were nowhere to be seen. Miss Osborne had alighted from the phaeton, and everyone had gone inside the cottage without her.

Well.

Lucy clambered down from the carriage, basket threaded over her arm, and made her way to the cottage door. She swept into the room, smiling beneficently. From their seats at the cottage's small table, Miss Osborne and the confined woman regarded her warily.

"We haven't been properly introduced," Lucy said, shooting Miss Osborne a look of her own, "but I'm Lady Kendall."

The pregnant woman gaped at her.

"And I brought you a basket," she added brightly. She swung around, holding the basket out to the children. "There are sweets inside," she tempted, dangling the basket in front of her.

The children shrank away, huddling into the corner with expressions of abject fear. The smallest one, a tow-headed boy who couldn't have been above two years old, clutched his sister's leg and began to cry.

"All right," said Lucy, slowly backing away. "No need to get upset. I'll just leave it on the table, see?" She deposited the basket on the table.

"Thank you, my lady." The pregnant woman's reply was barely audible, and her eyes remained downcast.

"You're welcome." Lucy clasped her hands in front of her. "Miss Osborne, I suppose I'll wait in the carriage."

The young lady's gaze did not turn from her patient. "Yes, that would probably be best."

A quarter-hour later, Miss Osborne returned to the phaeton with her little valise. Well, Lucy thought. That had not gone entirely as planned. She refused to show her disappointment in front of Miss Osborne, however. Of course the children would be terrified of an elegant lady who was a stranger to them. Given the fact that the previous Lady Kendall had died several years ago and been in declining health even longer than that, the children could not know how a proper countess behaved. On her next visit, they would all be tugging at her skirts.

They drove on to the next cottage. This time, Lucy did not allow Miss Osborne to leave her behind. She grabbed up the basket and followed the young woman up to the tiny, thatched-roof dwelling. She knocked on a door, and they were admitted to a small, dank room. The light that struggled through the single window revealed the room's two occupants. A boy, no more than twelve or thirteen years of age, held the door open with a bandaged hand. On the narrow straw-tick bed, a young girl sat quietly, her legs crossed beneath a threadbare brown wool skirt.

"Albert, Mary. This is Lady Kendall."

The door slammed shut behind them. Lucy wheeled about to regard the boy.

"What?" he asked, registering Miss Osborne's disapproval. "Surely her royal highness here don't expect me to bow?"

"How is your hand?" Miss Osborne asked, changing the subject.

The boy shrugged, still staring up at Lucy. "Better, I suppose. It still hurts like the devil, but it don't seem to be festering."

Miss Osborne set her valise on the small table and opened it. "Let's have a look at it, then. Come sit." She beckoned him with a tilt of the head. Albert obeyed, eyeing Lucy with all the suspicion and scorn a twelve-year-old boy could muster.

Lucy decided to focus her charitable efforts on Mary.

She crossed the room—a matter of only two paces, it being a small room—and sat on the bed beside her. The child's mousy hair hung around her face in wild, tangling curls. Big brown eyes stared out at Lucy from a thin, pale face.

Lucy smiled. Mary mirrored the expression with a gap-toothed grin.

"How old are you, Mary?"

The girl kept smiling.

"She don't talk," Albert called from the table. He winced as Miss Osborne prodded his wound.

"But she understands me. Don't you, Mary?"

Mary nodded. She held up one open hand, her bony fingers fanned wide.

"You're five?"

The girl nodded, and her smile spread wider still.

Lucy uncovered the basket on her lap. "What luck! I have a special biscuit here baked just for a five-year-old girl." She held out a circle of shortbread. "Do you like biscuits, Mary?"

The girl snatched the treat from Lucy's hand and lifted it to her mouth.

"Don't eat it, Mary." Albert's voice was tight with pain. "It's a Kendall biscuit. It's probably poison."

"Poison! Wherever would you get such an idea? Of course it isn't poisoned." She couldn't understand where these ridiculous notions had originated, but they began to grate on her nerves. It was one thing for Lucy to think disparaging thoughts about her own husband, but quite another to hear him maligned by complete strangers.

Lucy turned back to the girl. "You go ahead, Mary. Eat it right up." The girl clutched the biscuit in her hand, uncertain. "Or," Lucy said gently, "you may wait to ask your mama and papa first, if it will make you feel better."

"They haven't any parents." Miss Osborne dabbed at Albert's wound with a rag soaked in pungent liquid.

Albert gritted his teeth. "My father ain't dead."

"Perhaps he isn't. But he isn't here to settle the matter, now is he?" Miss Osborne wound a strip of clean linen over Albert's palm. "You may eat the biscuit, Mary." She silenced Albert's objection with a look. "It isn't poisoned."

Mary devoured the biscuit in a flash, then held out both hands for more. By the time Miss Osborne finished dressing Albert's hand, Mary had downed three biscuits, a hunk of hard cheese, and most of a cold chicken leg. Lucy wished she'd brought a bigger basket. The child was clearly underfed. She glanced at Albert. He looked rather scrawny, too.

As they rose to leave, Lucy fished in her reticule for a shilling and held it out to Albert. "Here," she said. "Buy yourself some biscuits. Mary ate them all already."

Albert snorted. "No thank you, your highness." He walked to the door and held it open, pulling himself up to what approached a manly height. "I don't take Kendall charity."

Lucy raised her eyebrows. "Oh, you don't take Kendall charity?" She approached the boy, staring him straight in the face. The flinty defiance in his eyes never wavered. Lucy checked the smile tickling the corners of her lips. Eight years ago, she might well have viewed an identical expression in a mirror. "Well then," she asked cagily, "will you take a Kendall wager?"

She plucked an apple from the basket on the table and walked outside. She beckoned to Mary, and the girl scampered happily after her. "Mary," she whispered, placing the apple in the girl's palm, "would you kindly run and place this on the fence there?" She tilted her head toward the stone border edging a nearby oatfield. "Quickly now, and there's a shilling in it for you."

The girl did as she was bid, and Lucy rewarded her as promised. "There's a shilling well-earned," she said loudly, shooting the older boy a look. She straightened and faced him, holding out her hand. "Now, about that wager. Albert, may I borrow your sling?" She nodded toward the leather strap protruding from his pocket.

He squinted at the distant target, then eyed her dubiously. "You can't hit that."

"If I miss, I'll owe you a shilling. And if I hit the mark —"

Albert snorted.

"If I hit the mark," she repeated coolly, "you must accept a half-crown." She took the scrap of leather from the boy's hand and bent to select a suitable stone from the path. "It's a wager, then?" she asked, fitting the stone to the sling.

He nodded. Lucy glanced briefly at Miss Osborne, who appeared to be watching the exchange with great amusement. Lucy felt a brief pang of conscience. Striking wagers with obstinate boys probably didn't befit the Countess of Kendall. But hang it all, the "fine lady" routine didn't seem to be fooling anyone. It certainly wouldn't buy Mary more bread.

Miss Osborne's gaze met hers. Lucy shrugged and smiled. She took aim at the apple, set the sling in motion with a flick of her wrist, and released.

The apple exploded in a cloud of white pith. Albert's mouth fell open.

Lucy dug a half-crown from her reticule. She handed it and the sling back to the slack-jawed boy. "If it's pride you're concerned about, Albert—next time, take the charity. It will cost you less."

Albert blinked. He looked down at the coin and the sling, then the fence, then back at Lucy. Flashing an amused glance in Lucy's direction, Miss Osborne reached out and tweaked his ear.

"Albert, I believe the words you're searching for are, 'Yes, my lady.' "

"You have a problem."

Jeremy looked up from his letter, surprised. Why he should be surprised, he didn't know. After their argument that morning, he'd spent the day expecting—hell, even anticipating—the imminent descent of Lucy's wrath. At least, he noted from her determined stride, her ankle appeared to have mended.

"I have a problem?" he repeated.

"A serious problem. Your tenants hate you."

He sat back in his chair. She wanted to talk about his tenants? "Yes, I know."

"No, I mean they truly hate you! When the name Kendall is spoken, old people spit on the ground. Mothers threaten their children with your name. 'Do as I say, or I'll have Lord Kendall come and take you to the poorhouse.' People *despise* you."

"And you see this as a problem."

"Of course! Don't you?"

He sighed, laying his quill on the desk. "A problem is something I can attempt to remedy. This—this is more of a reality. If it makes you feel any better, it's my father they truly hated. Me, they intensely dislike. So far."

"I went visiting tenants today, and the children shrank from me in fear!"

"You went visiting tenants? With whom?"

"Miss Osborne, the doctor's daughter. And an escort of outriders." Her green eyes flashed. "My lord."

Jeremy rubbed his temples. He'd known that would come back to haunt him. "Listen, Lucy, about this morning . . ."

She cut him off with an impatient wave of her hand. "I met two children today who are orphaned, most likely. Their mother is most certainly dead, and their father has been transported to Australia. Can you guess his crime?"

Yes, he thought. He had a reasonably certain idea.

"Trapping one miserable partridge to feed his ailing wife and their children. One bird, worth a sentence of transportation." Indignation burned red on her cheeks. She bit the fingertip of one glove and pulled it off.

He rose from his chair and rounded the desk to stand beside her. "Lucy, my father was a very harsh lord. He was especially unforgiving toward poachers. It's regrettable, but there's nothing that can change it now."

"But your father is dead," she said, peeling off her other glove. "You're the lord now. Certainly you'd never go making orphans of poor children, just for the sake of a partridge." She untied her bonnet and flung it onto a nearby chair. "Yet the tenants still fear you, despise you. Why don't they understand that you're nothing like your father? That you're a kind and generous and not at all hateful man?"

Jeremy leaned against the desk, his head spinning. He felt drunk, giddy. Maybe it was the fact that his wife kept shedding articles of clothing like an opera dancer. He stared, utterly rapt, as she untied her pelisse with nimble fingers and tossed it carelessly on the mounting heap of garments. It was too much to hope that she might continue with her boots, her stockings, her gown, and her shift. But a man could dream.

Then again, perhaps it was her words that had set the room whirling. *Kind*, had she called him? *Generous*? During the course of one day, he'd gone from "addle-brained brute" to "not at all hateful"? If this trend continued, by tomorrow she'd be spouting poetry. And somehow, most strange and dizzying of all those descriptors were those so casually uttered words, "nothing like your father." As if she could know.

"It bothers you that much, what the tenants think of me?"

"Of course it does!" She sagged against the desk next to him. "Because if they hate you, they hate me!"

He chuckled. Ah, yes. He ought to have known there was a sensible reason behind this veritable outpouring of affection.

"I'm sorry, Lucy, but their opinion of me is not likely to improve anytime soon." He stood and crossed to the window, looking out over the uneven landscape. "You have to understand, this isn't Waltham Manor. There, a man can toss a handful of seed at the ground and reap a bountiful harvest five months later. This is hard land. Rocky soil, unevenly watered. The wheat harvest failed this year. Last year, the barley. I'm attempting to do now what my father ought to have done years ago—improve the land, rotate the crops. Irrigate the dry areas, drain the wet. But in order to make the reforms, we've had to coerce the tenants to cooperate. They resist change. It means more work for them, at increased risk. So they've been told they must farm by the practices the steward proscribes, or I will revoke their lease."

He turned back to Lucy. "You can well imagine, that makes me rather unpopular. In the end, they'll reap the benefit, but for now . . . for now, they hate me."

Lucy sighed, folding her arms across her chest. "They hate *us*."

Her brow furrowed with frustration, and her lips pursed in a sulky pout. Jeremy thought to remedy both conditions by crossing the room and taking her mouth in a long, deep kiss. Instead, he leaned against the windowpane. Because there she'd gone again, setting the room awhirl with the tiniest word.

Us.

CHAPTER
TWENTY-ONE

"So this is our breakfast room."

Jeremy looked up from his newspaper, eyebrows raised. He was obviously surprised to see her, but—Lucy fancied—pleasantly so. "*Our* breakfast room," he said with a bemused expression. "Yes. I'm glad you finally decided to search it out. Perhaps later you'd care to tour the rest of the house?"

She smiled. "I think I would." After all, it wasn't as though she could keep to her suite forever. Yesterday's outing hadn't quite matched her expectations, but Lucy's first taste of a countess's responsibilities had not been entirely bitter. In fact, she felt rather hungry for more.

She plucked a pastry from the buffet and circled the room slowly, pausing to study a portrait hanging above the mantel. It appeared to be a vague likeness of her husband. His general figure seemed about right—broad shoulders, erect posture. Those heart-stopping blue eyes were captured rather well. But Jeremy's hair was black as jet, not that auburn color. And his jaw—the artist had his jaw all wrong. Far too rounded.

"This is a terrible likeness of you."

His coffee cup clinked against its saucer. "That's because it's not me."

"Well, who is it then? It can't be your father; the clothes are too modern."

"My brother."

She wheeled to regard her husband where he sat at the table, calmly salting an egg. As if he'd simply asked her to pass the butter. "You have a brother?"

"Had. I had a brother. He died when I was a child."

Lucy looked up at the young man in the portrait. "How old was he?"

"When he died? I was eight, and he was eleven." Jeremy's hand paused, suspending a tiny spoon in midair. "Nearly twelve."

"But this is a portrait of a young man, not a boy of eleven."

"Yes, well. You can blame my mother's fancy for that. She never really stopped mourning Thomas." He replaced the spoon in the saltcellar and picked up his fork. "That was his name. Thomas." He took a bite of egg. He chewed it slowly. Lucy ground her teeth in frustration.

Finally, he swallowed and looked up at her. She tilted her head and raised her eyebrows. "Please, continue."

"She—my mother—commissioned a new portrait of him every year. Until she died, of course. So she could look on him as he might appear, had he lived."

That, Lucy's stomach decided, was a perfectly nauseating idea. Yet it didn't seem to affect her husband's appetite in the slightest. He reached for another piece of toast. Lucy swallowed around the lump in her throat. "And when did your mother die?"

"Four years ago."

She calculated on her fingers. "So if you're nine-and-twenty, like Henry . . . About twenty-one years your brother's been dead, minus four . . . That means there are *seventeen* portraits of Thomas in this house?"

Jeremy scraped butter on his toast. "Not including those painted before his death. The actual total is probably above twenty."

Good Lord, Lucy thought. There were probably fewer portraits of the Prince Regent in St. James. For that matter, St. Paul's cathedral probably had fewer paintings of Christ. "What did he die of? A fever?"

"No, he was . . . It was an accident." Jeremy set down his knife with a dull clatter. His brow furrowed. "It's a long story."

"Well, and it will seem longer still if you force me to wring it from you, drop by drop. It would be far easier on us both if you just had out with it." She walked back to the table and stood over his shoulder. He stared down at the toast in his hand, impassive. "I'll find out eventually, you know. Don't make me go asking the servants."

"You really wish to hear it?" His voice darkened. He dropped the toast onto his plate and flexed his hand.

Lucy rolled her eyes. "No. Please don't tell me. I'm enjoying the gothic suspense." She sighed and placed a hand on his elbow. "Yes, Jeremy. I really wish to hear it."

"Very well, then." He rose from the table, grabbed her by the hand, and fairly dragged her from the room.

He strode purposefully down the long corridor. His paces were so long, she was forced to take three steps to his one. He pulled her down the corridor, through the entrance hall, down an interminably long passageway, and finally into a narrow, marble-tiled gallery, where a row of massive, gilt-framed portraits seemed to simply fade into the distance rather than end. When Jeremy halted at the gallery's midpoint, Lucy nearly collided with his back.

"That," he said, turning her around, "was my father." He let go of her hand and stepped toward the large, square painting.

Lucy followed his gaze. The portrait must have been painted when his father was near Jeremy's age, or perhaps a bit older. The same stony features marked his face, edged by faint creases that would deepen with age. The man's jaunty, cocksure pose contrasted with his serious expression. He wore a black coat emblazoned with gold braid and buttons and held a tricorn hat tucked under one arm. His other hand rested flat on the head of a tiger.

An honest-to-God tiger. A snarling, untamed, orange-striped beast. Lucy knew next to nothing about painting, but she recognized effective artistry when she saw it. When she felt it in her blood. The painting was mesmerizing. She could see the tiger's striped fur bristling, sense the raw power rippling through its muscles. To stand before this painting was to sense danger and peril and irrational fear. And to feel a surge of resentful gratitude to this arrogant man, whose dominant pose and ice-blue glare seemed the only things keeping her from being devoured whole.

She edged closer to her husband.

"The tiger you see there now resides in the great hall, mounted above the hearth. My father shot it in India and brought it back—it, and a bull elephant's head. He was an avid hunter, my father. He had the woods around the Abbey stocked with all variety of game. Not just partridge and pheasant, but boar and stag." He looked over his shoulder out the window. "This is one of the last woods in England where one can still hunt stag."

He turned back to the portrait. "Hunting was everything to him. Therefore, hunting would mean everything to his sons. He put a rifle in my hand before I could properly hold a spoon. He took me and my brother on daylong shooting trips and drilled us in marksmanship."

"Marksmanship?" Her shoulders lifted with laughter. "You must have been a grave disappointment, then."

"I was. In many ways."

The shift in his expression was subtle, but unmistakable. A slight crease pulled on his brow, and his jaw tightened by an infinitesimal degree. Lucy wanted to bash her head against the wall. She was an idiot. An unfeeling, heedless, mutton-brained ninny. She resolved not to speak another word.

"I'm sorry." Well, besides those two.

"Don't be." His face hardened further. "I took great delight in disappointing my father. I had no great fondness for him, nor for shooting. But Thomas loved both, and I idolized Thomas. The two of us would steal out of the house at all hours to go tramping through the forest."

He turned around and walked toward a bank of tall windows, his slow footfalls echoing off the polished marble. Lucy followed, looking out on the round, hedged garden and the dense woods beyond. The trees climbed the distant bluffs like spectators in an arena, waving autumnal banners of amber and red.

"We weren't the only ones tramping through the forest. The well-stocked woods proved irresistible to poachers. Some came in organized gangs, trapping game for market in London or York. And then there were the tenants, who simply desired a bit of meat for their tables. My father resented both groups equally. Any poacher apprehended on Kendall land received the maximum penalty allowed by law—jail, hard labor, even transportation. He ordered his gamekeeper to set man-traps and spring guns."

Lucy's stomach knotted. Henry had described to her the cruel methods some landowners employed to deter poaching. Man-traps, like the smaller traps used to catch game, were spiked metal jaws designed to snap around a man's leg. An encounter with a man-trap could leave a man maimed, if he was lucky. If he was unlucky, the wound would fester and he'd die. Of course, death was the entire object of a spring gun—a loaded rifle rigged up to a tripwire. A poacher, or anyone, who stumbled over the wire would be shot instantly.

Lucy had a sick feeling she knew where this story was headed. She might as well spare him the difficulty of saying it. "So which was it, with Thomas?"

"A spring gun."

"And you were with him?"

He stared out the window, unblinking. "Yes."

She quickly renewed her vow of silence. Any words she might manage to utter would be most unladylike. She tried to imagine being eight years old and watching her brother shot down like an animal. Then she shook herself, cursing her imagination.

It was as though he heard her thoughts. "I didn't see it happen." He cast a sidelong glance at her. His voice grew gentle. "It was dark, and I had fallen behind him. I only heard the shot."

The words had the ring of a merciful lie. Lucy suspected he said them only to soothe her feelings. Bless him, it worked. A bit. But the very idea still tied her stomach in knots. "And then?"

He turned to her with a blank expression. "And then he died."

She shook her head. "No, I mean after that. You said it was a long story. There are twenty portraits of Thomas in this house. His death can't be the end of the story; it's just the beginning."

He turned back to the window and exhaled slowly. His broad shoulders shrugged beneath his coat. She was quickly learning to recognize that motion. A shrug, for Jeremy, was not a lazy rise and fall of the shoulders. It was a powerful action—an explosion of brute strength, barely checked. And when his shoulders heaved, she could practically hear the rusty creaking of armor about them. The heavy, plate-metal shell that a child constructed to shield himself from pain. Lucy knew the armor. She carried a fair bit of it herself.

She also knew the armor had chinks. "It's a long story," she repeated levelly. "And yes, Jeremy. I really wish to hear it."

He pierced her with an icy gaze. Lucy refused to blink. If he thought he could scare her off with that Look of his, he was mistaken. "And then . . . ?"

He looked out the window. "And then everything changed. My father had always been stern. Whatever heart he had, it died with Thomas. After my brother's death, he only doubled the man-traps and authorized his gamekeepers to shoot trespassers on sight." He shook his head. "I resented him for Thomas's death. He resented me for being the one who survived. But he could no longer ignore me, once I was the heir. He redoubled his efforts to mold me in his image, and I resisted his every attempt.

"My mother—" He turned back to the portraits and nodded toward a painting of a delicate-featured lady wearing the lace-trimmed sleeves and powdered curls that were the fashion some thirty years past. "She had always been fragile. Thomas's death destroyed her. She took to her chambers and went into permanent mourning. She couldn't bear to look at me, because I only reminded her of the son she'd lost.

"My father only spoke to me to criticize. My mother couldn't speak to me without bursting into tears. And I . . ." That shrug again. "I was sent off to school." He firmed his jaw and cast her a sidelong glance. "It's not such a long story after all. But there you have it. No need to go asking the servants."

Jeremy turned and locked gazes with her, clearly awaiting her reaction.

Her reaction. Several reactions battled within her for prominence, and they all involved an explosion of physical energy. The first was an irrational impulse to simply turn on her heel and run. Run away and hide. Her second thought, equally childish, was to pick up the china vase from a nearby table and hurl it against the wall. The third reaction that sprang to mind was to run at her husband, climb him like a tree, and kiss him until he forgot his own name, much less the fact that he belonged to this ghastly assortment of relations.

But none of these seemed the appropriate reaction for a countess. Moreover, she knew none of them were the reaction Jeremy needed. His eyes were clear and unwavering. Daring her to run away or fly into rage. Forbidding her to pity him. And were their situations reversed, Lucy knew pity to be the last reaction she would wish.

So she fought against all three impulses and a good dozen more for an age. And then, because the still air around them and the silence between them threatened to suffocate her, she spent all that hard-won equanimity to purchase a single, round syllable.

"Oh."

His mouth softened slightly. She had the terrible suspicion that he might be priming his lips to impart another grim detail. Desperation loosened her tongue. "Is that all, then?"

He blinked.

Lucy forced a smile into her voice. "No raving bedlamite locked away in the turret?"

He slowly shook his head.

"No bastard children peeling onions in the scullery?"

The corner of his mouth quirked. "No."

"Well, then. And here I was expecting something truly dreadful."

His face relaxed. Relief washed through her. They couldn't have been standing more than a dozen inches apart. It was twelve inches too many, but she settled for narrowing the gap to two. Lightly threading her arm through his, she pivoted him back to face the portrait of his father.

"When I was a girl," she said, "I used to lie on the floor and stare up at my father's portrait. I would look up at him for hours, just listening."

"Listening?"

She nodded. "He told me long, fantastic stories. About his childhood, or mine. Sometimes about Tortola."

"But . . ." Jeremy's gaze clouded with confusion. "Didn't your father die before you were born?"

"Oh, yes." When he continued to simply stare at her, Lucy decided to humor his lack of imagination. "I have found," she said quietly, "and perhaps you have, as well . . ."—she tilted her head toward the row of portraits—"these things have a way of speaking to me, whether I wish it or not. And it's more comforting by half to imagine they have pleasant things to say.

"For example," she continued, pulling him toward a portrait of a frightfully ugly gentleman dressed in Navy regalia, "your father is telling me that he was greatly relieved, on the day you were born, to see that you did not have your great-uncle Frederick's ears. Like bat-wings, those ears. Positively terrified him when he was a child."

She turned to the portrait of his mother. "And your mother says she was simply glad you didn't come out all puckered and orange, because she ate nothing but jellied quince for the whole of her confinement."

Jeremy shook his head. "Lucy, when you asked earlier if there was a bedlamite locked in the turret—I didn't realize you meant to apply for the position."

She ignored him and pasted a sweet smile on her face. Gently tugging Jeremy's arm, she led him down the row to yet another portrait of Thomas. "Now this handsome young man is complaining that it's dreadfully difficult to haunt twenty portraits at once. He's begging us to pare down the number to three or four."

"You may do as you wish, Lucy. You're mistress of this estate. It's your house now."

"Mine?" She tightened her grip on his arm. "Oh, dear. I had been under the rather comforting impression that it was *ours*."

He looked down at her, the corner of his lips slightly crooked. It was the barest suggestion of a smile, and the most wonderful thing she'd seen in the past week. "So it is."

He placed his hand over hers where it lay on his arm. "I believe I've had enough of *our* house for one morning. Would you care to go riding? I imagine Thistle would enjoy the exercise."

"I can ride Thistle?" She lifted an eyebrow. "But must I have a complement of footmen trailing along behind me?"

"No." His smile widened. "You've no need of an escort, if you're with me."

"Oh." Lord above, at that moment he looked dizzyingly handsome. But somehow Lucy managed to grasp a few strands of thought and braid them into a realization. "Well, that makes more sense now."

"What makes sense?"

"Why you never wanted me along, on the shooting trips." She leaned against his arm as they turned to leave the gallery. "All that talk about my being just a girl, it being unsafe—imagine, you truly meant it!"

"What, did you think I was just being severe?"

"Yes, of course," she replied with a shrug. "For the

first year I knew you, perhaps two—I thought you were put on this earth simply to vex me."

His eyebrows lifted. "And after two years?"

"Oh, then I figured out the truth," she said as they walked out of the room. "I was put on this earth to vex *you*."

If breakfast had been a pleasant surprise, dinner that night was a disaster.

Lucy watched from her end of the table in silence as her husband pushed food around his plate. Grateful the soup course was over, she took a long draught of wine, rinsing her mouth of the lingering film of salt and grease. How Jeremy could abide oxtail broth, she couldn't guess.

"Finally grew tired of lobster bisque, did you?" he asked, sawing into a hunk of mutton.

"Not really." Lucy stabbed at a bit of carrot with her fork, but it squirted off her plate and flew across the room. She looked up, mortified. Jeremy's attention remained focused on his mutton. She dared not look to the left, however, for she felt reasonably certain that the missile had connected with a footman. Fortunately Aunt Matilda was taking dinner in her room this evening, else she might have been the unhappy target. "It's just that . . . Well, I thought I should request the dishes that *you* like for a change."

After their conversation in the gallery that morning, Lucy felt like a shortsighted girl who'd just been fitted with spectacles. In preparation for their ride, Jeremy had checked the security of her saddle straps twice, ordered the maid to fetch Lucy's warmer gloves, and cast her more stern looks than she could count. And all these small actions that would have yesterday seemed simply overbearing, Lucy now understood to be . . . still overbearing, but protective at base.

He'd witnessed too much pain already. He didn't want to see her hurt, too.

Was it any wonder she hadn't seen it? Lucy wasn't at all accustomed to being protected—with two dead parents and a guardian like Henry, she'd learned to fend for herself. Jeremy's concern was completely unnecessary. But it was also touching, and she wanted, in some small way, to acknowledge it. To thank him for it. To *try*.

"I see." Jeremy placed a morsel of mutton in his mouth and chewed. And chewed. Taking a sip of wine, he asked, "And who informed you of my partiality for boiled mutton?"

"One of Aunt Matilda's nursemaids. Mrs. . . ." Lucy churned air with her hand, as if to conjure the name from the ether.

"Mrs. Wrede?"

"That's it. Mrs. Wrede. I asked her to give Cook the menu, since she said she's known you for ages."

Jeremy sipped his wine again. "Indeed she has. She was *my* nursemaid. Kept me on a steady diet of broth, boiled mutton, potatoes, porridge . . ."

Lucy groaned. What an idiot she was. Mrs. Wrede had given Jeremy's favorite menu, all right—from when he was five years old. She might as well have poured him milk in place of claret. Propping her elbows on the table, she buried her face in her hands. "I'm so sorry."

"Don't be." He dabbed his lips with a linen napkin. "Truthfully, I'm not very hungry anyway." He waved away the remainder of the dishes. "Let's just skip to dessert, shall we? Let me guess." He smiled. "Suet pudding?"

She propped her chin on her hand. "I didn't order any dessert," she said plaintively.

"No dessert?" He looked stricken. "Why would you do that?"

"You don't like dessert."

"On the contrary," he said, in a dark voice that made her ears tingle. "It's my favorite course of the meal. I had rather looked forward to dessert."

"But—" Lucy halted, at a loss for a response. What was he saying? That although, in eight years, she'd never seen a morsel of sherry trifle or gooseberry fool pass his lips, he suddenly desired suet pudding? How was she—how was any countess to guess *that*?

She folded her hands in her lap. "I'm sorry. There isn't any dessert."

He set his napkin aside. "Very well, then," he said, rising to his feet. "It's late. You must be wanting to retire."

She stared down at her hands, running her thumb along the callused ridge of her palm. "I said I'd sit with Aunt Matilda. I think she's a bit homesick."

"Is she?" His voice was quiet. "I see. Then I'll order some chocolate sent up for you both."

They remained in awkward silence for several moments. Lucy could not bear to look at him. It seemed so wretchedly unfair, how her mood, her existence, her life's happiness were now linked inextricably with his. And she—of all the intractable chits in England, *she*—now craved his approval and desperately wished to please him but seemed doomed to fail at even this smallest attempt. He gave her jewels and pin money and even knew to send up chocolate, and what did she offer him? Boiled mutton, when he wanted suet pudding.

There was only one method of pleasing Jeremy in which she had shown the slightest competence—the act she yearned to repeat, lay awake in bed remembering, dreamt of every night. She'd so hoped that their conversation today, the intimate history and thoughts he'd shared, might lead to intimacies of a different nature.

But no.

It was this place, Lucy decided as she lay in bed alone

that night. This cold, silent, tomb-like Abbey filled with his family's ghosts and his own demons. Before coming to Corbinsdale, she had never appreciated how joy permeated Waltham Manor—the way each room echoed with pleasant memories, and the cheerful din of dogs and children and servants who were permitted to hum. In this house, there was no noise, no warmth, no joy. It was an antidote to ardor if ever one existed.

And outside the confines of the Abbey, the misery only increased. Every man, woman, and child within a ten-mile radius reviled anyone by the name of Kendall. That could scarcely make a man eager to procreate. Perhaps that was why Henry kept getting Marianne with child, Lucy surmised. Good harvest or bad, his tenants adored him for his convivial manner and generosity.

She thought of insolent Albert, and the satisfaction of turning his expectations inside-out. And Jeremy—the pain of losing his brother compounded by the loss of his parents' affection. The whole of Corbinsdale was an orphaned estate. Lucy recognized that familiar combination of outward defiance and silent craving for affection everywhere she went—in the tenants, the staff, her own husband. Maybe she couldn't change the drapes or plan the menus like a proper lady, but she knew something about relating to surly orphans. She was one herself, after all.

Perhaps, Lucy thought to herself, she did have some hidden, buried potential to become a true lady. Maybe Jeremy didn't see it, but that didn't mean she couldn't unearth it herself. She might not be the sort of countess he wanted. She certainly wasn't the sort of countess Corbinsdale expected. But maybe, just maybe, she was exactly the sort of countess they *needed*.

And then it came to her—just drifted down from the embroidered canopy over her bed, as if dropped by a passing angel or revealed in a dream—the Idea. The way to solve both problems at once, to bring this house to life and make the tenants adore her husband. The brilliant Idea that would work her into Jeremy's good opinion, his bed, and his heart.

An Idea this perfect could not possibly go wrong.

CHAPTER
TWENTY-TWO

And it would not have gone wrong, had Jeremy not been late for dinner.

Lucy sat in the Abbey's great hall, drumming her fingers on the empty plate that ought to be her husband's. Her mood alternated between anxiety for his safety and fury with him for returning home so late. He had not missed dinner one night since their marriage. Now this night, of all nights, he was late. The night she'd been planning so carefully for days.

It had been remarkably easy. She'd simply mentioned to Jeremy at breakfast one morning that she'd like to invite a few guests for dinner. Perhaps on Friday next? He'd been so pleasantly surprised, he'd called in the housekeeper immediately and instructed her to obey Lucy's every command.

Of course, this probably wasn't quite the dinner party he'd imagined.

Where could he be? She tried to think, but between the musicians and the small army of servants and the clatter of cutlery, forming a coherent thought proved difficult. Lucy smiled. The deafening roar from this evening would echo through the Abbey for days. Perhaps weeks. Farewell to cold, sinister silence.

A chicken bone sailed through the air, causing her to dodge left. Her guests seemed to be enjoying themselves. She'd given up waiting for Jeremy a half-hour ago and ordered dinner to be served. One didn't keep upward of a hundred guests waiting about hungry. You could only let them sit around drinking ale for so long before an acceptable delay became simple rudeness. This might have been Lucy's first time hosting a party, but she knew that much.

She nibbled a bit of roast beef from her own plate. She'd ordered simple fare for the meal, and plenty of it. The long tables lining the center of the room were laden with platters of roast meat, boiled potatoes, game pies, puddings and sausages, and bread with fresh-churned butter. The men, women, and children lining the long tables seemed to have no complaints. Food was disappearing at a prodigious rate, and serving girls bearing flagons of ale kept up a steady procession from the kitchen to the hall.

Hetta Osborne pushed her way through the merriment. Lucy's smile widened. "I'm so glad you could come!" she shouted above the cacophony.

"My father!" Hetta yelled back, tilting her head toward a silver-haired man wearing spectacles and a black tailcoat. He bowed, and Lucy curtsied in return, holding up the skirts of her new gown. The *modiste* had finished it just yesterday—all silk, in a poppy-red shade that her maid called *coquelicot*, with gold braiding at the waist and a low, square neckline that enhanced the curve of her bosom.

"Albert and Mary?" Lucy mouthed.

Hetta shook her head. "They wouldn't come. Albert had a message for you if you care to hear it. He said, 'Tell her highness she can take her . . .'" Her voice trailed off in the din.

"I can't hear you!"

"Just as well." Hetta crossed to Lucy's side and shouted in her ear, "You *should* be glad we came—I doubt this evening will end without at least a few injuries!"

Lucy laughed. So the men were a bit drunk. And a few of the women, too. Hungry tenants were unhappy tenants. People well-fed and in their cups tended to look more favorably on their hosts. It was all part of the plan.

As were the servants who began clearing the tables away from the center of the room.

"What now?" Hetta asked.

"Games, then dancing."

"Games?"

"Contests of strength and skill. Arm-wrestling . . . lifting . . ."

The servants began piling straw bales at the far end of the hall, under the ever-watchful eyes of the late earl's mounted trophies. Two footmen entered bearing targets, and a third followed with bows and arrows.

"Archery?" Hetta shouted. "Indoors?"

"Well, we can't very well have them shooting rifles, now can we?" Hetta stared at her. "Next year," Lucy explained to mollify her new friend, "we'll have the harvest home at the proper time of year. Outdoors—with canopies and booths and hoops for the children."

The guests moved to the sides of the hall, buzzing with excitement. Lucy once more searched the crowd for Jeremy, in vain. She reluctantly swept to the center of the room. This was supposed to be his moment, drat him.

The crowd fell silent. A hundred pairs of eyes fixed on her. Lucy cleared her throat, suddenly feeling a bit anxious. She ought to have had some of that ale herself.

"Thank you for coming," she began. "It is my honor to welcome you as guests to Corbinsdale Abbey. I hope you enjoyed your meal."

Enthusiastic applause and cheers echoed off the hall's vaulted ceiling. Lucy smiled.

"I apologize for the delay in His Lordship's arrival, but I'm certain he will be joining us soon. In the meantime, we have prepared a few contests to entertain you before the dancing begins. We will begin with archery, and the champion will be rewarded handsomely." She pulled out a small purse and shook it, rattling the coin within. The crowd whooped.

"Who will step forward to test his skill?" she asked.

"I will." A tall, burly fellow with a bushy ginger beard stepped forward, and the crowd erupted. He raised his arms, spurring the cheers to an even louder pitch. A good portion of the guests began chanting his name. Lucy couldn't quite make it out, but it sounded like "Hanson."

A wiry youth was thrust forward into the center of the room by his laughing friends. A third pushed his way through the crowd, a dark, stocky man with huge mitts for hands and a grave mien.

"Excellent," Lucy shouted, raising her hands for silence. She motioned to the servant, who distributed bows and arrows to the three men. "Your mark will be here," she said, sweeping to the end of the hall near the entryway, opposite the straw targets. "Each man will have three arrows, and the best accuracy overall will earn the purse."

The men took their places and began fitting their arrows to their bows.

"But my lady," the man called Hanson called out, "I don't know that the purse is sufficient reward. Don't you think,"—he looked to the crowd for support—"you should sweeten the pot?" The assembly broke into wild applause.

Lucy frowned, bewildered. "What do you suggest?"

"To the winner goes a forfeit, my lady." He fixed her with a lascivious grin. "A kiss." The crowd whooped and resumed chanting his name. The ginger-haired ruffian pumped his fist in the air, egging them on.

Lucy sized up the competitors. None of them looked

particularly kissable, but she didn't know how to refuse without seeming rude. A little peck on the cheek couldn't do any harm, she supposed. She met Hanson's eyes. It was a challenge he'd laid down, she realized. A dare. And Lucy never backed down from a dare. She lifted her chin. "Very well."

The guests roared their approval so loudly, she worried the Abbey roof might collapse.

"On my signal, then," she called, cupping her hands around her mouth. The crowd hushed as the men drew back their bows. "Fire!"

Two arrows sailed into their targets, both landing wildly off-center. The third target remained unmarked. Lucy looked back to the dark, stocky man and saw he had not yet fired. Instead, he leaned back, releasing the arrow up and to the right.

The shaft soared up toward the rafters. The guests gasped and scrambled for cover, elbowing one another out of the way. Then the arrow reached the zenith of its arc and began its descent. Somewhere in the throng, a woman screamed.

Thwack.

The missile collided with the mounted head of a stag, piercing it straight through one glassy eye.

The crowd erupted into its loudest cheers yet. Several men stepped forward to clap the rogue archer on the back.

Hanson, not to be outdone, fitted another arrow to his bow and shot. The shaft buried itself in the leathery hide of the bull elephant trophy. The tenants went wild, stamping and howling with glee.

Now all of the men were refitting their bows, and Lucy began to grow more than a bit alarmed. Not because she cared one whit for the late earl's prized collection, but because the longer this went on, the greater the likelihood that someone would get hurt.

"Gentlemen!" she cried. "Stop!"

But then the dark, stocky man sent another arrow sailing into the mouth of a boar, and Lucy's cries were drowned out by the thunderous wave of applause. She marched across the hall to stand directly in front of Hanson. If he could incite the masses to this fervor, she reasoned, he could quell them.

She was right. He lowered his bow. With a wave of his arm, he silenced the crowd.

"You must stop this," she said firmly. "Someone could get hurt."

He smirked, eyeing her from head to toe with a leer that made her skin crawl. "Well, my lady. Does that mean you're ready for your kiss?"

The tenants exploded into the loudest roar yet. Whoops and whistles resounded from the rafters. Lucy's cheeks burned with rage. Hanson stepped toward her, and the din grew louder still. She wouldn't give him the satisfaction of shrinking away. He was only a bully, and she knew how to handle bullies. Bullies, as a rule, feed on fear. Refuse to flinch, and they quickly grow bored.

She would not flinch.

As Hanson approached her, however, and she was forced to crane her neck to maintain eye contact, she admitted with some trepidation another trait bullies typically shared.

They were big.

He pursed his revolting, bearded mouth and made a disgusting smacking noise. She grimaced. If that was what passed for kissing with him, she pitied Mrs. Hanson.

The crowd, however, did not share her revulsion. They whooped and hollered louder than ever, until the Abbey walls seemed to shake with the effort of containing their tumult.

Do not flinch, Lucy told herself. *Do. Not. Flinch.*

A loud crack rent the air.

Hanson flinched.

The tenants went dead silent. One hundred heads swiveled to face the hall's entrance. Jeremy stood in the arched doorway, a rifle at his shoulder.

One hundred heads swiveled the other direction, tracing the angle of his shot. A cloud of smoke rose from the snarling tiger mounted above the massive hearth. The acrid scent of singed fur filled the air. As the smoke dissipated, Lucy watched a round, black hole appear in the exact center of the tiger's head, like a third eye.

Jeremy lowered his gun and strode to the center of the room. Each footfall echoed off the stone floor. He stopped, standing eye-to-eye with Hanson.

"Get away from my wife," he said quietly, pronouncing each word as a distinct, murderous threat. Then he turned his ice-blue glare on the crowd. "And get out of my house."

No one moved. No one breathed.

"*Now.*"

The crowd emptied the hall faster than water pours through a sieve. Within the space of a minute, Jeremy and Lucy stood completely alone in the center of the hall.

Lucy surveyed her husband from the feet up. His typically polished Hessians were muddied to mid-calf. Her gaze wandered up the mile-long, muscled columns of his thighs. His shirt, she noticed, was rumpled and wet. The pungent odor of wet wool suggested his dark blue coat was likewise damp. He wore no cravat, and dark hair curled in the notch of his open shirt. Stubble shaded his throat and jaw.

His cold glare awaited her when she finally met his eyes.

She would not flinch.

"What the hell do you think you're doing?" she demanded.

"I," he forced out, "am preventing a riot. The more appropriate question would be, what the hell do you think *you're* doing?"

"I'm convincing the tenants to like us, you imbecile. And now you've gone and ruined everything!"

A harsh bark of laughter tore from his chest. He turned and stalked away, flinging his rifle to the ground.

Lucy clenched her fists in exasperation. She looked up at the still-smoking tiger. "How did you make that shot?"

"What?"

"You're a terrible marksman. You can't shoot a pheasant at six paces. How did you make that shot?" She tilted her head up at the striped, three-eyed beast.

He brushed past her in silence and stalked out of the room.

Gasping with indignation, she rushed after him.

"Don't you walk away from me," she called, chasing him up the stairs. She caught up to him in the corridor. "As you just so charmingly pointed out to all our guests, I am your wife." She followed him into their sitting room. He turned toward his rooms, but she rushed around him and blocked the door.

"Lucy," he warned, his voice a dark growl, "don't push me right now."

"Or what? You'll glare at me? Oh, dear. I may swoon."

He fumed at her in silence. Exasperating man. Tall, dark, brooding, exasperatingly attractive man. His hair was plastered to his head in damp, black locks. His shirt clung to the hard muscles of his chest. But the heat of his body radiated through the layer of cool damp, bathing her in heady, leather-scented steam. She melted against the door, suddenly remembering the whole reason behind this evening's debacle.

She loved the addle-brained brute.

Lucy drew a deep breath and composed herself. "Jeremy, it wasn't meant to happen like that. You were supposed to come back in time for dinner." She stroked the wet lapel of his coat. "Where have you been, anyway? I was worried sick."

She was worried sick.

Jeremy shook his head in disbelief. Lucy couldn't know the meaning of the phrase. It was a very good thing he'd missed his dinner, or he surely would have lost it by now.

He'd ridden home through cold and wet, but—as always—thoughts of her had kept him warm. After a week of increasingly pleasant days as husband and wife, Jeremy's patience was at an end. This, he had vowed, would be their first equally pleasant night. Then he'd come home to a scene that chilled his blood—tenants on the verge of a riot, men shooting up his hall, a filthy, hulking brute poised to assault his wife—and *she* was worried sick. Standing there in a devil-red dress and looking up at him with guileless green eyes and *petting* him like a cat. As if she were never in any danger from that mob. As if she were in no danger from him. With every bone and muscle and sinew in his body, he wanted to grab her. To hold her close or to shake her silly, he didn't know. But he trembled with the sheer effort of restraint. He'd been holding too much in, for far too long, and he felt perilously close to exploding.

Her slender fingers curled around his lapel. "Is it the expense you're angry about? You needn't be. I used my pin money."

The expense? Now she thought he was concerned about the expense. She was so utterly wrong about so many things, he didn't know how to begin to set her straight.

"Lucy, listen to me." She tightened her grip on his lapel. "A bridge was out, and I got caught in the rain. I don't give a damn about any expense. And just because I don't hit a pheasant, it doesn't mean I can't shoot." Her brow wrinkled with confusion, and she opened her mouth to speak. He jabbed a finger under her chin, cutting her off. "And now that I've answered all of your nonsensical questions, you're going to answer some of mine. What the devil were you thinking? That getting the tenants good and drunk would just magically solve everything?"

She blinked. "Well . . . yes. Why shouldn't it? You were supposed to be a kind and generous host, and then they would see that you're nothing like your father. And then they would like us, and you would . . ." Her voice trailed off as her gaze slanted to the floor.

"Well you were wrong, on several counts. I'm very much like my father, in too many ways. In every way that matters to them. This evening confirmed *that* perfectly. And those people did not come here tonight to like us. They came to take from us. They will eat our food and drink our ale, not because they enjoy your gentle company, but because they feel it's owed them. Because it's Kendall food, and Kendall drink. They shot at those trophies because they belonged to my father. And those men wanted to . . ." The vile words stuck in his throat. "*Kiss* you—and no doubt more—simply because you belong to me."

She laughed. A harsh, bitter sound.

He cupped her chin in his hand, his fingers pressing into her cheeks. "It's not a laughing matter."

"Isn't it?" Her green eyes glimmered. "If only they knew. They could kiss me a thousand times and not take anything from you. How can they steal something you've already thrown away?"

He pulled his hand away from her face. What the hell did she mean by that? Confusion swirled in his mind, and its mate, anger, coursed in his blood.

"Good night, *my lord*." She brushed past him, heading toward her chambers. He grabbed her elbow, whirling her to face him.

"Not so fast, *my lady*," he said, closing the distance between them. He struggled to keep his voice calm, but raw hurt frayed the edge of his words. His threadbare patience was nearly worn through. He had waited for her, so patiently, at no small cost to his sanity. He could continue to wait, if he knew she would one day turn to him. But if she meant to reject him, he wanted to hear it now. "I believe you owe me a forfeit. You did promise a kiss to the best shot, did you not?"

She swallowed and glared up at him. Ever so slightly, she leaned into his body. The firm swell of her breasts brushed against his chest. "I did. *One* kiss."

"One kiss."

He grasped her face in his hands, angled it back, and brought his mouth down on hers. Hard. She squirmed against him, but he held her close, tangling his fingers in that tightly coiled hair. Her lips were pressed together, and he ran his tongue over them in a desperate plea. *Open to me,* he willed. *Take me in.*

Then suddenly, her hands shot under his coat and slid up his back, pulling him tight against her soft, supple body. Her lips parted to release a breathy moan.

It was all the invitation he needed. He thrust his tongue in her mouth and drank in that moan. Drank deeply, tasting her essence—golden and cool and sweet and wild, like ripe pears and honey. His mouth moved over hers again and again, and she welcomed his tongue with her own.

She moved closer. Wriggling into his coat, flattening her breasts against his chest, tilting her hips against his. He worked one hand between their bodies to knead her breast. She sighed against his mouth. Her hands moved to his shoulders, cleaving his wet coat from his body and tugging it down. Without breaking the kiss, he let his hands fall to his sides, and she yanked the coat from his arms.

One kiss. One kiss that would never end. Not if he could help it. He cupped her face in his hands and held her mouth firmly against his as they sank down together. Down to their knees, then down to the carpet.

Then she was under him. So yielding and sweet, his body ached with desire. Her fingers worked beneath his shirt, burning trails of fire over the chilled flesh of his back. And words tumbled through his mind, so many words he longed to say. *Beautiful* and *lovely* and *dear* and *heart* and *please.* And *we* and *us* and *ours.* And *help me* and *hold me* and *take me in.* And *don't let me go* and *never* and *never* and *never ever leave.*

But he couldn't say them. He couldn't risk breaking this kiss. This one kiss that was everything. He pulled up her skirts in a rustle of silk and cambric, fumbling through the layers of petticoats and finding the slit in her drawers. She was hot and wet and clasping around his fingers, and the words changed to *hurry* and *want* and *need* and *oh God* and *now.*

He tore open his breeches and slid into her, and she whimpered against his mouth. He withdrew and thrust again. She bit down on his lip. He stayed in her, grinding slowly against her. Then she threw her arms around his neck and opened her mouth to his tongue. And she wrapped her legs around his hips and opened herself to him.

He lost himself in her mouth and her arms and her legs and her tight, wet embrace. Again and again and again. He felt her arching and tensing and convulsing around him, and when she cried out against his mouth, he took it all in. Tasted her pleasure. Felt it surge through him, send him over the edge into *yes* and *yes* and *bliss* and *heaven* and *thank you* and *always* and *mine*.

He kissed her gently now, savoring the sweetness of her tongue. The smooth, plump curve of her lower lip. The corners of her mouth, which tasted curiously of salt.

Salt and bitterness. Like tears.

Jeremy broke the kiss and raised up on his elbows. She was shaking against him and covering her face, but she couldn't hide the truth.

Lucy was crying.

CHAPTER
TWENTY-THREE

Lucy couldn't stop the tears.

She tried. She fought them with every ounce of her will, but she couldn't stop them. It was too much. Too many emotions battled inside her—relief, frustration, desire, anger, joy—churning in that dark confusion of her mind. And then in one bright moment, they were all swept away in a wave of exquisite pleasure. Followed by that flood, that same strange, powerful deluge she'd experienced the first time they'd made love. A roaring tide of emotion that surged from her heart and swept through her body—and this time, it overflowed.

Oh, and they were terrible, the tears. So wet and messy. So helpless and weak. No dainty, ladylike tears, these. No slow, trickling drops of emotion punctuated by a delicate sniff. Lucy's eyes spilled buckets, and her nose ran. Her shoulders shook, and her chest heaved. She pressed her hands to her face, to no avail. There were eight years' worth of tears inside her, and she'd been strong enough to store them away one sniffle at a time. But damming all of them at once—impossible.

"Lucy." His voice sounded muffled, far away. "My God, Lucy. What is it?"

Even if she knew what to tell him, she couldn't have managed to speak. She could scarcely catch her breath. Sobs racked her body, and hot tears spilled through her fingers, channeling down to her ears. He withdrew from her gently and rolled away, and she cried even harder, bereft of his warmth and strength. Feeling empty and hollow and cold. She curled away from him onto her side, hugging her knees to her chest.

"Don't cry, Lucy. I can't bear it." His anguished whisper tore at her heart. Strong fingers smoothed her hair, but she shrank from his touch. And she hated herself for pulling away, but she couldn't help it. She was too exposed, too raw, and even the most tender caress rasped against her skin. "I'm so sorry," he said. "I'll do anything. Don't cry."

He'd do anything, he said. But he'd already done too much. He'd made her love him so completely, the love would not be contained. He'd breached every last one of her defenses, and now there was nothing left to keep him out. Nothing left to hold back the tears.

And these tears, they were everything Lucy had tried so hard, for so long to avoid. Vulnerability. Helplessness. She couldn't stop herself from crying any more than she could keep herself from loving him—and what he did, with the tears or the love, was completely beyond her control. She was down on the floor, curled into a ball, sobbing into her hands. Defenseless and weak and utterly at his mercy.

And then he confirmed what she'd always known. Nothing good ever came of tears. Quietly, wordlessly, he rose to his feet and left her.

He left her all alone.

Jeremy had to leave. It was a matter of self-preservation.

He stormed through his antechamber and into the sanctuary of his bedroom, barely managing to slam the door shut before crumpling against it.

A stronger man would have stayed—would have gathered her into his arms and held her tight and kissed the tears away. But he wasn't a strong man at that moment, in his heart. When Lucy shrank from him and wept, twenty-one years of strength peeled away, leaving only a vulnerable boy. An eight-year-old boy who'd witnessed the sudden, violent death of his brother. A confused, grieving child who needed a mother's comfort, but found only tears. Tears that poured salt and shame over raw, open wounds.

And it hurt. God, did it hurt.

Jeremy slammed his fist against the door, once. Twice. But the pain splintering through his bloodied knuckles did nothing to dull the agony twisting in his chest.

How many years had it taken, before he could enter a room without his mother weeping? How many times did she turn from him in tears, begging his nursemaid or tutor to take him away? Take him out of her sight, because she couldn't look at him without seeing Thomas.

Thomas was the fortunate son.

Thomas would never feel this gnawing visceral agony, knowing his very existence caused heartache and pain. Knowing that when she looked at him, she saw only someone he wasn't. Someone he could never replace. What was a boy to do, when a simple word or a laugh dropped into the air so innocently could land in a deluge of bitter tears?

He spoke softly, trod lightly, stayed out of his mother's sight. He never laughed or ran or played too loudly, for fear of disturbing her fragile peace. He escaped the house and went riding, hard and fast across the open countryside. He went off to school and surrounded himself with friends, taking comfort from their jollity even when he did not share it. He occupied his mind with books and studies, to keep unpleasant thoughts at bay.

The boy grew into a man. And between Cambridge and London and his friends' invitations, he rarely came home. He found gratification in the arms of women who would quite willingly shed their clothes, but never shed a tear. Women who gave of their bodies but withheld their hearts. Women he could never love.

Women he could never hurt.

But when Lucy turned from him and wept, she resurrected that boy. She brought back all the hurt. And that wounded, grieving eight-year-old child—he didn't know how to protect, or console. He only knew how to survive.

Tread lightly. Speak softly. Stay out of sight.

Leave.

In the following weeks, they were like two spirits haunting the same house. While Lucy went about her daily routine, Jeremy disappeared. Into his study, sometimes. More often to places out of the Abbey. He always returned for dinner, always on time. He made the minimum of conversation courtesy required, speaking in cool, measured tones.

There were no more kisses.

Although she and her husband barely spoke, Lucy found some solace in an entirely novel form of communication.

Letters.

She received weekly letters from Marianne. Chatty, rambling missives filled with all the homely details of life at Waltham Manor. The latest escapades of the children or the servants or the dogs. Even in the Abbey's oppressive stillness, Lucy could hear laughter and music in those letters. She read them so many times, the paper wore thin at the creases.

Sophia sent rapturous, effusive reports of her engagement and wedding plans, penned in perfectly looping script. On first reading, Lucy scanned the lines with a broad grin. The second time through, her smile would inevitably fade. Sophia's accounts of her betrothal and betrothed were unflaggingly cheerful. *Too* cheerful. Lucy suffered the niggling sensation that something must be wrong. After all, experience had shown Sophia to have a rather vivid imagination where letter-writing was concerned. One need only ask Gervais.

The identity of Lucy's most faithful correspondent came as a great surprise. Henry wrote to her two or three times a week. He had little to say in these missives—a few random remarks on the weather, or an update on the winter wheat crop. Perhaps a few words about the hounds. But the message beneath those few hastily scrawled phrases was clear. Lucy responded to each letter with her own assortment of off-hand observations, always the same answer writ between the lines.

Yes, Henry. I miss you, too.

She was learning to measure her happiness by small sources of comfort. Any day that brought a letter was a good day, in relative terms. The particular day that brought two letters, both brimming with exciting news, stood out as a banner occasion.

"We've received our invitation to Toby and Sophia's wedding," she told Jeremy at dinner that evening. "It's to be in December."

"That soon?" He did not appear to share her excitement. "Did you wish to attend?"

"Why, yes. Of course."

He took a slow sip of wine. "Very well, then."

Lucy pushed a bit of potato around her plate. "I was thinking . . . perhaps we could stop at Waltham Manor for a visit, after the wedding."

Silence.

She fortified her resolve with a sip of claret. "It's just that, I also had a letter from Marianne today. She's increasing again. I've always been there to help during her other confinements, and I'm a bit anxious for her. The first few months are always the hardest. And we will be passing through the neighborhood."

Jeremy shook his head slightly. "Your brother and I did not part well. I think a visit would be ill-advised." He cleared his throat and picked up his fork again. "Besides, I can't be absent overlong. Estate business, you realize."

Lucy let her fork clatter to the table. "Estate business. Yes, of course." She could taste the acid in her voice, and she knew he had to hear it. "Well, it was only an idea."

Jeremy sat back in his chair and regarded her. The cool detachment in his gaze froze Lucy's heart. "Perhaps," he said calmly, "you would prefer to visit on your own. I can deposit you at Waltham Manor after the wedding. The carriages will be available to retrieve you whenever you wish."

Deposit her? *Retrieve* her? What was she to him? Just some bothersome parcel to be shuttled about from place to place?

She stared at her husband. There he sat, His Lordship, positively monolithic at his end of the table. Ever calm and composed. Suggesting their indefinite separation over the fish course, in the same tone of voice he might speak of the weather. Lucy wanted to pick up the plate before her, hurl it against the wall, and watch it smash into as many pieces as her heart.

Instead, she curled her fingers around the stem of her wineglass and bit her lip until she tasted the coppery tang of blood. "If that's what you prefer," she finally managed. "I'll write to Henry tomorrow." She looked into those ice-blue eyes, scanning his gaze for any flicker of hurt or disappointment. Even a flash of annoyance would be welcome. "Perhaps,"—she swallowed slowly—"perhaps I should just stay until the babe is born."

Nothing.

"If you wish," he answered, returning his gaze to his plate. Lucy stared at him in disbelief as he casually forked a bite of salmon into his mouth. "I'm going to London tomorrow."

"To London? Tomorrow?"

"I have some business there with my solicitor, regarding another of the family properties. I'm riding instead of taking the carriage, so I shan't be gone long. I'll return on Thursday."

"I see." He was leaving for London, *tomorrow,* to be gone for the better part of a week, and he'd tossed that bit of information at her like one throws a crust to a dog. Lucy supposed she should feel fortunate he'd bothered to inform her at all. Her eyes burned. The dishes swam before her in a miasma of welling tears. She blinked furiously. She would *not* cry.

She laid her napkin down on the table. "I expect you'll want to retire, then. You'll need an early start."

He drained his wine slowly before responding. "Indeed."

Lucy let him go.

The next morning, she woke with the dawn. Even so, she stayed abed late and kept to her chambers until she was certain he must be gone. There was no sense in bidding him farewell. After dinner yesterday, any goodbyes they might exchange would feel redundant.

The Abbey did not seem quieter in his absence—it could scarcely become more silent than before. But for once, it wasn't the outward silence that oppressed her. It was the stillness inside her that ached. A strange, quiet void that she might have described as hollow, except that nothing echoed there. Each beat of her heart, each word, each breath was instantly dampened, smothered by this weightless burden of silence in her chest.

And she couldn't escape it. Couldn't crawl out from

under it or break free of its spell, because she carried it within her. Out on long, rambling walks. Through dark, foggy dreams. Around the vast stone confines of the Abbey, which she took to haunting during the day, wandering through the ancient chambers in aimless fashion.

One afternoon, while drifting through the music room, she wandered into Aunt Matilda.

"Aunt Matilda!" Lucy wrapped an arm about her aunt's indigo-draped shoulders. "Where is your nursemaid?" Familiar scents—spice and chocolate and snuff—opened a cache of fond memories. She felt a sharp pang of homesickness for Waltham Manor. "Never mind," she said, hugging the old lady close. "I'm glad to see you."

Aunt Matilda wandered over to the pianoforte and opened the instrument. The housekeeper had insisted on having it tuned Lucy's first week at the Abbey, no matter how much Lucy insisted she didn't play. Aunt Matilda sat down, touched her fingers to the ivory keys, and launched into a lively reel. Her blue turban bobbed in time with the music, and a helpless giggle burst from Lucy's throat.

Music. Laughter. For the first time in weeks.

The last strains of the reel stretched out into silence, and Aunt Matilda's hands dropped to her lap. Lucy went to sit beside her on the bench.

"Thank you, Aunt Matilda. That was lovely." The old lady smiled up at her with the same benign expression she'd worn every day in Lucy's memory. If only Lucy could borrow that unflagging optimism. Lucy grasped her aunt's papery hand in hers. "What's to become of me, Aunt Matilda? I've changed somehow. And I can't go back home, I just can't. I miss the Manor desperately, but I would miss him more." She gently laid her head on her aunt's shoulder. "I miss him now."

A turbaned head settled heavily against hers, and

Lucy squeezed her aunt's fingers. The bony hand lay limp and cold in Lucy's grasp.

"Aunt Matilda?" Lucy straightened, and her aunt's frail body slumped against her own. Lucy lifted the old lady's head, pressing a hand against her clammy cheek. "Aunt Matilda?"

CHAPTER
TWENTY-FOUR

"She'll be all right, won't she?" Lucy paced the Persian carpet of Aunt Matilda's suite, endlessly circling the blue-and-gold pattern. "She has to be all right."

Hetta squeezed each of Aunt Matilda's hands in turn. "Lucy, your aunt is eighty if she's a day," she replied from the bedside. "She won't live forever, you know."

"I know, but—"

"Shhh." Hetta laid her ear to Aunt Matilda's chest. Lucy ceased her pacing and held her breath until Hetta straightened. "You must face facts, Lucy. Your aunt cannot be expected to live much longer."

Lucy shut her eyes and whimpered softly.

"But," Hetta continued, "she isn't going to die today. So far as I can tell, at least." She helped the old lady into a sitting position and plumped the pillows behind her. "In fact, she seems to have suffered no lasting effects from her little spell." She began repacking her black valise. "Just make certain that she rests. Give her some beef tea; solid food, if she'll eat it. She'll be wandering around again in no time."

"All right." Lucy sniffed and swiped at her nose with the heel of her hand. "Thank you for coming. Shall I see you out?"

"That won't be necessary," Hetta said briskly, standing and smoothing the wrinkles from her fawn-colored skirt. "I know my way. I know this house better than you do, I'd wager."

"How so?"

"I practically grew up here." Hetta draped her pelisse over her shoulders and tied it in front. "My father was the late Lady Kendall's personal physician. Didn't you know?"

Lucy shook her head.

"That was the whole reason he moved our family from London," Hetta explained. "To treat Lady Kendall's 'nervous condition.' "

"Nervous condition?" Lucy handed Hetta her bonnet.

"Well, that would be what my father called it. He always was rather generous. 'Incurable grief,' the Lady herself would have said." Hetta knotted the bonnet ribbons under her chin. "Personally, I was inclined to think of it as 'insufferable moaning,' but then—I never was the sympathetic type."

She picked up her gloves from the bedside table. "Anytime her ladyship went into one of her fits, my father would be summoned to the house. Twice, three times a week. Sometimes daily. I didn't mind—he'd bring me along and I'd explore the Abbey while he bled her or dosed her with sedatives." She lowered her voice. "Have you found the naughty tapestry yet? The one with all the depictions of sinners in Hell, being . . . *sinful*?"

Lucy shook her head. She wasn't interested in tapestries—not at the moment, anyway. "Lady Kendall had fits? What sort of fits?"

"Oh, all sorts of fits. The more dramatic, the better. A word, a look, a sudden change in the weather—the slightest provocation sent her into hysterics. And then she would go on and on, crying for hours until my father could calm her. I don't know how he had the patience to treat her for eight years. And she'd been that way for ages before we even came here." She stepped away and began pulling on her gloves.

A chill crawled down Lucy's spine. She thought of her own helpless bout of tears, and Jeremy's panicked reaction. Was it any wonder he had left for London? He must have thought she was becoming another hysterical female. Perhaps she *was* becoming another hysterical female.

"My father said one must feel sorry for her," Hetta continued. "She had a fragile constitution, he said. She married a very harsh man, and then she lost a child." She looked up at Lucy with a wry smile. "But as I said, sympathy isn't my strong point. So if you've a mind to develop a nervous condition of your own, you'd better send for my father. The best you'd get from me is a smart slap across the cheek and a slug of brandy."

"I think I need both." Lucy sank down on the side of Aunt Matilda's bed. "I don't know what's to become of me, truly."

Hetta looked at her sharply. "Oh, no. Don't ask me for counsel, Lucy. I'm brilliant with poultices, but I'm not at all accustomed to giving advice."

"Believe me, I'm not accustomed to needing it," Lucy replied. She looked up at the whimsically painted ceiling, where gilt-haired cherubs peeked down at her from billowing white clouds. "What am I doing here? I don't belong here."

With an air of resignation, Hetta sat down next to her. "Your husband seems to think you do. If you want to know what you're doing here, I suggest you ask him. Unless you came with pots of money,"—she eyed Lucy dubiously—"he must have had some reason for marrying you."

"I didn't come with any money." Lucy picked at the lace trim of her sleeve. "He had to marry me. I bullied him into it."

Hetta burst into laughter.

"No, really," said Lucy. "I was perfectly shameless."

Hetta only laughed harder.

Lucy began to feel a bit indignant. "I'm telling you the truth! I threw myself at him like . . . like a wanton dairy-maid!"

At length, Hetta caught her breath and wiped her eyes with a gloved hand. "Lucy, please. First, your husband is an earl, ridiculously wealthy, and—if you won't mind my noticing—not unpleasant to look at. He couldn't have remained unmarried this long without learning to deflect unwelcome advances. Even from wanton dairy-maids.

"Second," Hetta continued, cutting off Lucy's objection, "Lord Kendall does not strike me as a gentleman who would be bullied into anything. Quite the reverse. Surely you've noticed that he need only flash that glare of his to send people scurrying. He's considered more than a bit intimidating."

"Well, I'm not one to be bullied, either," Lucy said. "And he can't intimidate me with that Look. Believe me, he's tried for years, but I just know him too well to believe there's anything behind it. And if you think he's pleasing to look at when he's glowering . . ." She sighed. "You ought to see him when he smiles."

Hetta looked at her for a moment, eyebrows raised. Then she rose to her feet and gathered up her valise. "Well, that's a relief," she said, already heading toward the door. "You didn't need my advice, after all."

"I'm glad you're here," Toby said, sipping his Madeira. "You can give me a bit of advice."

"Advice?" Jeremy snorted. "Why would you want my advice?"

"Well, you're a married man now, aren't you? Don't

you want to give me a speech about the duties of matrimony?"

Jeremy sighed. He should have known better than to come to the club. Of course, Toby would be in Town making wedding arrangements. Jeremy had perfectly good whiskey at the town house. Why had he not simply stayed at home?

"Toby, if you still don't know how to perform your marital duties, you need more than my advice. I can recommend you to a few capable tutors, if need be."

"You know I don't mean *that*." Toby chuckled. "I mean, don't you have some profound wisdom to impart on the care and feeding of a wife? Everyone else has. Felix won't give up on the subject. He's become quite insufferable."

Perhaps Jeremy ought to be talking to Felix. "Sorry to disappoint you, but I shall maintain my sufferable silence."

"Suit yourself." Toby drained his Madeira. "I'm surprised to even see you here. Cutting the honeymoon a bit short, aren't you?"

"I had business," Jeremy grumbled into his whiskey. He was not interested in discussing his business, estate or personal, with Toby. "I return home tomorrow," he added, lest Toby extend any unwelcome invitations.

Toby winked at him. "Eager to get back, I'll expect."

Jeremy didn't know what to say. The truth of it was, he had no business being in London. He ought to be at home, as Toby kept insinuating, honeymooning with his new bride. But life with Lucy was killing him, one dinner at a time. He'd gotten exactly what he'd demanded—a sedate, proper wife—and he couldn't have been more miserable. She scarcely seemed to eat anymore, and certainly not with any enjoyment. She dressed in new gowns and wore lace gloves; her hair was always perfectly coiffed. Jeremy couldn't remember the last time he'd seen her hair tumbling down to her waist in that clamor of chestnut waves. Neither could he recall a cross word from her since . . . *Since.*

Jeremy sipped his whiskey and swallowed the bitter taste of tears.

And then had come the eventuality he'd been dreading since their wedding day. She wanted to leave him.

So he'd left her first.

London offered no end of diversions to keep his mind off Lucy. But his thoughts were with her more than ever. Or rather, she was with him, in his thoughts. Everywhere Jeremy went, he saw sights he wished he could show her, experiences he felt certain she would enjoy. Balls, opera, the theater, Vauxhall. Oh, and why stop with the traditional amusements for ladies? Knowing Lucy, she would not be satisfied until she'd attended her share of boxing matches, too.

"Shouldn't you be with your intended?" Jeremy asked, wishing to change the subject. "You know, taking her to the theater or having dinner with her family?"

"Oh, Sophia hardly has time for me these days. I scarcely see her, unless she's dragging me off to shop for lace or select blooms for her wedding posy. I'm telling you, Jem, you did things right. License, vicar, man-and-wife. It all happened so fast, I could scarcely believe it. Not that I was surprised, mind."

Jeremy looked askance at him. "You weren't surprised?"

"Of course not. I knew that was not 'nothing' between you and Lucy in the orchard, no matter what you said. Then there were Sophia's little hints. And that letter sealed things nicely. But I knew even before the letter—else I wouldn't have proposed to Sophia the way I did."

Jeremy shifted in his chair. "What do you mean?"

"Come on, Jem. Do you honestly think I would have

done that in front of Lucy if I thought she were still in love with me? What kind of boor do you make me out to be?"

Jeremy wasn't certain what to make of anything at the moment. He drained his whiskey, hoping for answers at the bottom of the glass.

"No, I knew," Toby continued. "I've charmed many a young lady, Jem. Thousands, I'd guess. It's not the sort of achievement that lends meaning to a man's life, but it's the one talent I've got. I know exactly the moment I have them hooked. That pretty blush spreads across their cheeks, and they look up at me through their eyelashes, lips pursed just so. It's a thrill, every time. But just as I know the instant they fall for me, I can tell— with most distressing certainty—the precise moment they pick themselves up."

He motioned to the waiter for another drink. "After you had your little row with Henry that day in the woods, I walked Lucy home. Somewhere between the woods and Waltham Manor, she grew out of loving me. And I don't mind telling you, I didn't take it well. Eight years, she'd been mad for me—suddenly over." He cast a guilty look at Jeremy. "I was a bit jealous, I expect."

Jeremy stared at him.

"But it all came right in the end," Toby finished, accepting a fresh glass of wine from the waiter. "You and Lucy, me and Sophia. You should come to Kent for a visit next Easter. See the bluebells and all."

Jeremy leaned forward in his chair. "Toby, even you must have noticed, Lucy wasn't precisely thrilled to marry me. I . . . Henry . . . er, the circumstances forced her into it. She had no choice."

"No choice?" Toby laughed. "I was there at the wedding, Jem. I don't recall seeing Lucy bound or gagged or dragged to the altar. And that's the only way anyone could persuade that girl to recite vows against her will."

He chuckled into his glass. "Lucy, 'forced' to marry. A good laugh, that."

Jeremy had only downed one glass of whiskey, but his head was swimming. He couldn't comprehend what Toby was saying. He was a bit afraid to even try. Even if—and he mentally emphasized *if*—Lucy had indeed grown out of Toby and somehow grown into *him*, it meant only one thing. That Jeremy had managed to cock things up even worse than he'd thought previously.

"Say, Toby," he said, running a hand through his hair. "What do you plan to do when the charm wears off on Sophia? What if *she* grows out of you?"

Toby's face grew solemn. "I don't like to think about it, Jem." He shrugged, and a shadow of that rakish grin crept back to his face. "I expect that's what jewels are for."

It was a damned fool thing, carrying jewels on horseback at night. Aside from the obvious hazards of riding in the dark—the risks of becoming unseated, laming the horse, or losing one's way entirely—highwaymen were always a threat. To be sure, thieves would little expect a lone rider to be carrying a small fortune in gems, but desperate men would not hesitate to kill him for his horse alone.

But then, Jeremy was a rather desperate man himself. And anyone who tried to touch the necklace coiled neatly in his breast pocket would meet first with the cold steel of a pistol. Caution would tell him to stop at an inn, complete his journey tomorrow. But caution be damned. It didn't matter that it was dark, or late, or dangerous. It was Thursday, and he had a promise to keep.

He had several promises to keep, in fact, and he intended to start making good on them.

He'd told Henry he would give Lucy the opportunities she'd never had. He'd promised Lucy he would do his best to see her happy. And he'd vowed before God that he would honor and cherish his wife all the days of his life. Yet he'd fled to London, running away from those promises like an eight-year-old boy.

Yes, she had turned from him and wept, and it had hurt. It had damn near killed him. But tears didn't dissolve duty. Perhaps he could never give her what she truly deserved, but that fact didn't excuse him from trying.

He would do what he should have done from the first. He would bring Lucy to London. She would be within a half-day's journey of Waltham Manor—she might visit her brother and Marianne as often as she wished. He would present her at court and introduce her to society. They would attend as many balls and operas and exhibitions as she desired. She might even find a reasonable use for her pin money. And Jeremy could finally take up his seat in Lords. His obligations to his wife weren't the only duties he'd been dodging. Perhaps he could even do some good there, work toward outlawing the use of man-traps. That would be a more fitting tribute to Thomas than any fabricated portrait.

He tried not to dwell on Toby's words the night before. It was too much to hope that Lucy might love him. He told himself it didn't matter whether she did or not; his duty to her remained the same. Despite all this, Jeremy was feeling giddily optimistic. Which, for him, was an entirely foreign sensation. But not an unpleasant one. Not in the least.

It was a full day's ride on horseback from London to Corbinsdale Abbey, if one started with the dawn and changed horses halfway. If, however, one waited for the jeweler's shop to open, then spent the better part of an hour waving away trays of tawdry baubles before the officious clerk brought out the best wares, then wasted yet another quarter-hour while one's purchase was wrapped—the journey home stretched into evening, and the dark made for slower progress still.

But it was Thursday, and he'd told Lucy he'd be home on Thursday. And somehow, keeping that casually uttered promise became as important to him as honoring his wedding vows. It might not make a difference to her whether he returned tonight or never, but it did to Jeremy. Just as the necklace weighing down his breast pocket was less a gift to her than it was a symbol to him.

She was his jewel. Rare, precious, beautiful, and possessed of an inner fire that it was a crime against nature to dull or hide. He would expect nothing of her, make no demands. That base, brutish lust would not escape his control again. But he would protect her, and cherish her, and place her in the setting that allowed her to sparkle brightest. He hoped that setting would be London; he intended to use whatever powers of persuasion he could muster to plead that case. If Lucy still wished to return to Waltham Manor, he would buy up the surrounding land and build her a manor house of her own, with a stable full of docile mares and the finest French chef his English coin could hire.

It was nearing midnight when Jeremy finally reached the Corbinsdale stables. Lucy would surely be abed, he thought, handing his reins to a sleepy groom and making his way up to the house. Mounting the stairs two at a time, he considered whether he ought to rouse her. Certainly not in his present state, he thought ruefully. A day of hard riding on dusty roads did little to recommend a man when his object was persuasion. He would have a bath drawn, and then he would wake her. He hadn't looked on his wife in five days, and he didn't think he could wait until morning to see her again.

He didn't have to wait another minute.

Jeremy entered the sitting room to find his wife curled

up on the ivory damask sofa, asleep. He quietly crossed the room to stand before her. She did not wake. He sank down on the carpet next to his wife, his legs suddenly weak. He couldn't blame physical exhaustion, or mental fatigue. Lucy was just so damned beautiful, it brought him to his knees.

She lay on her side, one hand slid between the sofa's creamy upholstery and the golden skin of her cheek. Thick, dark eyelashes fluttered fetchingly as she dreamed. Her hair was unbound, rippling over her shoulder and glowing almost red in the firelight. And what she was wearing—dear God. It was a very good thing Lucy was asleep, because anything tender or honorable or gently persuasive in him instantly went up in flames.

A thin strap of black lace looped over the enticing curve of her exposed shoulder, and Jeremy's eyes followed it down, and down, to where plunging black lace framed the valley between her breasts. Red silk skimmed over the flat planes of her belly and the rounded swell of her hip, then diverged in another V of lace. The narrow slit began at the crest of her thigh, then widened as it wandered down the side of her leg. The silk fell away completely just below her knee, exposing the sweet curve of her calf as it tapered to her ankle.

Her ankle flexed.

A sleepy sigh pulled his gaze back up to her face. To heavy-lidded emerald eyes and slightly parted, sweetly bowed, dusky red lips.

"Jeremy?"

Lucy blinked again. Perhaps she was dreaming. She often dreamt of him like this, coming to her fresh from the stables—rumpled and unshaven, cool wind clinging to his hair and clothes. And sometimes, in her dreams, he murmured her name in this same reverent whisper and reached out like this to gently touch her cheek.

"Come with me to London."

But never in her dreams did he say *that*.

She rose up on her elbow, rubbing her eyes with her other hand. "What?"

"Come with me to London," he repeated, smoothing a lock of hair from her brow.

Lucy shook herself, trying to dispel the sleepy fog in her brain. "Now?"

He smiled. For the first time in weeks, he smiled. Her heart turned over in her chest.

"No, not now. But soon. I'm having my town house— *our* town house—prepared. Your suite is being redecorated. You'll have a carriage for your own particular use, and the phaeton, of course. Anything else you wish."

"But—"

He put a finger over her lips. "Don't answer yet. I'm getting ahead of myself." He reached into his breast pocket and withdrew a velvet pouch. Loosening the knotted string at the top, he said, "I know I've been remiss in my duty to you as your husband. I want you to know that's going to change."

He opened the pouch and emptied its contents into his palm. Filigreed gold and glowing red stones coiled in his hand like an exotic snake. Lucy gasped and clapped a hand to her mouth.

"To match your ring," he said, pulling her hand from her mouth and draping the necklace over her palm. "Come with me to London. I'll make no demands on you, I swear it. Just let me take care of you. Whatever you desire, whatever you need—it will be yours."

Lucy tore her gaze away from the jewels in her hand and looked up at her husband. Drat him. His little impassioned speech was wreaking havoc with all the words she'd practiced so faithfully and waited up late to say. That she didn't want to go back to Waltham Manor.

That the past five days had been sheer agony, and she never wanted to be parted from him again. She would go with him to Cornwall, if he asked it. Or Australia, or the moon.

But he wanted her to go to London. He wanted to buy her jewels and carriages and take care of her. He would make no demands on her, he said.

Even if she wanted him to?

Lucy loved him too much to let him go, even if she wasn't loved in return. If he had wanted her enough to marry her, then being wanted would have to suffice. So she'd practiced her seductive speech and donned this tarty red negligee of Sophia's—after all, something similar had worked once before. And now he was here on his knees, with jewels and promises and that beautiful, sincere blue gaze of his. Vowing not to desire her at all. Retreating back into that shell of indifference. Offering her a lifetime of opulent misery.

She didn't know how to respond.

Her fingers tightened over the necklace. The polished stones felt like liquid under her fingertips. "It's lovely, Jeremy. But I don't need this. And I don't need carriages, or a redecorated suite, either." His brow furrowed, and his jaw tensed. Lucy sat up. This was coming out all wrong.

Pulling on his lapel with her empty hand, she slid the necklace inside and let it drop back into his pocket. Then she ran both hands up to his shoulders.

"Jeremy, can't you see?" She swallowed hard, meeting his now-troubled gaze. "I don't need you to take care of me. All I need is—"

A soft knock on the door interrupted her. The door creaked open a foot, and the head of a ghostly-pale chambermaid poked through the gap.

"B-begging your pardon, my lord. My lady." The head bobbed a bit—a motion Lucy took for a curtsy. "I just thought . . . that is to say, we believed you should know . . . that someone ought to inform you . . ."

"For God's sake, what is it?" Jeremy rose to his feet.

The chambermaid shook. "Her Ladyship's aunt has gone missing," she squeaked. Then her head disappeared and the door slammed shut.

Lucy leapt to her feet. "Oh, no," she moaned, picking up the red silk dressing gown draped over the sofa's back. She shrugged into the robe and cinched it about her waist before dropping to the floor to hunt for her slippers. "We have to find her. She doesn't know this place, and the Abbey is so big. She could be anywhere. And it's so cold, and she's so frail. If she gets lost . . ." She jammed the slippers on her feet and scrambled up to a standing position, only to find herself nose-to-nose— or rather, nose-to-throat—with Jeremy.

"Don't worry." His hands went to her shoulders. "We'll find her," he said simply.

She nodded, staring stupidly at the open collar of his shirt.

"The servants have no doubt begun searching the house," he said. "Stay here and help them. It's unlikely she'd have made it outdoors, but I'll take some footmen out to the gardens, just to be certain." He tilted her face to his. "We'll find her. And then we'll continue this talk."

"All right, then."

Then he was gone. Lucy heard him thundering down the stairs, barking orders to servants as he went.

She crossed the corridor and entered Aunt Matilda's suite. It seemed best to first verify that she was indeed missing, and not simply huddled behind the draperies. That had happened once at Waltham Manor—the whole house had been turned upside down before her nursemaid finally found Aunt Matilda squirreled away in the window seat.

Lucy combed through the chamber, peeking in cupboards and ducking under the bed. Finally she strode to the windows and pulled back the drapes.

Nothing.

Or something.

A flash of white outside caught her eye. She scanned the darkness. There it was again. Moonlight glinting off something pale and wispy, like a ghost. Or an elderly spinster's shift. She pressed her face to the glass, straining to make out the landscape below. This window looked out over the front of the Abbey; the gardens were behind the house. Aunt Matilda was heading down the gently sloping green that bordered the woods, and the woods hid the narrow, winding valley of the stream.

Lucy rushed down the stairs and out the massive, open door. There were no footmen about. Jeremy must have led them all around back, to the gardens. She grabbed a carriage lamp from its hook beside the door and started off across the green. There was no time to go off in search of the men. By the time she found them and pointed them in the right direction, Aunt Matilda could be wandering lost in the woods, or worse—plunging into the icy stream.

Lucy caught a glimpse of fluttering fabric again, just at the border of the woods. She cupped her hand to her mouth to call out, but decided to save her breath. As Sophia had once so helpfully pointed out, it made little sense to shout at a deaf lady. Instead, she doubled her pace across the green, her silk slippers crunching over frosted grass. She hurried to the copse of trees she'd seen Aunt Matilda approaching and plunged into the forest.

She swung the lantern around, scanning through the trees. Nothing. She looked down. There were footprints, of sorts. Small depressions in the ice-crusted mud about the size of a woman's foot. She followed the trail, holding the lantern aloft with one hand and clutching the neck of her dressing gown with the other.

Heavens, but Aunt Matilda moved quickly. It seemed impossible that Lucy would not have caught up with her by now. She could hear the gurgle of the stream already.

The footprints ended at a rocky outcropping. She approached it cautiously, a bubble of dread rising in her throat. The stream's low gurgle became an ominous roar below. Holding on to a branch with one hand, she swung her lantern out over the edge with the other, peering down into the gorge. Praying she wouldn't see a tattered scrap of muslin shift somewhere down below.

Her shoulder exploded with pain. Lucy pitched forward with a scream. The lantern sailed from her hand and tumbled down, landing in the river with a splash.

The whole world went black.

CHAPTER
TWENTY-FIVE

Jeremy didn't find Aunt Matilda.

Aunt Matilda found him.

Having started the footmen searching the garden, Jeremy rounded the front of the house. Aunt Matilda greeted him in the entrance hall, barefoot and dressed in a shift nearly as translucent as her skin.

She was shuffling her feet around the parquet floor and humming a lively tune. When she looked up and saw Jeremy, she paused just long enough to utter a single word. "Lovely."

"Lucy," he called, ushering the old lady up the stairs. "Lucy! I've found her." He looked into the sitting room as he passed their suite. "Lucy?"

No response.

Jeremy shrugged off a whisper of anxiety. Casting a pointed look at a maid down the corridor, he steered Aunt Matilda into the Blue Suite. The maid hurried in after them, quickly assuming care of the elderly lady.

"Where is Her Ladyship?" he asked the maid brusquely.

"I . . . I don't know, my lord. I believe I saw her heading downstairs."

"Downstairs?" That made no sense. If Lucy had gone downstairs, why hadn't she found her aunt? Jeremy turned to exit the room, but something stopped him. The damn drapes were all pushed to the sides. No wonder the old lady went wandering off. The draft must be ice-cold. He crossed to the window and reached with both hands to gather the blue drapes together.

Then he saw it.

A tiny light, winking at him from the edge of the woods. Bobbing and weaving through the darkness. Like a fairy light.

But Jeremy didn't believe in fairies. What he believed, with a sick certainty, was that when it came to wandering into danger, his wife clearly took after her aunt.

He bolted from the room and took the stairs at a run, for the second time that evening. This had already seemed the longest day of his life, but every second now felt an eternity. He barely mustered the patience to duck into the study and grab up his gun before charging out into the dark.

Damned fool chit. He watched the flickering light recede into the woods, and he redoubled his pace. He was running now, the heavy necklace in his pocket slapping against his chest with every step. How was he supposed to cherish and protect his wife when she kept hurling herself into harm's way at every opportunity?

And she didn't need him, she'd said. She didn't need him to take care of her. Well, he thought bitterly as he began weaving through the trees, someone had to. She sure as hell couldn't take care of herself. When he caught up to that flickering light that kept teasing him in the distance, he would have a thing or two to say about taking care. And his wife would bloody well listen.

Jeremy came to a halt. He'd lost track of the light. He scanned the woods in the direction he'd seen it last. The night was overcast, but the clouds were thin enough that the moonlight filtered through them as a faint, silver glow. He blinked, his eyes slowly adjusting to the murky dimness. He stared down at the ground until his boots came into focus, black wedges against the leaf-strewn mud.

His breath was heaving in his chest. Perhaps if he rested another moment, he could gather it enough to call out. But it wasn't only the exertion that had him gasping for air. Panic seized his lungs like a vise. He hadn't been out in this part of the forest at night in years.

Twenty-one years.

He'd lost so much to these cursed woods already. And now he'd lost sight of that damn light. The cold wind whipping through the trees felt like death itself, and he couldn't breathe, he couldn't call out. It was all he could do to keep standing.

The faint babble of the stream reached his ears, and he turned instinctively toward the sound. He stumbled forward a few paces, then stopped again to scan for the light. To listen.

A scream rent the air.

Lucy's shoulder hurt like hell.

But she couldn't stop to wonder what it was that had struck her, or where the devil it had come from—because at the moment, she was a bit preoccupied trying not to fall headlong into a ravine.

Her other arm—the uninjured one—clutched a tree limb, and there she clung until her slippers found purchase on the rocky outcropping. Even once she had regained her footing, she held on to that tree branch for several deep breaths. Then slowly, cautiously, she released the branch and turned around.

What she saw surprised her so greatly, she reeled anew. "Albert?"

The boy stepped forward, dim moonlight delineating a baffled countenance. "Your highness?"

"What are you doing here?" This they spoke in unison.

Neither rushed to answer.

Lucy took advantage of the mutual silence to size up

her attacker. The sling that dangled from his hand told her the source of her pain. What a ninny she'd been. Thinking how fast Aunt Matilda was moving—of course she could never walk so quickly. Those footsteps hadn't been old lady-sized; they were boy-sized. And it hadn't been her aunt's shift Lucy had seen fluttering in the distance; it had been Albert's oversize, tattered homespun shirt.

He was swimming in it, that shirt. It must have belonged to his father.

His father, transported for . . . And Lucy realized she didn't need him to tell her what he was doing here. She already knew.

"You're poaching!" she accused.

The boy maintained his sullen silence.

Lucy stepped toward him. "So you won't take Kendall charity, but you'll steal from your lord as you please?"

"He ain't *my* lord." Albert turned his head and spat. "Anyway, it's his fault my father's in Australia. How else are me and Mary supposed to eat?"

"It's not Lord Kendall's fault; it was his father's. And you're old enough to work, aren't you?"

Albert strode boldly forward. He crouched beside her and picked up a small rock. "I do, when there's work to be had. Planting time. Harvest. But now—there's no farmer as needs me now."

She watched him pocket the small stone. The rock that struck her shoulder, she concluded. As he stood, Albert eyed her silk-clad form with an expression that had turned unmistakably adolescent.

"What the devil are you wearing?" he asked.

Lucy chose to ignore the question. She also chose to wrap her arms about her chest and change the subject. "Do you really fell much game that way?" She nodded at the sling and stone he'd pocketed away.

Albert shook his head. "I'm not really a good shot with it."

"You hit me well enough." The throbbing in her shoulder attested to the veracity of that statement.

"Well, yes." The boy paused, squinting up at her. "But I was aiming for your head."

"Oh." Lucy suddenly felt a bit dizzy. She folded her legs under her and sat on the ground. "What do you do then, take from the traps?"

Albert didn't answer. She saw him flex one hand at his side, as though shaking off an ache or pain.

"That's how you hurt your hand," she said. "Before."

He walked a few paces away and leaned against a tree.

"You ought to be more careful, you know," she scolded. "A wound like that can fester easily. My father died from a wound like that."

He shrugged. "Folks die for all sorts of stupid reasons."

"True. But that's not an excuse to go around acting stupid."

The boy snorted.

It was a fortunate thing he had poor aim, Lucy decided, because her brain had just produced a rather brilliant idea. "Come to work at the Abbey."

"What?"

"Come to work at the Abbey," she repeated.

"Like hell I will."

She frowned. "Why not? I'll ask my husband—I'm sure there's some work he can find for you. You'll have steady income, and you won't have to go wandering about the woods at night."

"No!" Albert's voice grew suddenly deep. He straightened and marched toward her where she sat on the ground. "Don't you tell him anything about me. He'll find me work, all right. In the poorhouse."

"Don't be ridiculous." The ground beneath her was icy cold, and Lucy hugged her legs to her chest. "He isn't like that, I swear. He's very understanding."

Albert scoffed. "I heard how understanding he was at that party of yours."

"That was . . . different. Just allow me to speak with him. Let me help you."

"Thanks, your highness, but I don't need your help."

Her hands clenched in frustration. What would it take to get through to this boy? She wasn't just trying to be superior. She *cared* about him, the stubborn ingrate. "I will tell you what you need," she said, her voice clipped. "You need to put your sister's welfare before your own pride. You need to stop running about the woods at night, where who knows what peril could befall you. And you need to learn some propriety. In private, you can curse me however you wish, but to my face, you will address me as *my lady*!"

There was a shocked silence. And the majority of the shock was on Lucy's side. Albert might have been wondering where that rant had come from, but she knew its precise source. She was echoing Jeremy, of all people. Was this how he felt, too? Concerned for her safety, desperate to help, but frustrated beyond measure when she refused to let him?

And how many times had she refused him?

Lucy's heart squeezed. He truly cared for her. He always had. And all this time, *she* had been the stubborn ingrate.

Albert was still looming over her, his hands balled into fists at his sides, looking rather uncertain as to what came next. She tried to make her tone soft and soothing. Motherly. "Albert, listen . . ."

But what they heard next was anything but soft or soothing.

"Lucy, don't move." Jeremy's voice thundered from somewhere unseen.

Followed by the unmistakable click of a gun being cocked.

"Get down!" Lucy cried, lunging forward.

A shot cracked through the dark.

CHAPTER TWENTY-SIX

Lucy tackled Albert about the knees. He fell to the ground, and in the same instant a shot whistled overhead.

She released his legs. "Run!" she whispered. "Run all the way home, and don't stop for anything!"

Albert scrambled to his feet and dashed off into the trees. A few seconds later, Jeremy thundered by in breathless pursuit.

"Stop!" Lucy struggled to her feet and grabbed her husband by the arm. "He's gone. You'll never catch him."

Jeremy pulled his arm away and swung his gun over his shoulder. "Oh, I'll catch him all right." He moved in the direction Albert had fled, and she grabbed his arm again.

"Wait! You can't just leave me here alone." She could play the helpless lady, if necessary. She hugged herself and shivered, only partly for effect.

Jeremy pulled to a halt, staring off into the woods with frustration. Then he turned back to her reluctantly. "No, I won't leave you." He fixed her with a fierce look. "Damn it, Lucy. What the devil were you thinking?"

"I saw him from a distance. I thought he was Aunt Matilda, so I—" she gasped. "Aunt Matilda!"

"She's fine," Jeremy said impatiently. "I found her in the entrance hall. She may be old and senile, but at least *she* knows better than to go wandering out in the woods at midnight, dressed in . . ." His eyes swept over her silk-clad curves with a possessive gaze that mingled anger and desire. "You have to stop behaving in such an imbecilic fashion. I can't always be around to save you."

Lucy felt pride, hot and rebellious, surging within her. *He cares for me,* she reminded herself. She just needed to calm him down, let him know she was all right. "Jeremy, I'm sorry I alarmed you. But I didn't need saving." She wrapped her dressing gown tight across her chest. Bloody hell, it was cold. "It wasn't how it looked. I had the situation in hand."

"*In hand.*" Jeremy let the gun slide from his shoulder and flung it to the ground. He stalked toward her with a strange expression, his eyes black as midnight. His breath came uneven and ragged, breaking up his words. "You had the situation in hand. Alone in the woods. In the dead of night. With a violent criminal."

She swallowed. "He wasn't a criminal. Not a violent one, at least."

It was as though he didn't hear her. He approached her slowly, step by deliberate step, until his chest grazed hers. She could taste desire on his breath. The blue of his eyes was swallowed by black, and a wild intensity radiated from him. A fierceness she'd only glimpsed before, he kept it so deeply buried. Now it seethed to the surface, exuded from him in potent waves, sweeping over her body. And her body roused to it. Craved it. Her skin came alive with exquisite awareness, every hair standing on end.

Lucy didn't know how to calm him down.

She didn't want to.

"Dressed in a few scraps of silk and lace." He hooked a finger under the collar of her dressing gown and pulled, exposing one shoulder to the night. She felt his finger graze along her collarbone, press against the hollow of her throat, then trace the column of her neck to her chin, lifting her face to his. "But you didn't need saving. You had the situation . . . in hand."

"Yes," she breathed. He moved forward again, his chest pushing against hers. Her back collided with the trunk of a tree.

He grabbed her wrist and wrenched her hand from its grip on her dressing gown. "In hand," he repeated, interlacing his fingers with hers. He tightened his grip until the bones in her wrist ached. In one swift motion, he pulled her arm up over her head and pinned it to the tree with his own. Her dressing gown fell open to the waist. She gasped at the rush of cold night air that assailed her throat and drew her nipples to hard peaks against her nightgown.

With his free hand, he palmed one breast through the shivering silk. He drew his thumb over her nipple. She gasped again, this time with pleasure.

"You didn't need saving," he said, sliding his thumb over the silk in tiny, maddening circles. Waves of sensation flooded through her, heat rippling beneath the gooseflesh that covered her neck, her belly, her thighs. Lucy bit her lip and closed her eyes. "Look at me," he growled. "Look at me, damn it." He gave her nipple a sharp pinch. Her eyes flew open.

"You don't need my money." He tore at the strap of her nightgown until the fragile lace gave way. The silk slid down, baring one breast.

"You don't need my gifts." He covered her breast with his warm, heavy hand, teasing the taut peak of her nipple, rolling it under his thumb until a tiny cry escaped her throat. He pressed his body against hers, pinning her to the tree with his weight. The heat of his arousal pulsed against her belly.

"You don't need my protection," he said through gritted teeth. His hand shot to her thigh, gathering up fabric, hitching up the hem of her nightgown in impatient tugs. His eyes bored into her.

"Damn it, Lucy, you are going to need me. I will make you need me." He lowered his head to her breast, drawing her nipple into his mouth.

Pleasure surged through her—hot, white light arcing through the darkness. His tongue flickered over the sensitive peak, making her writhe with a sweet, torturous ache. One of her hands remained pinned above her, but she reached for him with the other, digging her fingers into his neck.

His hand tightened around her hip, then snaked beneath the silk of her nightgown, pushing it up to her waist. He curled his hand under her thigh and lifted it, wrapping her leg over his hip. Icy cold rushed under the silk, over her thighs and between her legs. Then he pulled his hips back slightly, swept his hand over the crest of her thigh and plunged his fingers into the gap between them.

There was no more cold, only fire. Liquid heat coursing through her veins, churning in her belly and that space between her legs. He slid a finger into her. Then two. His touch was rough and artless, but she was slick and ready, and it wasn't enough. It wasn't nearly enough. His thumb found her most sensitive bit of flesh, and her mouth fell open in a startled cry. He clamped his mouth over hers, filling it with his tongue. Lifting her with his fingers and working her with his thumb until she nearly came apart.

And then it was gone. His hand was gone. His lips were gone. He leaned on her, pressing his chest to hers, all his weight bearing down on her aching breasts, and she writhed against him, desperate for more. She heard him gasping for breath against her ear, felt him fumbling with the buttons of his breeches. Then she felt *him*, hot and heavy and jerking with impatience against her thigh. She arched toward him instinctively, but he grabbed her hip, pushing her back down. His other hand tightened over hers, still holding her arm above her head.

"Tell me you need me." His eyes held her, dark and fathomless as the midnight sky.

"I—" Her voice failed. She couldn't think how to speak, couldn't remember how to make her mouth form words. Speech had no meaning. Her lips' sole purpose was to kiss; her tongue existed to lick and suck. She burrowed her face into his neck and ran her tongue along his throat. He inhaled with a sharp hiss and pressed his thumb deeper into the flesh of her hip.

"Tell me you need me," he insisted. He teased her with his shaft, brushing against her, and when he pulled away, a strangled sob wrenched from her throat.

"Jeremy," she cried. "Please."

"Tell me."

"I need you." God, did she need him. She was nothing but a quivering mass of desire and longing and *need*. "I need y—"

He crushed his mouth to hers, cutting off her words, cutting off her air. He released her arm and grasped her hips with both hands, lifting her up. In one quick, desperate thrust, he sheathed himself inside her, filling her. Filling that aching void of need. She dug her fingernails into his neck and held on tight. He withdrew an inch, tilted her hips, and thrust into her again, burying himself to the hilt.

Yes. Yes. Yes.

This was where they belonged. Together, in the dark. In firelit rooms and shadowed gardens and deep, black ebony wardrobes. Fighting themselves, fighting each other. Fighting to get closer. Fighting to become one.

He braced his head against her shoulder, grasping her hips to thrust deeper still. Harder, faster. Again, again,

again. Until the delicious tension threading through her pulled tight and snapped, releasing her into the darkness.

Then he pulled her back to earth with a tortured groan and a final, anchoring thrust. The power of his release racked through them both, and they quivered together in its aftermath. His fingers bore into the flesh of her hips, and his weight crushed against her breasts, and his shoulders heaved as he fought for breath.

"Damn it, Lucy," he said, his voice muffled against her shoulder. "Tell me you need me." He turned his head and laid his cheek against her breast. "Tell me you need me, because God knows I can't live without you. I'll kill the man who tries to take you away, and I'll be damned if I'll let you leave."

His hands slid up from her hips to wrap around her waist, laying claim to her, squeezing her to him until she owed him the very air she breathed. "I won't let you go."

She cradled his head where it lay against her heart. "Don't," she whispered, twining her fingers into his hair. "Don't ever let me go."

He didn't let her go.

Somehow, once his ragged breathing and his pounding heartbeat had slowed to a normal rhythm, Jeremy gathered the edges of her dressing gown and pushed the sleeves back up over her shoulders. Without letting go, he pulled her nightgown back over her waist and let it fall below her knees. Holding her against the tree with his body, his shrugged off his coat. Then he gathered her trembling form into his arms and wrapped the coat around her like a blanket. Without letting go.

He hefted her quivering body with one arm and reached down with the other to pick up his gun. He slung the weapon over one shoulder, tucked her head against his other, and silently struck a path through the woods.

He was drained physically and weak at heart, and the house was too far away. He carried her toward the low gurgle of the stream. Toward the hermitage. He covered the ground at a steady pace, pausing only occasionally to rebalance her weight in his arms. He cupped her shoulder in one hand and her thigh in the other, and somehow her hand had worked under his shirt to rest flat against his chest. Right over his heart.

He looked down at her face, cradled against his chest. Her eyes were closed, dark lashes resting against the pale curve of her cheek. In the moonlight, her skin glowed white and pure, and her lips were an ashen pink. Chestnut curls cascaded over his shoulder, and if he bent his head a fraction and inhaled deeply, he could catch the scent of pears wafting from her hair.

She was beautiful. God, how he loved her.

And he had never hated himself more.

Self-loathing weighed his every step, sucking his boots down into the mud. Pulling him down into the earth, to sink through the layers of rock and fire and fall straight down to Hell where he belonged. He'd come back from London pledging to care for her, protect her. If only she'd give him one more chance, he'd never drive her to tears again. All those noble sentiments, and what had he done? He'd pushed her up against a tree and savaged her like the brute he was.

Lucy needed protection, all right. She needed protection from him.

They reached the hermitage. Jeremy kicked in the door, splintering the wooden latch inside.

Something inside him splintered as well. Something painfully close to his heart.

The air inside the cottage was close and thick. He couldn't breathe. A desperate panic seized him, the urge to turn and run. He'd avoided this place for twenty-one years, and he'd meant to never visit it again. But now . . . now he had Lucy in his arms, and she had no one else. He would face this, for her.

Moonlight filtered in through the open door behind him, slowly illuminating the small room. It looked just as he remembered. A row of lead soldiers keeping watch above the mantel. The fishing tackle strewn across the small table. Two pairs of small, muddied boots by the door. Frozen in the past, all of it. Only a thick layer of dust evidenced the passage of time.

Jeremy carried Lucy in and laid her down on the rug before the hearth, slipping her hand out from under his shirt. She was asleep.

His chest constricted with anguish. Every struggling breath felt like a sob. The stale air was thick with loss and love—these two inexorably connected forces that it seemed, for him, would never divide. He was doomed to lose whomever he loved, and he was doomed to do it here.

But there was plenty of time to mourn tomorrow. The next day. The lifetime after that. Right now, his wife was cold. He pushed thoughts aside, setting his body to mechanical tasks. Focusing on simple goals. Light. Warmth.

After closing the door as best he could, he heaped her with furs and placed a folded blanket under her head. He stacked the fireplace with tinder and wood. Once the draw of smoke from a single lit branch assured him the chimney was clear, he added the burning twig to the rest of the kindling. The fire caught quickly, snapping and sparking and filling the room with sweet, smoky warmth and an amber glow. He knelt beside her, watching her chest rise and fall with every breath. Drawing a grateful breath of his own when the color returned to her cheeks and her lips. He reached out to caress her cheek, and she stirred, nuzzling into his touch. Cupping her face in his palm, he brushed his thumb across her lower lip.

He would hold this moment forever. Hold her face in his hand, her lips grazing his thumb in a secret kiss. When she woke up, it would be over. She would gather up her hounds and her cat and her senile aunt and leave, taking everything good in his life along with her.

She stirred again, shifting under the blankets. Her eyes fluttered open.

"Jeremy?" His name flowed from her lips slow and thick and sweet, like honey. It wouldn't last, he told himself. She'd be cursing him soon.

"Don't move." He pulled his hand away from her face. "Just rest."

She slid one arm out from under the blankets and rubbed her eyes with her fist. She might as well have driven her fist straight into his gut. Red, angry bruises blossomed along the skin of her wrist. Bruises from where he'd grabbed her arm and pinned it to the tree. Bile churned in his stomach. He'd hurt her, and not just there. He had to see.

He lifted the blankets gently, casting them to the side. She made a small sound, but he placed a finger on her lips.

"Let me look at you," he said, drawing aside the edges of her dressing gown. She nodded drowsily.

The red silk nightgown clung to her body in tatters. Jeremy tore the remaining strap of lace and drew the fabric aside. He steeled his jaw, swallowed hard, and forced himself to take a good, long look at what he'd done.

There were little marks on her neck and shoulder, where he'd kissed and sucked and bitten her flesh. Between her legs she was swollen and red, where he'd wedged himself and rutted like a beast.

"Turn over," he choked.

She obeyed in silence, and he forced his gaze to wander her body from the feet up, noting every scrape and scratch the tree bark had wrought on her perfect, golden skin. The marks were sparse on her calves and the backs of her thighs, but her back was a crosshatch of red streaks. He followed the curve of her spine up.

And then he saw it, and his breath caught in his chest.

A round, angry welt on her shoulder blade. A deepred circle of raised, swollen flesh. This was no scratch. This was nothing he had done. He traced the wound with his fingertip, and Lucy winced.

"He did this to you."

She nodded.

Jeremy stood up. He picked up his coat and shrugged into it before looking about for his gun.

"What are you doing?" she asked, rolling onto her side and propping herself up on one elbow. "Where are you going?"

"I'm going to kill him." Where had he put his damn gun? "I'm going to find that bastard and shoot him dead."

She sat up, grabbing the red silk dressing gown and pulling it on. "Jeremy, no. You can't."

"I assure you, I can." He must have left the gun outside. He put his hand to the door, but suddenly she was there, pulling on his sleeve.

"He's only a boy, Jeremy!" With a sharp yank on his arm, she wheeled him to face her. She repeated gently, "He's only a boy."

Only a boy.

The words ripped through him like a shot. Jeremy choked on a curse. Lucy reached for his other hand, but he recoiled from the touch. He couldn't even look at her. "How—" His voice was a rusty creak. He swallowed and tried again. "How old?"

"Twelve. Thirteen, perhaps." Jeremy stared mutely at

Lucy's hand where it clutched his arm. Her grip softened. Her voice, as well. "I tried to explain to you earlier. His name is Albert. His father's been transported for poaching. His mother is dead. He has a five-year-old sister to look after, and they're hungry. I took him by surprise in the dark. He can't be blamed for injuring me."

He shook her hand from his arm and turned away. He ran his hands through his hair, then slammed the table with his fists. An earthenware mug crashed to the floor. Behind him, Lucy gave a startled cry.

Damn him. Another crash.

Damn him. Damn him to hell. He pounded the words into the table again and again. He wasn't even certain which "him" he meant. His father, himself—it didn't matter. They were one and the same. Both destructive. Both damned.

For twenty-one years, he'd feared this moment. For twenty-one years, he had known it would come. Jeremy had lived his life to distance himself from his father's mistakes. That quiet, cold cruelty that made enemies of his tenants, a wretch of his wife, and a ghost of his eldest son.

Even as a boy, Jeremy had tried to resist. He'd tried to cheat fate. If his father said "Turn left," Jeremy went right. If his father urged, "Go faster," Jeremy slowed down. None of it mattered in the end. He was right back in the same damned place, paying for all the same sins. The tenants despised him, even before he'd chased them all off with a gun. He was pushing his wife up against trees and driving her to despair.

Then tonight . . . God. Tonight, he'd shot at a twelve-year-old boy.

A bitter compulsion forced him toward the open door. He had to leave. He had to get far away from her, before he hurt her again.

Lucy blocked his path. "Jeremy, this is madness! You can't honestly mean to go hunt down a child."

He grit his teeth and flexed his hands at his sides. Of course he didn't mean to go hunt down a child. He didn't mean to hurt anyone, but he did all the same. He was his father's son. He was cold and cruel and heartless, and it wasn't safe for him to stand here and belabor the point. He had to leave, and he had to leave now.

"Lucy, just get out of my way." She planted her feet wide and crossed her arms defiantly. He clenched his jaw and glared at her. "Move. *Now*."

"Why are you behaving like this?" Lucy's hands balled into fists. "Listen to yourself—scowling and making ridiculous threats. Why? Because your father treated his tenants that way?" She jabbed a finger into the center of his chest, poking at the raw, open wound that was his heart.

"Don't do this." *Jab*.

"You are not your father." *Jab*.

"You're good and kind and generous." *Jab, jab, jab*.

"Jeremy," she sighed. "For God's sake, you can't even bring yourself to shoot a blasted partridge. You wouldn't hurt anyone. You're just not that sort of man." She flattened her hand against his chest, lightly stroking the linen of his shirt. Her voice softened as she met his gaze.

"If you were, I wouldn't love you."

CHAPTER
TWENTY-SEVEN

He stared at her in silence, his expression inscrutable. If it weren't for his heartbeat pounding hard against her palm, Lucy might have mistaken him for stone.

Or ice.

"It's freezing in here." She kicked the door shut and leaned against it. If he planned on going anywhere, he'd have to get through her first.

"You're wrong," he said. His voice vibrated through her palm, sending shivers up her arm to curl around her neck.

"No, I'm not. It's cold as Hades. Look." She huffed a breath into the space between them. It swirled into frosty vapor.

"You're wrong about *me*."

"Oh. Well, I'm not wrong about that, either."

He shook his head. "Don't make me out to be kind, or generous, or anything approaching good. Of all people, you should know better. In all my life, marrying you was the most selfish thing I've ever done. I told your brother, I told myself—I wanted to protect you. Take care of you." His voice lowered as he closed the distance between them. "I lied."

His flinty gaze roamed over her face, her body. Hot breath tickled her ear as he leaned in close. "I wanted you. More than I've wanted anything in my entire life. I wanted you so much, I couldn't see straight. Couldn't sleep at night."

His voice shook, and Lucy trembled along with it. She sank against the door, borrowing its strength.

"I knew you wanted to marry for love. But I wanted you, and I didn't care. And tonight," he whispered fiercely, running a finger down her throat. "I've wanted you like that ever since that afternoon in the orchard. I wanted to press you up against that tree and spread your legs and rut with you like an animal. So tonight I took you, and I hurt you, and I didn't care."

His finger stroked down into the valley between her breasts. Lucy sucked in her breath. He pulled his hand away, made a fist, and slammed it against the door behind her. The force of the blow rattled her teeth.

"So don't make me out to be a good man. I'm an addle-brained brute, just like you said. I've hurt you inside and out, and don't you dare love me." He pounded the door again. "Don't you dare."

He fixed her with a burning gaze. Lucy was grateful for the door behind her holding her up, because without it her knees would surely buckle. She couldn't let him see. She couldn't fall to pieces, because he needed her to be whole.

"Oh, Jeremy. You know I can't back down from a dare." Forcing her lips into a half-smile, she reached up to smooth a lock of hair from his brow. He closed his eyes for a moment, and his Adam's apple bobbed in his throat. She longed to fall into him and press her lips against it, but she settled for cupping his cheek in her palm.

"I love you, Jeremy. And the only way you could hurt me is to walk out that door and leave."

He straightened. His hand shot to hers where it cradled his cheek. "The only way I could hurt you?" He pulled her hand away and turned it over between them. Lucy looked down. Bruises covered the skin of her wrist.

"Look," he said gruffly, giving her arm a shake. "Look at how I've hurt you."

She looked up at him, eyebrows raised. "I'd imagine the back of your neck doesn't look too pretty, either." When his face didn't soften, she said, "Jeremy, they're just a few bruises. I've suffered far worse from falling out of a tree, much less being loved against one."

His pale blue eyes were chips of ice. Lucy shook her head slowly. "You've been trying to frighten me away with that glare for years now, Jeremy. It's never going to work. You think I didn't know that there was something beneath that cool surface? Of course I knew. I always have, in some way, or else I wouldn't have been forever provoking you to get at it."

"No." He shook his head. "Lucy, you don't know—"

"Yes, I do." She placed her hand against his chest. "I know you. I know what's in there, because it's in me, too. There's passion and loyalty and pride and desire and a hundred other things. And not all of it's good, and none of it's gentle. It's fierce and wild and so intense that it scares you. You're afraid to let anyone see."

Lucy fisted her hand around his shirt and pulled until he met her gaze. "Don't let it scare you." She swallowed. "I see it. All of it. And it doesn't scare me."

She slid her hand inside his shirt, splaying her fingers over his heart. "Inside here, there's a warm, generous, loyal, compassionate man. His tenants are going to respect him. One day, our children will adore him." His eyes softened, and he drew a sharp breath as if he would speak.

"But not me," she added.

His face shut down. "Not you?"

"No." She shook her head and smiled. "I'm in love with the addle-brained brute."

She trailed her fingers over his bare chest, feeling hot sweat and hard muscle and a fierce, thumping heart.

"You know, you've a very inflated opinion of your charm if you think you convinced me to marry you against my wishes. I wanted you, too. That day in the orchard. Earlier tonight. Every minute in between. I wanted to marry for love, and I did. I loved you the day I married you. I love you now." Her voice quivered. "I will love you always, and . . ."

"Lucy," he groaned, pressing his thumb against her lips. "Stop. Just stop."

"*Stop?*" She brushed his hand away. What did he mean? Stop speaking? Stop loving him? Lucy didn't intend to do either. "*You* stop," she said, her voice suddenly bold. Using the solid strength of the door behind her, she pushed against his chest with both hands. He stumbled back a step.

"Stop arguing with me." She pushed him again, backing him up to the table. He sank his weight down on it, losing a good four inches of height in an instant. His legs sprawled wide, and Lucy stepped between them.

She met those ice-blue eyes, now situated just a few inches above her own. "You want to hear that I need you?" He nodded—a bob of the head so slight, she doubted he did it consciously. "Jeremy, I do need you. I need you desperately, and *that* scares me. I don't need your money, or your gifts, or even your protection. I need *you*. And right now, for the love of all that's holy, I need you to *stop interrupting*. I need you to look me in the eye and hear me when I say I love you. And damn it, Jeremy—I need you to believe it."

He opened his mouth to speak. She clapped a hand over his lips and lowered her voice to a growl. "Stop. Interrupting."

He shut his eyes, sighing with resignation against her palm. Lucy withdrew her hand. She allowed her thumb to linger over the curve of his lower lip. "Look me in the eye," she said softly.

He did.

With the full force of that Look burning into her, she whispered, "Hear me." She put her hands on his shoulders, bracing him. "I love you, Jeremy." His weight shifted under her, and she tightened her grip. "Believe it."

Then Lucy held his gaze, dug in her heels, and waited.

Stop this, his eyes commanded, his stern brow creasing for emphasis. *I forbid you to love me. Get away. Move. Now.*

She shook her head slightly. "You know that Look doesn't work on me. I'm not going anywhere."

Blue bewilderment crept into his gaze. "Why?" His voice was rough, demanding. "Damn it, Lucy, why? I've given you no reason to love me."

"I don't need a reason. But you've given me many. Because you want to make me happy and keep me safe. Because you know me in the dark. Because when I'm near you, every bit of me comes alive. Because I make you come alive, too. Because . . . just *because.*" She firmed her chin. "Because I do, and you can't stop me."

Then his brow softened and his gaze turned pleading, and Lucy's heart ached.

"Don't ask this," he said, his voice a soft rasp. "I don't know what to do with those words. I don't remember the last time I heard them, if I ever did, and . . ."

"And they scare you. I know."

He swallowed. "I'll do anything for you, Lucy. I'll give you whatever you wish. Let me take care of you. Let me buy you things. Ask me anything else, but don't ask this."

"But this is all I want." She dug her fingers into his shoulders. "This is all I need. And I'm scared, too, because I need it so much. I don't need you to say it back, not now. But I need you to hear it, and believe it, and be strong enough to bear it."

She would never know how long they stood there, gazes locked. Moments. Minutes. Perhaps hours.

But Lucy wouldn't back down, and she wouldn't release him. She held his shoulders and held his gaze. Until, at last, he drew in a slow breath and heaved a rough sigh. She felt his muscled shoulders roll under her hands, as though shrugging off a heavy weight. Strong hands reached out to encircle her waist. He closed his eyes briefly, then opened them again. And it was a fortunate thing that he held her waist tight, because her knees buckled the instant those brilliant blue eyes met hers.

Now this . . . this was a Look. One even Lucy could not ignore. With all the force that his usual glare demanded distance, this Look reached into her heart and pulled, tugging her close.

Then his jaw softened, and his lips parted, and his deep voice echoed what his gaze already said. Three little words that set Lucy's heart pounding and her blood singing with joy.

"Say it again."

"I love you, Jeremy."

He still felt it, that wince of doubt. The urge to push her away. She said it so simply. As though there was nothing easier, more natural in the world. The words themselves hung in the air, so tiny, so bare. Jeremy felt as though she'd thrust a frail, delicate, birdlike thing into his big, clumsy hands, charging him to keep it safe. And God forgive him, his first impulse was to shove it away. He would destroy it, surely. In his desperation, he would grasp it so tightly it would break into a thousand pieces—and his own heart would break along with it.

But then she smiled at him, so sweetly. Her cheeks dimpled with that infectious, impish joy, and he knew he could never push her away. Not her, not her love. He would prove to her—and prove to himself—he could be strong enough. He would be the man she believed him to be. He could cradle that frail, delicate love in his hands and guard her heart as though it were his own.

Because, in truth, they were one and the same.

Jeremy gathered her to his chest, pulling her heart against his. But something came between them. A lumpy weight knocked against his chest.

The necklace.

He let go of her waist and reached into his breast pocket to draw out the chain of jewels. In the firelight, the rubies glowed like hot coals.

"I know you don't need this," he said.

She shook her head. "I don't."

"But I want you to have it." He brushed her hair from her neck. "May I?"

She nodded slightly, lifting her hair to one side. He fastened the necklace around her neck, trailing his fingers along the delicate curve of her throat.

"Well?" she whispered, rolling the jeweled chain under her fingertips. "How do they look?"

"They look . . . jealous."

She laughed. It was the sweetest music he'd ever heard. "I didn't know jewels could be jealous."

He nodded solemnly. "Oh, yes. They're most certainly jealous. Jealous of you. And furious with me, for fastening them about a neck so beautiful. They feel like dull, misshapen rocks hanging there."

She laughed again. "Jeremy, please. I thought gentlemen bought ladies jewels so they could forgo the pretty phrases."

He grasped her waist again, pulling her close against him. "Pretty phrases be damned," he whispered. "You're beautiful, Lucy. And there's no jewel or phrase pretty enough to do you justice."

And there were no gifts, no words extravagant enough to tell her how much he loved her. He would have to show her instead. Tonight. Tomorrow. Every day for the rest of his life. She felt so delicious, pressed up against him, and he was already longing to taste her. Pretty phrases be damned. He would put his lips to better use.

Her own lips curved in a wicked smile, as though she read his thoughts. He gazed down at her, watching her smile spread slowly across her face and all the way up to her laughing green eyes. "Aren't you going to kiss me now?"

He lowered his lips almost to hers, until there was nothing between them but breath. "Yes, I am going to kiss you now. I'm going to kiss you long, and slow, and deep. I'm going to kiss you all night long, and into tomorrow, and every last day that God gives me beside you."

He cupped her face in his hands, and her lips trembled under his. "I'm going to kiss you here," he murmured above her mouth. He slid his lips over to her ear, letting his breath caress her earlobe. "And here," he whispered, nuzzling into her hair. Angling her head back, he buried his face in the sweet curve of her neck. "And here." He rubbed his rough jaw against the delicate skin of her throat, thrilling to her little gasp.

Then he pulled away and looked down at her face. Until her eyes fluttered open in a sweep of dark lashes that he felt brush against every inch of his skin.

"I am going to kiss you from the crown of your head, all the way down to the tips of your toes. And then I'm going to kiss my way back up your body and stop about halfway"—she shivered in his arms and he locked his thighs around her hips—"and I am going to kiss and kiss and *kiss* you until you are crying out my name."

"So," he said, standing up. He lifted her into his arms in one swift motion. "If you—my wife, my heart, my love—have anything else to say, I suggest you say it now." He carried her over to the fire, sinking down with her into the nest of furs and blankets. "Because for the next several minutes, I intend to keep your lips pleasantly occupied, and after that—after that, I promise you, you will forget."

She wrapped her arms around him, pulling him close. "Just one question," she breathed, as his hand slid beneath silk to curve around her breast.

"What would that be?"

Her tongue flickered against his ear. "When do I get to kiss *you*?"

CHAPTER
TWENTY-EIGHT

Several hours and countless kisses later, morning dawned, quiet and bright. Lucy rolled onto her elbow and smoothed the hair from her husband's brow as he stared up at the ceiling.

"What are you thinking about?" she asked, settling her chin on his chest.

He folded his arm around her. "I am thinking that I could stay here with you forever." She smiled and planted a kiss on his collarbone. "But," he continued, stroking her hair, "I'm thinking that if we don't get back to the Abbey soon, someone is going to come find us." He rolled over to face her and dropped a gentle kiss on her lips. "Why? What are you thinking about?"

She wound a lock of hair around her finger. "I'm thinking about Albert."

He grimaced. "Him again?"

"You should give him work," she said, trailing her finger across his chest. "Then he wouldn't be skulking about the woods at night."

"Give him work?" Jeremy snorted. "Like hell I will."

She frowned. "That's what Albert said, too. I don't understand why it's such a preposterous idea. He needs work; surely you have something he can do. It seems perfectly logical to me."

"Lucy, he's been poaching from the estate. He hurt you." He kissed the objection from her lips. "Intentionally or no, he hurt you. It would be hard enough to forgive him that. I can't reward him for it."

"Don't you see? It's not about rewarding Albert's wrongs. It's about righting your father's."

With a sigh, he rolled back to face the ceiling. "I don't think so, Lucy."

"Are you sure?" She ran her hand over his chest, flicking his nipple with her fingernail. "I can be very persuasive when I wish to be." She traced the same path with her tongue, and he groaned. "What do you think now?" she asked saucily.

"I think—" He rolled to face her again and wrapped one arm around her, crushing her close. "I think you said you like me better when I'm not thinking."

He kissed her deeply, running his hand down her back to squeeze her bottom. She sighed as he lifted her leg and hooked it over his hips, pulling her tight against his arousal. Even after a night of blissful passion, Lucy's body responded with surprising urgency. She rocked her hips, sliding over his hard length on a slick sheen of moisture. Exquisite pleasure rushed through her.

She reached between them, angled her hips, and guided him into her moist, aching heat. Slowly, slowly. Just an inch. Then two. Stretching out the pleasure by infinitesimal degrees. Jeremy's hand tightened over her hip. With a low moan, he thrust into her, hard.

"Oh," she cried, breaking the kiss.

"God, Lucy. I'm sorry." His expression went from desire to distress in an instant. "Did I hurt you?"

"Don't be ridiculous." She pulled away slightly, then rocked against him again. "I liked it. Where did you get this notion, that you have to be gentle with me? I'm still the same Lucy. I'm still the sturdy little chit who can outride and outshoot you. I won't break."

He kissed her neck, laughing softly. "You can't outride me."

"Oh, now that sounded suspiciously like a dare." She rolled him onto his back and straddled him, sinking onto him with a sigh. "Who's outriding you now, hmm?" She straightened her spine and tossed her hair over her back. His gaze fell to her jutting breasts. With a fierce growl, he grabbed her hips and thrust upward.

She gasped. "That's it!"

He thrust into her again. "You like that, do you?"

"No. I mean, yes." He thrust again. "Oh, yes," she sighed. She put her hands flat on his chest and leaned over him, her hair cascading around them like a tent. "I mean, that's it. That's why you married me. Because I won't break."

He stared up at her in puzzlement.

She countered his bewildered frown with a defiant smile. "You told Henry, you told yourself—you wanted to keep me safe. And that *was* a lie. Because deep down, you knew I wouldn't need saving at all. Not from this place, not from these people—and certainly not from you." She planted her index finger in the center of his chest. "I can take you. All of you. Everything you have inside, everything you are. You can do your worst, and you can give me your best. And I won't break."

"You won't break."

"I won't. And you knew it the first time we kissed."

He laughed. Laughed so deep in his chest, she felt his joy rumble through her whole body. It felt heavenly.

"Not the first time," he said. "Definitely not the first time." He slid his hands up her arms, pulling her down for a kiss. "Perhaps the third."

It was a long, muddy walk back up to the Abbey. Lucy's slippers only made it halfway. After that, Jeremy carried her.

As the prospect of the Abbey loomed closer, Lucy looked on it with new eyes. The façade of the rambling stone building caught the morning sun and came alive with brilliance. For the first time, she thought it resembled a structure built to praise God.

For the first time, it looked like home.

"Jeremy, stop."

His arms tightened around her. "What is it? Are you uncomfortable? Don't demand to be put down. I'll not allow you to walk barefoot through the—"

She silenced him with a smile. "I don't want you to put me down." She looked around her slowly, taking in the sunlit Abbey and craggy bluffs, then craning her neck to survey the frost-tinged woods behind them. "It's just so beautiful."

She looked up to meet Jeremy's puzzled gaze. "I'll go to London with you if that's what you want. You're my husband, and if you want to reside in Town—or Scotland or Egypt, for that matter—I'll follow you." She paused, allowing the silence to underscore the import of her words. It wasn't an everyday occurrence, for Lucy, pledging to follow a man's lead to the ends of the earth. Or to Scotland. "But I hope our home will always be here. I love this place."

"*This* place? Lucy, we could live anywhere you wish. Travel the world, if you like. Of all the homes I could give you, you tell me this is the home you want?"

She nodded.

"For God's sake, why?"

"Because this is the home you need." She smoothed a lock of hair from his brow. "You wouldn't be here if you didn't love it, too. Lord knows, you could have left it in the care of a steward and never looked back. Jeremy, we can make Corbinsdale a home again . . . fill it with light and laughter." She dropped her gaze, then snuck a glance at him through lowered lashes. "And children."

He winced. "Children? Here?" He looked over his

shoulder toward the woods. "Lucy, how can I even think it? This is a horrible place for children."

"It's not a horrible place at all. It's a good place." She put her hand on his cheek and waited for his eyes to meet hers. "It's a good place," she repeated. "It's also rough and wild and intractable, but that's why I love it. It's *us*."

"*Us*." He blinked away a glimmer of emotion. "Do you know, I love hearing you say that word."

He bent his head to hers, and for several moments Lucy could not have said anything. Even when he broke the kiss, all words had vacated her mind, save one. "Jeremy," she sighed.

"And that—" he dropped another light kiss on her lips—"is the word I adore hearing most of all." He shifted her weight in his arms and resumed walking toward the manor. "Thank God you stopped calling me by that infernal nickname."

"I did stop calling you 'Jemmy,' didn't I? How curious. I don't even recall when that happened."

"Don't you? I do."

The dark note in his voice reverberated through her body, and desire echoed back. Lucy formed an immediate suspicion of which occasion that might have been. But then she realized something else. She gasped. "Thomas called you Jemmy, didn't he? That's why you could never abide it."

His silence—and a brief hitch in his stride—served as confirmation.

Lucy laid her head against his shoulder. "Oh, dear. Why didn't you ever tell me?"

Again, he said nothing. But she needed no response. Of course, he *had* told her, scores of times, not to call him that. He scarcely could have explained why. She shut her eyes and burrowed into his shoulder, feeling acutely every example of her insolence over eight years.

"I'm so sorry. You were always so rigid, so proper—I couldn't resist needling you. I never meant to . . . to stab you in the heart."

He chuckled. "That's a bit dramatic. Don't apologize. You couldn't have known. If it makes you feel better, for the most part, you *were* simply annoying." She gave his arm a playful swat, and he squeezed her tight. "But I suppose, in a way . . . you never allowed me to forget him. I wasn't always glad of that." He paused. "But now I am."

"Does that mean we can stay here at Corbinsdale?"

"It means . . ." He sighed heavily. His boots echoed over the cobbled stone entryway as they approached the Abbey's thick wooden door. "Lucy, I don't . . ."

His voice trailed off as they entered the foyer and a throng of wide-eyed servants rushed to greet them. From the back of the horde emerged a most familiar, yet most unexpected figure.

"Henry?" they exclaimed in unison.

Jeremy slowly lowered Lucy to the floor. With one sweeping glare, he cleared the room of servants. She had to admit, that Look had its uses.

She clutched Jeremy's coat around her body. Henry approached her slowly. He took in her disheveled state, eyeing her from tangled hair to bare toes. "My God," he said, his voice shaking with rage. "What has he done to you?"

He turned his burning gaze on Jeremy. "I'll kill you. I warned you before, and now I'll kill you. And—" His nostrils flared. "I'm going to enjoy it." Henry started toward him, his hands in fists.

Lucy threw herself in her brother's path. "Henry, no! You don't understand."

Henry glared over her shoulder at Jeremy. "You said you'd take care of her, you bastard!" He gestured toward Lucy's tattered clothing. "Just look at her! She's a disaster."

Lucy clenched her jaw and let the words bounce off her pride. "I had a little accident. You know how clumsy I am. Just a little mishap in the woods, that's all. Jeremy—" She swallowed. "Jeremy came to my rescue. You should thank him." She looked over her shoulder at her husband. "I should thank him."

"I'll thank him to go to hell." Henry glanced down at her bare legs. "What the devil were you doing in the woods half-naked?"

She shut her eyes. "Henry—"

Jeremy interjected, "She's cold, Henry. I'll be glad to explain everything. But let us go wash and dress, and then we'll sit down to breakfast and discuss this like civilized people."

"Civilized people? You call this civilized?" He advanced on Jeremy, backing Lucy up between them. "If you think I'm allowing my sister to spend another minute in this house, you're mad. I'm taking her back to Waltham Manor, where she belongs."

"You can't just take her," Jeremy said, his voice growing rough with anger. "She belongs here. She's my wife."

Henry's eyes narrowed. "Not if I kill you, she isn't. Then she's your widow."

They lurched toward each other. Lucy put out her hands, one on either man's chest, bracing her outstretched arms to hold them apart.

"Stop it, both of you! No one is killing anyone. This is absurd." She turned to her brother. "Henry, why are you here?"

"Why do you think I'm here? The minute I got your letter, I ordered the carriage. If you're miserable enough that you want to come home, you can come with me now. You don't have to wait until Toby's wedding." He glanced down at her briefly before directing his cold stare back at Jeremy.

Lucy cringed. She'd forgotten she'd sent him that letter, the day Jeremy left for London. Of all the times for her brother's protective instincts to surface. "Henry, I'm not miserable."

"But your letter said . . . Why else would you want to come home?"

"To help Marianne, of course."

"Marianne?" Henry blinked. His green eyes went from blazing to puzzled. "Why would you need to help Marianne?"

"With her confinement, you dolt!" Henry blinked again. Lucy turned to him, putting her hands on her brother's shoulders. "She's increasing again. You mean she hasn't told you?"

"No, she hasn't." He turned and looked at the ceiling, dragging a hand through his hair. "Damn it, no one ever tells me anything."

"Congratulations," Jeremy offered weakly.

Henry shot him a look. He turned back to Lucy. "So you're saying you don't want to come home?"

Lucy shook her head. "I'm happy here." She felt Jeremy step up to stand behind her. He placed his hand on the small of her back, and she leaned against it.

"Are you certain?" Henry asked, eyeing her with suspicion. "Because it looks as though you've been to hell and back." He cast a wary glance at Jeremy. "Maybe you're just afraid to tell me in front of him. Maybe we should discuss this alone."

Lucy laughed. "Afraid? Me? Henry it's been only a matter of weeks. You can't have forgotten me so thoroughly as to think that."

"I haven't forgotten how much you dislike him, either. Nor the way he compromised you, the blackguard." He shouted over her shoulder at Jeremy. "I should have called you out then. I should have shot you dead."

The two men lunged at one another again, and again Lucy forced them apart, arms outstretched. "Stop this, both of you! You're behaving like children."

But they weren't children, these two seething idiots whose chests struggled against her palms. They were men. The two men Lucy loved most in the world, and the two people who would do anything for her. They cared for her, but they cared for each other, too. And Lucy sensed that she could hold them together as much as she'd pushed them apart.

"Listen to yourselves," she said, looking back and forth between her husband and her brother. "The two of you have known each other since you were boys. You've been the best of friends for ages. Like brothers, really." She let her arms fall back to her sides. "Well, now you're brothers in truth."

Lucy turned to her brother. "Henry, I will always love Waltham Manor." She glanced at Jeremy. "I suspect we all will. We had a kind of family there every autumn. None of us wanted it to end. I think . . . no, I *know* that's why I was so desperate to stop Toby from getting married. That's why Jeremy kept coming back, year after year, even though he detests hunting. And that's probably why you never sent me to school or to Town, and why you kept putting off my debut." A shadow of guilt crossed her brother's face. She placed her hand on his arm. "It's all right. I didn't want to leave you, either. You're my brother, and I'll always love you. But Jeremy is my husband now, and my home is with him."

"Just because you married him doesn't mean you have to live here," Henry said. "I won't permit you to stay here suffering, just to satisfy his pride." He shot another glare at Jeremy.

Lucy grabbed the lapels of her brother's coat and

shook him until his gaze dropped to hers. "Henry, stop it! You're being ridiculous." She spoke slowly, enunciating every word. "I *want* to be here. I am not suffering. Not in the least."

He opened his mouth to object, but she silenced him with another shake. "For God's sake, Henry! We're madly in love, can't you see?"

"Madly in love?" Henry snorted. "Impossible. I don't believe it."

She released his coat with a growl of frustration.

Jeremy moved behind her, his chest pressing against her back, his strong hands resting on her shoulders. "Henry," he said. "Believe it."

Henry's forehead smoothed. His steeled jaw went slack. He inhaled sharply, as though he might speak, but then released the breath in a bewildered sigh.

Just then, the door burst open behind them. All three wheeled about to see a grizzled man in homespun garments enter, leading a scrawny boy by his ear.

Not just any scrawny boy. Lucy gasped. "Albert!"

"Caught him nosing around near the traps, the little mongrel." The man, whom Lucy presumed to be the gamekeeper, twisted the boy's ear. Albert winced and stomped down on the gamekeeper's toe.

"Filthy vermin," the gamekeeper spat, wrenching the boy's ear harder. "A good whipping will beat that out of you. Or perhaps you'd prefer a few years of hard labor with your father?" The gamekeeper turned his attention to Jeremy. "Well, my lord? What shall I do with the cur?"

Lucy grabbed Jeremy's arm. She opened her mouth to make an impassioned plea for the boy's release, but his stern mien silenced her. He shook his head slightly in warning. "Trust me," he said in a barely audible whisper.

She bit her lip and glanced over at Albert. The boy

was watching her intently, waiting to see how she would react. She would never convince him to trust Jeremy if she didn't trust him herself. Sliding her grip from her husband's sleeve to his hand, she interlaced her fingers with his. She cleared her throat, casting Albert a pointed look. "Yes, my lord."

Jeremy gave her hand a brief squeeze before releasing it. He stepped toward the boy, pulling himself up to his formidable full height. Even in a tattered shirt and worn breeches, he still looked every bit the lord. Albert's eyes flashed with fear and anger.

Jeremy addressed the gamekeeper. "Release him," he ordered, in a tone that would brook no argument. The gamekeeper complied.

"There's been a mistake," Jeremy continued. "I meant to speak with you today, Tomkins, but it seems the youth's enthusiasm has preempted my announcement. Andrews hired the boy as an apprentice gamekeeper. I believe we've discussed your need for additional help. The boy here will take over the traps."

Tomkins looked as though he would object, but Jeremy silenced him with a look. He turned his gaze on the boy. "You weren't to start yet," he said sternly. "You were to wait until Mr. Andrews introduced you to Mr. Tomkins properly. I gather you simply couldn't wait?"

Albert looked to Lucy, bewilderment in his eyes. She swallowed the anxious lump in her throat and nodded encouragingly, silently willing him to accept this chance. *Yes, my lord.* She mouthed the words to him, adding the most persuasive look she could muster. Silence reigned for a long moment, and Lucy watched pride and confusion and hunger battling in Albert's countenance.

Finally, the boy looked back up at Jeremy. "Yes, my lord."

Jeremy gave him a slight nod. "You are dismissed,

then. Tomkins will acquaint you with your duties tomorrow."

Albert looked back at Lucy, and she grinned her approval. She ducked her head and made a small motion with her hands.

The boy caught on. He was a quick one, after all. He bowed stiffly in Jeremy's direction. "Yes, my lord." He repeated the gesture in Lucy's direction, with a bit more feeling. "My lady." Lucy's heart swelled. With a small parting smile, Albert fled the room eagerly. The gamekeeper moved to follow.

"Tomkins," Jeremy called.

The gamekeeper halted.

Jeremy tilted his head toward Henry. "My guest, Mr. Waltham, has just arrived. He has expressed a desire to see your kennels." He turned to Henry. "Tomkins has a new breed of harrier you'll be interested to see. And when you've finished, we'll join you for breakfast."

Henry stood impassive.

Jeremy crossed back to Lucy. He took her hand from where it dangled at her side, kissed it tenderly, and tucked it into the crook of his elbow. "Believe it, Henry."

Henry looked from his friend to his sister, shook himself, and shrugged. "No one tells me anything. All right, then." He turned to the gamekeeper. "What's this about harriers?"

Jeremy did not wait for the men to make their exit. He steered Lucy toward the staircase, leading her up the steps at a determined pace. The moment they turned the corner of the landing and the entrance hall disappeared from view, he hefted her into his arms without a word. He mounted the remaining stairs two at a time—an exertion that ought to have winded a man, but Lucy was the one becoming breathless.

He carried her into their sitting room, kicked the door

shut, and then leaned against it, taking her mouth in a thorough kiss. Lucy threaded her fingers into his hair and kissed him back hungrily, suckling his tongue until she pulled a deep moan from his chest. He broke away, shifting her weight in his arms.

"I've waited weeks to have my wife in my bed," he said, sweeping her into his bedchamber. "And I'll be damned if I'll wait a minute longer." He dropped her into the center of the enormous mahogany bed and then straightened to peel off his shirt. He sat on the edge of the bed and tugged off his boots before setting to work on the fastenings of his breeches. Lucy rolled onto her side, looking on with unabashed enjoyment as he wrestled out of his remaining clothes.

He noted her amusement. "You could be doing the same, you know."

"What, and miss the show?" He pulled his small-clothes down over his hips and kicked them onto the floor. Lucy sighed. She reached out to trace the muscled slope of his thigh. "You are a beautiful man."

She cast off Jeremy's coat and what remained of the red silk dressing gown, tossing them onto the floor. She crept toward him on her knees to where he sat on the edge of the bed, sidling up behind him and brushing her breasts over his back. He pressed back against her, molding her body around his. He felt strong and warm. Her hands skimmed over his powerful arms and snaked around to caress his chest. Settling her chin on his shoulder, she brushed a kiss against his ear. "Thank you," she murmured. "For Albert."

He snorted. "Don't thank me for his sake. That was for you. I'd send the little reprobate off to jail without a thought."

Lucy ran her tongue across the nape of his neck and up to his other ear. "No, you wouldn't."

"I would, if you asked it." Turning, he slid out of her

embrace and knelt on the floor before her. She sat back on her heels. Situated like this, they were the same height. They looked one another directly in the eye.

He braced his hands on either side of her, caging her with his body. "I told you last night that I can't live without you."

She nodded. "I remember." God, how could she forget?

"That was a lie."

Lucy blinked. That hadn't been exactly what she was expecting to hear.

His hands went to her shoulders. "I *can* live without you, and that's the hell of it. For close to thirty years I've done it. And if you leave me, I'm certain I'll continue a miserable existence for thirty more. So it's not that I *can't* live without you. It's that I *won't*. Whatever it takes to keep you here with me, I'll do it. If I have to make stablehands of every last miscreant in the county, I will. Because . . ." He hesitated.

She swallowed the lump rising in her throat. "Because . . . ?"

He slid his hands up to cup her face. Not gently, but with the full force of passion. His darkened gaze searched hers. "Lucy, I . . ." He brushed a thumb over her lips. "I don't even know how to say it. The words don't seem like enough."

"They aren't enough. But they're a start."

His grip tightened, bracing her so there was nowhere to look but at him. Nothing to see but his eyes, and nothing to hear but his voice. "I love you."

She reeled. The words—just the words, spoken rough and fierce—unleashed that terrible flood within her. That powerful, all-consuming surge of emotion she now understood to be love. Lucy trembled with it, felt it welling up within her and threatening to overflow. She shut her eyes tight. She would *not* cry. He needed her to be strong.

Jeremy gave her head a little shake, and she opened her eyes again. "I love you," he repeated, his voice husky with emotion. "Now and always. More than my own life. More than anything."

Oh, dear. There it went. A big, round drop of love spilling over her eyelashes and trickling down her cheek.

He pressed his lips to her face, kissing it away.

Another tear fell, streaming down the other cheek. Lucy pressed both hands to her face, desperate to stop them. She couldn't drive him away again, not now.

He pulled her hands down and grasped them tightly in his. "Please don't hide from me."

"Please don't leave." She choked back a sob. "I'm not a hysterical female, truly I'm not. I'm just"—*sniff*—"just—"

"I know," he said, smiling gently. "I'm a bit over-whelmed myself. But I'm not going anywhere. *We* are not going anywhere. This is our home. It's where we belong. We're going to fill it with children, and light, and laughter. But Lucy,"—he reached up to brush a thumb over her lips—"your tears belong here, too. You're safe with me."

Oh, and now there was no stopping them. Tears fell from her eyes like a hot summer rain, streaking down both cheeks, sliding down the edge of her nose, running into the corners of her mouth. And he kissed them away, murmuring sweet words of love and heart-swelling oaths and her name. Over and over again, her name—so she knew the words were for her. So she believed it.

"Lucy." He pressed his lips to her trembling eyelids. "I love you."

Somehow her hands found their way to his cheeks, and she pulled him away slightly, bracing her forehead against his. "I love you, too." She sniffed. "Oh, but I've been such a fool." Smiling, she wiped her eyes with the back of one hand. "The drapes, the dinner, that tarty negligee. I didn't know how to be the wife you wanted. You said men want an angel, or a dream. But Jeremy—I'm just not an angel."

He chuckled, sweeping a curl behind her ear. "No, you're not. And thank heaven for that. I shouldn't like you to be a dream, either. I'd live in fear of waking up." He cupped her chin in his hand, and his expression grew serious. "Lucy, you *are* the wife I want, just as you are. I'm sorry I ever gave you reason to doubt it. I was just so afraid of seeing you hurt . . . of hurting you myself . . ."

"I understand now." She bit her lip. "But you needn't have worried. I—"

"You won't break, I know. And do I love you for it." He dropped a gentle kiss on her lips. "But let me love your softness, too. Your strength and your tenderness. Lucy, you're so much more than an angel or a dream. What you are is a goddess. *My* goddess. And you have me completely at your mercy."

Smiling, Lucy wound her arms around his neck and pulled him onto the bed. "I believe I like the sound of that."

EPILOGUE

Christmas came a bit early to Waltham Manor.

Lucy sat on the drawing-room carpet with her nieces and nephew, presiding over the merriment as they unwrapped a prodigious number of gifts. She looked up to catch Jeremy watching her from his armchair with a very familiar expression. She felt herself flush. That Look of his never failed to stir her blood.

She rose to her feet casually, shaking the wrinkles from her skirts, and paused to look out the window before crossing to her husband. Leaning over his chair, she brushed her lips against his ear and whispered, "Meet me in the wardrobe later?"

Jeremy choked on his whiskey. "What, again?" He put an arm about her waist and pulled her into his lap. "What's wrong with the bed?" he whispered into her neck. "I have a rather sentimental attachment to that bed."

She took the drink from his hand. "Yes," she murmured from behind the glass, "but we have a bed at home. We don't have the wardrobe. And we'll be leaving tomorrow morning for Toby and Sophia's wedding. After that, we'll be in Town—you've got the whole session of Parliament ahead." She wriggled her bottom against his lap, eliciting a soft growl. "Who knows when we'll have another chance?"

He ran his hand down her back and hooked a finger under her laces. "There's always next autumn."

A smile tickled the corner of her lips. "I don't think we'll be visiting next autumn."

"Why not?"

"Papa!" Tildy and young Henry ran to their father where he stood in the entryway, leaving poor little Beth to crawl alone on the carpet. The children swarmed over their father, climbing his legs like tree trunks and foraging in his pockets for sweets. He sank to his hands and knees on the carpet, dutifully admiring the shiny playthings and stooping to kiss Beth's pudgy cheek.

"That will be you someday," Lucy whispered to her husband.

Jeremy's arm tightened around her waist. "I hope so."

"Hope all you wish. I, however, have no talent for hoping. I know, I believe, I expect." She set the glass down on the side table and twined both arms around his neck. "As I believe I once told you—to your great amusement—I *know* how mating is accomplished. I *believe* it's been"—she looked up at the ceiling, calculating—"three-and-forty days since I last had my courses. And therefore I am—or rather, we are—*expecting*."

His eyes widened. "Lucy." He swallowed hard. "That's too soon to be certain. Isn't it?"

She smiled. "I'm certain." She leaned forward to kiss the adorably bewildered expression from his face.

"Good Lord, not in front of the children." Disentangling himself from his progeny, Henry rose to his feet. He gave Jeremy a stiff nod. "Jem."

"Henry."

Lucy felt Jeremy tense. Only a few weeks had passed since her husband and her brother had been at one another's throats, but she'd hoped they would greet one another more charitably than this. Would they never be friends again?

"How are you, Lucy?" Henry asked, true concern in his eyes. "Well, I hope?"

"Quite well, thank you."

"Really? You look a trifle pale." Henry turned his gaze on Jeremy. "Has he scolded you for changing the upholstery this time? Or perhaps you discovered his dungeon full of bones and ghouls."

"Not yet," Lucy said. "Henry, you know I'm happy with Jeremy. Must you persist in tormenting him?"

Henry shrugged. "Of course I must. He's family now."

Lucy gave him a cool look, but her heart warmed. No, the two men would never be friends again. Now they were brothers, and they would remain so forever, whether they liked it or not.

"Besides," Henry continued, "what would you have me say?"

"Oh, I don't know," Lucy replied. "Perhaps, 'I'm sorry,' or 'I forgive you,' or 'I'm so thrilled for you both'?"

Both Henry and Jeremy laughed.

"What's so amusing?" she asked, mildly annoyed.

"For God's sake, we're men," Henry said. "We don't say things like that. At best, we keep them tucked in the pockets of our best waistcoats, to pull out at weddings and funerals."

A commotion in the corridor headed off Lucy's response.

Toby and Felix burst into the room, wearing riding clothes and grim expressions.

"And speaking of weddings," Henry said without missing a beat, "what are you doing here? Aren't you getting married in a few days?"

"She's gone," said Toby. He struggled to catch his breath. "Sophia's gone."

"Gone?" Lucy untangled her arms from about Jeremy's neck. "Wherever did she go?"

Felix leaned on a nearby chair, red-faced with exertion. "My . . . parents-in-law," he huffed, "telling everyone . . . Sophia . . . is ill . . . sent to seaside . . . for her . . . constitution."

"Perhaps you ought to go with her, man." Henry crossed to the bar. "You're not looking so hale yourself."

"She hasn't gone to the seaside," Toby moaned, slinging himself onto the divan. "She's eloped. We're on our way to Gretna Green. If we hurry, we might catch them before they reach Scotland."

"Eloped?" Jeremy asked. "With whom?"

"Some painter." Toby threw his head back and covered his eyes with his hand. "A Frenchman, no less."

"What was his name?" Felix wheezed. "Germaine . . . Jarvis?"

"Gervais?" Lucy asked. A nauseous feeling curled in her belly. Not an infrequent occurrence of late, but dread compounded the queasy sensation.

"That's the one," Toby groaned against his forearm. "I've been jilted for Gervais." He straightened and looked at Lucy. "How did you know? I mean, I hoped you might know something. She left you a letter, too." He fished a folded paper out of his breast pocket and leaned forward, hand outstretched. Lucy took it from his hand, sliding her thumb under the broken seal. "You'll forgive me for opening it already," Toby said.

"Of course." Lucy unfolded the tear-stained missive.

Ma chère Lucy,
Remember how it seemed, once upon a time? That if we imagined something and wanted it deeply and believed it with all our hearts, we knew it could come true?
Well, I've decided to give it one last try. This time, I've eaten all my porridge. I'm closing my eyes tight . . . and when I open them, I shall be far, far away.

I'm quite fond of Toby, but I could never make him
happy. Still, he'll take this rather hard, I fear. Please
console him as best you can.
   Ton amie,
   Sophia

"What the devil does that mean, she ate all her porridge?" Toby asked, throwing his hands in the air. "She must know I'd buy her all the porridge she liked."

"Oh, Toby." Lucy shook her head as Jeremy took the letter from her hand. "I wish I could tell you where she's gone, but I can't. But I'm certain she hasn't gone to Scotland with anyone named Gervais."

"But . . . if not . . . Scotland," Felix managed, "where?"

Lucy shrugged. There wasn't anything she would put past Sophia. "She could be anywhere."

Toby groaned and sank back onto the sofa, covering his eyes with one hand. "I've been jilted. *Me!* I can't comprehend it. Every girl in England wants to marry me."

Lucy turned to face her husband. "Poor Toby," she murmured.

" 'Poor Toby' nothing," Jeremy said curtly. "*Console him as best you can?*" he read aloud with eyebrows raised. His arm tightened around her waist. "Don't even think it."

Lucy gasped in indignation. "I would never!" She snatched the letter from his hand and folded it neatly. "And don't tease. Sophia's wild imagination may be Toby's misfortune, but we owe a great debt of happiness to her absurd letters."

"I suppose we do." His hand slid to cover her belly. "And a very tiny debt, as well."

Lucy laid her head against his shoulder and tapped

the letter against her smile. "I wish Sophia nothing but happiness," she said thoughtfully. "But cling as she might to those girlhood dreams"—she craned her neck to brush a light kiss against her husband's jaw—"I am exceedingly grateful that mine did *not* come true."

ACKNOWLEDGMENTS

Becoming a published author is the fulfillment of a lifelong dream, and it never would have been possible without my family. I'm so grateful to my husband, for his love and support, and to my two children, for their patience with a highly distracted mother. My parents gave me the best gift imaginable by encouraging my early love of books, and my grandparents always believed I'd someday publish one of my own.

In writing this book, I was blessed to have two brilliant critique partners who helped me every step of the way: Courtney Milan and Amy Baldwin. Several other writers, readers, and friends read early drafts of the book and provided invaluable feedback. Lindsey, Sara, Lenore, Maggie, Michelle, Susan, Pamela, Kalen, seton, Darcy, Elyssa, and Lacey—I am indebted to each of you.

Many thanks to my amazing agent, Helen Breitwieser, and to the entire team at Ballantine, especially my editor, Kate Collins, and her assistant, Kelli Fillingim.

Thank you to Kelly and Brian, for all the Starbucks, sympathy, and Internet savvy.

I wouldn't be writing historical romance if not for the works of Jane Austen, and the inspiring creative environment fostered by her many online fans in the Lounge, the Gardens, and the Tearoom.

Finally, I want to acknowledge the wonderful network of friendship and support that grew out of the 2006 Avon FanLit competition and to thank Mary, for all her encouragement and advice.

Read on for a preview of the next tale of
romantic escapades from Tessa Dare

SURRENDER
OF A SIREN

GRAVESEND, DECEMBER 1817

In fleeing the society wedding of the year, Sophia Hathaway knew she would be embracing infamy.

She'd neglected to consider how infamy *smelled*.

She paused in the doorway of the fetid dockside tavern. Even from here, the stench of soured ale accosted her, forcing bile into her throat.

A burly man elbowed her aside as he went out the door. "Watch yerself, luv."

She pasted herself against the doorjamb, wondering at the singular form of address implied in "luv." The man's comment had clearly been directed toward *both* of her breasts.

With a shiver, she wrapped her cloak tight across her chest.

Taking one last deep breath, she sidled her way into the dank, drunken confusion, forbidding her gray serge skirts to brush against anything. Much less any*one*. From every murky corner—and for a squared-off tea caddy of a building, this tavern abounded in murky corners—eyes followed her. Suspicious, leering eyes, set in hard, unshaven faces. It was enough to make any young woman anxious. For a fugitive young lady of quality, traveling alone, under the flimsy shield of a borrowed cloak and a fabricated identity . . .

Well, it was almost enough to make Sophia reconsider the whole affair.

An unseen someone jostled her from behind. Her gloved fingers instinctively clutched the envelope secreted in her cloak. She thought of its brethren, the letters she'd posted just that morning, breaking her engagement and ensuring a scandal of Byronic proportions. Seeds of irrevocable ruin, scattered with the wind.

A cold sense of destiny anchored her rising stomach. There was no going back now. She could walk through far worse than this shabby pub, if it meant leaving her restrictive life behind. She could even endure these coarse men ogling her breasts, so long as they did not glimpse the secret strapped between them.

Her resolve firmed, Sophia caught the eye of a bald-headed man wiping a table with a greasy rag. He looked harmless enough—or at least, too old to strike quickly. She smiled at him. He returned the gesture with a completely toothless grin.

Her own smile faltering, she ventured, "I'm looking for Captain Grayson."

" 'Course you is. All the comely ones are." The gleaming pate jerked. "Gray's in the back."

She followed the direction indicated, moving through the crowd on tiptoe in an effort to keep her hem off the floor. The sticky floorboards sucked at her half boots. Toward the back of the room, she spied a boisterous knot of men and women near the bar. One man stood taller than the others, his auburn hair looking cleaner than that of his company. A brushed felt beaver rested on the bar nearby, an oddly refined ornament for this seedy den.

As Sophia angled for a better view, a chair slid out

from a nearby table, clipping her in the knee. She bobbled on tiptoe for a moment before tripping forward. The hem of her cloak caught on her boot, and the cloak wrenched open, exposing her chest and throat to the sour, wintry air. In her desperate attempt to right herself, she clutched wildly for the wall—

And grasped a handful of rough linen shirt instead.

The shirt's owner turned to her. "Hullo there, chicken," he slurred, his breath rancid with decay. His liquor-glazed eyes slid over her body and settled on the swell of her breasts. "Fancy bit of goods you are. By looks, I would have priced you beyond my pocket, but if you's offerin' . . ."

Had he mistaken her for some dockside trollop? Sophia's tongue curled with disgust. Perhaps she was disguised in simple garments, but certainly she did not look *cheap*.

"I am not offering," she said firmly. She tried to wriggle away, but with a quick move, he had her pinned against the bar.

"Hold there, lovely. Jes' a little tickle, then."

His grimy fingers dove into the valley of her bosom, and Sophia yelped. "Unhand me, you . . . you revolting brute!"

The brute released one of her arms to further his lascivious exploration, and Sophia used her newly-freed hand to beat him about the head. No use. His fingers squirmed between her breasts like fat, greedy worms burrowing in the dark.

"Stop this," she cried, making her hand a fist and clouting his ear, to no avail. Her efforts at defense only amused her drunken attacker.

"S'all right," he said, chuckling. "I likes my girls with plenty o'pluck."

Desperation clawed at her insides. It wasn't simply the

insult of this lout's hands on her breasts that had her panicking. She'd forfeited her genteel reputation the moment she left home. But his fingers groped closer and closer to the one thing she dared not surrender. If he found it, Sophia doubted she would escape this tavern with her life intact, much less her virtue.

Her attacker turned his head, angling for a better look down her dress. His grimy ear was just inches from her mouth. Within snapping distance. If she bit it hard enough, she might startle him into letting her go. She had all but made up her mind to do it, when she inhaled another mouthful of his rank sweat and paused. If her choices were putting her mouth on this repulsive beast or dying, she just might rather die.

In the end, she didn't do either.

The repulsive beast gave a yawp of surprise as a pair of massive hands bodily hauled him away. Lifted him, actually, as though the brute weighed nothing, until he writhed in the air above her like a fish on a hook.

"Come now, Bains," said a smooth, confident baritone, "You know better than that."

With an easy motion, her rescuer tossed Bains aside. The brute landed some feet away, with the crunch of splintering wood.

Sagging against the bar with relief, Sophia peered up at her savior. It was the tall, auburn-haired gentleman she'd spied earlier. At least, she assumed him to be a gentleman. His accent bespoke education, and with his dark-green topcoat, fawn-colored trousers, and tasseled Hessians, he cut a fashionable silhouette. But as his arms flexed, the finely tailored clothing delineated raw, muscled power beneath.

And there was nothing refined about his face. His features were rough-hewn, his skin bronzed by the sun. It was impossible not to stare at the golden, weathered hue and wonder—did it fade at his cravat? At his waist? Not at all?

The more she peered up the man, the less she knew what to make of him. He had a gentleman's attire, a laborer's body . . . and the wide, sensuous mouth of a scoundrel.

"How many times do I have to tell you, Bains? That's no way to touch a woman." His words were addressed to the lout on the floor, but his roguish gaze was fixed on her. Then he smiled, and the lazy quirk of his lips tugged a thin scar slanting from his jaw to his mouth.

Oh yes, that mouth was dangerous indeed.

At that moment, Sophia could have kissed it.

"The proper way to touch a woman," he continued, sauntering to her side and propping an elbow on the bar, "is to come at her from the side, like so." In an attitude of perfect nonchalance, he leaned his weight on his arm and slid it along the bar until his knuckles came within a hair's width of her breast.

Mouth of a scoundrel, indeed! Sophia's gratitude quickly turned to indignation. Had this man truly yanked one lout off her just so he could grope her himself? Apparently so. His hand rested so close to her breast, her flesh heated in the shadow of his fingers. So close, her skin prickled, anticipating the rough texture of his touch. She wished he *would* touch her, end the excruciating uncertainty, and give her an excuse to slap the roguish smirk from his face.

"See?" he said, waggling his fingers in the vicinity of her bosom. "This way you don't startle her off."

Coarse laughter rumbled through the assembled crowd.

Retracting his hand, the scoundrel lifted his voice. "Don't I have the right of it, Megs?"

All eyes turned to a curvy redhead gathering tankards. Megs barely looked up from her work as she sang out, "Ain't no one like Gray knows how to touch a lady."

Laughter swept the tavern again, louder this time. Even Bains chuckled.

Gray. Sophia's heart plummeted. What was it the bald man had said, when she asked for Captain Grayson? *Gray's in the back.*

"One last thing to remember, Bains," Gray continued. "The least you can do is buy the lady a drink." As the tavern-goers returned to their carousing, he turned his arrogant grin on Sophia. "What are you having, then?"

She blinked at him.

What was she having? Sophia knew exactly what she was having. She was having colossally bad luck.

This well-dressed mountain of insolence looming over her was Captain Grayson, of the brig *Aphrodite*. And the brig *Aphrodite* was the sole ship bound for Tortola until next week. For Sophia, next week might as well have been next year. She needed to leave for Tortola. She needed to leave now. Therefore, she needed this man— or rather, this man's *ship*—to take her.

"What, no outpouring of gratitude?" He cast a glance toward Bains, who was lumbering up from the floor. "I suppose you think I should have beat him to a pulp. I could have. But then, I don't like violence. It always ends up costing me money. And pretty thing that you are"—his eyes skipped over her as he motioned to the barkeep—"before I went to that much effort, I think I'd at least need to know your name, Miss . . . ?"

Sophia gritted her teeth, marshalling all her available forbearance. She needed to leave, she reminded herself. She needed this man. "Turner. Miss Jane Turner."

"Miss . . . Jane . . . Turner." He teased the syllables out, as if tasting them on his tongue. Sophia had always thought her middle name to be the dullest, plainest syllable imaginable. But from his lips, even "Jane" sounded indecent.

"Well, Miss *Jane* Turner. What are you drinking?"

"I'm not drinking anything. I'm looking for you, *Captain* Grayson. I've come seeking passage on your ship."

"On the *Aphrodite*? To Tortola? Why the devil would you want to go there?"

"I'm a governess. I'm to be employed, near Road Town." The lies rolled effortlessly off her tongue. As always.

His eyes swept her from bonnet to half boots, stroking an unwelcome shiver down to her toes. "You don't look like any governess I've ever seen." His gaze settled on her hands, and Sophia quickly balled them into fists.

The gloves. Curse her vanity. Her maid's old dress and cloak served well for disguise—their dark, shapeless folds could hide a multitude of sins. But as she'd dressed herself for the first time in her life that morning, her fingers shook with nerves and cold, and Sophia had assuaged their trembling with this one indulgence, her best pair of black kid gloves, fastened with tiny black pearl buttons and lined with sable.

They were not the gloves of a governess.

For a moment, Sophia feared he would see the truth.

Balderdash, she chided herself. No one ever looked at her and saw the truth. People saw what they wanted to see . . . the obedient daughter, the innocent maiden, the society belle, the blushing bride. This merchant captain was no different. He would see a passenger, and the promise of coin.

Long ago, she'd learned this key to deceit. It was easy to lie, once you understood that no one really wanted the truth.

"Lovely, aren't they? They were a gift." With a gloved flourish, she held out her letter. The envelope bore the wear and marks of a transatlantic voyage. "My offer of employment, if you'd care to examine it." She sent up a quick prayer that he would not. "From a Mr. Waltham of Eleanora plantation."

"Waltham?" He laughed, waving away the letter.

Sophia pocketed it quickly.

"Miss Turner, you've no idea what trials you're facing. Never mind the dangers of an ocean crossing, the tropical poverty and disease . . . George Waltham's brats are a plague upon the earth. One your delicate nature and fine gloves are unlikely to survive."

"You know the family, then?" Sophia kept her tone light, but inwardly she loosed a flurry of curses. She'd never considered the possibility that this merchant captain could claim an acquaintance with the Walthams.

"Oh, I know Waltham," he continued. "We grew up together. Our fathers' plantations shared a boundary. He was older by several years, but I paced him for mischief well enough."

Sophia swallowed a groan. Captain Grayson not only *knew* Mr. Waltham—they were friends and neighbors! All her plans, all her carefully tiered lies . . . this bit of information shuffled them like a deck of cards.

He continued, "And you're traveling alone, with no chaperone?"

"I can look after myself."

"Ah, yes. And I tossed Bains across the room just now for my own amusement. It's a little game we seamen like to play."

"I can look after myself," she insisted. "If you'd waited another moment, that revolting beast would be missing an ear."

He gave her a deep, scrutinizing look that made her

feel like a turned-out glove, all seams and raw edges. She breathed steadily, fighting the blush creeping up her cheeks.

"Miss Turner," he said dryly, "I'm certain in that fertile female imagination of yours, you think sailing off to the West Indies will be some grand, romantic adventure." He drawled the phrase in a patronizing tone, but Sophia wasn't certain he meant to deride *her*. Rather, she surmised, his tone communicated a general weariness with adventure.

How sad.

"Fortunately," he continued, "I've never known a girl I couldn't disillusion, so listen close to me now. You're wrong. You will not find adventure, nor romance. At best, you'll meet with unspeakable boredom. At worst, you'll meet with an early death."

Sophia blinked. His description of Tortola gave her some pause, but she dismissed any concern quickly. After all, it wasn't as though she meant to *stay* there.

The captain reached to retrieve his felt beaver from the bar.

"Please." Sophia clutched his arm. Heavens. It was like clutching a wool-sheathed cannon. Ignoring the warm tingle in her belly, she made her eyes wide and her voice beseeching. The role of innocent, helpless miss was one she'd been playing for years. "Please, you must take me. I've nowhere else to go."

"Oh, I'm certain you'd figure something out. Pretty thing like you? After all," he said, quirking an eyebrow, "you can look after yourself."

"Captain Grayson—"

"Miss. Jane. Turner." His voice grew thin with impatience. "You waste your breath, appealing to my sense of honor and decency. Any gentleman in my place would send you off at once."

"Yes, but you're no gentleman." She gripped his arm again and looked him square in the eye. "Are you?"

He froze. All that muscle rippling with energy, the rugged profile animated by insolence—for an instant, it all turned to stone. Sophia held her breath, knowing she'd just wagered her future on this, the last remaining card in her hand.

But this was so much more thrilling than whist.